Ardagh awoke wit[...] ness that he was in [...] feet, dizzy, wondering [...]

Something attacked. Ardagh staggered back, tripping over a protruding root, frantically trying to ward off whatever it was and gather his dazed senses. The Something lunged, a great dark mass swirling through a hundred shapes at once. No time for defense: the prince threw himself aside, feeling branches lash at him and thorns catch at his clothes. He landed with Sidhe lightness, rolling, scrambling up again, never taking his gaze from the Other, realizing in that moment *demon* and desperately hunting through his mind for a combat spell. Nothing! There was nothing that would work in this Realm that was strong enough!

"Ae!" The demon's sudden swipe with suddenly-grown talons just barely missed slashing him open. The talons lashed out again, and Ardagh abandoned bravado and ran, twisting, wriggling, struggling his way through the tangled forest. He burst out into a clearing, gasping—only to find the demon facing him as if it had been there all along, radiating such sadistic joy it sickened him. No combat magic, no sword . . .

What can I do? Ardagh thought wildly. *Throw rocks at it?*

Despairing, he drew his dagger. As the demon came plunging down over him, he lunged up at it with all his might, feeling the blade cut into something that felt nothing like flesh.

And the demon screamed.

BAEN BOOKS BY JOSEPHA SHERMAN

A Strange and Ancient Name

King's Son, Magic's Son

Bardic Choices: A Cast of Corbies
(with Mercedes Lackey)

Castle of Deception: A Bard's Tale Novel
(with Mercedes Lackey)

The Chaos Gate: A Bard's Tale Novel

THE SHATTERED OATH

JOSEPHA SHERMAN

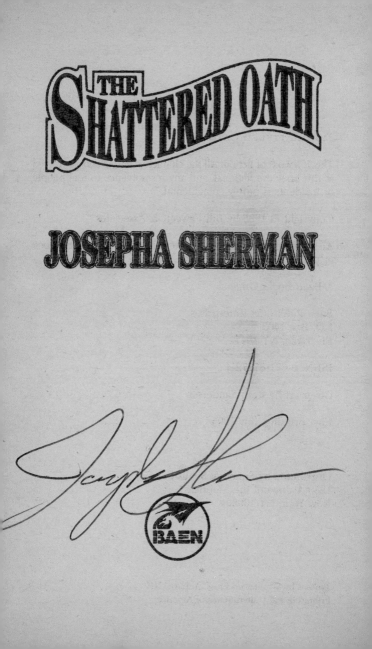

THE SHATTERED OATH

Copyright © 1995 by Bill Fawcett & Associates

A Baen Books Original

Baen Publishing Enterprises
P.O. Box 1403
Riverdale, NY 10471

ISBN: 0-671-87672-4

Cover art by Ruth Sanderson

First printing, July 1995

Distributed by Simon & Schuster
1230 Avenue of the Americas
New York, NY 10020

Typeset by Windhaven Press, Auburn, NH
Printed in the United States of America

A PRINCE AT HOME

CHAPTER 1

The garden was a subtle mix of tame and wild, of rocky outcroppings and soft green slopes, all beneath the sunless sky of Faerie. The quiet air was fragrant with the scents of pure white roses and a multihued riot of wildflowers; off by herself in a little bower, a green-haired servant stroked music from a silver-stringed harp.

And Ardagh Lithanial, Sidhe prince and lord of this garden and its surrounding estate, sat seemingly at ease amid all the tranquil beauty, his airy palace with its slender columns and gleaming white walls to his back, and appeared to give all his attention to his guest.

But behind the narrow, sharply planed mask of his face with its slanted, fiercely green eyes, the prince brooded. Tall and elegantly slender as all his race, Ardagh was of the dark-haired branch of the royal line (some whispered, though seldom where the prince could overhear, that such hair, sleekly black as sorcery, meant a taint of human blood somewhere in the past), the son of his late father's second wife. It was his older half-brother, Eirithan Lithanial—green-eyed as he but silvery-fair of hair—who sat the throne.

Which was quite to Ardagh's satisfaction.

Not that anyone seems willing to believe it. Least of all Eirithan.

They'd had some friendly moments together, the brothers, some times of sharing jests and tales. Eirithan wasn't

1

all that much Ardagh's senior, after all; barely twenty years separated them, a mere blink of time to the Sidhe. But, Ardagh thought bitterly, the shadow of the crown had always hung over them. Even at their friendliest, they'd both known the rightful heir had never quite been easy about this . . . unnecessary younger brother. And now that Eirithan ruled, the happier days seemed gone for good, replaced by end-less suspicion.

Suspicion shared, it would seem, the prince thought with a touch of dark humor, by his guest. "Must we have that servant forever lurking behind us?" Lord Iliach snapped suddenly.

"What's this, my lord?" Ardagh asked, brow raised. "Are you afraid of being overheard? Have you a need for fear?"

"No, no, of course not."

Of course not, the prince echoed silently. Lord Iliach would never be crass enough to actually accuse him of ambition. Instead, the Sidhe lord, most fashionable in deep blue silks that made the most of his golden hair and blue-green eyes (and clashed most jarringly with Ardagh's own red-violet robes) merely smiled and began chatting of small matters. But the smile never quite touched his cool, slanted eyes.

"What a lovely garden this is!" Iliach exclaimed suddenly. "How clever of you, Prince Ardagh, to allow the land itself to shape its own design. *Such* a pleasant touch of wildness."

Now what games are you playing? Ardagh wondered. Iliach was, after all, a true Sidhe of the royal court: clever, sly and subtly malicious; there was never a word he said that didn't contain several hidden meanings. *He reminds me,* the prince thought wryly, *of why I shun my brother's court.* "Why, my lord Iliach," Ardagh asked with feigned amusement, "what are you hinting? That I was, perhaps, too weak to impose sufficient magic on it? Too weak to shape things properly?"

Iliach straightened as though genuinely dismayed. "Oh, never that! I only meant to frame a comparison. Might it not be said a garden is symbolic of a realm?"

"Might it?"

"Why, indeed! A foolish ruler tries to force his subjects to his will. A wise ruler, however, is like a wise gardener, knowing when to impose some will on his subjects, when to allow them a touch of freedom."

"As," Ardagh said mildly, "does my brother."

Iliach raised an elegant golden brow at the implicit warning, and fell silent. Somewhere in the garden, Serenai, Iliach's wife, wandered with her ladies, cooing over this flower and that, gathering specimens for her own garden; it was Iliach's excuse for being here. The women's voices, light and inconsequential as birdsong, drifted back to where the two men sat, and Iliach smiled anew.

"My Serenai is such a charming creature!"

Ardagh dipped his head politely; "charming" was the kindest word one could apply to pretty, vapid Serenai. Iliach purred, "What a pity, Prince Ardagh, that you haven't yet taken a wife of your own. Unlike your brother, of course, and his lovely Karanila."

Karanila, Ardagh thought, with her coldly perfect face and unreadable eyes that just might hold a hint of malice behind them . . .

"And what a pity," Iliach murmured, "that our ruler has no child of his blood as yet. But then," he added delicately, "he does have you as his heir."

Just once, Iliach, come to the point! All at once overwhelmed by impatience, Ardagh snapped, "Does that please you, my lord?"

"I beg your—"

"Look you, I know you and my royal brother have quarreled in the past. Oh, don't give me that so-innocent stare! Being who and what I am, how could I not know?"

Iliach waved a graceful hand in surrender.

"I also know," Ardagh continued, "that you have been trying for long and long to reinstate yourself in my brother's favor. Without success."

"Ah, but you—"

"But I do *not* envy my brother his role. I do *not* wish to usurp it. You and he and everyone at court knows I have so sworn! I have given my word to do nothing to

harm him or his reign. Do you think me an oathbreaker,
my lord?"

Oathbreaking was one of the worst crimes possible to a
folk who never lied. "Never that!" Iliach exclaimed with what
seemed real shock.

Ardagh smiled thinly. "Then you will believe me when I
say I wish my brother a long, prosperous life and many heirs
of his body."

"Doesn't every loyal subject wish the same?" Iliach smiled
his charming, insincere smile, and added, "Why, Prince
Ardagh, don't glower so! No need to be upset. We were
merely talking . . . gardening."

Of course. Just like Lady Tathaniai and Lord Charalian
who'd come here before him, and the other half-dozen who
happened to have remote blood-ties to the current royal
line; the Sidhe might not actually be immortal, but they
boasted such long lives few of them could puzzle out all
the eons-long twists of genealogy. There were always possible claimants to any throne.

Ambition, Ardagh thought, was one way for shallow minds
to ward off boredom.

*But not one of you would-be traitors will believe I won't
be used in your games!*

If only Eirithan wasn't so capricious a ruler none of this
nonsense would be necessary. Ardagh clenched his teeth,
thinking of all those endless, expensive, time-and-magic-
wasting court revels—which, of course he, as prince, had
to attend—with his brother watching with cold suspicion.

*And then you punish our people for your own waste and
neglect of our land. You're ruling over Sidhe, brother, not
some magickless little humans aching for a master!*

Ardagh knew something about humanity. The prince had
once, out of curiosity, crossed Realms into their mortal
lands—warily at night to avoid the alien and, for all he knew,
deadly to Sidhe, earthly sun—and been bemused by the
barbaric vitality he'd seen, even though he didn't pretend
to truly understand those bizarre, short-lived creatures. (A
flash of memory: sharing the tale of his adventures with
Eirithan, the two of them agreeing humanity was hardly

something on which any sensible Sidhe would care to spend much time.)

No, my brother, we don't have anything in common with those master-and-slave folk. And I only wish I could get you to see that.

Enough of this. "I see that your wife has finished her gathering," the prince said shortly. "She wishes to leave. Good day to you, Lord Iliach."

Ardagh waited, chin resting on steepled hands, till the lord and lady were well out of hearing, flown away in their graceful winged chariot, then got to his feet in a restless surge of energy, and paced down the narrow paths of his garden. The green-haired harpist froze when he strode past her bower, staring up at him, her golden, slit-pupiled eyes widening in alarm.

"Angry?" she whimpered.

"Not at you, Ninet."

"Certain?"

Ardagh sighed. "Yes, little one. I'm certain. Here, look."

A flash of will sent a cascade of rose petals fluttering down about Ninet: an easy illusion to draw from the magic-rich essence that was Faerie. Ninet giggled, then snapped at the petals, trying to catch them in her teeth before the tiny surge of magic faded and the illusion-petals vanished.

"Gone," she said with a little sigh. Putting down her harp, the being flowed to Ardagh's side, no taller than a Sidhe child against his height, slim and sleek as a cat, more innocent than either. "Music?"

"I heard it, Ninet. It was very pretty."

Ninet, as far as the prince could tell, was the result of someone's experiment, not quite animal, not quite sprite, abandoned to wander aimlessly till she'd turned up on his estate. Her intelligence was hardly human, let alone Sidhe, expressing itself mostly in music. Ardagh glanced down at her puzzled face and dropped a reassuring hand to the smooth green hair. Ninet pushed into the caress like a cat, and the prince smiled faintly.

"Ninet, I am so very weary of political games! I want—" He stopped with a sharp laugh. "I admit it, I don't know quite what I want from my life." *Adventure,* his mind told him suddenly, unbidden. *Excitement. A chance to use my magic for something more than gardening!*

Bah, ridiculous. He wasn't a child to dream such foolish things. And yet . . . "There has to be more than this—this green quiet," Ardagh said, "lovely though it is. But that doesn't mean I lust for a crown!"

Ninet blinked. "Crown?" she repeated blankly.

"A form of bondage," Ardagh told her dryly. "Ae, never mind. What I want hardly matters: I can hardly back away from my bloodline until and unless Eirithan can finally sire an heir." That was no easy thing for a member of such an infertile race; their father had been considered truly amazing for having sired not one but two healthy sons. "Ha, and once my brother has a child, I become even more 'unnecessary'! Isn't *that* a charming thought?"

"Means?"

"That means, little one, that for now we can expect more visits from malcontents."

Ninet, of course, understood almost nothing of what he was saying, but she nodded wisely, eyes solemn. "And as for my brother," Ardagh continued, stroking her hair absently, "Eirithan may not trust me at his side, but he certainly won't let me out from under his eye, either!"

Ninet blinked. "Not happy?" she asked nervously. "Go?"

"I can't! Don't you see— No. Of course you can't." Very slowly, Ardagh told her, "As long as I remain Eirithan's heir, I can't just up and disappear. Do you understand that?"

"What?"

"Ae, Ninet. I may not be sure what I want, or what my future holds, but this is my estate, and I have no intention of surrendering it." He paused thoughtfully. "I do wonder, though, just how many of my servants are reporting to my brother." The prince had long ago cast a security spell over the entire estate; no one could work magic without his knowing it. "But there are always more mundane ways of transmitting information." He ruffled the little being's hair. "Enough."

"Music?" she asked hopefully.

"Yes, Ninet, I think I would like to hear more of your music, and— What is it?" Ardagh snapped at the servant who had suddenly appeared at his side.

The slender, silver-haired being bowed warily. "Your pardon, my prince, but had you forgotten your royal brother's revel this night?"

Ah yes, he had. Ardagh sighed. "Very well. Have my spidersilk robes laid out. The . . . red ones, I think." He paused. "*Now* what?"

The servant licked its thin lips nervously. "The theme, my prince! The theme of this night's revel is—"

Oh Powers, he was sick of these endless, meaningless themes! "I don't care what it is!" Ardagh exploded. "The red robes are suitably royal, and the red robes will do!"

Eirithan Lithanial, tall and regal in flowing silver robes, silvery hair framing his impassive face, listened without stirring to what his spy was telling him. This Iliach was such a slippery creature, noble enough of blood and never quite treasonous, but willing to bend to whomever promised him the best reward. Look at him now, smiling so ingratiatingly, saying absolutely nothing of use. Eirithan held up an aristocratic hand for silence.

"In short," he said coldly, "no matter what you tried, my brother would not be baited."

"Ah . . . no, my liege. He claimed most vehemently that he remains true to the vow he swore to you."

"So. Leave me."

Eirithan watched the Sidhe lord leave, then got to his feet in a swirl of silver robes. He began pacing restlessly through the small audience hall, ignoring the precise beauty of walls magicked so they seemed lined with windows into fantastic realms rather than with mere paintings, glad that there was no one else in the hall to see his uneasiness.

What games are you playing, Ardagh? So seemingly innocent, there in your pretty gardens far from my court. You are my brother, we share the same ambitious blood—you can't be content like that. You must make a move against me, but when? How?

He never had been able to understand Ardagh, not even back when they both had been boys and could share some jests, some hints of friendship.

No. It had never quite been friendship. How could it be? How could he ever forget, even for a moment, what his brother represented? Though up to now Ardagh had never provided the slightest reason for action (*for murder*, whispered Eirithan's mind, making him shiver: *He is my brother, I will not shed his blood*), he might someday prove the greatest threat to Eirithan's reign in all the realm—

"My liege." The voice was smooth and rich as velvet. Eirithan stopped dead.

"Karanila. What would you, wife?"

She moved softly to his side, almost as tall as he, beautiful, slender and graceful as a hunting hound, her long, moon-pale hair caught in a hundred intricate, jewel-studded braids. The scent of her subtle fragrance, the delicate touch of her hand on his arm, sent a sudden flash of desire through him.

So beautiful, so beautiful . . . if only I could trust her!

Malicious for malice's sake, that was Karanila.

With a surge of will, Eirithan forced himself sternly back under control. Karanila smiled. "So distraught, husband, so remote. What troubles you?"

"Nothing to worry you."

She stiffened slightly. "It's Ardagh, isn't it? Ae, again."

Eirithan glanced sharply at her. "What does that mean?"

She turned away, toying with the end of one gleaming braid. "Nothing to worry *you*."

"Don't play games! What is it? Has Ardagh dared approach you?"

Her sideways little smile was infuriatingly innocent. "Would he dare?"

Eirithan caught her by the shoulders, forcing her to face him. "I told you, don't jest with me! Has Ardagh tried to betray me?"

Karanila's eyes were unreadable, her mind closed to him. She hesitated just long enough to set his nerves on edge, then pulled free, raising a hand to gently trace the lines of

Eirithan's face. He jerked his head back angrily, and Karanila chuckled, deep in her throat. "No, my husband," she purred, "he has not." She paused a heartbeat longer before adding thoughtfully, "Yet."

"Stop that." Eirithan pulled Karanila to him again, more gently this time. "Dance with him tonight, yes? Talk with him. A woman can learn things from a man he never meant to tell her."

Karanila chuckled again. "Shall I? Shall I, indeed? And do you trust me that much, my husband?"

Eirithan froze, reluctant to admit the truth, unable by his Sidhe nature to lie. Karanila disengaged herself gently from his grip and walked away, her laughter trailing lightly back to where he stood.

Lord Iliach looked neither left nor right as he strode down the intricately intertwined corridors of his estate, but every psychic sense was alert and quivering. At last he allowed himself the smallest sigh of relief. Serenai was off with her women in her garden, cooing over her plant cuttings. No one else was watching or following. Iliach dared one bold look about, just to set his mind at ease, then slid behind a billowing hanging, barely noting the woven, magic-worked figures moving slowly through a never-ending dance. Beyond lay a small, secret room, barely large enough to hold those who sat within.

"My lords, lady." His welcoming sweep of hand took in them all: icy-eyed Lady Tathaniai in ice-blue silks, sturdy, impassive Lord Charalian, and the brother-lords Sestailan and Teretal, elegant as ever, their hair bright as spun gold— all those ambitious souls who were his allies. For now. Until they no longer needed each other. "My pardon for arriving so late, but . . . as you can guess, I was detained."

"Well?" Sestailan asked coolly. "Does he suspect?"

Iliach sighed. "Of course he does. Our liege lord remains his usual suspicious self. But he can prove nothing." The Sidhe lord sank into a chair, calling a wine-filled goblet to him with a twist of will. "And no, I did not give him anything about us. For all that he listened so closely to every word I said, our dear Eirithan never once suspected I was anything but his humble servant."

"And the other?" Teretal wondered, leaning forward.

"Who? Ardagh?" Iliach took a long sip from his goblet. "What a tiresomely honest creature he is!"

"But is he with us?" Lord Charalian snapped.

"No. Not yet. He remains *his* usual self: haughty, hostile, and so proud of his honor he has no sympathy for any . . . weaker sorts."

Lady Tathaniai raised a warning hand. "Don't scorn the prince too much, my lord. Haughty he may be, but he's no fool."

Sestailan laughed softly. "True enough. And that pride of his may prove very useful."

Iliach matched their suddenly sly smiles with his own. "Useful, indeed. Play one brother against the other carefully enough, and—" He gave a graceful little shrug. "Who can say what will result? Or who may remain in power?"

"Or," Teretal purred, "who may end up there?"

The theme of this night's revel, Ardagh saw, was winter sorcery. Aristocratic dancers in drifting silks the many cool shades of snow under moonlight, glittering here and there with drops of silver, moved smoothly to music from crystalline flutes and silver-strung harps, all within a vast hall of the royal rath, his brother's ornate fortress, transformed by enchantment into the illusion of a gleaming blue-white cave of ice.

It all, Ardagh thought dryly, looked like one great, overblown sugar cake.

The prince stood straight-backed and silent at the side of his brother's throne, refusing to admit that his servant had been right: the red of his robes was jarringly loud against so much silvery-white. He also refused to acknowledge the cool glances a good many of the Sidhe nobles turned his way as they whirled by. He knew well enough they thought him overly proud because he kept to himself, because he kept his vows and refused to play their subtle games.

Ardagh glanced sideways to where Eirithan sat all in silver, pale face and hair all adding to the illusion of an icy statue. Only the eyes were alive, studying the dancers as though puzzling over their innermost thoughts.

Probably wondering which of them are plotting against him. Or with me.

"So solemn," purred a velvety voice, and Ardagh started, then dipped his head in a polite little bow.

"Karanila."

If her husband was an icy statue, Karanila was a statue come to life, the floating folds of her pure white gown shimmering like winter mist, her hair and face frosted with a haze of glittering silver. Her smile was coolly amused. "I find myself without a partner for this dance." Her eyes glinted slyly. "My husband refuses to join me. Will you not take his place?"

Ardagh refused to take her words at anything but face value. "I'm not in the mood for dancing."

"Come now, Ardagh. I promise you a mere dance won't compromise your precious honor."

The prince bit back an impatient oath. Karanila was beautiful as ever, the cold silver frosting of face, hair and costume making the woman beneath the chill facade seem all the more sensual for the contrast. If she were anyone else, he would probably have enjoyed the mutual game of seduction and surrender. But she was who she was, and the only way to stop her slightly malicious teasing was to yield to her more open demand. Her hand resting lightly on his arm, Ardagh led Karanila out onto the dance floor, moving gracefully through the intricate steps with her, aware that many of the others had retreated to watch.

As Eirithan was watching.

"How my husband stares," Karanila purred, as the dance brought them nearly into each other's arms. "Almost as though he expected us to be plotting something devious."

"Nonsense."

The dance drew them apart. Ardagh moved through the pattern with this lady and that till he found himself confronted by Karanila again.

"Or," she added with an odd little smile, "as though we were planning to betray him."

"I'm not. Are you?"

"Why, Ardagh! Such a question!"

The dance drew them apart once more. Ardagh waited impatiently for it to end, hoping it would before he had to face Karanila and continue their ludicrous duel. Ae, no, here they were again, face-to-face, and her eyes alive with mischief.

"And can you really say you never even thought about betraying him?" she murmured. "Never? Not even for me?"

Her lovely face was turned to his, her body so close he could feel its warmth, so close they were nearly touching. But Ardagh could have sworn he *felt* a subtle, chill undertone beneath the flirtation, and glanced up at Eirithan again, seeing the sudden tense alertness.

So that's it. You're using Karanila, brother, trying to trick me one way or another. Damn you!

He stopped short, the dancers eddying about him in surprise. With a curt bow to Karanila, Ardagh stalked from the dance floor, ignoring her indignation. Eirithan stiffened as he approached, and the prince snarled, "Don't worry, brother. I'm not trying to assassinate you."

"What—"

"How *dare* you try trapping me?"

"Mind your tone!" With an intricate wave of his hand, Eirithan created a barrier of secrecy about them, a vague shimmering of the air that held in sound.

But the courtiers could still see through that barrier. Belatedly aware of them staring in wild curiosity, Ardagh turned his back on them, adding in a fierce whisper, "When are you going to stop these ridiculous games?"

"I play no games."

"Oh no, of course not! Since the day you took our father's throne, everything you've said or done where I'm concerned has been aimed at forcing me to break my vow!"

"Now that is *truly* ridiculous," Eirithan said coldly. "I am doing nothing more than keeping my throne secure."

Powers, they might as well still be boys! Mixed in with the moments of friendship Eirithan had given him had been unpredictable bouts of anger, bewildering to the younger boy. It wasn't until he'd become an adult that Ardagh had realized the reason behind that rage. Of course Eirithan had never quite dared destroy his unwanted younger half-brother; not even the most jealous of princes would kill anything as rare and precious as a child. But that hadn't stopped him from forcing Ardagh into duels with sword or spell—practice duels, he'd claimed, but vicious enough.

And just as stupid as this whole discussion! "Look you, Eirithan, there are times when I very much regret my vow to you—but swear it I did! And if you paid as much attention to your people as you do to trying to trap me, you wouldn't have to worry about your throne!"

Ignoring Eirithan's command to stop, Ardagh destroyed the magical barrier with a surge of his own Power and began to stalk angrily away. But before he'd gone a dozen steps, he nearly collided with a breathless, wild-eyed messenger. As the startled prince stepped aside, the messenger gasped to Eirithan, "My—my liege, we n-need help—Wyvern—village—"

Ardagh felt the shiver of magic brush him: someone was casting a restorative spell on the exhausted man, who staggered, then began more strongly, "A wyvern has attacked a village, killed a man and two children."

There was a collective gasp of horror from the courtiers: precious children slain! Eirithan sprang to his feet, the very image of outraged royalty.

"Come, my friends!" he shouted. "We shall have a royal hunt! This monstrous killer shall be slain!"

Melodramatic, a cynical part of Ardagh's mind whispered. But he wondered aloud, inexplicably uneasy, "The wyvern normally hunts deer and other such creatures. Why should it leave the forest? Why take on prey foreign to it?"

But in all the sudden swirlings of excitement, no one heeded him.

HUNTED

CHAPTER 2

The courtiers, Ardagh noted wryly, were taking to the excitement of preparing for a royal hunt with all the fervor of long-lived folk too familiar with boredom. They were laughing and calling to each other with all the glee of children, the air about them sparkling with Power as they altered elegant robes to more practical riding gear, had their shining Faerie steeds brought to them, and summoned this bit of armor or that favorite weapon. Ardagh barely managed to do his own summoning of hunting armor from his estate without having his conjuration spell interrupted by all the furor. He glanced about at the wild confusion and gave up any hope of finding a servant to help him.

Ah well, impractical armor it would be if I couldn't don it all by myself.

Fighting his way out of a sea of people, the prince worked his way into a quiet little alcove.

Not so quiet at that. As he finished fastening the leather cuirass, muttering to himself at the idiots who'd designed the thing with clasps at the back, the prince looked up and fell silent, raising a wry brow at the small group of nobles who'd so suddenly joined him.

"My lord Iliach. Ah, and Lords Teretal and Sestailan as well. And with such wary looks on your faces! Dare I ask what this is about?"

Iliach glanced uneasily over his shoulder. "We have only

14

a few moments of privacy before anyone starts suspecting," he murmured.

"Have we?"

"Prince Ardagh, all at court saw your quarrel. All know how your royal brother feels towards you."

"Do you, now?"

"None would blame you if you—"

"If I what?" Ardagh interrupted coldly.

"Why, made a move towards—"

"Treason?"

"So strong a word!"

"So accurate a word." Ardagh glared at them without trying to disguise his contempt. "Have you finally grown tired of masked allusions, or are we going to dance delicately about the subject one more time? For the last time, my lords," he continued before they could protest, "I am *not* interested in betraying my brother. I have, whether you like the fact or not," *or*, a cynical part of his mind added silently, *whether I like the fact or not,* "sworn my vow of fealty to him. None of you, singly or together, can make any offer strong enough to turn me into an oathbreaker. Ah, you flinch at that word! Yet that is exactly what you'd make me, my lords!"

They started to disagree, then fell awkwardly silent, unable even now to utter falsehoods. Ardagh grinned at them like a wolf. "One thing more, my lords, I *will not* be anyone's puppet! Is that understood?"

One by one, reluctantly, they bowed their heads in submission. But a little prickle of worry cut through Ardagh's contempt as he watched. Even the smallest scavengers may bring down a dragon if there are enough of them. And he'd just declared himself a threat to these scavengers, particularly now that they'd as good as announced treason against their ruler. They dared not risk letting him speak to Eirithan.

Oh, you idiot! For all that his heart was suddenly racing, Ardagh kept his voice regally cold and level. "Don't fear, my lords. I shall say nothing to my brother—as long as you do nothing against him."

The Sidhe were capable of incredibly devious actions, but no matter what plans they might think he was fomenting, the scavengers had to believe he meant what he'd said. And that, in turn, Ardagh told himself, would have to serve as the best security he could find for now.

Defiantly turning his back on the nobles, the prince rejoined the safer swirl of Sidhe and horse and hounds, all the while half-expecting an assassin's spell. He could *feel* the plotters' hatred burning at him even as he swung into the saddle of the arched-necked Faerie steed a servant brought for him. Grimly ignoring his uneasiness, Ardagh took the handful of light, silver-tipped javelins offered him, settling all but one into the sheath set in the saddle for that purpose, thoughtfully hefting that one in his hand, approving of its balance, musing that it would work as well against a Sidhe as a wyvern, should it come to that.

But with a clear blare of horns wild enough to set the blood racing the hunt was away, and there was no more time for worry. Bent low over the neck of his silvery horse, Ardagh felt its smooth muscles working easily beneath him, building up greater and greater speed as it ran with eager delight till the wind fairly shrieked in his ears. The prince buried his head in the long, silky mane, grinning. Ahead, the royal hounds coursed like sleek arrows, low to the ground, their hides burning white, their ears blazing red. Silent hunters, these, till the prey was roused; their very silence made them all the more chilling.

Finally, the blast of a horn—a tangle of confusion and baying of hounds—the wyvern burst from concealment, rearing up on its powerful hind legs, short, ridiculous forelegs clutched at its chest. Something seemed wrong with the viciously fanged mouth, and after a moment Ardagh realized what it was, and knew why the beast had turned from its natural prey to easier kills: one side of the long, narrow jaw hung askew, broken by accident or by some hunter too fearful to finish what he'd begun. Ardagh rose in the stirrups, javelin raised—

But too many branches were between him and the wyvern,

and he settled back with an angry sigh. Let the hounds do their work and flush the beast totally out of hiding.

The wyvern roared its pain and rage as one of the hounds nipped it on the flank. The long, poison-tipped tail came lashing savagely about, but the hounds were too battle-wise to be so easily stabbed. One dog, not quite as quick as the rest, yipped as the weight of the wyvern's tail caught it broadside and hurled it aside, but the others darted in to harry the wyvern, biting at flank or legs.

"Be wary!" someone yelled. "It's going to charge!"

Ardagh's hand tightened about the javelin. Steadying his nervous horse with knee pressure, he told the wyvern silently, *Come. Give me just one clear shot.*

Without warning, the wyvern rushed from cover. Ardagh grinned fiercely, javelin raised. Just another moment . . . But another horse jostled his own, and the prince glanced sideways— Eirithan, fierce-eyed and angry, wanting the kill for his own.

Sorry, brother, the honor is mine!

Ardagh raised his javelin again, but Eirithan's horse was charging forward, blocking his aim. And the prince—

—all at once could not lower the javelin, could not drop it, could not do anything but *feel* the pressure on him from five other minds. Damn them, damn them, how could he have been so stupid? A trap, it was all a trap, even the wyvern; its jaw had been deliberately broken, he didn't doubt it now, though which of the traitors had actually—

—the traitors led by Lord Iliach—

—the traitors who were using him as their royal assassin, forcing his arm back for the throw—

They will not! Ardagh thought fiercely. *I . . . will . . . not . . . do this thing!*

But he had no choice. Heart pounding, breath coming in gasps, the prince realized that though he might be stronger magically than any one of the traitors, he couldn't overwhelm all five. His arm continued preparing the throw no matter how much he fought, the javelin aimed straight at Eirithan's heart—

Damn you, no!

As the javelin left his hand, Ardagh hurled every bit of will not against the traitors but at the javelin itself. Powers, there wasn't enough time, it wasn't going to work, it would never—

But the weapon merely grazed Eirithan's face, whirring on to strike the wyvern cleanly. The beast roared its pain, staggering back, off balance. The hounds lunged, dragging it down, and a dozen flashing javelins made an end of it. And Ardagh, suddenly released, struck out at the traitors with all the raw Power in him, hearing someone cry out in pain, *feeling* someone fall.

In the next moment, magic seized him from all sides. Held helpless by the sudden flood of Power, the prince tried to cry out to the courtiers to let him go, that it wasn't *he* who was the traitor, but he could barely drag enough air into his lungs to breathe. They had all seen him hurl the javelin; they weren't about to release a would-be assassin.

But I'm not, damn you, I'm not!

Eirithan, hand to bleeding face, was staring at Ardagh, eyes wide with shock. "Traitor!" he gasped at last.

Ardagh managed to choke out a defiant "No!" but could get no further.

Eirithan kneed his horse to the prince's side, still staring. "I always knew you were not to be trusted, even when you were a boy, I knew it."

Oh, nonsense! You knew no such thing!

"But I never dreamed you would go this far," Eirithan continued. "I never dreamed you would actually try to kill me."

The effort to speak nearly strangled Ardagh. "I didn't!" he gasped.

"Silence, *liar, oathbreaker!*" Terror blazed from Eirithan, the terror of someone seeing his long-held fears proven true.

"No! You must—"

The magical bonds clamped down ever more severely. Sagging in the saddle, barely able to cling to consciousness, Ardagh could no longer utter any sound at all, and Eirithan continued sharply, to all the others, "We are returning, *now*! This traitor must be punished!"

⚜   ⚜   ⚜

It could not have been called a fair or honest trial by any
standards, Ardagh thought bitterly, not with everyone's
magical bonds still holding him so tightly he couldn't say a
word in his defense. No one else was saying anything in
his defense, either.

*Of course not. No one's going to be impolitic enough to
challenge Eirithan. Especially since everyone saw me cast
that cursed spear.*

At least the bonds had been loosened enough so the prince
could breathe and stand without aid. But cursed if he was
going to let anyone see the helpless horror he felt! The prince
stood as proudly as the bonds would let him, forcing his
face into a cold mask that revealed nothing at all as Eirithan
accused him of crime after crime. Almost worse than listening to the litany was seeing the true traitors (the remaining
traitors; he saw with a flash of fierce satisfaction that his
last, desperate attack had eliminated Teretal) standing to
one side in sanctimonious sadness. A good many layers of
these cursed magical bonds were their sendings.

Don't you feel *their falseness?* he screamed silently at
Eirithan. *Don't you realize that they're the real peril?*

No, Eirithan plainly realized nothing of the sort. He
seemed to be coming to the end of his accusations now,
and Ardagh braced himself, more afraid now than he would
have wanted to admit: the Sidhe were not a gentle people
when it came to punishment, and death would almost certainly be the least terrible part of a traitor's fate.

But Eirithan hesitated, then waved his counsellors to him.
They conferred for so long Ardagh wanted to shout at them
to make up their minds, no matter how terrible the decision, just make up their minds and end the suspense. He
could see the word "death" on many lips.

All at once Eirithan turned back to Ardagh, and the
prince was surprised to see a hint of . . . could it possibly
be concern mixed in with the fear and rage? "I should con-
demn you to death, Ardagh," he said hesitantly. "That is a
traitor's fate, after all. But you and I are the last of our blood.
I . . . I will not take my brother's life."

Then let me go, damn you. Let me show you the real traitors!

"No," Eirithan continued more resolutely, "I shall not take your life. Instead, my false, false brother, I shall exile you." His face suddenly devoid of all emotion, voice ringing out as cold and clear as a hunting horn, Eirithan cried, "Hear my words, my people! I hereby declare that he who was known as Ardagh Lithanial is of Lithanial blood no longer, prince no longer. He is a traitor, a nameless, clanless oathbreaker, and as such can no longer be allowed to live within our Realm.

"And so I hereby declare this nameless one shall be cast into exile! He shall be banished forever to the one Realm that will harbor such an oathbreaker, the one Realm I have found in which falsehood is no sin and the folk are as treacherous as he:

"This nameless one is hereby cast out to live whatever miserable life he can achieve not amid the lordly Sidhe but amid the lowly humankind. And never shall he return!"

No, oh no, Ardagh thought in panic, *I am Sidhe, still Sidhe no matter what you claim! I cannot survive in that barbaric world! Eirithan, no!*

But, helpless in his bonds, he could say nothing. Half-choking on rage and despair, the prince watched Eirithan and his sages, with an extravagant waste of magic, cast open a shimmering Portal.

That's my spell, curse you, the one I taught you when I first told you about humanity!

A spell that was about to be used on him. Ardagh fought his bonds savagely, uselessly, as two servants caught him by the arms.

No! I shall not be tossed away like some shameful slave!

Something of his despair and desperate pride must have torn free to touch Eirithan's mind, for at a commanding wave of his hand, the courtiers (murmuring in disapproval) dissolved their magical bonds. But Ardagh, poised on the very edge of the Portal, saw the coldness in their eyes and knew it was already too late for him. The slightest wrong move or word on his part would mean the hurling of a storm of spears. He must step through the Portal into wrongful exile, or die here and now.

I will not let you slay me, curse you! Ardagh thought. *And at least I can take this much vengeance.* He shouted with all the helpless fury in him, "Look to your back, Eirithan! The traitors still live—"

The spears were thrown. Before they could strike, he leaped boldly through the Portal to meet his fate.

KINGS AND QUEENS

CHAPTER 3

Aedh mac Neill, High King of Eriu for nigh these five years, woke with a start, staring wildly at nothing, heart pounding as though he'd just been fighting a battle. Beside him, his wife Eithne stirred, brushing tangled chestnut hair back from her face, blinking sleepily at him.

"Aedh?" she murmured. "What's wrong?"

He took a deep, steadying breath, then touched her cheek with a gentle hand. "Nothing. Only a dream."

The woman straightened, raising herself on one elbow, eyes suddenly focused with alarm. "With enough power to it to wake you!"

"Eithne . . ."

"Don't give me that superior look! Dreams have meaning, love, you know—"

"Oh, I know nothing of the sort."

"What did you dream?" Eithne insisted. "Come, tell me."

Aedh sighed, rolling over onto his back, looking blankly up at the canopy overhead, considering. "It was an odd thing," he said at last. "Not a nightmare, not exactly . . . just strange. I dreamed I was in the midst of battle, alone, set round with foes."

"Och!"

"But just when things were looking very grim indeed," Aedh continued thoughtfully, "a stranger slipped through the foes to my side." He glanced sideways at his wife. "Now,

I don't know what made me dream him up, Eithne! He was the most foreign-looking fellow I ever could have imagined: tall, pale of skin, and almost as beautiful as a woman. But whatever else he was, that man could fight like a very devil! And between us, we won the day. I woke up just as we were grinning in triumph at each other." Aedh turned to look fully at Eithne. "So. That's the lot of it. Are you satisfied?"

Eithne wouldn't meet his gaze. "You were right," she murmured after a moment. "It could only have been a dream, nothing more than that."

He grunted in satisfaction. "Go back to sleep. The hour's still early."

"Mm-hmm." Eithne curled comfortably against him, all warm, cozy softness, head pillowed against his chest. Aedh smiled and held her close, for the moment wonderfully content.

But his dream-prodded mind refused to relax, insisting on remembering actual battle after battle. And at last he gave up all hope of sleep. He might be Aedh Ordnigh, Aedh the Ordained, rightful High King in the sight of God and man, but that wasn't making his reign any easier.

And had you expected it to be any other way?

Hardly. The land of Eriu was divided among a seemingly endless number of lesser kings—some of them ruling over as few as a hundred men—and all of them, great and small, were an ambitious, skeptical lot, not particularly willing to see anyone set over them. The very first year of Aedh's reign, when he should have had at least a short period of grace, had seen him having to ride out against the stubborn king of Meath to prove he, Aedh Ordnigh of the Ui Neill sept, the noblest, most powerful of dynasties, was, and would remain, ruler of all Eriu.

Not that such a victory made much of an impression on the rest of the kings. No, that would have been far too simple.

In these past four years, Aedh realized with a start, he could count maybe ten months all told when he hadn't been forced to ride out somewhere, sword in hand. And who knew but that someone else wouldn't be challenging him tomorrow, or the day after that. The king mentally ticked off the most blatant possibilities: There were the two ambitious sons of the late king of Meath to consider, and trouble out of Leinster that might yet lead to war. Add to that the various factions here at court, most of whom were related to other kings and burning with their own ambition. And just to keep matters nicely stirred, there were also those two swift raids to the north of Eriu by the Lochlannach, the seafaring barbarians come down from their frozen northern lands. Those raids just might not be isolated occurrences—

Och, well, nobody ever promised me this would be an easy way to live! And I certainly don't intend to meekly surrender the crown. The way Father did.

Aedh straightened carefully, not wanting to disturb Eithne (the one quiet, peaceful, loving part of his life, his Eithne, and the two children they'd gotten between them, brave young Niall and pretty little Fainche). He was sturdy of build and, he knew proudly, still fully as fit and strong as a younger man, but now and again he could feel the pull of old wounds warning him he wasn't invulnerable. There were few enough of those wounds, God be praised, and none of them truly serious: for a warrior king in his mid-thirties, Aedh admitted, he'd been remarkably fortunate—or (who knew?) shielded by some divine Power.

Father? Aedh wondered wryly. *Is this your doing?*

He sighed, softly so Eithne would not be disturbed. Niall Frasach had been a good man, some said a saintly man. Aedh could remember a boyhood filled with the ever-growing legends of his father quelling demons by sheer sanctity. Niall Frasach, Niall Condail: Niall the Pure of Mind, who had finally abdicated the throne for a monastery.

Ah, yes. And in the process, Aedh thought, his father had conveniently left behind all the unsettled problems and plots of the less pure of mind for his successor to solve, and involved his son in a ten-year struggle to claim the throne and prove himself High King. Being the son of a saint might be good for one's soul, but it certainly wasn't an easy thing for someone living in the here and now.

Well, he was High King now, damn all his enemies to the monks' Hell, and couldn't imagine being anything other than High King.

Pulling aside a bed-hanging a finger's breadth, Aedh glanced out at the cool grey light of early morning and sighed anew. A feather bed was a wonderfully comfortable thing, whether or not one had been sleeping, but the day was here and he could hardly lie abed any longer. The life of a king was ringed round with rules and prohibitions, including what he should and should not do each day. And today, the mid-day of the week, was the one deemed suitable for royal hunting.

"So be it," Aedh muttered, disentangling himself carefully from his wife, and got to his feet.

"You're not leaving?" Eithne cried from behind him, and Aedh turned to her.

She was sitting up in bed, bedclothes gathered about her, hair a wild cloud, looking as soft and vulnerable as a girl who'd never borne a child. And for a moment such a wave of pure tenderness surged through Aedh that he ached to rejoin her in their bed and never leave.

Nonsense. He was a man grown, not a romantic boy. "What's this, wife?" he asked lightly. "Still worried about my dream? Come now, we both know it was nothing but a silly, powerless little thing. Or . . . is there something you're keeping from me?"

"No, of course not." She said that just a touch too quickly, Aedh thought. "But everyone knows you go hunting on this day of the week. Anyone could be lying in wait—"

"Eithne. My dearest. My darling, loving, tenderhearted wife." Aedh bent to kiss her gently. "I've gone hunting before without this fuss. What would they think of a king who hid behind his fortress walls, afraid to stir? How long do you think I would keep my throne?"

"But—"

"I'm not a fool. I will be wary."

Eithne sighed. "Of course. I'm the one who's being foolish. Go on, and good hunting to you, love."

🌰 🌰 🌰

Queen Eithne stood at the open window, watching fervently as Aedh rode away. Och, but he was splendid and shining, sitting his horse as straight and proud as a man half his age (not that he was that old, she told herself sternly, no more than ten years her senior; there were only the fewest threads of silver amid the reddish hair and beard, and they gleaming like royal ornaments in the sun). Ahead of him coursed a slew of fine hounds, and all around him rode Aedh's own chosen guard; Eithne knew them man and dog, and trusted the lot.

At the king's side rode battle-wise Cadwal ap Dyfri, that rarity among mercenaries: a man who'd made it to middle years. A curt, crusty man, Cadwal, trusting almost no one, guarding his secrets like a miser his gold, but a truly skill-ful fighter, and in his own bought-and-paid-for way more loyal to Aedh than many a courtier. Eithne knew he would die before he let harm come to the king who'd never once treated him as anything less than a man of honor.

Then why am I so uneasy? What was the meaning of that cursed dream?

Feeling just a touch foolish, she snatched up a small handful of earth from one of the pots of herbs she kept to sweeten the air, and hurled it after her husband, a childish charm to bring him safely back to her. Arms hugged tightly about herself, Eithne stood watching as Aedh rode down from the royal keep, down through the many outbuildings and the earthen rings of defense, down into the endless expanse of forest, till she could see him no more. Only then did she turn away, calling for her women to come and dress her and bring her children to her.

As always, her heart gave a little leap at the sight of the two lovely young things. Niall, now nearly eleven, was straight-backed as his father but as lightly built as a young falcon, his stare Aedh's steady grey gaze. The boy was just at the age of not wanting to be embarrassed by a mother's hugs, but little Fainche, all of five, rushed eagerly into Eithne's arms. The woman lowered her face to the girl, nuzzling the curly reddish hair, delighted by the fresh, clean, baby smell of her.

With a reluctant sigh, Eithne straightened. "Off with you now. To your studies, the both of you. Niall, don't give me such a long look! Time enough to be following your father to the hunt when you're older."

"How *much* older?"

"Och, child, time passes soon enough, all too soon! Besides, do you think your father would be High King if he had neglected his studying?"

"He would be High King no matter what!" Niall said hotly, and Eithne stifled a smile.

"As will you, someday," she told him solemnly, "God willing." *But, oh please you listening Ones, not for many long years.* "But only if you finish your lessons! Now, off with you, I say! And you," Eithne added to her servants, "off with you, too. I wish to be alone."

She waited in sudden tension, listening, *feeling*, till she was sure no one was watching. Clutching her cloak to her, Eithne hurried to the one secret chamber not even Aedh had seen: the chamber that was barred with Words and Wishes from being discovered. Slipping inside, she shut and bolted the door behind her, then stood for a moment, biting her lip in anxious thought. Yes . . . this was the ritual she'd work.

Eithne hurriedly cast open a small chest and set out candles at north, south, east, west. She paused, willing everything from her mind but the words of her spell . . . the words, and an image of Aedh, proud and full of health . . . Aedh . . .

Holding that image firmly in her mind, she lit a taper, then the southern candle. As it caught fire, Eithne murmured, "Nothing from the south can harm Aedh, nothing cause him peril."

The western, northern, eastern candles were lit as well, the spell repeated. Eithne sat in the small space between the candles, watching them burn, concentrating with all her might on *feeling* any danger to Aedh burning as well, melting harmlessly away, leaving him safe, safe, safe. . . .

At last, drained, Eithne got to her feet, staggering a little, then damped the candle stubs and returned them to the chest. For a time she stood motionless, trying to regain her strength, then let out her breath in a long sigh. She'd done what she could to protect her husband. The rest was up to the gods.

Ah, yes, the gods, Eithne thought with the tiniest of shivers, the Dagda and Brigit—whom the Christians had tried so earnestly to turn into one of their saints—and bright, shining Aengus. Father Seadna, the High King's priest, was a tolerant man, but there *were* limits. And Aedh . . . oh, Aedh loved her, she never doubted that, but he must never, never learn, he who had been ordained king by the Christian priests, that his wife secretly practiced a far older religion, that she secretly worked her magics to protect him.

Wearily, Eithne returned to the royal chambers. Aedh was shielded by God and man and magic. Everything would be well.

Then why did a darkness still seem to hang over him for all her spells, to hang over them all?

Outside the grianan, the ladies' house, of the royal palace of Clonach, the small kingdom that lay several days' riding north from the High King's seat, the morning shone clear and fine, the distant sea deepest blue sparkling with sunlight. The roar of surf on rocks was far enough away to be muted to a familiar, soothing thrum, but Queen Derval of Clonach paid all that no heed. Slender and golden-haired, her pale, smooth skin the love of poets and despair of other women, she put down her needlework with an impatient sigh and sat watching her tall, auburn-haired husband pace restlessly back and forth till at last she could stand it no longer. "Now what's the matter?"

Donnchadh, King of Clonach, stopped short to stare at her. *Like a deer caught by wolves*, Derval thought in disapproval. *Or a little boy in fear of punishment*. "Am I doing the right thing?" he challenged her. "Am I?"

Derval let out her breath in a sharp hiss. "*That* again! Do you wish justice or not?"

"Of course, but—"

"But what? You are of the Ui Neill sept, just like Aedh, you are every bit as worthy as—"

"He has been crowned Ard Ri before God and man,"
Donnchadh said severely, and Derval sighed yet again.

"A man made king," she said as carefully as though speaking to a child, "can still be unmade. I thought we had settled all this, husband. We both agreed Aedh is too weak, son of a saint that he is, too . . . educated a man to properly guard Eriu—particularly with this new threat of longboat raids hanging over us."

"Yes. Yes. It's my lands that lie in direct peril from those raiders, not his."

"*Will* you stop that pacing?" Derval rose, nearly as tall as her husband, to block his path. "Listen to yourself! For shame, Donnchadh!"

"What—"

"Whining like this—you sound like a frightened child, not a king."

Face dark with sudden rage, he raised a hand to strike, and just for an instant, seeing the fury in his eyes, Derval felt a spasm of genuine fear. But even though her heart was pounding, she refused to flinch, staring steadily back at him. And Donnchadh was the first to give way, turning suddenly aside to look out the unshuttered window.

Weakling! Derval thought in contempt, and moved to stand beside him, staring out to where their son, golden young Fearghal, at sixteen already nearly as tall as his sire, was testing his swordplay against one of his comrades. A sudden unexpected pang stabbed her heart at the sight. Fearghal, though no one dared remind him of it, was the second-born, not the true heir to Clonach. That claim belonged to the firstborn son, to Breasal. Breasal, who was hostage for his father's good behavior, there at the High King's court so far from Clonach, where he'd lived for so many years he must now be King Aedh's creature. *You always were a sickly child, poor boy,* Derval thought, *so slight and gentle I could almost think you a changeling. You could never have held a throne.*

Look at this. She was already thinking of him in the past tense. Fiercely shutting her mind against the pain she felt, a mother's pain, Derval added, *If I must sacrifice you, my firstborn son, I will. Though it will tear at my heart to do it, I will do what must be done. At least one of my children will sit on the High King's throne.*

"Good," Donnchadh muttered, watching Fearghal closely. "Yes. Hit him again, there, and there. Ah, yes, well struck."

Does he even remember *Breasal?* Derval wondered, and in that moment hated her husband with all her heart.

Fearghal, meanwhile, beat his opponent back and back again, finally trapping him against a whitewashed stone wall. The other boy tried to surrender, but Fearghal struck the sword from his hand, then swept his feet roughly out from under him. As the other boy went crashing to the ground, Fearghal stood over him, laughing. "So," Derval said softly. "Do you want our son on the High King's throne or not?"

Donnchadh's hands tightened on the sill. "You know I do."

"Well, then."

The man's shoulders sagged in sudden resignation. "I know, I know." The glance he gave her was full of despair. "And I have done what I must. Treason though it might be, I have done what I must."

It is no treason if it sets my son, my Fearghal on the High King's throne, Derval thought, but said nothing.

THE EXILE

CHAPTER 4

How long had he been huddling here, too dazed to move? Ardagh Lithanial, exiled prince of Faerie, straightened slowly, aching in mind and body, trying to remember all that had happened. There'd been the passage through the Portal, the bewildering sense of being not here, not there . . . then a rough hardness all around him that he now realized must have been the stony walls of a cave. Somehow he must have staggered out of it, only to collapse . . . where?

Wait now, the cave . . . what if the Portal was still open within it? Ardagh whirled and saw—

"Ae, no . . ."

The cave was small, dank—and most definitely finite.

But I know the Portal spell, I can reopen it and . . . all I have to do is . . . is . . .

No, this couldn't be! He *couldn't* have forgotten, not so totally! A coldness settling in his heart, Ardagh fought and fought with his memory. He *must* remember, he had to remember!

He couldn't. The shape of the Realm-crossing spell was gone from his mind as though it had been cut away.

For the first time the full weight of what had been done to him fell upon Ardagh. His legs gave way beneath the burden and he crumpled, shrouded in a fog of mindless grief and terror, so overwhelmed by the size of his loss he had to catch a fold of his sleeve between his teeth to keep

31

from screaming. He had nothing, no rank, no home, no name—

No, curse it, he had *not* lost his name; no matter what else they'd taken from him, he was still Ardagh Lithanial!

Gradually the prince became aware of an odd warmth stealing through the chill, gentle on head and arm. Blinking in confusion, he looked down at himself, seeing a strange golden light. . . .

Sunlight! Mortal sunlight, and he was—

Obviously not about to be charred to ash. Maybe the rumors were true and his dark hair did mean a taint of human blood. A protective taint.

Ah well, if the sun wasn't going to kill him, he was going to have to do something about staying alive. Ardagh got slowly to his feet, looking warily about. He was standing in a small glade, surrounded by dense forest, though he couldn't have put a name to any of the not-quite-of-Faerie trees. The light that filtered down through the leaves seemed so strange that at first he couldn't puzzle out the difference.

Ah, of course! If a sun—a single, central fire rather than the glowing, overall Faerie radiance—was to be of any use, it would have to be strong enough to actually cast shadows!

How bizarre! Like a candle flame, but so much more powerful!

The strangeness of the concept sent a new shiver racing through him. And yet, as Ardagh raised a hand to the sunlight, turning his arm this way and that in Sidhe curiosity to see the effect, then twisting his whole body about to watch the alien, fascinating way his shadow stretched and shrank, he had to admit that the dappling, golden effects of sunlight weren't totally unattractive.

But this experimentation wasn't getting him anywhere. Ardagh took a deep, testing breath of air that was clean and cool, rich with the inimitable sweet-spicy scent of new vegetation. *One small stroke of luck,* he thought. *I might have been transported into the heart of winter.*

So, now. The sunlight wouldn't hurt him and the season was Earthly spring. But as he warily opened his senses to the world about him, Ardagh suddenly shivered. For all the pretty freshness about him, the air, the whole land, had a certain *flat* feel to it that sounded a warning chime in his mind. Where was the land's Power? He could hardly have expected this Realm to be as Powerful as Faerie, where the raw stuff of magic was literally everywhere, easily drawn from the very air and soil. But surely this couldn't be a world without any magic at all . . . ? Powers, Powers, surely he hadn't been abandoned in a Realm where he was totally defenseless?

Heart racing in renewed panic, Ardagh tried spell after spell. Nothing! Nothing worked, nothing roused, nothing—

No. Stop that. There *was* Power in this Realm; he could sense it, even if the shape of it was strange and weak. And some of his magic, the inner magic that was fueled only by his own mind and will and didn't depend on outside Power, still remained; Ardagh felt it shimmering within him. But oh, it was such a pale, pathetic thing compared to the splendors he had known!

The splendors from which the traitors had sundered him.

At that thought, the first hot stirrings of fury shot through him, cutting through shock. Ardagh, smiling without humor, welcomed that fury, carefully nursing it into full flame. Yes, yes, the traitors thought him safely out of their path, trapped here in this alien place. They thought he could never return.

"All the Powers hear me," he vowed savagely, "I shall go back. No matter how long it takes, I will find a way home. Powers hear me, I shall prove my innocence. And, oh Powers, I swear this: those who betrayed me shall pay!"

What wonderful melodramatics, a corner of his mind observed. And proclamations might be well and good in the right surroundings, but it was nothing short of stupid to make so much noise in a strange place.

Besides, Ardagh admitted with a touch of humor, vow-making or no, he could hardly stand here for the rest of his life.

And to think I once wished for adventure. Ay me, never make an idle wish: It just may be granted. I only hope some-one is kind to poor Ninet.

But what was he going to *do*? Where was he to go? Ardagh looked helplessly around at forest, and forest, and forest. A prince wasn't exactly well trained in wilderness life; he doubted he could have lived off the land even in Faerie. He hadn't the slightest chance of success here, where even the trees were unfamiliar. The weather had grown comfortably warm and soft, but surely it wouldn't stay that way forever. What was he going to do for food or shelter or—

Ardagh took a deep breath, willing his thoughts to calmness. If he wished to survive in this realm, he needed to find himself some humans as soon as possible, and make some manner of life with them.

With whom? Peasants? The prince tried to picture himself cutting wood or digging up roots or doing whatever other lowly things peasants did, and shuddered delicately. He might be an exile, but he was certainly not going to lose whatever shreds of honor might be left to him! No, somewhere out there must be what passed for a human aristocracy, no matter how pale a shadow it might be of Sidhe nobility. All he had to do was find it, then make himself a place as . . . as advisor, perhaps. Granted, he didn't even know the name of this land, let alone anything of its politics, but one could always learn what needed to be learned. Yes . . . humans being the short-lived creatures they were, any of them would surely be glad of Sidhe wisdom, even if Ardagh never risked revealing himself as Other. Work his way into a high enough position, and he would live as an honored guest.

At least till I can find the way back home.

Ardagh glanced down at himself. Good, serviceable hunting leathers and boots . . . strong, soft spidersilk tunic underneath the leather . . . Fortunate that Eirithan hadn't thought to relieve him of sword and dagger. And, the prince mused wryly, he did have his wits. Many a hero of many a tale had started with less!

A scramble up a tree showed him a darker shadow among the forest that must mean a road. Full of determination, Ardagh Lithanial, lost prince of Faerie, set forth on his journey.

Two days later, Ardagh wasn't feeling so sure of himself or his fortunes. Yes, the weather remained mild, but it seemed to rain every day, a soft, endless drizzle that worked its way down through the ceiling of leaves in a gentle, relentless mist. He was perpetually damp and tired and disgustingly dusty, aching from having slept on beds of gathered leaves, and hungrier than he could ever have imagined. There was a wealth of greenness all about, but of course, Ardagh admitted dourly, he had no way of knowing what was edible; the three small fish he had snatched out of a stream and the one scrawny rabbit he'd caught, Sidhe reactions swift as any predator, had hardly been enough to fill his stomach for long.

I'm a prince, curse it, not a—a vagrant!

But it was the smallest flare of insulted pride, half-smothered by the ever-present weight of fear that was worse than any physical discomfort: the fear that was composed mostly of terrible, endless loneliness and the knowledge that search this Realm though he might, he would never, never find another of his kind. Even at his most solitary, back on his estate, there'd never been a time when he couldn't seek out someone else.

Ardagh gave a shaky sigh. By now the sight of anyone, even the lowliest of humans, would have been more welcome than he ever would have cared to admit, but he hadn't seen the slightest sign of life—

Till now! The prince darted aside in sudden startled alarm, vanishing into the underbrush like a deer, staring at the newcomers. Rougher of skin than any Sidhe, stockier of build, broader of face . . . His eyes widened at the sight of their facial hair; save for eyebrows his people had none.

Animals, shaggy, hairy animals . . .

Not quite. Warriors, these, from the tough look of them, armed with sword and spear—

Iron swords! *Iron* spears! Powers, why hadn't he remembered humans used *iron*, that metal most dangerous to Faerie folk, sickening *iron*, a wound from which would almost surely lead to Sidhe death!

Eh well, the prince thought with desperate humor,

struggling with his new surge of panic, he would just have to take care not to get wounded.

But what were warriors doing here, so far from any habitation? Sidhe curiosity awakened anew, stronger than any alarm. Not quite ready to reveal himself, Ardagh stalked the men at a silent, wary distance. They were trying their best not to be seen or heard—though to his keen ears they were making enough noise for an army. But there didn't seem to be anything to hunt that was worth so much caution!

Ha, they were stopping for a rest, over the protests of the one who seemed to be their leader. The prince smiled thinly and settled himself comfortably on a rock. Now, let him try something. . . . The spell should work, since it was cast by him *on* him and required no external fueling. Silently, he mouthed the words, willing the magic into being. . . .

And suddenly he couldn't breathe, couldn't think, couldn't hear or see or—

It was over. The world cleared about him, and Ardagh, gasping for breath, trembling, head swimming, realized that he would have to be wary even with the sadly diminished powers left to him. The Language Spell certainly shouldn't have had such dramatic effects.

This world, the prince thought bitterly, *just does not care for Sidhe magics.* Here, like it or not, *he* was the alien.

Still the spell had worked. His mind was beginning to clear, and as it did, Ardagh realized with a little shock of relief that now he could actually understand what the humans were saying. Some of the panic of being lost in a totally foreign world diminished now that he had their language.

The humans certainly weren't in the mood to appreciate the fine, clear day around them. Ardagh heard complaints of, "Not used to fighting on foot," and, "Shouldn't have to crawl our way to battle!"

"Can't risk horses," someone muttered. "They make too much noise."

One warrior cursed under his breath. "I don't like it. Don't like it at all. This isn't some petty little under-king we're going after, it's the Ard Ri, the High King himself!"

High King! Ardagh echoed silently. A High King must

surely be one who ruled over all others, kings and com-
moners alike: a human of considerable might. He could
surely enjoy a comfortable life at such a king's court, at least
as comfortable a life as might be had among humanity—

Except that these men seemed determined to prevent it.

"You arguing with King Donnchadh?" their leader
snapped. "He's the one you swore fealty to, not some high
and mighty Ard Ri. And he's the one who gave us our
orders."

"Huh. Don't see Donnchadh here."

"You want a king to take part in an *ambush?*"

"How come it's not honorable for him, but all right for
us? We're free men, not slaves! I tell you, I don't like it!"

"Maybe you'd rather take on Aedh in his fortress? No?
This is his hunting day, our only clear chance at him, so
let's shut up and get ready!"

Why, the traitors! Ardagh thought indignantly. *Traitors
against their liege lord as surely as Iliach and the others!*

Cursed if he was going to let them wreck his safety
before he'd even won it! Ardagh stole silently ahead, hunting for this mysterious Aedh, this High King. Ah yes, now
he heard hoofbeats on the road ahead of him, rapidly
headed his way, and the idle yapping of hounds who hadn't
yet found a trail.

And what happens when the hounds catch my scent?
Ardagh thought in sudden alarm. *I most certainly won't smell
like a human to them. For all I know, they'll try to attack!*

Warily, he swung up into a tree and perched on a thick
branch, screened by leaves, and stared in open curiosity at
this new group of humans. They were better clad than the
first lot, wrapped round in what seemed to be long plaid
woolen cloaks over tunics that looked almost as sleekly
smooth as his own. Their saddles had no stirrups, but they
sat their small, sturdy horses with an ease that spoke of years
of training.

One rider caught and held the prince's glance: a strongly
built man, red of hair and beard, a warrior by his build, a
ruler by his bearing. At his side rode a second human, a
well-worn, grizzle-bearded warrior—Cadwal, his name

seemed to be—who deferred to the red-haired man as though to a king—

Ha, yes! Ardagh came so sharply alert he nearly slipped from his perch. This red-haired man was High King Aedh himself—the man the traitors meant to kill!

They shall not! Ardagh leaped down from hiding with a warning cry, "A trap! Beware the ambush!"

Swords shrieked out of scabbards, spears flashed up— For a moment Ardagh was sure he was going to be spitted, and hastily added, "Not me, *them*," even as the traitors came rushing out of their failed ambush.

The prince whipped out his own sword as a warrior closed with him, a pang of worry stabbing through him that Faerie metal might not hold up against iron. But the blades clashed together again and again without damage.

So be it! Ardagh thought. With a savage laugh, the prince dove into battle, his pent-up fury, loss and rage tearing free in one wild, deadly dance of combat. He was quicker than the humans, more graceful, swifter to react; he lunged, parried and slashed with feral joy, hardly aware of the burning sickness of iron all around him.

Caught in his battle-frenzy, Ardagh saw one of the warriors guarding the High King fall, and vaulted into the empty saddle with inhuman speed, blocking the downward swing of an enemy blade that would have cut into Aedh's neck, barely keeping his balance on impact with no stirrups against which to brace himself. He heard the king's hasty gasp of thanks, caught grizzled Cadwal's approving glance, then the three of them were fighting together, Ardagh and the human warrior guarding Aedh between them as though they'd been rehearsing it for days.

At last his mad strength began to ebb. Ardagh came back to himself with a jolt, drained and panting, glancing wildly around for more foes but finding none. Sudden shame overwhelmed him. Powers, how could he have done this? He had lost self-control as badly as any human!

But how good it had felt to know the joy of battle; not some sly treachery against which one was helpless, but an honest battle that could be fought and won.

Won, yes. The last of the would-be assassins was on the ground, gasping out his life, and the prince heard Aedh snarl, "Hurry! Find out who sent him!"

But the warrior who'd hurriedly bent over the man straightened with a sigh. "Too late."

"Damn!" That was Cadwal, sword still in hand. "Dunod, Iwan, Garwyn, scout out the woods. Make sure there aren't any more of the vermin lurking."

"There aren't," Ardagh said. "I was following them for some time."

The warrior gave him a wolf-fierce stare. "Why?"

"Better to have that lot before me than after me!"

"Easy answer, but—"

Aedh impatiently waved them to silence. "Then do *you* know who sent them?"

"I think," the prince began warily, "it was a king named Dun . . . ae, Dun something."

"Donnchadh?" Aedh snapped. "Is that the name?"

"I'm not sure," the prince admitted. "All your names sound foreign to me. Ah—is something wrong?"

The High King was staring at him as if seeing him clearly for the first time. "Good God," Aedh said with genuine reverence. "You're real."

"I . . . beg your pardon?"

"That dream—och, never mind. Let's just say my wife is going to be insufferably smug for a time." Aedh's voice sharpened. "Are you hurt, man?"

Ardagh, following the king's alarmed glance, looked down at himself and gasped to see a long, deep slash crossing the front of his leather armor. Powers! If it had cut just a bit deeper, *he* would have been sliced, and by poisonous iron! "No," he said after a moment.

"Now that's a fortunate thing, ah . . ."

"Ardagh Lithanial." Ae, why not be honest about it? "Prince Ardagh Lithanial."

"So-o!" Aedh's lift of a brow was skeptical. "And where might Prince Ardagh Lithanial be from? Nowhere near here, that's for certain!"

"Ah, no. My lands lie far away, indeed."

"Cathay?" one of the warriors asked tentatively. When Ardagh hesitated, not quite sure how to reply, the man continued as eagerly as a child reciting a favorite story, "I've heard traders' tales about men from that land who have such dark hair and such slanted eyes. Yes, and the tales say they wear silk even into battle, too!" At Cadwal's warning glance, the man added hastily, "Not that I mean to pry, Prince Ardagh!"

Ardagh waved a gracious hand, denying nothing. He'd never heard of Cathay, but if these men wanted to believe him from there, well and good; the land was apparently so far away none of them knew anything about it, either!

"Enough questioning," Aedh cut in. "Prince Ardagh, I owe you my life, my gratitude, and my hospitality." He must surely still be wary of this bedraggled stranger—Cadwal most blatantly was—even if said stranger had saved his life, but the king added without more than the slightest hesitation, "Will it please you to return with me to my fortress?"

Powers, yes! Ardagh gave the man an exceptionally graceful, elegant bow to hide his sudden surge of relief. Food and shelter and clean clothes—no, more than that, a home of suitably high status, even if it was among humans!

For a man who had narrowly escaped assassination, King Aedh seemed remarkably calm, mildly pointing out this landmark or that to the prince as they rode. Either the human had survived so many attempts on his life that he could almost take them for granted, or he had a truly regal amount of self-control. *Almost as much self-control as a Sidhe,* Ardagh thought with a touch of surprised approval.

"Travel is a fine and fascinating thing," Aedh said without warning.

"It can be," Ardagh agreed warily.

"I admit, being who and what I am, I've hardly had the chance to do much wandering."

Ardagh acknowledged that with a dip of his head. "A king has little free time."

"Ah, but you, surely, Prince Ardagh, would be able to speak about such matters as travel with authority."

Ardagh fought down a grin, beginning to enjoy this odd little duel of words. "Would I?"

"Why, are you not most remarkably far-travelled?"

"Farther than you could dream," the prince said with heartfelt honesty.

From the glint in Aedh's grey eyes, he was enjoying this game as well. Instead of coming right out and asking direct questions, he commented vaguely, "You must have seen many wonders."

"Indeed." Smiling to himself, Ardagh skirted falsehood in delicate Sidhe style; he certainly had seen things a human would find wondrous, even if travelling hadn't been involved. "I must tell you of some of them. At a later time," he added casually, watching for Aedh's reaction. When the king showed not the slightest sign of surprise at that, Ardagh smiled to himself; the man had as good as welcomed him to stay.

"You must admit," Aedh remarked in a sudden, offhand manner, "that it's a bit unusual to see a prince travelling alone."

"Sometimes one has no choice." Feeling the king's sudden sharp gaze on him, Ardagh added flatly, "Particularly when one is the younger brother of a most suspicious ruler."

"Ah. That would be an awkward thing."

Ardagh glanced his way. "Especially when one has no intention of breaking one's oath of fealty."

It was Aedh's turn to say, "Indeed," managing to put a world of meaning—skepticism, sympathy, approval—in the one word. "And how is it such a one is alone and afoot?"

My, how nicely this human king played the game, never quite overriding the bounds of courtesy. This was promising, Ardagh thought; the man had a sharp intellect to him. He would almost certainly welcome a clever advisor.

"Any man may fall afoul of bad fortune," Ardagh said, leaving Aedh to make of that what he would. "But now," the prince added smoothly, "my luck seems to have turned."

Aedh grinned. "So it has. See now, we've returned to Fremainn."

That? Oh, surely that couldn't be a royal home! Yes, it

was clearly a fortress of sorts, a series of earthen embank-
ments, rings within rings, over which the upper half of a
round, broad tower could be seen, but it was all so—primitive! No, there must be some mistake, or a jest, an odd
human jest, and they'd be riding on and—

No. Guards stood atop the earthen ramparts, saluting their
king, welcoming him back. A wooden gate was cast open
and the hunting party made its way through a narrow maze
of corridors that smelled strongly of earth and damp and,
Ardagh thought with distaste, garbage. They came at last
into a vast grassy space covered here and there by round
houses of wood and thatch; only the round central tower
Ardagh had seen from outside was of stone. The air was
cleaner here, but as the prince glanced about, misery settled
over his spirit.

This was indeed the royal home, the High King's fortress.
This was the finest, fairest palace to be found in human
lands.

This barbaric place of earth and wood and stone was to
be his home.

A HOME AWAY FROM HOME

CHAPTER 5

One thing these humans appeared to be, Ardagh mused, was enthusiastic. A swarm of them, plaid cloaks flapping as they ran, scurried from keep and outbuilding and craftsman's stall, bowing to their king, chattering with his warriors. Some took the hounds in charge, others the horses—but no matter what they did, all of them, the prince realized, were making excuses to stare at him. Their broad, ruddy faces—some of them actually covered with hair!—were so very different from the pale, narrow, elegantly planed Sidhe norm that Ardagh could hardly blame them for being curious; he was barely keeping from staring at them in turn. He also seemed to be the only one with dark hair in the entire fortress, and the prince had to fight a sudden, ridiculously self-conscious urge to raise a hand to smooth his battle-tangled locks.

But suddenly Ardagh forgot all about awkwardness. A tall, slender woman had come rushing out from the keep like a young girl, gold glinting from head and neck, long, chestnut-bright hair streaming out behind her, to fling herself into Aedh's arms, gasping, "You're safe!"

"Och, Eithne! Of course I'm safe. I told you all would be well." The brusque words were belied by the gentleness in Aedh's voice and in the equally gentle curve of his arms around her. "Come, wife, enough of this. We have a guest."

43

"Och!" The woman drew back in embarrassment, hastily arranging the line of her gown and cloak. "Your pardon," she began to Ardagh, then stopped short, staring.

Ardagh stared as well, seeing past the ruddy skin and green eyes to a glittering hint of—why, yes, the woman bore a trace of Power! Power carefully hidden, as though she didn't dare let anyone know about it . . . *Now, isn't this interesting?* Ardagh thought, and stored the fact away for future reference. And was she sensing something of who and what he was? Was her gift strong enough for that? No . . . it would seem not. She seemed perfectly willing to accept him as human.

Aedh was watching his wife with a hint of amusement in his eyes. "Eithne, may I present the Prince Ardagh Lithanial of Cathay? Ardagh, this lovely lady is my wife, Queen Eithne."

As Ardagh bowed politely, he heard the king add softly to Eithne, "He saved my life."

"Your dream!"

"Yes, if you insist, my dream." But Aedh's voice wasn't quite as condescending as his words. "There were would-be assassins— No, no, it's all right, I'm not hurt, in good part thanks to Prince Ardagh. Yes, love, just as in the dream. You have my permission to say 'I told you so' as often as you wish!"

But Eithne, face gone ashen, was offering Ardagh a curtsey of her own. "My thanks, Prince Ardagh, my true, heartfelt thanks."

"I did what needed to be done," Ardagh told her, which was true enough, even if what he'd done had been insuring his own safety.

"But we can hardly leave our guest standing here," King Aedh cut in, and signalled to some plainly clad men—more servants, Ardagh assumed—who came running eagerly forward. "See that Prince Ardagh is treated according to his rank, according to the full laws of hospitality."

The servants bowed obediently, glancing sideways at Ardagh, their eyes bright with curiosity. Aedh added to the prince, "We will, if it pleases you, sit together a bit later and . . . chat. And you will, of course, be my honored guest at dinner."

And beyond, Ardagh told him silently. But gently, gently—time enough to make himself an indispensable part of the realm once he'd learned the rules.

And so Ardagh said merely, "As it pleases *you*." With a polite dip of the head to Aedh and his wife, he followed the servants away. They led him not into the main keep, but down a narrow, grassy corridor between two wooden, thatch-roofed buildings, stopping before a small, round hut set apart from the others by a low wall.

"If it pleases you, Prince Ardagh?"

As they moved respectfully aside, Ardagh paused for a moment, looking into darkness, thoughts of treachery in his mind. But even if the walls of the hut were of woven wickerwork, they'd been whitewashed and polished to an elegant, gleaming purity, and the doorposts themselves were intricately carved wood inlaid with bits of bright silver. Hardly a place for betrayal.

By now, his eyes were adjusting fully to the dimness within. Ardagh saw that for all the hut's simplicity, it held a nicely built table, a chest for possessions, and what looked like a very comfortable bed with an enticingly thick feather mattress. There were no true windows, but slits in the wooden walls just below the shingled roof let in some light and air.

So now, a guest house—and one, presumably for honorable guests. Or what passes for a guest house in human society.

Aware that the servants were waiting for some response, the prince nodded. "Quite satisfactory."

An awkward pause followed, as it dawned on the servants that he had no belongings to be stored away. They glanced at each other, then at him, and one of them said warily, "You will want personal servants assigned to you, of course."

"Why?"

That caught the humans by surprise. "Why—uh—because—"

"I assure you, I am quite capable of dressing and taking

care of myself." *And the last thing I want is one of your kind sharing this place with me.*

The servants glanced at each other, blatantly thinking by this point that he was a complete eccentric. One of them asked, as if he wasn't at all sure of the response he was going to get, "If you will follow us, Prince Ardagh?"

"Lead on."

They led him on through the wooden maze to a second building, as dim and windowless as the first. Again Ardagh waited uneasily for his vision to adjust, then let out his breath in a sigh of relief.

A bathhouse. The humans' idea of hospitality, the Powers be praised, included a bath. Ardagh waited, fighting back impatience, as the servants laboriously brought bucket after bucket of hot water, then gladly surrendered his hopelessly travel-stained clothing—but not his sword, he wasn't quite that trusting, placing the weapon instead to one side where he could reach it should need be—and settled blissfully into the bath.

As he luxuriated in the hot water, feeling the aches of battle and long, hard travel seeping away, Ardagh found himself struggling to keep awake.

Idiot! These people may have the concept of laws of hospitality, but they are also capable of falsehood!

Ah, but when was the last time he'd slept in a bed? For that matter, when was the last time he'd slept the night through? Travelling through wilderness didn't exactly lend itself to peaceful rest.

Forcing his mind to stay at least reasonably alert, Ardagh mused that though the human way of life here might look impossibly barbaric, at least the folk did seem to place some worth on cleanliness; they all bore a faint, unavoidably animal smell that seemed to be the scent common to humanity, but their clothes and bodies were spotless. Maybe it wouldn't be quite as intolerable to live among them as he'd first feared.

"Your Highness?"

Ah well, he could hardly lie here all day. His own clothing had been whisked away, but surely other clothes of suitable quality would be provided. Ardagh let the careful

servants dry him (sensing their bemusement at his Sidhe
lack of body hair; they all seemed by comparison hairy as
animals) and gingerly comb out his tangled hair, then stood
courteously still as they dressed him in a linen tunic so finely
woven it was pleasantly soft against the skin and smelled
faintly of the sweet herbs with which it must have been
stored, snug-fitting woollen leggings, and over all one of
the apparently ubiquitous plaid woolen cloaks, this one in
a pattern of dark red crossed with sky blue that showed a
nice appreciation for the contrast it made with his fair skin
and dark hair. A servant showed him the proper way of
wrapping the cloak—the *brat,* the man called it—and pinning it in place with an enamelled brooch. Ardagh's hand
hesitated when he realized the pin of the brooch was iron,
but there was a minimal amount of the metal after all, and
it was well insulated by the thick wool of the *brat.* The prince
slipped his feet into his own soft boots, which had been
neatly cleaned and brushed during his bath, then glanced
at himself in the sleek bronze mirror a servant held for him
and winced at how unSidhe he looked.

"Your Highness, if you would follow me . . . ?"

Ah yes. The royal . . . chat. Now he must prove himself
worthy of further hospitality. Even though he knew nothing of the politics here or even the name of the land—Ardagh
straightened, channelling his thoughts to quiet self-control.
What wasn't known could be learned.

"So be it," he said. "Lead on."

The royal palace seemed to be more a collection of connected buildings than one cohesive structure. Ardagh was
led to a quiet little stone building jutting out from a wall
of the central keep. This, he was told, was "the conversation house," presumably, judging from the solid, secure look
of it, a place where one could talk in private.

It was windowless, as the bathhouse had been, though
a small central hearth cast a sharp, flickering glow and sunlight filtered down through the smoke hole overhead.
Ardagh kept his face properly impassive, but he couldn't
hold back a spasm of distaste. Didn't these humans know
the art of building proper windows or creating large enough

sheets of glass to fill them? Or, he thought in sudden wariness, was this closeness intended to ward off would-be assassins?

A pity they don't have magic to help them. It would make their lives so much simpler!

"Prince Ardagh," said a now-familiar voice. "Please, enter." King Aedh, his hunting clothes replaced by a fine, softly woven red *brat* and a linen tunic so white it glowed in the faint light, was sitting at the far end of the little house, gold glinting richly from neck and brow. He looked very much like a man totally at his ease, without the slightest sign of reaction from his narrow escape, though Ardagh suspected that the king's relaxed appearance was as much a disguise as his own mask of Sidhe calm.

As the prince approached, he saw two more men seated to Aedh's left and right. One, on the king's right, was almost as elegantly clad as Aedh, his hair and beard neatly combed. His tunic and cloak were of a more subdued blue and green patterning, but he, also, gleamed with gold here and there. The other man, who sat on the king's left, was clean-shaven, his grey eyes more tranquil than those of Aedh, deep as shadowed pools. He alone showed no sign of riches, wearing a plain robe woven of what looked like bleached white wool; the only real spot of color about him was the narrow ribbon of embroidery at the edge of his wide sleeves.

Ardagh, not completely sure how one judged human age, guessed that both men must be older than Aedh: the hair of the white-robed man had been severely trimmed, but enough remained to show liberal streaks of grey, while the hair and beard of the other fellow was a solid ash-grey, and his pleasant, plain face was lined. There was nothing old, however about his wise green eyes; they sparkled with life and a hint of a wry, clever wit.

"To my left," Aedh introduced, "is Father Seadna. Good Father, may I introduce you to Prince Ardagh Lithanial?"

Those quiet grey eyes studied the prince as though trying to puzzle out everything about him. "I have been told how you saved the life of our king. Please accept my gratitude in the name of the Church."

Ardagh was clearly expected to understand what that meant and make some ritual response. Lost, he bowed politely and hoped that was enough. Evidently it was, because Father Seadna returned the courtesy without any sign of surprise.

"And this," Aedh continued, giving the man on his right a quick, affectionate glance, "is Fothad mac Ailin, once my tutor, now my chief poet. And, I might add, my chief advisor in state affairs, just as Father Seadna is mine in less secular matters."

Ah.

But he could hardly have expected a king to lack for advisors. Besides, Ardagh reminded himself, he knew nothing of this land, not even its name; he would need someone willing to teach him what he needed to learn. What better way to deal with a potential rival than to turn him to an ally? Face carefully neutral, Ardagh sank smoothly to the small, cushioned couch he'd been offered and dipped his head to Fothad with the same polite courtesy he'd shown to Father Seadna, and received Fothad's equally polite bow in return.

"Thank you for answering my summons so promptly," Aedh said without irony. "I know you must be weary."

Ardagh brushed that off. "I can understand that you'd wish to question me, King Aedh."

"Och, no, Prince Ardagh, that's hardly our way!" the king said with such theatrical indignation Ardagh knew it was feigned. "To force a guest to submit to questioning would be against all the laws of hospitality."

Indeed. But, Ardagh thought cynically, there were always ways to sidestep such laws, particularly when one was a human. "I see," the prince said in a voice carefully empty of sarcasm. "What, then, shall we discuss?"

Aedh smiled slightly. "Why, I thought you simply might wish to . . . relax a bit after this strenuous day. Remember what you could of the name you overheard."

Ardagh sighed. "Believe me, King Aedh, if I could, I would. But at the time I hardly knew I'd need to remember it."

"Ah well, no," the king agreed, "how could you?" Aedh paused a moment. "Perhaps we could discuss something else—though of course I would not dream of questioning you."

"Of course not."

"But perhaps it just might please you to volunteer, if you would, some assurance that your royal brother isn't hard on your heels."

"That," Ardagh said shortly, "he most definitely is not. My brother has no intention of ever seeing me again, and I will swear to it by whatever oath you wish."

"And of course," Father Seadna murmured, "you have no desire at all to gather an army to yourself."

Ardagh raised a wry eyebrow. "From here, you mean? To attack my brother? With the distances between this realm and that being as vast as they are? My word on this, King Aedh, such a thing would truly be impossible."

"Would it, now?" Fothad wondered softly.

Ardagh stiffened. Did the human realize the insult he'd just implied? No, no, of course he didn't; he couldn't. With a sudden inner chill he remembered where he was. These people could never understand anything of Sidhe honor. They thought nothing of falsehood, and he was forever trapped among them—

No, damn Eirithan and all the rest of that treacherous royal court to the Outer Dark, he was *not* forever trapped! He *would* return. And right now he needed these humans; he must not let them alienate him. Struggling with despair and rage, the prince snapped, biting each word off sharply, "I have just given my word. My people do not lie."

Fothad flinched and held up an apologetic hand. "Forgive me. I meant no insult."

He seemed genuinely contrite, and after a tense moment, Ardagh dipped his head in acceptance. Aedh continued as calmly as though the moment of tension had never happened, "And what, I wonder, would a prince of Cathay wish from this far-off land?"

"The same thing any other man alone might wish," Ardagh retorted. "Food. Shelter. A safe place to rest."

"More than that, surely."

The prince hesitated, hating the thought of showing anything the humans might interpret as weakness. At last he admitted with reluctant frankness, "King Aedh, what I want just now is simply this: sanctuary. A place where I may stay and think on what to do next."

"That," Aedh assured him, "you have."

But Ardagh thought he caught the faintest hint of what could only be human pity in the man's voice. Stung, he added sharply, "I have no intention of accepting charity." With a quick glance at Fothad, the prince added, "I am sure you have truly wise counselors there at your side. But perhaps you can make use of someone not quite so familiar with this realm. There may be times when subjective wisdom might not be as useful as objective observation."

Aedh glanced at his ministers. Fothad waved a hand in wry salute, and Father Seadna smiled fleetingly.

"I promise you," Ardagh added with delicate irony, "I am not exactly untrained in the world of royal politics."

Aedh chuckled. "No, you wouldn't be, would you?" The king got suddenly to his feet, stretching. "It truly has been a most strenuous day so far."

"A master of understatement," Fothad murmured, and Aedh laughed.

"Come, Prince Ardagh, by now our dinner must surely be ready. You," the king added to Ardagh with an open grin, "could surely use a good meal, from the looks of you. No, man, don't glare at me. I doubt *I* could have survived in the wilderness for long, either. A peasant could probably have lived off that woodland with ease, but you and I are trained for more . . . civilized battles." Wry humor glinted in the grey eyes. "That fact," he said, almost casually, "speaks in your favor more than any fine words."

"I . . . beg your pardon?"

"Why, Prince Ardagh, had you been in better condition, had you not shown such blatant signs of hardship, such princely ignorance of woodsmanship—particularly with the forest so green and lush about you—I would never have believed you were who and what you claim. Now come, our dinner waits."

Following King Aedh and his Queen through the now almost total darkness, servants lighting their way with torches (disturbing the Sidhe's flawless night vision), Ardagh braced himself for the new flood of human curiosity that was sure to come at dinner. The dining hall proved to be—*of course,* the prince thought wearily—yet another separate building. Sensible, he supposed, since most of the structures here seemed to be of flammable wood and thatch, to keep the cooking fires isolated lest they—

Ardagh stopped short in the doorway, hit by such a storm of noise and smell and heat that for a moment he couldn't have moved to save himself. Humans all around, talking and laughing and shouting, the scent of them mingling with the reek of roasting meat and grease and the smoke from torches and central fire pits that wasn't quite finding the smoke holes in the roof, and the cold, cold burning of iron from everyone, everything—

I can't! I—can't!

Hardly aware of what he was doing, Ardagh raced wildly back out into the night. As his legs gave out from under him and he crumpled to his knees, the prince had time for one brief thankful thought that no one had followed him. Then he was lost in a time of seemingly endless misery as his too-empty stomach insisted, no matter how he fought with it, on continuing the useless struggle of trying to rid itself of food that wasn't there.

Then, just when he had finally won the battle for control, a sudden voice asked, "Are you ill?"

Ardagh started, glancing up, gasping and drained, and saw a woman's dark blue eyes staring down at him, set in a fierce, keen-featured face framed by a mass of deep red hair. Furious at having been caught in such humiliation, the prince ached to blast the impudent human where she stood—

Foolish. Even if he had wanted to so stupidly lose his sanctuary, he had no such battle-magic in this Power-feeble

Realm. Yet under the circumstances, he could hardly defend himself properly with words, either. *What can I say? "I can't stand the noise you humans make. I can't stand your animal smell. I can't stand the feel of your iron."*

No, no, all that was impossible to admit.

Contempt flared in the woman's eyes. "Now, aren't you ashamed of yourself?" she snapped.

Stunned, he glared wordlessly up at her, and she hurried on, "I mean, a fine royal man like yourself losing himself to drink, and here it is still so early in the evening!"

"I—am—not—drunk."

The words were bitten off with such savage force he saw the woman flinch. As though angry at herself for that weakness, she retorted sharply, "Oh, no, of course not. It simply amused you to grovel on the ground like a dog emptying his stomach."

Before Ardagh could find anything safe and sensible to say, the woman turned away, red braids snapping out behind her, and was gone, leaving him still crouching there, blazing with useless rage.

Struggling back to his feet, Ardagh forced himself back to the dining hall. Come what may, he was *not* going to show any further weakness to these people!

So, now . . . he froze in the doorway, his stomach trying its best to rebel all over again: the hall was just as noisy, just as thick with smoke and the *feel* of iron.

Come now, you fool, you have some Power left. Use it. Isolate the smoke . . . accept it, a natural scent, nothing terrible about it.

Yes. His will held true. The smoke was not truly foul, just a bit thicker than might be preferred. Only smoke. That much was conquered.

Now, you must isolate the smells of food.

It was just as natural for his stomach to rebel, since it had been nearly empty for too long. But food was life, and he would not let himself turn away from life. Ardagh carefully analyzed scent after scent . . . yes. He could hold the smell of roasting meat separate from the rest, an aroma no longer sickening but warm and savory and promising.

Now, isolate the human noise . . . separate out the animal sounds, hunt for the emotions underneath.

Delicately, Ardagh separated out anger and greed—the quick, transient emotions that seemed so much a part of what he'd seen so far of humankind; carefully he hunted for the true, basic shape of mood in that hall.

Which, he realized with some surprise, was happiness, the comfortable easiness of those among friends, at peace with what and where they were. And, again to Ardagh's surprise, he felt a little pang almost of envy shoot through him. How strange to have friends! How strange to be so totally at ease with others, to play with them so freely and boisterously!

One thing more must be considered. *Iron.*

But with the overwhelming distractions of sight and sound and odor reduced, the terrible *feel* of iron was, if not reduced, at least bearable. Ardagh took a deep, steadying breath and reentered the hall.

Silence fell. Hands froze on drinking horns, heads turned in his direction. Even the servants turning the iron spits over the central fires stopped to stare. Sure that every gaze in the hall was on him, the prince strode, straight-backed and proud, across the rush-covered floor to where King Aedh gestured to him. No true chairs here; the king and his wife sat, like everyone else, on low, hide-covered benches behind the length of the equally low, dish-laden table. As Ardagh took his seat at Aedh's side, between the king and Fothad, crossing his long legs in imitation of the others, the king glanced at him in sympathy.

"Delayed reaction to battle, eh? I've felt that a few times myself."

Powers, does everyone know where I've been and what I was doing?

Maybe not. Aedh, at least, had guessed. The clever grey gaze flicked over him, and the king smiled slightly. "Go easy on the ale till you've given your stomach something solid to work on."

Excellent idea. Ardagh ignored the bronze-studded drinking horn set before him and chewed slowly on a section of freshly baked bread. Then, when he was sure that would stay where it should, he warily helped himself to some of the roast being offered to him and bit into it. Ah, sweet and crisp, lovely. He could have closed his eyes in bliss, unable to remember the last time he'd tasted cooked meat. Such niceties as forks were unknown here, but he hardly cared about that right now. Besides, one could nibble daintily enough if one were careful and one's hands were clean.

"What would this meat be?" he asked after a time, and got a bemused glance from Fothad.

"You *are* from a far land if you fail to recognize boar."

Ardagh raised a wry eyebrow. "Does that mean you believe me?"

Fothad grinned. "Who am I to argue with my king?" But he softened the cynical reply by adding, "It must be a frightening thing to be a stranger in a foreign land. If you have questions about the rules of this realm, don't hesitate to ask me."

Ah. Good. That might have been said merely out of human courtesy, but Ardagh quickly returned the grin. "Oh, don't fear. I intend to do just that."

A woman stirred at Fothad's free side, glancing quickly at Ardagh then away, and the prince straightened. This was the sharp-eyed female who'd mistaken him for a drunken human. Her face now burning red, she was trying her best to ignore him.

So be it, Ardagh thought. *I don't want anything to do with you, oh sharp-tongued woman, either. Life is going to be difficult enough without any such complications!*

Fothad glanced from him to the woman, one eyebrow raised. Whatever he might have been wondering, his voice was carefully bland as he said, "Prince Ardagh, may I present my daughter, Sorcha ni Fothad? Sorcha, this is Prince Ardagh Lithanial of Cathay."

Ardagh dipped his head in curt politeness, and received an equally curt dip of the head in return.

His daughter. Wonderful. Nothing is going to be easy for me in this Realm, is it?

Ignoring father and daughter both, he bit savagely into the roast boar.

🌑   🌑   🌑

Eithne stole wary glances past the sturdy bulk of her
husband at the stranger. Right now, lost in a positive rapture
of eating, he looked anything but exotic, even with that glossy
black hair and those odd, slanted eyes: the man plainly hadn't
eaten well for some time. But, for all his hunger, his manners remained impeccable. A prince, indeed, Eithne mused.
And yet, and yet, underneath it all, there was the faintest,
strangest hint of . . . she wasn't quite sure what she *felt*. Not
for the first time cursing her small, unpredictable magic,
Eithne shivered suddenly, and Aedh glanced her way.

"Cold, love?"

She shook her head. "A thought, nothing more."

Ardagh seemed totally oblivious to her wonderings. But
somehow she was sure he knew. He knew who and what
she was, while she, oh she still knew nothing at all about
him. . . .

*Yes, I know he saved your life, and for that I shall never
be grateful enough. But . . . what have you welcomed into
our home?*

Much later, curled next to Aedh in their bed, Eithne lay
awake for what seemed an eternity, still wondering. At last,
when the night was at its deepest, she slipped silently from
the bed. Behind her, Aedh grunted in his sleep, stirring
restlessly, and she froze. But then he settled back into sleep,
snoring softly. Eithne let out her breath in a soundless sigh.
Moving to the window, she softly cast open a shutter and
looked out into the night.

It was the darkest hour. But even so, someone was moving
out there, a barely visible shape in the darkness. *A guard?*
Eithne wondered for a moment.

No. As that someone turned, Eithne caught the faintest
gleam of pale skin, as though it held its own light.

The stranger, the foreign prince who called himself Ardagh
Lithanial, was prowling through the night, graceful and silent
as a cat, the darkness clearly no barrier to him, going nowhere
in particular but pacing restlessly like a man unable to
sleep—or, Eithne thought uneasily, like one hunting for
something he knew he would never find.

Exile, she remembered with a sudden touch of pity, feeling as he neared her window a hint of his anguish. *A lost, lonely exile.*

But exiled from where?

As though realizing he was being watched, the prince stopped short. His green gaze, glinting in the darkness like the eyes of an animal, looked up and locked with her own, and Eithne, staring into those clear, cool eyes that were like a blank mirror giving up nothing at all, thought with a little chill racing through her, *Alien, alien.*

And in that moment, her own small magics rousing, she knew exactly how alien. "Sidhe," she breathed.

Oh no, that couldn't be. The Sidhe were only beings out of stories; he was human, he had to be. . . .

As though he'd heard her whisper, the prince gave her the most elegant, most mocking of bows, then moved silently off into the night.

IN A STRANGE LAND

CHAPTER 6

King Aedh glanced impatiently across the parchment map at his Chief Poet and counselor. "Oh come now, Fothad, no more lectures. What do you *think* I've done?"

Fothad sighed. They were alone in Aedh's private audience chamber. The walls were of good, solid stone, the roof of solid slating, but that didn't stop him from keeping his voice low. "I know, I know. You've sent out your spies. There hasn't been enough time yet for them to report back to you as to who was behind that bungled attempt at killing you. But . . ."

"I have also sent out friendly little messages to all the underkings, reminding them ever so politely that I hold their eldest sons at Fremainn."

"As fosterlings."

"Don't mince words. I hold them as every High King before me has held vassal children: as hostages against their parents' continued loyalty."

"But you treat the youngsters like fosterlings!" Fothad argued. "You'd never hurt a child!"

Aedh's glance hardened. "Wouldn't I? As High King I would do what I must, Fothad, never forget that. Unfortunately, the real problem isn't what I might or might not do, it's that some virile king might be ruthless enough to say, 'I can always make more sons,' and simply sacrifice the eldest."

"Oh, thank you for setting my mind at ease!"

"Look you, man, I am *not* taking the attack too lightly. But it could have come from a dozen sources." The king's finger stabbed at the parchment, pointing out Meath, Leicester, various clan-sites and lesser kingdoms. "Any one of these rulers could be bearing a grudge or carrying an unseemly ambition. The good God knows I have enemies enough here at court! I can hardly ride out against *everyone*."

"Well, no, but—"

"No, Fothad. Let it go. Like it or not, my friend, that bungled ambush can hardly be my prime concern. If I spent all my time worrying about personal safety, how long do you think I'd hold my throne?"

"Ah well, there is that," the poet admitted reluctantly.

"So now, on to other matters. What have you gathered?"

Fothad glanced down at his parchment scrolls, unrolling them one by one. "First: The two heirs of Meath are already at each other's throats."

" 'Already?' Say 'again,' rather." Aedh shook his head. "I hated to divide the kingdom between them—that's asking two ambitious young men to be as saintly as my father— but what else was there to do? Kill one of them at random and let the other live as the only heir? Better to let them settle it, and only step in if their quarrel threatens to spill over into the rest of Eriu. Go on, what else?"

Fothad studied his notes again. "Father Seadna has probably told you this already, but Breasal mac Segeni, the Abbot of Ia, has died."

"Hardly unexpected. He'd been in that abbey for . . . what . . . twenty or twenty-one years at least, and wasn't a child when he entered holy orders. Send royal regrets to Ia. What else?"

"The usual. Quarrels and minor battles between this sept and that. Lord Ailell of Cobba has lost a son in one of those fights."

"Not an Ui Neill clansman, thankfully. I don't have to get personally involved. Mmm, but I can't send him official condolences, either. It would look as though I were taking

sides in the quarrel. Private sympathies, then," Aedh decided.
"What else?"

Fothad hunted through the scrolls. "Nothing overly dramatic, God be praised. Various small quarrels among the
folk here at Fremainn. Nothing warranting your attention.
And before you ask: There have been no new Lochlannach
raids."

"Yet."

The poet glanced up from his notes. "Those raids *could*
have been isolated incidents."

Aedh snorted. "You don't believe that any more than do
I. That's a harsh, hard land those Northerners inhabit, and
I can't really blame them for envying us our fertile green
Eriu."

"Indeed." Fothad's voice was dry. "All it takes to become
a successful raider in the Northern lands is a good ship,
a fair amount of armed men, and a totally ruthless mind."

"And too much idle time. Most of those raiders seem
to be landless men or second sons shut out of inherit-
ances." Aedh smiled without humor. "The Lochlannach
aren't a genuine threat as of now, disorganized as they
are."

"But if they ever do come up with one unifying war
leader—"

"We'll worry about that if and when it happens." Aedh
pushed the parchment map aside. "What of our guest?"

Fothad blinked. "Ardagh Lithanial, you mean? The wandering prince of Cathay? 'He who is in straits must make
shift some way.' "

"And, 'There's no hearth like your own.' I can quote
proverbs, too. Stop evading. What of him?"

Fothad hesitated, then shook his head. "An amazing man,
that, truly amazing."

"You believe he's what he claims?"

"An exile from a far-off land? Och, yes. There's an unden-
iable hint of sorrow to the man. Besides, no one could carry
on such a perfect act of being so totally ignorant of everything about us—or feign such a hunger about learning how
to live here."

Aedh grinned. "You don't exactly mind playing the role of tutor once more, do you? Particularly when the pupil is an adult and not one of my offspring."

"Ah well, your children are both nice, bright students."

"When they're attentive."

Fothad grinned. "When they're attentive. They *are* very young, after all. And," he added slyly, "they do take after their father."

"So superior!" Aedh teased. "You weren't all that much older than I when you tutored me."

"True. And most terrified of my suddenly high rank. Och, but as for the prince, I must admit that after listening to childish prattle, it *is* a pleasure to deal with an adult mind."

Aedh chuckled. "So my wife tells me." He leaned forward, humor fading from his face. "Speaking of women, one thing more: While my Eithne is far too sensible for such foolishness, the other women of our court seem to be finding our elegant prince quite appealing. And he is not exactly repelling their interest."

"He *is* a rather handsome man," Fothad said carefully.

"So he is. Quite striking. And presumably the morals of Cathay are quite different from our own. But he is technically *cu glas*, after all, a 'grey dog' exile from overseas without legal standing."

"Though of course," Fothad added, "as a prince he has a good deal of status."

Aedh nodded. "But even so, we can't have a foreign exile causing trouble. Speak to him, Fothad."

"*Me?*" the poet said in dismay. "Shouldn't that be more of a job for Father Seadna?"

"What could he do? Our good monk has already told me Prince Ardagh has not the vaguest idea of Church dogma; the prince can hardly be harangued like some Eriu sinner. Besides," Aedh added with a wry quirk of the mouth, "what does a chaste monk know of the ways of a man with a woman?"

The wryness, Fothad knew, was because while Father Seadna was, indeed, celibate, it wasn't unheard-of for some monks of Eriu, and even some abbots, to wed. "No, my friend," the king continued, "the job, as you put it, is yours. Slip a touch of . . . prudence into one of your lessons."

Fothad sighed. "Prudence, my king, it is."

Ardagh leaned casually against the wall of his "home," pretending to be looking out at the grassy yard beyond and the maze of buildings, ignoring the usual light mist that couldn't quite be called rain. He kept his face absolutely clear of any trace of emotion. "And so, if I understand correctly, the ideal state of grace involves celibacy."

"Chastity," Father Seadna corrected, glancing at the prince as if hunting mockery. "The two are not exactly the same."

"Granted. But either way, if one loves and weds and creates young, one can no longer be in that state of grace."

The monk, unexpectedly, grinned. "You argue like an acolyte trying to stir up debate, Prince Ardagh, if you'll pardon me for saying so."

Ardagh hesitated, wondering what would happen if he should choose to take offense. It was amusing to play with the monk, even if these "chance encounters" were happening so often that "chance" was being stretched almost to the breaking point; it was amusing to try to puzzle out the convolutions of human religion even if the monk was almost certainly trying in a gentle, subtle way to convert him.

Odd thought, that, to claim to know the one true path to the Unknowable, and to try to make others worship that way as well.

But at the same time, there was a quiet radiance to Father Seadna, clear to Sidhe eyes, that kept the prince from open mockery; whatever else this monk might be, he took genuine joy in his faith.

Ah well. "I meant no harm," Ardagh said.

"I know that." Father Seadna's eyes were suddenly very serious. "And I know why whenever we meet you banter words with me like this."

"Do you?"

The monk paused thoughtfully. "You are a very lonely man, Prince Ardagh," he said at last, "and that, I think, not merely because of your exile."

Ardagh only just kept the surprise from his face. "What's this? Are you finally admitting you're seeking to convert me?"

Father Seadna never flinched. "Were I a priest of Rome," he retorted, a touch sharply, "in the heart of Mother Church, I don't doubt I'd be trying my best to convert you from . . ." he hesitated in an attempt at tact, "whatever."

"My people have their beliefs, I assure you." Not as rigidly shaped or held as those humans professed, of course; no Sidhe would be so arrogant as to claim to know every Answer, or name Names as lightly. "But you are not a priest of Rome. Nor, I think," he added, one brow raised, "would you wish to be."

"You misunderstand me. We may be far from Rome here in Eriu, but we are all still children of the one Church."

"Even King Aedh."

"Especially King Aedh! He was ordained by the Church in the sight of God and man."

"Even if he is not always a totally dutiful child of that Church? I have heard rumors of quarrels with this abbot and that, over politics, over status, over the fact that he never fostered his son in a monastery as they wished."

"A king's life," Father Seadna said sternly, "is not an easy one, particularly when that man is High King of Eriu."

"And he has only the one precious son and heir, and doesn't want to risk him."

"One can hardly blame him. And you are trying to stir up contention yet again, Prince Ardagh."

Ardagh grinned. "Perhaps."

Father Seadna shook his head. "You must surely be aware by now that there are many other monks here at court attending to the folk of Fremainn. The Ard Ri could have requested any religious man he wished to minister to his own soul's needs, up to the greatest of abbots, yet he chose me. I still am not certain why." *I am,* thought Ardagh. *Your sincerity shines like a light.* Being Sidhe, he added with cynical honesty, *It keeps you from being a political threat to him.* "That he has," Father Seadna continued, "is still a matter over which I fight a daily battle against the Sin of Pride."

"And you will not hear anyone speak out against him? Fair enough."

Father Seadna sighed. "You twist words nicely, Prince Ardagh. As a monk of Eriu, just as if I were of Rome, I should be doing my utmost to turn you to the Light. But—"

"But I am a prince," Ardagh cut in sardonically, "and a royal guest."

"But I will not," the monk corrected sternly, "I cannot force you to salvation against your will."

All at once, Ardagh was very weary of the conversation. "I will find my own salvation, thank you," he said. "Good day to you." With a curt bow, he left.

They really do speak so incredibly casually of Names of Power, without once considering the risk of angering those Names; they prattle easily of the Hereafter when they don't even know that much about the Here; they have one Church, but the branch of their faith that's based in Rome—I assume that's yet another far-off city—that Roman faith seems alienated from the one here in Eriu—

Bah, I will never understand their ways!

But how had that monk been so damnably sure-sighted? Ardagh's stride slowed to a stop. *"A very lonely man."* How had Father Seadna known—

"Ha." Easy enough to guess that an exile would be lonely, and to pretend from that guess to have great insight. All at once fiercely impatient with himself for having wondered, even for a moment, Ardagh stalked away.

Fothad mac Ailin, poet and minister, sat alone in his chambers, bent over his harp, all and only poet at the moment, lost in the song that insisted, come what may, on being created *now*. Every few seconds he would stop to scratch notes down on the scrap of parchment on the table at his side. *More work for my Sorcha to transcribe, poor lass!* the poet thought vaguely. But the song was still calling to him, and Fothad surrendered, diving into the sea of music once more.

A sea from which he surfaced after a time with a sigh of satisfaction. There were places in the melody that weren't yet quite right, and a few rough rhymes that definitely needed smoothing, but overall—

Fothad looked up with a start. "Ah. Prince Ardagh."

No telling how long the man had been standing there, watching with those clear, uncanny green eyes of his. Fothad knew better than to ask how he'd gotten into this private chamber; in the days since the prince's arrival, Ardagh had proven he could move as silently and secretly as a cat when the fancy took him, and had a very odd notion of what was or was not proper.

Uncanny, indeed. That the man really was a prince, Fothad had no doubt. As he'd told the king, Ardagh's every move spoke of noble breeding. But what was going on in that elegant, sharply planed head . . . even after these several days, Fothad still had no idea of that. Prince Ardagh was swift as the wind when it came to learning whatever he wished to know. But what he wished to know—there was no predicting that.

Odd man, odd man. But I don't think there's a bit of harm in him—or rather, the poet amended, *no harm in him for anyone who's helping him. There's something about those clear, sharp eyes . . . I don't think I'd like to be on the wrong side of his anger.*

"Forgive me," Prince Ardagh said. "I was enjoying your music. I didn't mean to disturb you."

Fothad waved a hand, feeling a little surge of pleasure at the genuine appreciation he heard in that melodic voice. "No matter. I need to take a rest from the song before I can put the final polish to it."

" 'A poem ought to be well made at first,' " the prince intoned with false solemnity.

" 'For there is many a one to ruin it afterwards,' " Fothad capped, smiling. "Adages come in handy, don't they?"

"In any language," Prince Ardagh agreed. "But as a poet of Eriu, you can wield more than mere adages, am I not right?"

"I don't quite understand."

"Isn't it true that a Chief Poet is able to compose Powerful satires?"

The emphasis on "Powerful" left no doubt the prince referred to magic. "The . . . ah . . . bards of the past were supposed to be able to create satires with enough strength in them to kill, yes."

"And now? Isn't one of your duties to protect the king from sorcery?"

Fothad stirred uncomfortably. "Prince Ardagh, you speak of the old, pagan days. Of course," honesty made him add, "any poet worth the title is quite able to take revenge on anyone who crosses him, and without needing a touch of magic. Just think of how catchy some tunes can be, haunting the mind and spreading from one person to another."

The prince chuckled. "And if those catchy melodies are linked to scandalous, equally catchy words about an offender, words that also linger in the mind and spread from one person to another—ae, yes, that would be as good a revenge as anything magical!"

Fothad decided to drop the subject before it went any further. "So now, adages and satires aside, do you wish a lesson?"

"Indeed."

The poet struggled to hide his pleased grin. He had to admit, born tutor that he was, that he took fire from the prince's seemingly endless hunger for knowledge about the land, about its customs and politics, its *duns* and monasteries and villages, and even the names of its birds and beasts and the tales of its people (particularly stories dealing with doorways into magical Realms: no accounting, Fothad mused, for what someone found interesting). The prince was absorbing social customs with ease, seemed puzzled by the tenets of Christianity—the poet gingerly decided to leave that topic to Father Seadna—and showed a fascination with Eriu's convoluted politics. Och, and he also revealed a most satisfying love of, no, a downright hunger for, music! There was a satisfaction in teaching such an eager student Fothad admitted he hadn't known since he was a very young man and King Aedh was a boy.

And even Aedh was never quite so quick. "What would you like to study today?"

The humor left Prince Ardagh's face. "I wish to know more about the laws of this land."

"Now, there's a broad topic! Can you give me a specific—"

"What," the prince asked flatly, "is a *cu glas?*"

He must have overheard someone talking about him. Hedging frantically, Fothad began, "Well, it literally means 'grey dog,' but it doesn't really apply to you."

"Does it not? Is not a *cu glas* an exile from overseas?"

"Ah, yes, but . . ."

"What I wish to know, Fothad mac Ailin, is how status is calculated in this land, and what constitutes honor. In particular," the prince said, fixing the poet with a steady green stare, "I wish to know my own legal standing here."

"It's a bit unusual," Fothad admitted. "In ordinary cases, a man such as yourself, an . . . ah . . . exile from overseas, would . . . well . . . be without an honor-price. You know what that is?"

"The fine one must pay when he has injured or slain another. Reimbursement, as it were, to the victim or the victim's family." A slanted black brow arched up. "Are you saying that anyone can try to slay me with impunity?"

"No, no, of course not! Even if you are a—a foreigner, you are still a prince, and so no one would dare raise a hand against you."

"Wise of them," Prince Ardagh murmured almost too softly for it to have been a threat; for a moment the green eyes were alarmingly cold. "Then, since I am a prince and do, apparently, have some manner of honor-price even though no one can puzzle out exactly what sort, does that mean I am bound by the restrictions you folk put on royalty?"

Fothad hesitated, considering carefully. "Yes and no. Wait, hear me out." The poet ticked the rules off on his fingers. "A king, and by extension any royal man, must not work at common trades. But I can hardly see you in that situation."

"Hardly," the prince agreed.

"A king—in theory at any rate—must never be defeated in battle. But since you are not a ruler, that law doesn't really apply to you, either. The good Lord willing, none of us shall see combat soon anyhow."

"Indeed. Go on."

"Let me think a moment . . . ah, yes. A king must never default on an oath—"

"My people," the prince cut in, "do not lie."

"I see. Then that isn't a problem, either, is it?" *You're babbling,* Fothad scolded himself. *Stop it.* He was used to dealing with emissaries from all the many kings of Eriu, reflecting all the aspects of human emotion, without so much as flinching. But there was something about the steady stare of these odd green eyes, revealing nothing of the thoughts behind their coolness, that was very unsettling. The next law that Fothad had been about to mention was the antiquated one that a king's body must be without blemish, but looking at the elegant creature before him, the poet didn't even bother mentioning it.

"Of course even a king must obey the law," Fothad continued hastily, "but once again, that should not be a problem. You are not a criminal, nor one who—"

He stopped short. Prince Ardagh had, without warning, dropped his gaze to one of the parchment scrolls that shared the table with Fothad's music, as though all at once bored with the whole subject of law. As the prince gently began unrolling the scroll, revealing a map of Eriu, Fothad asked warily, "Is there anything else you would like to know?"

"Yes. More about the geography of this land, if you would."

I cannot puzzle the man out. He shifts interests as swiftly as a child, but there's certainly nothing juvenile about that keen mind. Watching the prince study the map, a slight melancholy all at once surrounding him, Fothad felt a sudden stab of pity for this lost exile and asked impulsively, "Are you happy here?"

Prince Ardagh glanced up, not a trace of emotion in those cool green eyes. "What would you have me say? I am grateful for this sanctuary, yes, and for the time you and the High King have spared me. But I am still too well aware of being a stranger. As the people here are aware."

"You can hardly blame them for still staring," Fothad murmured. "We don't see one like yourself very often."

"No," the prince agreed, and Fothad caught the faintest hint of a smile on the fair face. "This edge of land, here." An elegant forefinger tapped the eastern coast. "What lies beyond?"

"Didn't you come that way?" Fothad asked. "Most travellers do pass through Cymru on their way to—"

"Cymru. That would be the homeland of the warrior Cadwal."

"Ah . . . yes."

"What is a man of Cymru doing here? Is there friendship between the two lands? I thought not."

"No," Fothad admitted, "not exactly. Though the folk there are said to be our distant kin." He glanced warily at the prince. "Then you *have* seen Cymru."

"No."

Fothad glanced at him in surprise. "Then how would you know how things stood between the two lands?"

"I have eyes and ears," the prince reminded him. "And I see how folk here look at Cadwal and his men. Or is that faint contempt shown because they are mercenaries?" He hesitated over that word, as though it was particularly foreign to him, then shook his head. "We do not have such a concept as 'mercenary' in my land."

"Ah . . . I see." Fothad felt like a man struggling upstream, fighting to keep up with the prince's unpredictable leaps of logic. "I suspect it's a little of both his origin and his profession with Cadwal. Though he's never once shown any desire to return to Cymru and stays as loyal to our king as any born of Eriu."

"More so, I should think," Prince Ardagh mused, with just the slightest touch of cynicism. "At least as long as the High King's gold continues. An odd thing, that, to *buy* a warrior's honor."

"Well, yes, in a way, but it is as fitting for a king to include such mercenaries in his retinue as those he has saved from injustice, servitude or— So now," the poet said firmly, determined to regain control of the conversation, "if you didn't pass through Cymru, which way did you travel? Down from the lands of the Lochlannach?" At the prince's blank stare, Fothad added with a small touch of triumph, "Then you had to have come through the land of the Franks. Now, there's a long way about to reach Eriu! I hope you are a good sailor."

An impatient shrug; Prince Ardagh, Fothad noted, managed to make even that simple gesture graceful. But then, such a beautiful fellow could hardly be anything but graceful.

Which reminded Fothad of that one rather awkward subject the king had instructed him to broach. *Thank you, Aedh*, he thought with heavy irony. *I truly appreciate your leaving this task to me.*

"Prince Ardagh . . ." the poet began hesitantly. "I don't mean to meddle in your affairs. . . ." Oh, ridiculous choice of words! "But I don't know how the laws of your land stand in . . . ah . . . one particular matter."

"I don't—"

"I mean in regards to . . . to women."

The prince stared blankly at him. Fothad sighed deeply and tried again. "Regarding the *courting* of women," he corrected.

The uncanny eyes sparked with understanding, then went very cold. "There is a limit to how I will obey your laws," Prince Ardagh murmured. "What I do or do not is not the business of any other. And I do no harm to any of your people or their honor."

"Uh, no . . ." Fothad began. "But . . . you can't court *every* woman."

To his astonishment, the prince chuckled. "If you mean by that delicate phrasing what I think, no. Even were I as hot-blooded as one of your sturdy little stallions, I could not possibly 'court' every woman in this fortress." But there was no matching warmth in his eyes. "Fothad mac Ailin, I do appreciate your teachings. But you are not to meddle in my life."

"Dammit, man, I'm not meddling! I'm trying to keep you out of duels!"

"Ah, that. I would not fear such things."

There was suddenly such chill, inhuman delight in the prince's smile that Fothad felt a thrill of horror stab through him. But before he could find anything to say in reply, the coldness was gone so swiftly he was left wondering what he'd seen.

"Don't fear," Prince Ardagh continued gently. "I will even vow this: I will not bring needless harm to you or yours or any here, nor will I do damage to the hospitality King Aedh has granted me." He paused, this time smiling quite charmingly. "There. Does that set your mind at ease?"

Not exactly. But one could only argue with a prince so far. Particularly a prince with such uncanny eyes. Fothad grinned wryly and held up a hand in surrender.

"My lady?"

At the servant's hesitant voice, Sorcha ni Fothad looked up with a start, blinking in surprise at how dark the little chamber had grown. Och, it couldn't be nightfall already?

"Do you wish me to light a lamp, my lady?"

"No. I've done enough work for now." Sorcha rubbed her eyes with a weary hand, then got slowly up from the table, stretching stiff muscles, feeling far older than the young woman she was. "Just cap the ink bottle, if you would, and rinse the pens." Glancing down at the newly drawn lines on the precious sheets of parchment, she added, "Don't touch these. Let them dry thoroughly. I *don't* want to have to draw them again."

"Ah, no, my lady." The woman paused. "Will you be joining the royal court for dinner?"

Was it *that* late already? "Of course. No," Sorcha added, wiping her hands clean on a scrap of linen, "you don't have to escort me." Not a man of King Aedh's court would ever dare to raise a hand to a woman of that court, let alone one who was the Chief Poet's daughter.

No time to change clothing, not if she didn't mean to make a dramatic entrance long after the other women had retired. Well, what she was wearing was decent enough. Sorcha hastily checked hands and face for inkstains, peering into the precious little glass mirror the servant held for

her. Snatching up her soft woolen *brat* and wrapping it
about herself, she paused long enough for the woman to
pin it securely at the shoulder, then hurried out of the
chamber.

The day had passed so cursedly fast! Not that she had
done much with it, no, even though her father would have
claimed she had earned her keep by transcribing his songs
from those ridiculous scrawls of his (easier, he admitted to
her, to decipher the old druidic ogham) into something more
easily read by those who came after him. Sorcha flinched
from the thought of her father not being there someday,
and set her mind instead to complaining about being used
like some priestly clerk.

Might as well be a clerk stuck in some monastery— That
made her laugh aloud. *Not that I'd ever be suited to a
monastery, not mentally and most certainly not physically!
But isn't there anything else I can do, not as my father's
daughter but as myself? As an adult?*

But that was the way the law was written, like it or not:
a woman was under her father's protection until she wed, and
then she was under her husband's protection. Well, Sorcha
thought, she'd been a wife once, however briefly. Even if
Meallan hadn't exactly been the husband of every girl's
dream, he had at least allowed her to think for herself.

*Allowed? Ha, no, he was thankful someone else could take
charge of things for him.*

While he lived. Meallan's unexpected death had brought
her back here to where she'd been raised. She was her
father's legal heir, since Fothad had no other child—at least
the law granted her that much, woman or no—with nothing much to do now that she was a widow but follow Fothad's
wishes and wait to inherit.

*I don't want to inherit, not if it means my father's death.
But oh, I don't want to be trapped here, either!*

Fothad had expected his daughter to use her brain, teaching her everything from music composition (though she knew
her songs were pale imitations of his own) to writing, and
she thanked him for it. But what good was all her learning? If only there was something different for her to do with

it, something different to see, someone with whom she could discuss what she knew!

Lost in these frustrating thoughts, hardly watching where she was going, Sorcha nearly collided with a tall, dark-haired man—

"Prince Ardagh!" she gasped.

Of course she knew he had been studying with her father on and off in the past few days, learning about the land of Eriu, but up to this time Sorcha had managed to avoid him. How could she possibly face the man? Sorcha reddened every time she thought of how she'd found him huddled in misery on the ground, how she'd harangued him for drunkenness.

"I'm sorry," she blurted.

His eyes—those amazing green eyes—studied her coolly. "No harm was done." His voice was smooth as flowing water.

"No, you don't understand. I—I'm talking about the other night. When I . . ." She shook her head. "I had no right accusing you as I did. You are a royal guest. What you do or don't do isn't my business."

But a small voice in her mind was protesting, *But he's a hero; he shouldn't have been wallowing on the ground like a sot. Like Meallan.*

"I was not drunk." This time the words were said without rancor. His eyes really were most remarkably green, Sorcha thought uneasily, clear as glass yet revealing absolutely nothing of the mind behind them.

"Of course not," she said hastily. "I—"

"You don't believe me? Do you think me a *liar?*" There was a hint of barely controlled anger in the smooth voice, as though she'd accused him of something obscene.

"I'm sorry," Sorcha said, and meant it. "Look you," she added in sudden fierce honesty, "my late husband, Meallan, was a man of good, noble birth, but he drank too much. He often rushed out into the night to—to—"

"Empty his stomach?" the prince finished delicately. "I see. And you thought I, too, was in a similar state."

"You don't understand. Meallan died that way. One night,

he just . . . didn't return. By the time we found him, sound
asleep in the cold and wet, he—he had caught a fatal chill."

"Ah." The eerie, too steady green gaze gave up nothing
of his thoughts. "You were concerned for the royal guest."

Was he mocking her? "I was disappointed," Sorcha said
flatly, "that a prince of Cathay should prove just as weak
as anyone else."

This time he did laugh. "Whatever else I may be, I am
not a supernatural creature, Sorcha ni Fothad. Don't try
to turn me into something more than I am."

His eyes were still cool as before, but a new warmth hinted
in his elegant voice, a new music glinted in its smoothness.
Sorcha was astonished to find herself taking a step forward
in spite of herself, fascinated by the strange, finely carved
beauty of his face and the lithe, graceful lines of his body.
Meallan must have been a fine-looking man in his youth,
but time and drink had done their damage. Being of noble
birth, daughter of the Chief Poet, Sorcha had never been
allowed to do more than dream about any other men (not,
she thought wildly, like the old, pagan days, when a woman
could take any man she wished without shame). Now, without warning, here she was wondering what it would be like
to lie in the arms of this elegant stranger who—

This was ridiculous! She didn't know the prince, she didn't
even truly *like* the prince, and she was not some silly little
servant girl to let a smooth voice sway her! Backing up in
sudden fury, Sorcha snapped, "No, Prince Ardagh, I wouldn't
dream of turning you into something you're not. Royal blood
or no, you're nothing more than a man, just like any other."

His smile was infuriatingly amused. "Not exactly that."

Sorcha didn't wait to hear more. She turned and stalked
away. Behind her, she could hear Prince Ardagh calling her
name, a touch of surprise in his voice, but Sorcha, trembling with anger, refused to listen.

King Donnchadh of Clonach cut and slashed and cut again
at his opponent, driving the hapless warrior back across the
grassy practice field, hardly noticing the frantic light in the
man's eyes, taking out in this bout all his savage frustration.

Why had he been given such terrible luck? He was of the royal clan, the Ui Neill sept—as Derval never failed to remind him. Oh, granted, his was a distant branch, but he was Ui Neill just the same. And yet here he was, stuck in his rocky little ancestral kingdom while Aedh mac Neill held the Ard Ri's throne.

Stuck with a shrew, Donnchadh thought with petty malice.

No. Whatever else Derval might be, she was never anything as small-minded as a shrew. The woman frightened him sometimes: it was like living with a sword crafted by a master—sleek, sharp, and ever dangerous. Derval, Donnchadh mused, had nothing of womanly softness to her; there were times when he wondered how she'd ever managed to bring children to term. And he knew she held him, her husband and king, in contempt as a weakling.

I'm not weak, damn you, he snapped at her (but silently, always silently), *I am a king. I cannot act as rashly as you would like.*

And yet, Donnchadh reminded himself, he had let her persuade him to send those assassins. Aedh might be dying, dead, even now.

Then why have I had no word? Where are my men, curse them all? Where are they?

Donnchadh's sword wavered, and the warrior, laughing in surprise, pressed his sudden advantage. The king came back to himself with a start just in time to ward off defeat, and drove his opponent staggering back.

A sudden commotion broke his concentration, making Donnchadh turn in anger to see who dared interrupt him. Several servants were gathered about a fallen warrior, helping the bedraggled, tattered man to his feet.

Dear God. Oh dear God.

It was one of the men he'd sent to kill the High King. Fierce with panic, Donnchadh strode forward, brushing the servants away. "Well?" he asked sharply, catching the warrior before the man could crumple again. "What news? What happened to the rest of your men?"

"Dead." The man's voice was a weary whisper. His eyes closed and he sagged in Donnchadh's grip. "Betrayed."

"Betrayed! By whom?"

The warrior shook his head slightly. "Never saw him before . . . we were in ambush . . . the way we planned. King . . . King Aedh would never have known we were there . . . not till too late . . ."

For a time he was sure he wasn't going to get an answer. But then the warrior roused enough to repeat vaguely, "Never saw him before . . . he was beautiful as an angel . . . but he could fight like a devil." The man chuckled weakly at his own wit. "Like a devil . . ."

"And the king! What of King Aedh?"

The warrior stared up at Donnchadh with wry, feverish eyes. "King Aedh lives, never fear . . . King Aedh lives . . ."

"But does he know who sent the ambush?" Donnchadh asked fiercely. "Answer me! Does he know?"

But with a small, weary sigh, the warrior slipped away into death and left Donnchadh alone with his fear. He let the body fall with a shudder, turning away—

To be faced with Derval. Her face a beautiful mask, she said only, "We must talk."

When they were alone in her grianan, Donnchadh began to stammer out his fears. But Derval held up a restraining hand. "There are only two possibilities. One: Aedh has no idea who sent those men, and we are safe. Two: He knows, and we must prepare accordingly."

"Easily said!" Donnchadh snapped. "What would you have me do? Declare open war on him? Try my tiny army against the forces of the Ard Ri?"

"No. Of course not. Whether or not Aedh knows what you attempted—"

"Me!" Donnchadh exploded. "It wasn't my idea alone. As I remember, dear wife, it was you who goaded me on!"

Her perfect mouth tightened ever so slightly. "Whether or not Aedh knows what *we* attempted," she said, "we must find ourselves a powerful ally."

"And who would you suggest?"

"There are other kings. Many who are not happy with Aedh holding the throne."

"Many who are not happy with *any* of the Ui Neill sept!

Would you have me deal with my enemies? Or maybe you'd rather I allied myself with the Lochlannach!" To his horror, Derval actually fell silent at that, eyes thoughtful. "You *can't* be considering that!" Donnchadh gasped.

After a long moment she shook her head. "No. That would hardly be wise."

He snorted. "Of course not. I'm not stupid enough to deal with those Godless barbarians!"

"You're not strong enough," she corrected quietly. "And no, I am not insulting you, husband, merely stating a fact. You are not as strong as them."

But Donnchadh, astonished, surprised a flicker of fear in Derval's eyes. *She's as frightened as me! Frightened of Aedh—* "We must have an ally before our luck runs out," Derval murmured. "But who? Who?"

Husband and wife fell silent, thinking feverishly. But neither could find an answer.

DISTANT CLOUDS

CHAPTER 7

The morning of this early summer day was pleasantly warm, the sky for once a clear, bright blue as Ardagh stood in the doorway of his guesthouse. All around him bustled busy human life, the usual tangle of visiting dignitaries, various courtiers, and the horde of servants scurrying about with sacks of grain or buckets of water and taking care of the hundred little tasks necessary to keep a fortress this size running smoothly. But the prince's house, positioned well, stood in a small circle of blessed quiet.

Thank you, King Aedh, for that.

Since there was no one to watch the lapse of dignity, Ardagh threw back his head like a child to let the sunlight pour down on his upturned face. One of the nicer things about this Realm was the sunlight—rare enough in a climate that often seemed as much mist as air—though he'd been warned by just about everyone not to let the sun shine too brightly or too long on his fair skin. Well, it didn't seem to be doing him any harm, though his skin was gradually taking on an odd golden tone. *Intriguing,* Ardagh mused, looking down and turning a hand this way and that to study it. *Rather attractive, in a way.* The women here seemed to like it well enough, too, Fothad's prudish warnings notwithstanding.

Ah yes, Fothad. Ardagh let his hand drop to his side, tranquility shattered. Fothad, with his endless fund of information, his wonderfully satisfying music—and his odd, odd questions. *"Are you happy here?"* Happy *here*? Had he ever known happiness, truly known it, even back in the Sidhe Realm?

Ae, and wasn't this ridiculous? In his native Realm, he'd had a rightful place, a purpose. Here, in this alien place, he was lost, and between the poet and his warnings and Father Seadna with his "you are a lonely man" it was no wonder they had him confused and—

Bah, he shouldn't be worrying about what humans thought! Oh, they had their points: a love of laughter and music, a gift for metalwork that was nearly the equal of anything of Sidhe-work. But at best, they were hardly a study in logic, and at worst a mass of unpredictable contradictions. That woman, now, that Sorcha ni Fothad, Fothad's sharp-tongued daughter . . . any woman of the Sidhe would have understood he'd only been jesting with her the other day, flirting to make her smile. But she'd thought he had genuinely been out to seduce her!

As if I'd risk complications with her father. Even if I were attracted to such a—a prickly woman.

No, no, *all* these folks were confusing! Monasteries, now: From what Father Seadna had told him, monasteries dotted Eriu; the man came from one of them himself. According to him, the places were centers of learning, which was a good thing—but Ardagh had teased out of Fothad the information that they were also independent, sternly managed little cities containing (with a few odd exceptions) nothing but male clerics.

How can humans possibly believe that men and women are separate creations, one superior to the other? And why do they make such a ridiculous fuss over something as natural and joyous as mating?

Ah well. He could not expect humans to be as advanced as the Sidhe. But, like it or not, frustrated and confused and out-and-out bewildered though those humans made him, he must learn to live among them.

I've been here . . . what, perhaps a month of their time, and what have I accomplished? Gathered a few pretty tales

*of Doorways that don't give me the slightest clue as to how
to get home, learned some facts about the people and customs of this land . . .*

Honesty made him admit that a month wasn't long in
which to study an entire culture. And even a Sidhe could
only absorb so much knowledge at a time. But how, the
prince mused, was he going to use that knowledge? Oh yes,
the High King would almost surely give him sanctuary for
as long as Ardagh requested. But what honor was there in
being a mere idler? The prince suddenly rubbed a hand
over his eyes.

Curse it to the Darkness!

Fortunate humans, able to lie even to themselves. He,
however, couldn't hide from the fear forever nagging at his
mind: Was this Realm weakening him? Was it changing him?
Would it, at the last, make him forget who and what he was?

*Of course not! It's the lack of magic in this cursed Realm
that's bothering me. If only I could find some good strong
source of Power!* Yes, oh yes, how wonderful it would feel
if only he could cast some genuine spell, no matter what
or why, just to shake his senses, just to remind him of himself!

The sound of swords clashing together brought the prince
sharply back to his surroundings. Every morning, Cadwal
and his warriors exercised in the grassy field behind the royal
keep, within sight of Ardagh's guesthouse, practicing their
weaponry in the unromantic, matter-of-fact fashion of men
whose lives depended on those skills. Watching them now,
the prince felt his own hand close reflexively about an
imaginary hilt. He'd gone without his own weapons practice too long—not a wise thing when the edge of a blade
was the best weapon available to him.

*I wonder what they would say if I asked to practice with
them. Or is the thought of a prince dueling with common
mercenaries so outlandish they'd be mortified? There've been
enough misunderstandings already. I don't want any—*

The prince whirled at a sudden sound to his left, then
froze in utter astonishment. A child! By the Powers, a child!
A human child, a small girl, standing as frozen as he, staring at him with wide, astonished eyes. Ardagh crouched

down to his unexpected visitor's level, studying her in wonder.
Look at this, look at the perfection of the small face, the
delicate lashes and charming little nose! The Sidhe being
the barely fertile people they were, he'd only seen children
twice in his life, and never this close. Oh, what a marvel-
ous thing, this beautiful, perfect new youngster!

"Now, who may you be, little one?" Ardagh asked gently.

She continued to stare, thumb going nervously to her
mouth. Ardagh sat back on his heels in dismay. Didn't she
understand him?

"Can you talk?" he asked doubtfully, not at all sure when
intelligence first showed in human children. "Are you old
enough for that?"

She lowered the thumb in contempt. "Course I can. I'm
five."

"Oh, I see." The prince bit back a delighted laugh. "Forgive me, my lady. I didn't mean to insult you."

She accepted his apology with a wave of a chubby hand.

"But how is it my humble home is graced by so charming a visitor?" No, that was far beyond the little one's understanding. "What are you doing here?"

The child hesitated, then said firmly, "Running away."

"I see. But why?"

"It's Niall's fault."

"Niall," Ardagh repeated blankly.

"Uh-huh. He's always teasing me. Says I'm just a baby.
But I'm *not* a baby."

"I know, I know," Ardagh assured her, struggling to keep
his voice solemn. "You're five. A grand age, indeed. But who
is this bothersome Niall?"

Her contemptuous stare told him he didn't know *anything.* "My brother."

"Do you mean Prince Niall?" Ardagh asked in sudden
comprehension. "Yes? That means you must be Princess
Fainche."

"Course I am."

Ardagh got to his feet and bowed deeply. "I am honored.
But you don't *really* want to run away, do you?"

"Yes, I do."

But she didn't sound very sure. Ardagh crouched down again. "It's a big, lonely world out there," he told her solemnly. "The nights are quite dark, and full of wild animals."

Her eyes were very big. "Don't care."

"You're very brave. I suppose even a raging boar wouldn't frighten you. There are many of them in the woods, you know. Wolves, too. And bears. You really *are* very brave. So brave, indeed, that no silly brother like Niall is going to bother *you!*"

She nodded fiercely.

"Well, then," Ardagh said, getting to his feet, "there really isn't any reason for you to run away, is there? If you do, Niall will never be able to see just how brave you are."

She eyed him warily, then nodded again.

"Good!" Ardagh exclaimed. With any luck at all, no one would have noticed yet that the child was missing, and he could put her back where she belonged before anyone had a chance to panic. "Come, we'll go back together so you can tell Niall you won't let him tease you any more."

To his utter delight, she put her small, warm, slightly sticky hand trustingly into his. How perfect it was, each tiny finger tipped by a precise little nail! Did humans appreciate the wonder of their own young? Or did they, easily fertile creatures that they were, take children as a matter of course?

Ardagh's nocturnal prowlings had made him familiar with every way into the royal keep. If they slipped in by this out-of-the-way entrance, he should be able to get the child back to—

No.

"Fainche!" Queen Eithne came rushing forward, flanked by half a dozen flustered servants, and the prince sighed. The little girl pulled back at her mother's cry, but Ardagh wouldn't let her go. "Come, my brave one," he whispered. "You must prove just how brave you are."

He heard Fainche's soft little intake of breath. Then she slipped her hand from his. Fighting back a grin, Ardagh saw her march as proudly as any ruler to her mother, who looked plainly torn between the urge to slap or hug her wandering daughter. At last Eithne drew the little girl fiercely into her arms, staring over Fainche's head at Ardagh like a wild thing defending her young. Stung, the prince assured her, "She's unhurt."

Eithne ushered the child into the arms of the servant women, who scurried off with Fainche into the keep. But the queen remained. "What were you doing with her?"

"I?" Ardagh said in surprise. "Seeing her back home. I believe she was running away." Smiling at the memory, he added, "The child told me quite emphatically that she wasn't a baby, no matter what her brother said."

Eithne showed not the slightest trace of a smile. "But why was she with you?"

"I found her standing just outside the guesthouse. Probably trying to figure out what she wanted to do next. The little one wasn't too enthused at the thought of—" Ardagh broke off in sudden horror, staring at the grim-faced Eithne. "You don't think I would have *hurt* her, do you? What manner of folk am I among? Who would ever hurt something as precious as a child?"

Eithne's fierce gaze never wavered. "Not hurt her, Prince Ardagh. Steal her. That is what your people do with human children, isn't it? Steal them away?"

Ardagh let his expression go absolutely blank. "My people?"

"The Sidhe, Prince Ardagh. The Fair Folk, the People of Peace, whatever you want to call them." Eithne stopped short, as though longing to hear him argue with her, to deny the whole thing.

"For what it's worth," Ardagh said, "I have never stolen a changeling in my life."

"Don't mock me."

"I wasn't. Merely stating a fact. Have you told anyone else your suspicions?"

She shook her head, eyes wary. "Who would believe me?"

"Who, indeed?" *Feeling* her flicker of fear, he added, "What I told your husband is a fact, too: I really am a prince, I really do have an older brother on the throne, and I really am in exile to, among other things, preserve the security of the realm. And," he added, "I really do appreciate this sanctuary."

"But you are of the Sidhe. Y-you aren't human."

Ardagh sighed. "Yes. I am, indeed, of the Sidhe. No, I am not human. But I assure you, that does not make me a monster, either." He paused, studying her. "Now, I wonder, are you going to be as honest with me?"

"I . . . don't . . ."

"Come now, Queen Eithne. If no one else here has doubted I am from far-distant Cathay, why are you the amazing exception?"

"I guessed the truth. I am good at—"

"Oh, please. Even I can tell that's a lie."

"What of it? I am not honor-bound to tell you anything."

"Such melodrama. I'll make a pact with you, Queen Eithne: you keep my secret, I keep yours."

"My—"

"Secret, yes. Magic calls to magic, if one has the ears to hear."

"That's ridiculous! I don't—I'm not—"

"I think I know why you hide your Power. Father Seadna has cornered me often enough to lecture me about the Christian faith. It does not take kindly to magic, does it? And your husband's reign is sanctified by the Church. How awkward it would be should the High King's wife prove to be a—"

"I am a good Christian!"

"Queen Eithne, it hardly matters to me what you are or are not, what you practice, what you believe. I simply don't want to have to watch my back every waking moment."

"What are you trying to say?"

He smiled without humor. "What do you think? As I told you, I'm offering a pact. A royal treaty, if you would. I will keep your secret if you say nothing of mine."

"That is nothing short of blackmail!"

"Call it, rather, practicality." He paused, watching her stunned, furious face. "So. Have we that pact? I would much rather have an ally than an enemy. What about you?"

She was silent a long time, then suddenly burst out, "First

you must swear, on your honor as a prince, that you mean no harm to my family or any of my people."

Ardagh frowned. "I have already given that vow to Fothad."

"Not to me!"

"Humans! If it will soothe your mind, I do so swear to you as well: I mean no harm to you and yours nor to any of your people. Though of course," he added darkly, "I will defend myself if attacked."

She never flinched. "Fair enough."

"So. The oath is sworn. And my people never lie."

"S-so I've heard."

"Enough games!" the prince snapped. "Look you, I really would appreciate having one soul in this place of humans with whom I don't have to pretend. And I suspect you feel the same." He watched her gaze flicker. "Well? Are we agreed? Are we allies?"

Eithne sighed. "What choice have I? Yes, Prince Ardagh, for the moment at least, we are allies."

The prince cocked his head in a sudden burst of Sidhe curiosity. "Now that we have that matter settled, perhaps you can tell me what's bothering you." He permitted himself a quick grin. "Besides me, I mean."

"I don't—"

"You can hardly hide it from me. There's an aura of uneasiness dark as a cloud over you."

"You sense that, do you?" Eithne's shoulders sagged. "The maddening thing is that I don't *know* what's bothering me." She glanced sharply up. "And please don't say something soothing; it's not just my imagination."

"No. Your Power is too true for that."

"I suppose I should thank you for that." Eithne shuddered, hugging her arms about herself. "I've been feeling the vaguest sense of a premonition for some time now. I thought it had vanished after the assassination attempt, and I told myself, 'That's it, the danger's over.' But the premonition hasn't faded. Something is going to happen, something terrible, and I—I don't know what it is or how to stop it."

Ardagh stood rigid, refusing to show anything of the sudden panic he felt. Anything that was perilous for the humans would probably be perilous for him, as well.

But only humans panicked over What Might Be. "Precognition was never one of my best abilities," the prince admitted, "even in the Sidhe Realm. But you have an ally now. Whatever happens, remember that."

For whatever good it did in this magic-poor Realm.

This seemed to be his day for seeing children. Not at all displeased, Ardagh, on his way back from his newfound and unexpected royal alliance, paused to one side of the grassy central court as a whole horde of shouting, laughing youngsters scurried by. All boys, they ranged from barely older than little Fainche to nearly adult. *The royal hostages,* the prince realized suddenly.

Hostages, maybe, but they didn't look abused in any way. A bit overwhelmed by all their young energy, Ardagh stood watching them, still laughing and roughhousing, settle into groups sorted by general age and size. Ah, they were here for weapons practice; Aedh was plainly taking his host responsibilities seriously. *And by making their lives here so pleasant,* the prince thought, wise in the ways of royal politics, *he's also raising a whole generation of important allies who will think fondly of him.*

But not all the youngsters were out there on the practice field. Ardagh noticed a slender figure hovering wistfully to one side, not far from where he stood. A boy—no, a young man—no, a boy, Ardagh finally decided, a skinny youngster just at that age when it was so difficult to decide whether a child had quite reached adulthood.

"Aren't you supposed to be out there with the rest of them?" the prince asked, and the boy gave a little gasp of surprise and whirled, revealing a face too finely drawn, too pale for human health, and blue eyes far too weary for a boy.

"P-prince Ardagh."

"You recognize me, lad, but I'm afraid I don't know you."

"Oh, I—I'm Breasal mac Donnchadh. My father is king of Clonach."

"Yes, I know that much." Ardagh dipped his head in an amused little salute. "Pleased to meet you, Breasal mac Donnchadh. But why *aren't* you at weapons practice?"

"I . . . cannot." It was the merest whisper. "I haven't the strength. The last time I tried, I—I . . . fainted."

"I see," Ardagh said helplessly. The Sidhe, with their low rate of fertility, had their share of sickly children, but those either began to thrive as their magic matured or simply died as babes. What did one say to a nearly grown boy who looked frail enough to fall over at a push?

And yet, and yet, this was still a child, and as such to be cherished. The prince continued awkwardly, trying to find comforting words a human child would understand, "Ah well, swordplay isn't the whole of life. Look at Fothad mac Ailin—he's definitely not a swordsman, but he certainly is an asset to the king. And the scholar who's the royal judge . . . ae, what's his name . . ."

"Neasan mac Dubhan."

"Exactly. Thank you. Neither of those men are warriors, but the court couldn't function as well without them. Learn all the other lessons you're being taught, and you'll still prove an asset to your father."

A shadow passed over the weary eyes. "My father does not care what befalls me." It was said with such matter-of-fact calm that a shiver raced through Ardagh.

"Nonsense."

"It's true, Prince Ardagh." Breasal shrugged slightly. "I would never have the strength to rule Clonach. I am no use to him."

"B-but a parent doesn't just abandon a child! Surely he at least sends you messages—"

"Your pardon, Prince Ardagh, but I haven't heard a word from Clonach since the day I was brought here." Color suffused the pale face as the boy added fiercely, "And please don't feel sorry for me. King Aedh has been more of a father to me than my own blood kin, and I will be happy to stay here and—and serve him as well as I can for as long as he'll let me." Breasal broke off, gasping, but before Ardagh could move, the boy seemed to pull himself back under control, saying with desperate pride, "Now, if you will excuse me, Prince Ardagh?"

Watching Breasal hurry off, the prince shook his head in confusion. *I will never understand humans, never, never!*

Ae, but he still had a chance to learn something more about them, Ardagh remembered with a little jolt. Royal judge Neasan mac Dubhan was trying Fremainn legal cases today, and any of the nobility who cared to observe was welcome to attend; most did, finding attendance politic. With one last rueful shake of his head over human foibles, the prince started off for the king's court of law.

Ardagh glanced subtly about. The court of law consisted of one rectangular hall, part of the royal keep, with the door on one end and three rows of seats along the remaining three sides. He had been seated on the left-hand side, the side reserved, so he'd been told, for higher nobility or visiting royalty.

The prince recognized most of the aristocratic lot near him. To his immediate left was young Eirnin mac Flainn, ruddy hair and face clashing splendidly with the brilliant blues and yellows of his tunic and *brat*. Amulets disguised as ornaments hung from about his neck and glittered on his fingers, but not one of them, Ardagh *felt* contemptuously, had a shred of Power to them.

He also has a most decidedly . . . slimy feel to him. If he were a merchant, Ardagh mused, *he'd be giving short measure. If he wasn't poisoning his customers outright.*

Still, unpleasant fellow and superstitious fool though he was, Eirnin was still a kinsman to the warring brother-kings of Meath, which meant he must be granted respect.

The man to Ardagh's right wasn't much more appealing. This was Odran mac Daire, lean as a grey-haired hunting hound, his eyes grim and cold and devoid of humor, elegant in his more subdued violet and wine-red.

Unpleasant fellow. He, if I'm not mistaken, is every bit as nasty a soul as Eirnin: the sort who would arrange quiet "accidents" for his enemies.

But Odran was of the Ui Neill sept, which made him kin to King Aedh himself.

Human politics aren't all that different from those at my brother's court. Smile and keep smiling and never quite say what you're thinking. Bah. I thought I was through with that nonsense.

Behind the prince in the second row sat several other men of varying degrees of distinction, all with close ties to this king or that important clan.

And not a one of them, I would guess, who doesn't envy Aedh up there on his royal dais. I can feel enough ambition swirling among the lot to stun Ethenian the Jealous.

There at the head of the hall sat King Aedh on a slight dais, flanked by Fothad on one side and Father Seadna on the other. This once, however, the king sat behind someone: Neasan mac Dubhan, a quiet, competent, plain-featured man of middle years, who ruled the hall—at least in theory—while the royal law court was in session. Ardagh guessed that Aedh would be quick enough to intervene if he saw anything of which he didn't approve, but so far there hadn't been the slightest need to overturn any of the judge's rulings. Neasan had cut right through the dozen or so minor cases before him without once even raising his voice.

I'm sure that everyone's glad there are only minor cases to be heard today, Ardagh thought. *But I doubt I would have been so patient about the whole affair.*

A Fremainn worker brought suit against a carpenter because he had been injured by a splinter flying from the carpenter's adze. Neasan had dismissed the case, mildly commenting that splinters flew where they would without any human malice being involved. The judge also ruled invalid a land contract made between two lesser nobles after witnesses swore one of the men had been drunk at the time, and ordered one guard to pay honor-price to another whose nose had been broken during a fight over a matter neither of them could recall.

At least I see that humans are capable of logic, the prince admitted, watching Neasan with grudging admiration. *Sometimes. Ae, but these petty matters are hardly the stuff of great drama! All I've learned so far is that humans get muddled by drink and sometimes have short tempers. Nothing that I hadn't already guessed.*

Stealing a sly glance at King Aedh, Ardagh decided the man looked every bit as bored as he felt.

"If there are no more cases," Neasan began.

"Your pardon," cut in a woman's voice, sharp as the call of a trumpet, and Ardagh sat bolt upright in surprise.

Sorcha ni Fothad came striding into the court, green gown swirling about her legs, to stop short before the judge with a curt bow and a deeper one for the king and her father. Ignoring Fothad's scandalized whisper of "Sorcha! You shouldn't be here!" she said fiercely to Neasan, "There is yet one case that has not been heard. I cry justice for one of my maidservants."

A wild murmuring spread throughout the court, and a puzzled Ardagh took advantage of the confusion to ask Odran, "What is so unusual about her being here?"

That earned him a stern glance. "She is a woman!"

"Yes, obviously, but—"

"The testimony of a woman is not legal."

"Whyever not?"

But just then Aedh thundered out a commanding, "Silence!" In the sudden stillness that followed, Neasan said gently, "Lady Sorcha, you know this procedure is most irregular."

"I also know that my maidservant has no living father to protect her. She is under *my* protection and, woman though I may be, she has no one else to speak in her behalf."

Neasan hesitated a moment, plainly mulling over the laws. Aedh leaned forward impatiently, as though about to prod him, but the judge said, "There is precedent for women speaking in defense of the helpless. Tell us the crime."

"Rape," Sorcha said bluntly.

" 'Rape?' " Ardagh whispered to Odran. "I don't know the word."

He received a second sharp glance and a hissed, "Forced fornication."

Ardagh sat back in shock. What foulness was this? Powers, what manner of perverse creature could even dream of—

"Can you be more specific?" Neasan asked, seemingly unruffled.

Sorcha glared, hands on hips. "Must I name her? Surely the poor woman has been harmed enough already!"

Neasan paused, then shook his head. "Your concern for your servants' well-being does you credit, Lady Sorcha. You may withhold the woman's name for now. But I really must have more details."

Sorcha took a deep breath. "Yesterday night, my maid-servant felt faint and left her bed for a breath of air. It was foolish of her to go alone, perhaps. But she felt quite safe in the king's fortress—wrongly, as it turns out! She was seized upon in a corridor by—by one I shall name in a bit. He made some attempts to woo her, she told me, but when she refused him, he took her against her will."

"And yet she said nothing to you or anyone else till today?"

"She was too terrified to speak of it till this day! He was far above her in rank—and he threatened to kill her if she told a soul. It was only when I questioned her at length that the poor thing broke down and admitted what had happened."

"And can you name her alleged attacker?"

"Oh, I can, indeed!" Sorcha snapped. "It was this man!"

Her finger stabbed at Eirnin mac Flainn. As the startled murmurings burst out again, the noble stiffened in outrage. "I protest! I have had nothing to do with a—a *servant!* And I will not be verbally assaulted by this woman or anyone else!"

And you, Ardagh realized in sudden disgust, *are as guilty as the Darkness. I can* feel *the ugliness spilling from you.*

"No one is assaulting you, my lord," Neasan murmured. "Lady Sorcha, this is a harsh charge you've made. But I must ask if the woman in question made any outcry at the time."

Sorcha winced. "Of the attack? No. She was too afraid."

"I see." The judge settled back in his chair with a sigh.

"You know the law, Lady Sorcha. If she is assaulted while within a settlement, a woman is obliged to call for help."

"Not if she's afraid the man will kill her if she screams!"

"I'm sorry. That *is* the law." Neasan paused. "Were there any witnesses?"

Sorcha's shoulders sagged. "No."

"Well, then. I am sorry, but . . ."

Powers! They're actually going to let the creature escape!

Not if he could help it. "A moment, please," Ardagh called out, and heads turned his way. "If I may be allowed to speak?"

At Neasan's startled nod, the prince left his seat to stand beside Sorcha. "What are you doing?" she hissed.

"Trying to correct a wrong," he hissed back. "Quickly, does the maid have any marks on her?"

"What—"

"Does she?"

"Y-yes. There's a purplish birthmark, like a star, on her left thigh, but—"

"Excellent!" To Neasan, Ardagh said, "My lord, there is no such thing as this 'rape' in my . . . land. In fact, I find it difficult to believe such a crime can exist at all. But I do believe I can learn the truth of guilt or innocence for you, if I may."

Neasan hesitated, frowning, then glanced back at King Aedh, plainly at a loss. Aedh, just as puzzled, hesitated as well, then nodded. "Go ahead, Prince Ardagh," the judge said.

"Thank you." He strolled over to where Eirnin sat. "My Lord Eirnin, in my land we have ways of determining guilt or innocence that may surprise you." So much was quite true. "Why, some might say we need only stare into a man's eyes." *"Some" might say anything.*

"What nonsense is this?"

"No nonsense. You see," Ardagh continued, skirting false-hood, "it just may be that we can read in those eyes exactly what has happened, and if that is so, then there is no way to hide that truth from us. Will you let me stare into your eyes, my lord?"

Eirnin's face was nearly as red as his hair. "I—no! My Lord Neasan, I must object to—"

"Come, come, my Lord Eirnin," Ardagh purred. "What harm in this? Surely you are innocent?"

"Yes, but—"

"Then let me stare into your eyes." Ardagh stared, putting into that steady look every bit of Sidhe arrogance.

Eirnin stood the alien green gaze for a few tense moments, the fear radiating from him. And then he scrambled to his feet, one hand clutching at the amulets about his neck. "Sorcerer!" he shouted.

"I? But I have done nothing but stare, my lord. While you, I think, have done much more. Was it possible that I saw a woman in your eyes, my lord, her clothing torn?" *No, it was not possible. But you don't know that, human, do you?* "Was it possible that I saw her lips move in entreaty? Ah, and was it possible that I saw a mark on her left thigh, one shaped most fetchingly like a star?"

"You couldn't have known about that!" Eirnin shouted, then froze, realizing he'd just as good as confessed his crime. "But—but I am Eirnin mac Flainn! And it was only a servant!"

"No great person in herself," Neasan agreed. "But a servant of Sorcha ni Fothad, which is to say of Fothad mac Ailin, Chief Minister and Poet to the Ard Ri himself."

Satisfied, Ardagh glanced at Sorcha. But instead of the joy or relief he'd expected, he saw only tight-mouthed tension. "What is it?" he whispered.

"Not now!" she snapped back.

Of course no real harm could come to Eirnin; his rank was too high for that. "But you must pay an honor-price," Neasan ruled, "equal to the honor-price of the woman's guardian."

"That cannot be another woman!"

"No," the judge agreed. "The proper legal guardian in this case would be, perforce, the guardian of Sorcha ni Fothad, namely Fothad mac Ailin. Oh, and of course since the woman you have admitted raping is most surely of marriageable age, the law states that you must pay half her honor-price as well."

Ardagh watched Eirnin's mouth fall open in shock as he

realized the extent of the two fines. Paying them—particularly matching the honor-price of the Chief Poet himself—would most certainly bankrupt the man. He would not dare return to his own estate, not with all knowing why he fled.

Instead he must stay here, totally dependent on King Aedh for charity. How nicely ironic.

Trembling slightly, Eirnin bowed to the king. "With your leave." At Aedh's cold nod, the man hurried off.

But now, Ardagh realized, all attention was on him. And not a few hands were surreptitiously making signs against evil. *Oh, you superstitious idiots!* He laughed sharply, the sound ringing out loudly in the suddenly quiet hall. "What," Ardagh shouted, "did you think I used *magic?* All I did was use his own fear against him!"

"The birthmark," Neasan said. "How did you know of the birthmark?"

"Powers, how do you think? The lady here told me!"

There was a new moment of confused silence. Then Aedh broke it with a hearty laugh. "Clever, Prince Ardagh, most clever!"

But the laugh sounded forced. *I've made you a new enemy, haven't I?* Ardagh thought. *Or at least sharpened an enmity that already existed. But what else was there to do?*

At Aedh's nod, Neasan mac Dubhan stated, "This court session is hereby declared closed."

Before anyone could stop him, Ardagh maneuvered his way out through the bustle of folk leaving the hall and caught up with Sorcha ni Fothad.

"What's wrong?"

She glanced quickly his way. "Don't you know who Eirnin mac Flainn is?"

"Indeed. No deed is without its complications, is it? But you must have considered that before you made your attack."

Sorcha sighed. "Yes. And . . . I . . . you . . ." She stopped short. "Well now, to be blunt, I didn't expect any help from you."

Stung, he asked, "Why not?"

"Why, because, Prince Ardagh, you are a—you—"

"I have never," Ardagh snapped, "taken a woman against her will. Nor will I ever do so."

She stared at him, eyes wondering. "You mean that."

"Of course I do! Once and for all, Sorcha ni Fothad, *I never lie!* That creature was about to walk away from the perversion of something joyous into an evil act, and I—simply could not fail to act."

For a moment more Sorcha looked up at him, her face just then open and defenseless, and Ardagh, with a pleasant jolt of surprise, found himself thinking, *Lovely eyes. Lovely woman. When she isn't on the attack.*

As if she'd heard his thoughts, Sorcha reddened and looked away. "I thought I understood who and what you are. Apparently I was wrong."

"Very probably," Ardagh agreed with a wry little laugh.

"But what you are," she added sharply, "that I haven't decided. Watch your back, Prince Ardagh. Eirnin mac Flainn can make a deadly foe."

"So," Ardagh said, "can I."

"I don't doubt it. Oh, and . . . thank you."

Before he could reply, Sorcha ni Fothad had hurried away.

THE VISITOR

CHAPTER 8

Bishop Gervinus, no longer young but still tall and strongly built as the noble Frankish warrior stock from which he came, walked in welcome solitude. Elsewhere in the teeming maze that was the Vatican complex was the usual crowd of bishops and deacons, notaries and accountants necessary to keep such a complicated organization functioning. But this one slightly out-of-the-way hall was quiet and private, faintly scented as nearly every hallway was with incense and candle wax, and glowing softly with gold in the ever-present candlelight. There was not the slightest hint of turmoil, religious or political.

Almost, Gervinus thought, *as though there wasn't undeclared war between the Roman Church factions and those of my own Frankish lands. Were I a truly religious man, I would be horrified by such hatreds within the faith.*

The bishop continued on down the quiet halls, hearing his own footsteps seeming loud against the inlaid marble floors by contrast with the surrounding silence, his thoughts still on politics.

Undeclared war between the two factions, indeed: Barely a year ago, Roman agents had actually attacked and nearly killed the pope himself, angry at his alliance with the mighty Emperor Charles, he who was as often named Charlemagne. Only that alliance had rescued the badly injured Leo from a most unpleasant death, and it was he who would soon, barring further turbulence, crown his rescuer as emperor.

Charlemagne. My own family's liege lord. And which side should I back in this ecumenical battle, I wonder? Which side is most likely to win?

Had matters been slightly different, there wouldn't have been a question. After all, as the son of a high-ranking Frankish noble, a man of some importance at Charlemagne's court, Gervinus had been born into a predictable, well-regulated world.

Unfortunately, he had been born the second son. *The superfluous son.* It had been many years since older brother Conrad, solid and strong as their father and brainless as a true warrior, had brought that fact home to him, but the bitterness remained. They'd both been children back then, Conrad nine and Gervinus seven, but as fierce as any older foes. That day, Conrad had been sitting on his younger brother's chest after yet another of their vicious fights, taunting him with, "You'll never be anyone of worth. You'll be nothing but a musty old priest."

Gervinus' mouth tightened with the memory, remembering even now his shock, his pain. His pride. He hadn't let any tears show then, for all his rage and hurt. Nor had he wept later, when his father, that tall, grim man who almost never laughed, had beaten him for getting into and losing yet another fight. Instead, ignoring his aching body, the boy had asked coolly, "Why must I be a priest?"

As always, his father had looked away from his steady gaze. Gervinus had learned at an early age that he was considered by everyone in the keep as a frighteningly bright, frighteningly cold child. "What else is there for you to be?" his father had asked. "Conrad is the eldest, and of course the firstborn boy must inherit all."

"But *why*?"

That had brought a frown. "A noble's estate can hardly be portioned out like some peasant's land! Come, boy, you're surely old enough to realize that there's no other honorable post for a second son than the Church."

"But I don't *want* to be a priest!"

For a moment, he'd been sure his father was going to strike him. But then the man, unexpectedly, had smiled. "Think about it, boy. Think of how high a clever priest might rise. The power behind the throne, boy. The power behind the throne. Ah yes, I see the ambition flickering in those cold eyes of yours. Young as you are, you know exactly what I mean."

So he had. But later that night, he'd methodically set about destroying every one of Conrad's weapons and noble dress.

Fortunate my father didn't beat me to death for that. But then he wouldn't have had a son to donate to the Church.

The bishop stopped in front of a door as though readjusting the drape of his robes. Beyond, he knew, lay a small council chamber, empty as it usually was and far more private than his own spartan quarters. Hearing voices behind him, Gervinus turned, nodding politely to the two deacons who were passing him, chatting softly together. The young men fell silent, shying slightly from him like two startled wild things, then returned his nod and hurried on.

Idiots.

Once he was alone again, Gervinus bent to the door's lock and murmured a phrase that was neither Latin nor the Frankish tongue. The words were nonsense to him, but he had learned from the first memorization that they were enough to focus Power: with the softest of clicks, the door swung open. He slipped inside, closing the door silently behind him, and repeated his small spell in reverse. The room was now guarded against any chance intruders.

Ignoring the religious images watching somberly from every wall, Gervinus sat at the heavy oak table that dominated the room and waited to catch his breath. Maybe the tales told of sorcerers casting spell after easy spell, but he knew the truth: one could only work sorcery after long study and careful concentration, and even then only in limited fashion.

One did what one could. Recovered, the bishop drew out of his robes a plain, leather-bound book sealed with a small, intricate lock, and an equally plain little mirror. For a moment he sat studying them. Such ordinary-seeming objects. Yet the mirror had taken long months to make and had nearly cost him his life: only at the last moment had he remembered that it was perilous for any sentient being to be the first to glance at the polished surface. The dog he'd forced to gaze into the mirror had died in convulsions from the uncontrollable surge of Power that set the mirror to functioning. And as for the book, his precious grimoire—

Gervinus shook his head. Every now and then the sheer strangeness of the path his life had taken struck him like a blow. He had never actually intended to study sorcery. No, in the Frankish monastery where he'd first been sent (a quick memory: the disquieting glint of relief in his father's eyes at being rid of his troublesome son), the boy-Gervinus, thrilled by his introduction to the literate world, had devoured whatever his tutors had given him to study, whether letters, psalms, mathematics or grammar, but always with an eye towards purely normal, purely temporal power. Even when he'd stolen into the monastery's small library at night to read every precious book or scroll he could find, he had certainly never dreamed of anything more.

Until that night when he had found one crumbling little scroll on which was scrawled what was undeniably a spell of Summoning. Too curious to be afraid, the boy-Gervinus had carefully carried out each step, standing, trembling just a bit, in a chalked circle, whispering the ugly, alien syllables.

And Something had come, Something strange and chill and . . . empty. Gervinus tensed slightly even now, remembering the moment his life had been forever changed. For that Something had whispered to him that he, too, was empty, that he believed in nothing, in no one, but himself . . . night after night, that same chill voice had whispered in his dreams, telling him the same terrible truth, until at last the terror was gone and only the truth remained. After all, even back then, he *had* believed only in himself, in what he could win through wit and will.

Why not? Look what the supposed One True Faith pro-duced: my father, illiterate and proud of his ignorance, who never once showed that so-vaunted Christian love to his own

*son, and my brother, equally illiterate and stupidly content
in his ignorance, who showed most unChristian hate towards
his own brother yet never once suffered for it—*

Bah, what could such a faith possibly hold for him? And
if there were times after Its visits that his dreams turned
dark, warning of endless nothingness, why, what were dreams
but foolish fancies?

So, now. If the only path of power open to him meant
he must spout Churchly dogma even if he believed none
of it, so be it. Granted, he'd expected, being a noble's son,
to be rewarded with a post at the emperor's court, Charlemagne, who thought nothing of creating his own bishops
when he pleased, taking papal consent for granted. Even
though the emperor was seldom at that court, off battling
Saxons or Slavs or anyone else who debated his rule, there
would have been no end to how high an ambitious cleric
might rise at the royal court.

Instead, Gervinus thought with a touch of impatience,
here he was trapped in Rome, watching Pope Hadrian die
and Pope Leo replace him, watching this faction try to oust
that one, doing nothing much else all these tedious years.
He'd been pulled from the Frankish monastery at his father's
whim. Why? Some misguided attempt of the man to enter
international politics? Or merely the urge to separate warring brothers as far as possible? Why bother? Dear Conrad
was and remained as he had always been, in excellent health,
and his brood mare of a wife had by now given him two
equally healthy sons. Gervinus snorted. Short of murder-
ing two generations of kin without leaving a trace, there
wasn't a secular hope for him.

Ah well, one took power where one found it. And the
learning to be found here had been so intoxicating: the books,
so many more than could be found in any Frankish monastery, the chance, for the first time in his life, to fully use
his mind and stretch his knowledge—even, Gervinus added
silently, beyond the limits allowed the clergy.

Oh, yes. Secret excursions into the depths of the Vatican
library had unearthed some very strange books, ostensibly
hidden there to keep them out of the reach of Darkness,

books so much more powerful than that one pathetic little spell-scroll back in the Frankish monastery. He already had a talent for sorcery, surely; that Summoning, amateurish but effective, had proved it. And now at last he'd had a chance to expand that talent. The grimoire had come from that sorcerous cache of books, and hour after hour of study, Gervinus knew, had made him quite proficient in its use.

But what good is it? I don't dare risk anything truly Powerful, not here in the very heart of the Church! Looking back at himself as the brash, bitter, lonely young man he'd been, hating Rome, hating everything about the Roman Church that was so alien to a Frankish boy, Gervinus shook his head at opportunities lost. What a fool he'd been! *No matter how I despised them, I should have wooed friends, allies.*

Instead, his early aloofness had branded him unpleasant, unsociable, coldly brilliant. All, Gervinus admitted frankly, quite true: he *was* brilliant, and he had no desire for the weaknesses that were good fellowship or the sins of the flesh. But that coldness meant that while he had at first managed to rise rapidly through the clerical ranks, it had been only so high and no higher. Yes, he had gained the status of bishop, but Auxiliary Bishop only, without a diocese, without a purpose, without a use save to serve as errand boy to the Curiate.

He came sharply alert. No time now for reflection. Deep within the Vatican's maze, members of that Curiate had just begun their meeting, activating the spell he'd set in their chambers. Unlocking his precious grimoire, staring into his sorcerous mirror, Gervinus began his muttered chant. Soon a wavering image formed in the highly polished silver, soon he could hear voices, thin and faint as though from a great distance. Straining, the bishop could make out tantalizing bits, just enough to let him know they were discussing, as was everyone these uncertain days, the politics of Church and empire.

And . . . him? Was that his name being mentioned? Something about . . . "troublemaker . . . cold-blooded . . . can't tell which side he's on." Frowning, Gervinus struggled to hear

more. Something about, " . . . must be rid of him." "But
how?" " . . . can't just see he vanishes . . . noble-born . . ."

They were silent a good while, so long that Gervinus' spell
began to fade. Just when he thought it would disappear
altogether, he saw one of those Churchly bureaucrats
straighten and say, "Mother Church's reach . . . stretched
. . . over the far realms . . . not enough news from the distant
lands." There was a frenzy of excitement from the others,
a good deal of jabbering he couldn't hear. And then the spell
dissipated and was gone. Gervinus slumped in his chair,
drained and exhilarated at once.

They were going to rid themselves of him, those bureaucrats, and never once see the favor they were granting him.
He would at last be free of this prison! It only remained
to see to which far-flung land he would be sent, and then
he could begin to plan, to act, to finally use his talents.

Bishop Gervinus, late of Rome, originally of the Frankish lands, stood at the ship's rail, mysterious in his hooded
cloak, hiding his impatience behind a mask of tranquility
as he looked out over the flat expanse of blue. With the
ship becalmed, there was nothing to do but wait. He was
pretending not to hear the whispers of the sailors around
him—not an easy thing to do, what with no sound from the
motionless ship or the limply hanging sail and Church standard, or the utterly tranquil ocean.

Bah, whispers were nothing. Gervinus was used to such
foolishness as these idiots were sharing; the lower classes
were full of their superstitions. If the commons thought him,
despite his clerical garb, somehow in league with Darkness
just because he held himself aloof from them, what man
of any importance would stoop to listen to them?

Even, Gervinus reflected with a moment's sardonic humor, *if they might happen to be correct.*

His thoughts were interrupted by a nervous sailor, doing
whatever it was sailors did when a ship was becalmed. The
bishop raised a hand in casual benediction as the man passed,
and the sailor dipped his head in uneasy thanks.

Idiot. Idiots all.

"Your pardon, Holiness." It was the ship's captain this time, a roughly made, weather-worn man whose hodgepodge of an accent indicated someone who spent more time in foreign ports than at home. Diffidence sat most uneasily on him. "You asked for me?"

"Indeed," Gervinus said. "We have been becalmed for nigh a day now. What do you intend to do about it?"

"Well . . . uh . . . there isn't too much we *can* do, Holiness, not without wind. Unusual for it to turn so calm this far into autumn, but," with a helpless shrug, "there you are." He glanced hopefully at the bishop. "I don't suppose you . . ."

Gervinus stared. Did the idiot really think he was going to get down on his knees here and now and pray for wind? "I shall do what I can. In my cabin."

The ship was crowded with his retinue of guards and servants, but at least he needed to share the cramped little room that was misnamed the cabin of honor only with the acolyte Arnulf, a youngster of Frankish blood like himself; a valuable find, not for his intellect (dubious) or cunning (low) but because he shared certain sorcerous views.

The bishop paused in the doorway in distaste as the stench of sickness reached him. Gervinus had the stomach of a sailor, but his acolyte did not. Closing and bolting the rickety door behind him, the bishop snapped, "Get up, Arnulf. The sea's as still as glass. You can't possibly still be ill."

Arnulf's face was a ghastly green, but he staggered to his feet, a slight young man asking hopefully, "Is Eriu in sight?"

"No. Nor is it likely to be any time soon unless we do something about it."

Arnulf's eyes widened. "The others—"

"Will hear nothing unless you keep shouting like that. And," Gervinus added grimly, "I'm sure you will continue to keep a discreet tongue in your head."

"Of course, Master!"

Of course, Gervinus mocked silently. It had nothing to do with priestly obedience. Arnulf longed for Power far more than for Salvation.

Reaching into his belt-pouch, the bishop pulled out a

simple copper ring set with a small red stone, slipping it
onto his left hand. From the clothes chest at the foot of
his narrow bunk, he extracted his precious grimoire with
its intricate little lock. Gervinus paused, studying it for a
moment. Lately he had felt the oddest *pull* whenever he
attempted sorcery, as though some outside Something was
enticing him to use Power whether he would or not.

Nonsense.

His glance sharpened, noticing the faintest of scratches
marring the smooth surface; Arnulf, the young idiot, had
been trying to steal a bit of his master's knowledge.

*I should let him open the book. Let him learn for him-
self what true Power means—and how perilous it can be.*

But a dead acolyte would be a nuisance. He needed
Arnulf, for now at least.

At a murmured word from the bishop, the lock fell open.
"Clear me a space," he said over his shoulder, "and fill that
bowl with fresh water."

"You're not going to call on *him* again, are you?"

Gervinus turned to stare so coldly that Arnulf shivered
and dropped his head in submission. "What I do or do not
is not for you to question," the bishop murmured. "Now
do as I tell you."

As Arnulf hurried to obey, Gervinus stood motionless,
focusing his thoughts, ignoring the fierce, distracting surge
of joy his sorcery always brought him, then opened the book
and began, quietly, to read Words that were in no human
tongue. The cabin's stale air began to stir, ruffling his robes,
but the bishop never faltered. Midway through the calling,
he thrust his ring-bearing hand into the water, submerg-
ing ring and stone, continuing without pause to read the
spell to its final twisting end.

The cabin shook to a sudden blast of cold, dank air.
Something came, something vaguely manlike yet so shrouded
with mist even Gervinus couldn't make out its true shape.
But it could only be the being he'd summoned.

"Arridu."

"What would you?" The soft voice was the sound of wind
whispering over ice.

"Something of your power."

Arridu glanced about the cramped cabin and laughed coldly. "*A storm? While you are trapped on this fragile little piece of wood? That would be . . . amusing.*"

One did not show strong emotion to a demon. "Not a storm," Gervinus said in a perfect counterfeit of calmness. "Merely a wind. A steady wind to carry this 'piece of wood,' as you so poetically call it, west and northwest to the land known as Eriu."

"*Why should I do this thing?*"

"Because, Arridu, I know your true name. I bear your ring."

The misty shape swirled and shifted. The air filled with the rank stench of wind over swampland. "*True, true,*" the demon said at last. "*But I must be paid. Give me a sailor's life. A life for a wind.*"

Gervinus hesitated a careful moment. "A sailor's life," he repeated. "Neither I nor my acolyte are sailors, understand that."

"*Understood.*"

"A sailor's life you shall have, then. Done."

Arridu laughed and vanished in a swirl of mist and a roar of wind. Gervinus staggered, bracing himself against a wall as the wind rose and rose. "So be it," he murmured.

It would be a simple thing to see that a sailor slipped overboard during the windstorm. All knew that sailors could not swim. It would be thought a sad accident, nothing more.

And soon enough, they would be in Eriu, and he would never have to see this ridiculous ship again.

"Uh . . . your Holiness?" It was the captain, nervously approaching Gervinus where he stood at the rail, wind tangling his robes about him.

"What?" Gervinus just barely kept from snarling. The demon had kept its pledge, but with a touch of true, demonic malice: The howling wind that had followed, driving the ship before it, had been only one small degree removed from a storm, shredding sails and standards, nearly snapping the mast itself. Only the one unfortunate sailor had been dragged screaming overboard, but the survival of the ship had been a narrow thing.

"You asked me to inform you when Eriu was in sight. Well . . . uh . . . it is, although it's going to take us a while to limp into shore, the sails being torn the way they are."

Idiot. I already knew that. But Gervinus dipped his head in a curt bow. "Thank you. You may leave me. I would not keep you from your duties."

After a moment, the captain bowed just as curtly, and left Gervinus to his brooding. He glanced up at the once-proud Church standard where it hung in sad, useless tatters, and clenched his teeth.

Arridu nearly escaped my control. And yet that is such a minor demon, its powers only of one Element! If I cannot control it, if I cannot wield true, stronger Power, I am naught.

He would manage, Gervinus told himself. He would, in fact, triumph. Not one of the Curiate had expected him to give in so graciously when they'd told him he was being sent to Eriu "to see that our far-off brethren do not sink back into the ways of Pagandom." Not one of them had guessed why he'd been so humbly willing to travel such a vast distance and endure so many hardships along the way. But all those pious bureaucrats would have been horrified at his smile just now, thin and cold as the edge of a knife.

In this far-flung corner of Christendom, so far from Rome and the reach of Mother Church, he would settle. The people here would have no sophistication. How could they, the ignorant louts, sitting out here on the edge of the world? They would know nothing of Rome, or even of the secular splendor of Charlemagne's court, and be easily fascinated by anyone coming from so far away. Ah yes, through sorcery and cunning, he would bend their High King to his use, turn the man into his puppet. In this far-flung corner of Christendom, he would build his realm.

And if it meant rousing Darkness to do it, why, so be it.

FINDING A PURPOSE

CHAPTER 9

Eithne turned her head on the pillow to look at her husband, a shapeless mass lying beside her in the darkness. "Aedh?" she asked softly.

"Mmm."

"Aedh, are you still awake?"

He grunted. "I am now."

"Aedh, I've been thinking."

"Good. Keep it up."

That made Eithne giggle in spite of herself. "Stop that! I'm trying to be serious."

Aedh sighed and turned over with a great creaking of the bedframe to face her. "I see I'll get no sleep this night unless I hear you out. What's troubling you, Eithne?"

The words burst from her before she could stop them. "Prince Ardagh." Feeling Aedh tense, Eithne added hastily, "Oh, I don't mean he's laid a hand on me or said a word out of place, nothing at all like that." *I am of the Sidhe. I am not human*—no, she would not think of that. "But . . . what is to become of him?"

"Who knows? By the Laws of Hospitality, he is free to shelter here as long as he behaves himself. And I wouldn't throw out a man of royal blood, one who has no means of support."

"That's just it. He's a prince; he can't be expected to work like a crofter or turn mercenary like Cadwal."

"What are you proposing?"

To her amazement, Eithne suddenly realized she was on the verge of tears. "I—I don't know. He needs something to do, something with a purpose."

"Here now, since when have you started worrying about the man? I thought you didn't like him!"

"I . . . don't, not really. But . . ." *He is a creature of magic, of wonder, that's what hurts my heart, because our poor mortal realm diminishes him.* "He has a fine, sharp mind. You told me how cleverly he handled himself during the law court."

"Clever. He sharpened Eirnin's enmity and possibly allied the kings of Meath against me."

"I doubt that. They'd never be able to agree long enough to muster an army."

Aedh snorted. "Well put. And I must admit Prince Ardagh has been useful enough in my council meetings."

"Only useful? That wasn't what you said when he solved that argument over . . . what was it, cattle? . . . with a few neat words."

"Acerbic words that left the claimants too embarrassed over their behavior to fight. God knows, I don't dare loose the man against any royal emissaries—no predicting what he'd do to them!—but I agree, when he chooses, our princely guest can be close to brilliant in his own odd way."

"Exactly! There must be some way you can make better use of him. Aedh? He saved your life. Don't you trust him by now?"

"Do you?"

Eithne remembered the vow the Sidhe had sworn to her, his eyes coolly earnest: his folk never lied. "Yes," she said softly.

"Eithne, Eithne," Aedh murmured, amusement in his voice. "My strange, unpredictable wife."

"Hey now, what does that mean?"

"So sensible at most times, so dreamy at others—you should have been a bard, Eithne."

She snorted. "I have small gift for music."

"True," he admitted, and Eithne smacked his shoulder.

Chuckling, Aedh added, "Sensible and dreamy she is, and most wonderfully full of love and pity as well. And I thank the Lord each day that she's mine."

But even as her husband drew her into an embrace that was more sleepy than lustful, Eithne thought with a sudden pang of guilt, *I am not honest with you, Aedh, I cannot be. It's not for pity or love of Ardagh that I try to help him. No, my dearest love, it's because by giving Prince Ardagh a purpose, keeping him content, he is far less likely to betray me.*

"Cadwal."

The mercenary whirled, going into an instinctive battle stance. But in the next moment he straightened, hand dropping from the hilt of his half-drawn sword. "*Dewi Sant*, man, you move like a cat!" In the next moment, he could feel his face burning, because you didn't talk like that to royalty.

Prince Ardagh didn't seem offended. "Your pardon. I sometimes forget . . . others' hearing isn't as keen as my own."

Now, what did that slight hesitation imply? Without warning, a half-forgotten wisp of childhood lore brushed Cadwal's mind. Instead of "others," could the prince have been about to say "humans"?

Pw, no, of course not. Enough years had passed, with enough hardship and fighting to fill them, for him not to harbor foolish fancies. "Your pardon for my bluntness, Prince Ardagh, but you look like a hunting beast ready to pounce. I do something to offend you?"

The startling green eyes blinked in surprise. "No, of course not. Cadwal, I have recently seen you teaching young Niall some of the fine points of swordplay."

Cadwal grinned, feeling the usual little thrill of pride that King Aedh had entrusted him, the Cymru foreigner, the mercenary, with the training of his son. "The young prince has the making of a fine warrior. God grant," he added hastily, "he not need those skills for many years yet."

"Indeed. But if it is not considered odd for you to be

training one prince, then surely you may duel with me as well. If," Ardagh added with what was very clearly an after-thought, "you wish it."

Arrogant creature, aren't you? Cadwal asked silently. *But then, so are most princes.* "I've seen you once in battle," the mercenary drawled, "and I wouldn't mind crossing swords with you, see more of your Cathayan style of fighting. Do us both a bit of good."

To his surprise, that sparked a genuine grin from the aloof prince. "When and where?"

Cadwal felt himself starting to grin as well. "Now's as good a time as any, as soon as we get ourselves some blunted training swords from the armory." *No way I'm going to risk drawing a prince's blood.* "And we can use the same training field my men and I always use."

The prince followed him without argument to the sturdy oaken building. Figuring that a man who—royal or no—was a good swordsman would enjoy seeing the weapons in the High King's armory, Cadwal stepped aside to let the prince enter.

But to his surprise, the man stopped short in the door-way, his face gone pale, almost as if he was struggling against sudden nausea. *Or,* whispered an unbidden little voice in Cadwal's mind, *against the presence of so much massed iron?* But then the mercenary snapped at himself, *Stop that, you idiot! You sound like an old woman!* "Something the matter, Prince Ardagh?"

"Nothing." But in his eyes glinted definite distress. *He scared of the dark? Maybe. Or maybe he's one of those folks whose sight doesn't adjust to darkness quickly.*

Whatever the cause, it wouldn't be wise to embarrass a prince any further. The mercenary said lightly, "Wait here. I'll get the swords. Won't take a minute."

He hardly needed light to find weapons he and his men used every day. Picking a handful, Cadwal brought them out to where the prince was waiting, then frowned. "You sure you're all right?"

"Quite sure." Prince Ardagh selected a sword, testing it in a few efficient moves. "This will serve. Shall we?" He gave that unexpected, infectious grin again, eyes laughing too, and Cadwal forgave him a good deal of his arrogance.

"We shall, indeed!"

Och, this was a fine swordsman, indeed, quicker on his feet than it was right for a man to be, smooth to lunge or parry, so graceful Cadwal felt clumsy as a fool by comparison. But the prince had clearly fought in few actual battles, at least not battles won by the sword; he lacked the downright cunning of a successful mercenary. Cadwal, unable to so much as touch the fellow, still managed to hold his own, even managed to drive the prince back a few steps, vaguely aware that they'd gathered quite an audience, his men and Aedh's.

Making wagers, are they? You better not be wagering against me, my boys, or I'll have you running laps round the fortress till your eyes cross.

Best to stop this duel right about now, before either one of them got embarrassed by a loss. But something very odd was happening. Bit by bit, the prince's clear green gaze was changing, hardening, growing alarmingly cold, inhumanly wild.

Och, we've roused some old memories, have we? Nasty memories, to look at those eyes. You're not even really seeing me any longer, are you?

Enough of this. Cadwal hastily stepped back and lowered his sword, yelling, "Cease!"

For a moment he wasn't sure that was going to mean anything to his now savage opponent, but then the prince stopped short, almost as if he'd been slapped, eyes still inhumanly fierce.

"Why did you halt?" he asked hoarsely.

Cadwal forced himself to meet the fierce glare without blinking. "Because you were getting too serious," he said, and saw Prince Ardagh flinch. "It stopped being merely a test of skill to you. Look you, I'd as soon face a raging boar with not a weapon in my hand as a swordsman who's lost control of his emotions."

For a moment he was sure the prince was going to strike him. But just as Cadwal was wondering what he'd do if that happened, Ardagh shuddered and turned away, admitting softly, "You're right."

Their audience was watching with rigid fascination. Cadwal moved to Prince Ardagh's side so he wouldn't be overheard by those idle idiots and murmured, "It's no easy thing to be an exile. I know that, believe me." That earned him a quick glare, but Cadwal continued in a burst of anger, "Maybe I'm not a prince or anything fine like that, but do you think exile's been any easier for me?"

He wasn't prepared for the sudden sympathy that flashed in the green eyes. "No. Of course it hasn't. But . . . how do you bear it?"

"Och, you do," Cadwal said gruffly. "You live each day as it comes, and you bear it."

The prince turned to study him, frowning slightly. "There is more to you than the man who fights for pay. How did one like you ever become a mercenary?"

A quick stab of pain, an unwanted flash of memory, death and pain and despair—*He doesn't know, he doesn't understand.* "I killed a man who needed killing," Cadwal snapped. "If ever we come to share a few drinks together," *as if royalty and mercenaries ever do,* "then maybe I'll tell you about it."

"I'm sorry." To Cadwal's surprise, that sounded genuine. "I didn't mean to bring old pain to the present."

The mercenary brusquely waved that away. "*Hiraeth* makes fools of us all."

"*Hiraeth?*"

"It's a Cymreig word. Means . . . well, it doesn't translate, not exactly. *Hiraeth* is something more than mere homesickness, more like . . . like the bittersweet ache for what you can't ever have again."

"Ah." It was the barest whisper. "*Hiraeth,* indeed."

He might have said more, but just at that moment there came a shout:

"Prince Ardagh? Ah, Prince Ardagh, there you are!"

"Fothad mac Ailin," Cadwal said. "It's been . . . interesting, Prince Ardagh. But it looks like this is where we both go back to work."

◉   ◉   ◉

Ardagh, still shaken by his odd duel and the odder conversation, stood waiting for Fothad, hurrying down the grassy
field to reach him. *Did Cadwal realize why I couldn't enter
that armory? That sudden surge of iron . . . and did he guess
who I was seeing during the duel? Did he guess how close
I came to cutting him down because I ached to kill my
brother instead?* Ardagh shuddered, repinning his woolen
brat more closely, chilled by more than sudden inactivity.
*Eirithan, we were never friends, but I never knew till now
just how much I hated you.*

But here was Fothad, and here was an end to musing.
As the Chief Poet paused to catch his breath, his face was
practically beaming with delight. "I have exciting news for
you, Prince Ardagh, news that I think you'll enjoy."

"Indeed?" the prince asked warily.

"Why, yes. A merchant has just arrived at court—and he
has travelled all the way from Cathay!"

Ae.

Fothad, taking the prince's surprised dismay for subdued
pleasure, chattered on, "Just think of it, Prince Ardagh.
Someone who can share your native tongue with you. Someone who can give you news of your home."

Someone who can betray me as an imposter, Ardagh
thought. But there was no plausible excuse he could give
for not seeing the man, so he grimly followed in Fothad's
wake.

The merchant, a stout, sturdy, brown-haired man, was
standing in the open meadow before the royal keep, surrounded by his goods and a bevy of bargain-hunting
women. Queen Eithne, Ardagh noted with a quick flash
of humor, stood to one side, clearly aching to be foraging
with the others but held back by her rank. Aedh stood
with her, red hair and gold crown bright in a glint of sunlight, a hint of a smile crooking up the corner of his mouth.
But then his gaze met and locked with that of Ardagh.
And there was something very odd about the suddenly
speculative stare.

Testing me, are you? Ardagh wondered. *Human or Sidhe,*

it would seem that a king is always a suspicious soul. But then, he has to be such, if he is to survive.

"So, Prince Ardagh," Aedh said, as lightly as though not the slightest wisp of suspicion was troubling him. "I have someone for you to meet: Seanan mac Cian, far-wandering merchant."

The merchant turned to face Ardagh, a smile on his broad face: the sort of man, Ardagh guessed, who can go anywhere because he sees no difference between this culture and that. "So now, Your Highness, they told me . . ." He stopped, running a hand through his thick brown hair. "Funny, now, I've seen lots of Cathayan folk, but I've got to say I never saw anyone who looked quite like you, begging your royal pardon."

Ardagh heard Queen Eithne draw her breath in sharply, plainly seeing the end of everything for both of them. *Don't panic,* he told her. *Not yet.*

He couldn't make any specific statements about Cathay; he didn't know anything specific to say! "There are many folk," Ardagh mused aloud, using vague truth to skirt falsehood, "and most amazingly far-travelled though you are, you could hardly have seen them all."

Seanan mac Cian, of course, could only assume that " . . . in Cathay" was included in that ambiguous statement. He nodded enthusiastically. "Och, and isn't that the truth, Your Highness? I've travelled a good deal, indeed, long years of travel, but it's a big land, Cathay is, so much vaster than this one, as I don't have to tell you. Yes, and it's a land with a good many kingdoms in it. I certainly can't claim to have seen them all, or all the inhabitants, either. I'm sorry that I seem to have missed your kingdom entirely." He grinned apologetically. "Still, you might enjoy hearing the sound of this."

The merchant burst into a spate of oddly cadenced, totally incomprehensible words.

Cathayan. And I'm supposed to understand what he's saying. Suddenly inspired, the prince replied in as rapid a flood of words in his native Sidhe tongue, saying nothing much, then stopped at the merchant's puzzled frown, smiling inwardly.

"Sorry, Your Highness," Seanan mac Cian said after a moment. "I'd forgotten just how many dialects there are in Cathay. It looks like I never did touch on yours." He scratched his head again. "I really am sorry about this. Haven't seen your kingdom *or* learned your language. I hope you'll not hold my failure against me."

Ardagh waved that away with a gracious hand, and the human's face brightened. "But at least I can give you some news of what's going on in the parts of Cathay I did see, if you'd like."

"If you would." Ardagh politely listened to a recital about places he'd never seen, people of whom he'd never heard. Since he was surely expected to ask, the prince inquired about his brother, his lands, keeping his expression eager as though he really hoped for an answer, knowing it was impossible for the merchant to give him anything more than an awkward apology. He hardly listened to that, looking instead directly at Aedh, who gave him the most subtle of smiles before turning away.

Ardagh paced restlessly about the confines of Fremainn, mulling over what had happened between him and the trader, between him and Aedh. At last he found a perch on the edge of a low wall, and wondered, *Ae, Aedh, do you finally accept the story you humans have placed on me? Do you believe I do come from Cathay? Do you truly trust me?* The prince settled the folds of his clothing more comfortably, the feel of wool and linen against his skin all at once very alien. *I can't let things come so near to crisis again. I must make myself so valuable to the king that no one will dream to question me. But how? I am a being of magic; I never realized it so strongly as now, when that part of my self is all but denied me. I need magic about me to sharpen my mind and will. And yet where am I to find any at all in this Power-weak Realm?*

A small, solid body plumped down beside him on the wall. "Princess Fainche! Where did you come from?"

"Bored," she told him.

He couldn't resist the temptation to tease the little thing. "You come from Bored?"

"No!" the child said with an indignant stare. "The *lessons* were boring. Boring, boring, boring!"

"I get the image," Ardagh cut in hastily. "What were you studying?" At her not-quite understanding frown, he amended, "Ah, that is, what were the lessons about?"

She sat, kicked her legs back and forth for a bit, then shrugged. "Things. People and—and—things."

"I see." History? Geography? "But *all* stories are about people, and people can be quite fascinating."

"Tell me a story."

Ardagh just barely managed to bite back a laugh at the autocratic tone. "Only if you ask me politely, youngling. You are a princess, after all."

She considered that carefully, then nodded and said quite seriously, "*Please* tell me a story."

That pretty little face! She wasn't at all aware of her own power yet, but Fainche was going to make quite an appealing woman someday. With a jolt, Ardagh realized that with his long Sidhe life, he just might come to see that woman grown while he, himself remained unchanged.

Shaken at the sudden reminder of the gulf between him and humanity, the prince began the first tale that came to mind, a true story as it happened, a Sidhe tale of a captured prince and the heroic band who had set out to free him. It was an exciting adventure, what with monsters and sorcery the band had faced. It was also such a strong reminder of home that Ardagh, caught in a surge of nostalgia, lost himself in the tale, seeing it in his mind as firmly as if he stood beneath the clear, sunless Sidhe sky, unknowingly casting a spell of wonder along with his words.

Wonder or no, he had to catch his breath after a wild battle with a dragon. Jarred back to the present the prince realized for the first time that he had attracted quite an audience of children, some of them lingering on the edges, wary as wild things drawn by a lure, others flopping right down at his feet to listen with openmouthed awe.

What a . . . bizarre situation!

There beyond the children, not quite hidden in shadow, stood King Aedh and a whole bevy of aides and attendants—

and the maidservants who were surely supposed to be in charge of Fainche. This time the smile the king gave Ardagh was full and quite genuine.

Ae, but his audience was growing restless. Ardagh hastily returned to the tale, and the rescue of the captive prince from his forest prison, this time refusing to lose himself so totally.

The forest prison . . . the forest! Powers, how very obvious! The forest, of course, there was the answer to his lack of magic!

"And so," Ardagh concluded hastily, "the prince and his gallant band returned home, where he ruled wisely and happily all his days. The end. Now, go back to whatever you were doing before this. Except for you," he added, catching Princess Fainche by the hand. "You, I will deliver personally. King Aedh, I believe this child belongs to you."

"Indeed." He caught his daughter by the shoulders. "Fainche, you must *not* run off like that."

She met his glare bravely. "I was *bored!*"

"Life can't always be as fascinating as one of Prince Ardagh's stories. This isn't a joke, Fainche! Do you want the servants to be hurt because you ran away from them? They will be, you know, if that happens again. Do you want that?"

"N-no."

"Good! I don't want to hear that you've left your lessons without permission again. Is that understood? Well? Is it?"

Crestfallen, biting her lower lip, Fainche nodded.

"Remember it! Remember that if you want to be treated like a princess, you must act like one. And that," Aedh added, "includes sitting through your lessons even if they bore you! Now, off with you." He pointed Fainche in the right direction and swatted her on the rump to send her hurrying into the arms of the anxious maidservants.

Sensing Ardagh's gaze on him, Aedh turned back to the prince. "My apologies, Prince Ardagh. Fainche's a good little girl for the most part, but she's just at that 'very much independent' stage."

"And it worries you."

"Of course it does! Every time I hear that she's run off

again, I think, 'A foe has her!' And the terrible thing is that
it just could happen. My son and daughter would make
incredibly valuable hostages." He shook his head. "Now I
see why the rule of fosterage started. Not that I'd worry
the less if Niall and Fainche were being raised and trained
by someone else."

"But surely your children are safe within Fremainn."

"Och, probably. I still worry." Aedh paused. "I take it you
aren't a father."

"No. My people are . . . not particularly fertile, and so
we cherish all children. I cannot understand the idea of
anyone willingly harming such a precious being. Or simply abandoning one."

"I assume that means you've met Breasal mac Donnchadh."

"Yes."

Aedh sighed. "I doubt he'll make it to manhood, the poor
sad, sickly boy, and I suspect he had a miserable time of it
at home, but I try to give Breasal at least some chance at
happiness while he's here."

"I know." Ardagh, paused, frowning. "What is it?"

Aedh shook his head. "You are a bewildering man, Prince
Ardagh, quite bewildering. Gentle and cold, aloof and gen-
erous—och, well, Father Seadna would say that all humans
are such a muddle of contradictions!" At the smallest of
impatient "ahems" behind him, Aedh glanced back at the
eagerly waiting aides and gave a wry little smile. "If you
will excuse me, it's time for me to stop being the father and
go back to being the king."

He disappeared back into the royal keep, closely followed
by his entourage. But for the first time, Ardagh thought,
there had been genuine friendship warming his voice.

*Is that all it took? The kindness I would have shown to
any child? Is that all it took to finally make you trust me?*

Ah, but now that he was alone again, Ardagh could let
himself think about the forest. He hadn't had a chance to
notice much of anything before, when his only concern had
been to find shelter and food, but *any* forest had a strong
life-force—one from which magic could be drawn, even in

this Power-weak Realm. Ae, yes, out among all that green, vibrant life, he would find restoring Power. And then, and then . . .

Tomorrow is the High King's hunting day, the prince realized. *And I shall most definitely see that I am included in his party!*

PLOTS

CHAPTER 10

Bishop Gervinus, late of Rome, stood on a narrow, muddy street, a rickety wooden dock washed by the sea on one side, ugly little wood and stone buildings on the other, and fought with himself for patience as he'd been fighting since he and his retinue had come ashore a day ago.

Did I really think of rousing Darkness to win myself a kingdom? No, no, far easier if I'd set myself to rousing stupidity instead!

For surely he had never been surrounded by such dolts, here in this provincial little Eriu excuse for a seaport. There was nothing more than the one dock and hardly any town worthy of note. The buildings were mostly small, mostly smelling strongly of fish. The people were mostly tall, mostly fair of hair and skin—but they, too, smelled strongly of fish. Gervinus frowned at their gaudy woolen cloaks, which were checked in the loudest combinations of color. What sane mind would dream of weaving sky blue and sun yellow and bilious green into the same pattern?

Rather alarmingly, no Church messenger had put into this port. Not one of the local folk seemed to have been expecting his arrival. Perhaps the messenger had never arrived; perhaps he had been swamped in a storm or slain by bandits. Or, thought Gervinus, perhaps he had never been sent at all. Maybe the Curiate really did mean to be rid of him.

No matter. I shall still win.

At least these idiots had been clever enough to recognize him right away as a man of the Church, giving him nervous little bows whenever they looked his way. But not one of them spoke more than a few mangled words of Latin or any other civilized tongue.

"My Lord Bishop." It was the head of his guards, going quickly to one knee. "Your pardon, Your Grace, but there is not a horse-litter or carriage to be found."

"But have you found sufficient mounts?"

"That, yes, Your Grace, though the horses here are little taller than ponies."

"No matter." As the son of a Frankish noble, Gervinus had grown up knowing how to ride anything on four legs. "I will ride astride. It will do me no harm to be reminded of humility." *Even if I feel it not.* "See to it that we have sufficient provisions for the entire retinue."

"I have already done that, Your Grace."

"Excellent," Gervinus murmured, and held out his hand so the guard might kiss his holy ring. "But have you yet found anyone to serve as guide?"

The guard winced. "Not yet, Your Grace. We've all tried, but no one here seems to understand exactly where you want to go."

Gervinus drew his hand back sharply. "Get up, man. I will try this myself."

He had studied the Celtic language back in Rome; it was not *that* complex a tongue. "Tara," he said to the local folk, then bit back a sigh of frustration at the blank stares he received. "Take me to Tara," he repeated slowly and carefully. But the language he had studied back in the refined libraries of Rome seemed to be almost as alien as Latin to these idiots. "Do you understand me? Take—me—to—Tara." God, wasn't there anyone here with something besides mist between the ears?

The locals were chattering together, gesturing wildly, plainly debating what this odd stranger really wanted. Suddenly one of them, a stocky little mouse of a fellow, as brightly redheaded as though he'd been topped with a live

coal, said, "Aha!" in sudden inspiration and turned to
Gervinus. "Your—ah—Grace?"

His accent was like nothing the bishop had studied back
in Rome, lilting and unexpectedly musical, but with the stress
placed in equally unexpected places. "Would it be Teamhair
you're wanting?"

"That's what I've been saying all along," Gervinus said
with great restraint. "Tara."

"Ah. Well. I'm not sure why you'd be wanting to go there,
Your Grace, not that it's anything of my business, but I do
know the way to Teamhair."

At last! "Very good," Gervinus said shortly. "I wish to be
in Tara without further delay."

"*This?*" Gervinus erupted, staring up at the earthen rings,
the grassy, tranquil mounds where buildings might once have
stood. Oh, it was an impressive enough site in its way, this
series of ancient hill forts dominating the gentle landscape
about it—but it was never what he had expected. "*This* is
Tara, Fortress of Kings?"

The little guide scratched his head. "It's Teamhair, sure
enough, just as My Lord Bishop wanted."

"But where are they? The king and his court—where is
everyone?"

The man frowned in confusion. "I thought you knew, Your
Grace. Teamhair's still the—ah—ritual home of the High
King, it's where he was crowned king and all. But no one's
actually *lived* here for . . . well now, it must be over a hundred years."

Why had no one back in Rome thought to tell him this?
Was their information so very much out of date? Were they
trying to make him look a fool? "Then where—"

"High King Aedh—I'm guessing that's who you're seeking, Your Grace, King Aedh Ordnigh, you being of the
Church—well, he and his court would be at Fremainn, his
royal fortress, this time of year."

"Then *why didn't you tell me this before?*"

"You didn't ask, Your Grace! 'Teamhair,' you told me, plain
as can be, 'take me to Teamhair.' And here we are."

For one wild moment, Gervinus ached to call back Arridu to rend this *idiot* to bits. But of course that would have been downright foolish; even if he dared risk it, his whole retinue would serve as perilous witnesses. Instead, the bishop managed to grate out, almost steadily, "Fremainn. That is where I wish to be. Fremainn. Do you understand me? I wish—no, wait. If this is such a sacred site, why are no guards surrounding it?"

The guide scratched his head. "Never thought about it much. But I guess Teamhair's powerful enough to protect itself. Who would dare harm it?"

Dolt. "I see. Then there is no reason for me not to see it at closer range myself. Stay here, all of you."

As the guide and his retinue both watched in bewilderment, Gervinus climbed up the long, grassy slope to stand at last, catching his breath, amid the wide plain and mounds of Tara. Ancient fortifications, as he'd guessed, worn down by time and covered with grass. Burial mounds, also ancient: those he had seen in his Frankish boyhood days. *I wonder what ridiculous legends the locals have built up around them.*

There was not a sound save for the soft whisper of the wind and the light, cheerful chirping of a few sparrows, but the sense of the past was very strong. To the bishop's left loomed what must be the heart of the site, the sanctuary where the High Kings of Eriu were crowned, and Gervinus snorted at the mix of Christian and pagan: Church masses might have been performed here under the open sky, but that standing stone so near the altar had nothing whatsoever to do with Christianity. It reminded him instead of the *menhirs* of Frankish lands, but he didn't doubt it was the Lia Fail, the stone that was supposed to cry out when a true king touched it.

What if . . . ? the bishop thought in sudden fierce curiosity, and raised a hand to touch the stone. But he froze just short of its surface. What if something *did* happen, and not anything he might want? What if there was some sorcery here that would recognize him for the outsider he was and—

Nonsense. It was just a stone, nothing more than that.

So short a time here and already he was acting like one of the superstitious idiots.

Pagans, Gervinus thought with a rush of contempt. *Christianized pagans. How easy they will be to corrupt.*

If he had the time and the solitude, he would have worked a testing spell to prove the stone's lack of Power. But revealing his sorcery so soon would be truly stupid. And without sorcery, there was nothing more to be learned here.

He stopped short. Someone had laid down a floral offering here, hiding it amid a little jumble of rocks. Now, why would anyone try to hide—ah. The offering hadn't been made to the Christian site at all, but to the standing stone.

Pagans, Gervinus repeated, this time in genuine shock. *Ah, but here is my lever by which to move a king: these pagans must be removed by whatever means I deem necessary. This land, I will state in horror, must be restored to the True Faith—and what man will dare stand against me?*

Gervinus hurried back down to the others and told the guide, enunciating carefully, "I wish to be in Fremainn. Take me there. Now."

The little man shrugged as though he wasn't about to be surprised by anything this stranger demanded. "Whatever you say, Your Grace."

It was starting to rain. Of course it was starting to rain, Gervinus thought, pulling the hood of his cloak up over his head. What else could he expect from this barbaric place?

Still, barbaric or not, it was a kingdom. And it would yet be his.

Earlier it had been raining in the gentle, determined way that seemed so typical of the land, but with equally typical suddenness, the weather had turned sunny. Ardagh sat outside his guest house, sword in one hand, soft cloth in the other, polishing the straight, slender blade with meticulous care, enjoying the way it gleamed in the autumn sunlight. At first he'd been rather worried about what the mortal sun might do to Faerie metal, but obviously the blade was taking no more harm from it than did he. Instead, as he turned the sword this way and that, being careful he hadn't missed a spot, it seemed to take on a new light, so brightly clear Ardagh fancied he could almost use the blade as a scrying mirror. Surely he really could catch the quickest, most fleeting glimpses of Sidhe splendor . . . Sidhe faces . . . his brother's face—

Bah, no. This was ridiculous. All he was doing was dazzling his vision and—

He was being watched. Ardagh looked down the length of the sword at a small, straight-backed figure: yet another child, a boy this time and older than Fainche, though there was something to the set of his cheekbones that reminded the prince of her. The boy was slender in an agile, fierce young way, his eyes a familiar grey stare . . . ah, of course. The only one of the children here who'd been rather distant to him. Shy? Or just regally wary?

"Prince Niall." Ardagh dipped his head politely and received an equally polite bow in return.

"Prince Ardagh."

Silence fell. Ardagh returned to cleaning his sword. The Faerie alloy wasn't liable to corrosion the way mortal iron rusted, but that didn't mean it didn't need care. He had no intention of being left having to rely on an iron Eriu blade which, though it would undeniably be of fine design, would sicken him every time he drew it. Out of the corner of his eye, he saw the boy follow each stroke of the cloth with fascination. "You have something to say to me, Prince Niall?"

The boy started. "My sister likes you."

"So I gathered. Why does that bring you here?"

"I wanted to—to see if you were safe."

Ardagh glanced up at the intent young face. So, now, for all his teasing, the boy did care for his sister. "Safe?" the prince echoed, letting his voice and eyes go Sidhe chill and watching Niall blanch slightly, though the boy never flinched. "I am not *safe*, boy. I never will be safe. But I also will never, ever harm a child. Is that understood and accepted?"

Niall blinked as though suddenly released from a spell.

Hesitantly, now very much a child himself, he nodded, then asked, almost shyly, "That blade isn't silver, is it? No, it couldn't be; silver's too soft to hold an edge, Cadwal told me that."

"Cadwal's right. There's silver in here, indeed." Ardagh turned the blade to catch the light, then sheathed it. "But there are other, stronger metals in the mix as well. The same is true of my dagger."

He drew that and began to work on it as well. After a nervous moment, Prince Niall crouched at his side, watching intently. "I like the hilt," he said suddenly. "It echoes the hilt of your sword."

Ardagh grimaced. "It should; the set took long enough for the smiths to make." *Even with magic.*

"What are those twining ornaments? I mean, I can guess they give you a better grip, but what are they? Some sort of birds of prey?"

"Nothing you'd recognize in this land, but yes." Ardagh held the dagger lightly by the quillon for a moment so the boy could get a better look at the elegant, fierce *thierien,* then went back to his polishing. "You enjoy weaponry, do you?"

The solemn grey eyes blazed into life. "Och, yes! Sometimes I get hurt or so weary I ache all over, but it's . . . well, Cadwal would be angry at me for 'making light' of his livelihood, but it's fun."

Ardagh chuckled. "I've been there." *Though not for longer than you would believe.* "And you're right, for the most part, it is." *More so for you, my little human friend, since you don't have an older brother trying his "accidental" best to kill you during practice.* "Eh, but you must have other lessons as well."

"They can be fun, too," Niall said with such careful tact that Ardagh nearly laughed.

"I see you've already learned one of the lessons of politic behavior." Returning his dagger to its sheath, the prince got to his feet. "But our political meeting is at an end, I fear. You will be accompanying your father on today's hunt?"

"Yes! He finally—yes!"

"So be it," Ardagh said with a formal little bow, face showing not a trace of his amusement. "I will see you there."

"Damn him. Damn him. *Damn him!*"

The young man paced savagely back and forth in his small chamber, brilliant blue and yellow *brat* swirling and tangling about him. He was Eirnin mac Flainn, cousin to the kings of Meath, he was *somebody*. Or he had been. But now, thanks to that cursed prince of Cathay—

"May demons drag him to the deepest pit of hell!"

Thanks to the prince, Eirnin was now little more than a beggar. He couldn't stalk off home, not with his honor-price so badly damaged, and calling for aid from his royal cousins was impossible; even if he could get a message to them, Conchobar and Ailill were too busy trying to kill each other for the throne of Meath to bother with him. That left Eirnin with nothing to do but live off the High King's charity, while his friends—

"Ha! Friends!"

They had dropped him quickly enough, the treacherous, worthless wretches, with not a word of explanation, not a word of sympathy, not even a jesting, "How was she?"

"How was she!" Eirnin spat. "She was a damned *servant*, a *nothing*. How *dare* everyone make such a fuss over her?"

Rape. How could you call the taking of a nobody like that rape? Just because she'd put up a struggle—they all did, it was part of the game! Hundreds of nobles before him had helped themselves to hundreds of women, and yet here he was, singled out and disgraced just for—for being a normal, virile man!

Of course his friends had deserted him. In a flash of honesty, Eirnin admitted he would have done the same had it been another in the same situation. One did not risk association with someone fallen out of the royal favor.

Never mind that. The question was how to get back into that favor. And . . . what was he to do about the prince who'd brought him to this ridiculous pass? At the thought, Eirnin stopped short, heart racing, and his hand stole, almost of

its own accord, to one of the amulets dangling from about
his neck.

But then he tore the little clay trinket from him with a
savage oath. What good had it done him? The sorcerer who'd
sold it to him had sworn it would ward off all magic, but it
certainly hadn't stopped Prince Ardagh from looking right
into his mind and dragging out the truth! Who knew what
other dark powers the prince possessed?

God, maybe he's reading my thoughts right now and—

No. What had happened in the law court had been a trick.
And even if it hadn't been, even if maybe the prince did
have some eerie powers, he was mortal, just like any other
man. He could bleed and hurt and die.

And die, Eirnin repeated, and clenched his hand about
an imaginary hilt. Aedh had taken most of his retinue from
him, but he still did have a few of his own servants left,
and one or two of those might actually be loyal.

No, wait. One of them *was* totally loyal. It wasn't out of
any love for him, Eirnin knew, but because one night the
man had made the mistake of getting drunk and letting his
master overhear his secret. Self-preservation was a strong
motive for loyalty, Eirnin told himself with a sudden fierce
smile, and when you added the man's total ruthlessness to
the mix—

Och, but nothing must happen within Fremainn. There
were too many potential witnesses here, too many chances
for discovery. But what about during the hunt? Everyone
knew accidents could happen when all were excited and
weapons were close to hand. The prince was such an odd
creature that he might be caught away from the rest of the
hunting party. If that happened, oh, perfect. It would look
like the work of a bandit. Everyone would go running off
on a useless search. And he, Eirnin thought with a savage
grin, would be avenged.

Go hunting, Prince Ardagh, he urged. *Go hunting, and
be hunted—to death!*

Sleek hounds loping in the fore, the High King's hunting party rode down from the fortress of Fremainn, cloaks

flying, horns sounding. And in their midst, sitting his sturdy little horse with ease, rode Ardagh. They passed beneath the first canopies of leaves, and were suddenly taken from a world of shifting grey clouds and flashes of sunlight into one of soft green mystery. Ardagh drew in a deep breath of sharp, clean vegetable scents and laughed. Although the month was late, the last of summer still clung to these lands. The wild, strong life-force of the yet-unsleeping forest surrounded him, striking him so strong a blow he swayed in the saddle.

King Aedh glanced sharply his way. "Are you all right?"

"Quite, quite." Aware how both the king and young Prince Niall were staring, the prince bit down on his tongue before he could keep from babbling like an idiot, *feeling* the wonderful life surging at him from all sides. "King Aedh," he continued, carefully skirting falsehood, "I . . . quite lost track of days." *True enough.* "There is something I must do in this forest. You might call it a . . . personal ritual." *Among other things.*

He saw uneasiness in the king's eyes. Aedh's full title was, Ardagh reminded himself, High King Aedh Ordnigh, Aedh the Ordained, ordained by the Church; even if, as the prince had teased Father Seadna, Aedh had his occasional quarrels with the equally strong-willed abbots who ruled the monasteries as he ruled Eriu, the king could hardly be comfortable with what he had to assume would be a pagan rite.

But, bound by the Laws of Hospitality, Aedh could not argue, except to ask, "You are not thinking of hunting alone? A prince who hunts alone," he added at Ardagh's puzzled frown, "loses some of his honor-price in the eyes of men— and in courts of law."

Once more confused by the maze of human rules, Ardagh assured the king, "No. I am not going to hunt alone."

"I take it you will not need a bodyguard?"

The implication of that, at least, was clear: if they needed to send out a search party for Ardagh, the king would *not* be pleased. The prince smiled slightly. "No," he promised. "I will not get lost. And I will catch up with your hunting party in a bit."

Giving the reins of his horse to a bewildered guard, he waited, forcing his face to stay a polite, tranquil mask, until the last of the hunting party was gone. Then at last Ardagh threw himself full-length on the ground, breathing in the rich, loamy scent, digging his fingers into the earth as if he meant to take root. Ae, Powers, Powers, how wondrous this felt! Yes, this was an alien Realm, yes, the *feel* of the very ground was alien to him, but the life-force was there, the magic. It was not at all as casually strong as that of the Sidhe Realm, it was not that easy to absorb, but it was wondrous just the same, slowly seeping into mind and body, giving him new strength, new sharpness, new life. . . .

But he dare stay apart from the others no longer. Aching with reluctance, Ardagh disengaged himself from the forest and sat up, dizzy and elated and feeling truly Sidhe as he had not for so long. Perhaps there wasn't the easy Power to be had from air and earth and water of his native Realm, but this would do, ae yes, this would do. He raised his arms, casting up an extravagant fountain of magical sparks, red, blue, gold, laughing at the sheer triviality, the sheer delight of it.

Powers, yes, yes, now I can bear to live among the humans and yet stay me. *All I need do is let them think it a religious need that I make regular pilgrimages out here, and I can regather my strength.* Aedh would probably think him a worshipper of the human's Mother Earth. *Ha, well, in a manner of speaking, I suppose I am, and if there's any One who can hear me, thank you!*

The prince got to his feet, then froze, frowning slightly, listening, *feeling* with every newly restored magical sense. He wasn't yet familiar enough with humanity to be sure what he'd *felt*: trouble, surely, but of what sort or from whom . . .

Ardagh shook his head impatiently. There was only one human he knew who might be able to find the exact source of the trouble. Not Aedh, of course. Clever king though the man might be, he had no magic to aid him—no magic of his own, that was.

Eithne is not *going to like this,* Ardagh thought with a wry smile. *But, like it or not, we have no choice.*

With that, he went in search of King Aedh and the hunting party.

The murderer crouched in foresty shadow, knife in hand, waiting, tense with suspense as he always was before a kill. There was no guarantee Prince Ardagh would return this way, none at all. Still, this was the most clearly marked trail back to the hunting party.

Then where was the man? Maybe something had already gotten Prince Ardagh. Ha, like what? Boar would have made enough noise to bring everyone here in a rush, and nothing much else was going to attack a man, not when there was still so much regular prey to be had.

So. The prince was alive. For now.

But if I miss, and Eirnin mac Flainn learns I failed, he'll kill me.

Naw, the young idiot's too squeamish for that. More his style to have me accused of some crime or other and watch someone else do the dirty job for him. Be just as dead either way.

Staying nice and safe under a noble's protection had seemed pretty good at first, what with there being not many places left for a killer to hide. *Damn him, I never should have been so stupid. Never should have gotten drunk. Never should have let that idiot know I'd done in a few targets.*

Well, one more wouldn't matter, royal blood or no: once it was spilled, all blood looked the same. Eirnin had given him a nice, heavy pouch, though they both knew the contents were merely a token payment for services rendered. Eirnin's continued protection was the main reward. One more target, then he was safely back under that protection.

Ardagh froze, every sense alert, Sidhe vision easily spotting the human hiding in shadow, the plainly clad man without the slightest hint of who he was or who'd sent him out here. Sidhe instinct *felt* the cold bite of the iron blade in the man's hand, *felt* the coldness of the man himself, the dim echo of others' dying gasps, the dim scent of spilled blood. A murderer. An assassin.

And it's me for whom he waits this time, the prince realized with a shock of surprise. *A bad mistake, human, a fatal mistake.*

Silent as a predator, Ardagh stalked the human, stood for a moment, calculating, then reached out and coolly tapped the man on the shoulder. As the man spun about with a strangled yelp, the prince asked mildly:

"Waiting for me?"

To his surprise, the human reacted almost as swiftly as a Sidhe, lunging at him with the deadly iron blade. Ardagh sprang hastily back, realizing with a shock that the Realm hadn't given him enough Power for a death-spell, whipping out his own silvery dagger instead, even as part of his mind was screaming, *What are you doing? You're a prince, not a trained knife-fighter!*

What else could he do without battle-magic? Running was out of the question: no Sidhe fled from combat, not without so much as a wound being delivered. Ardagh circled the human, seeing how easily the man kept pace with him, seeing how low and steady he held that iron dagger. Not a good sign, that, not at all. It meant the human knew how to do fatal damage with one upward stab, so Ardagh burst into motion, lunging, leaping, feinting, making up in Sidhe speed and grace what he lacked in practical experience, dodging the iron blade again and again. But if the human couldn't touch him, he couldn't quite get past the human's guard, either.

It's going to depend on which of us has the greater stamina. Which one of us makes the first mistake.

Ardagh sprang back—and his heel slipped on an exposed root. As the prince flailed wildly for balance, the human threw himself into Ardagh. They both crashed to the ground, the prince landing with bruising force on his back, struggling to catch his breath and block the human's knife. *I will not die from* clumsiness! Ardagh vowed, and caught the human's descending knife-hand with his own free hand, the impact jarring all the way up to his shoulder, battling to bring his Sidhe dagger into play. The human slammed his own free hand down on Ardagh's knife-hand, pinning it against the ground, then slowly began forcing his iron knife down, point aiming relentlessly toward the prince's unprotected throat.

He's too strong! I can't hold him!

Gambling wildly, Ardagh suddenly released the man's wrist, twisting to one side with all his might, feeling the knife plunge down into the tangle of his clothing, not into him. In the bare instant that the human was off-balance, the prince tore his pinned hand free and lunged blindly up with his blade. He heard the human grunt, felt him roll aside, and stabbed again, then scrambled to his feet, knife poised. The human stared up at him with puzzled eyes, as though hardly believing what had just happened. He might have tried to speak, but all Ardagh heard was the softest of sighs. And then there was nothing, not even breath.

Aware at first only that he was, amazingly, alive and no worse than bruised—although his clothing was rather repulsively stained—the prince stood shaking with reaction and struggling to catch his breath. Ae, Powers, that had been a close thing, far too close! A shame, though, that the human had died before confessing who'd sent him.

If anyone did. He could have been a bandit.

And the woods could be full of flying fish. Glancing down at his dagger, Ardagh shuddered and wiped it clean on the human's clothing, then straightened, listening. The sound of the struggle was bringing the royal hunting party here to investigate. The prince hastily dropped to one knee beside the body to search for any clues he could find. A pouch . . . coins, and something else. His hand closed about a small, hard object. Pulling it free, Ardagh stared for a moment, then smiled.

Ah, yes . . . clumsy of you, Eirnin, very clumsy.

As King Aedh and his men came crashing through the underbrush on their horses, Ardagh quickly slipped the tell-tale pouch and its contents into the folds of his *brat*, then scrambled back to his feet. The humans were all staring at him, little Niall's eyes wide with horror. Aedh's glance swept down from the disheveled prince to stop at the body, clearly registering *bandit*, then swept back up again.

"None of that's yours, I hope?"

Ardagh looked down at his bloodstained self in distaste and shook his head, waiting for the lecture he was sure was going to follow.

But all King Aedh added was a laconic, "Now you see yet another reason for a prince not to go hunting alone. Let's get you back to Fremainn, shall we?"

. . . AND COUNTERPLOTS

CHAPTER 11

Slipping into the room unseen that night had been no problem for one of the Sidhe. Ardagh stood silently watching his enemy for a time as the man prepared for bed without the slightest sign of alarm, savoring this moment of keen anticipation. But if he waited any longer, the element of surprise might be lost, so the prince said quietly, "Eirnin mac Flainn."

The man turned so quickly he nearly fell. And to Ardagh's pleasure, Eirnin actually blanched, eyes wide with horror at the sight of the prince. He opened his mouth to shout, but Ardagh snapped, "I wouldn't."

"You—how did you—"

"How did I what?" the prince purred. "Get in here? Did you really think mere doors could keep me out? Ah, or were you, perhaps, wondering how I survived that little surprise you had waiting for me in the forest?"

"I—I didn't—"

"Tsk. Anyone setting an assassin in place should not be so careless—or so foolish—as to leave any evidence behind." Ardagh held up the little clay amulet he'd found within the assassin's pouch. "You didn't mean to give him this, I'm sure. I see that the thong has been snapped, as though you tore it from you—ah, you did, didn't you, probably when you realized it didn't hold any Power at all against someone like me. You should have checked to see where it landed, Eirnin.

135

But, alas, you didn't. You dumped the assassin's payment into his pouch without once looking at what you did. And so there it lay, all tangled up in with that payment."

"What did you do to him?" It was the barest whisper.

Ardagh smiled. "Do you really need to know?" He kept his voice silken-smooth, gently edged with menace. "I don't approve of people who try to kill me. I don't approve of *you*, Eirnin mac Flainn."

He took a slow, menacing step forward, a predator stalking his prey. Eirnin backed up and continued to back up until he came to a sudden halt against the far wall. "Don't . . ."

"Don't what, Eirnin mac Flainn? Don't kill you? Oh, I have no intention of . . . killing you. Dead, you are no longer amusing. Alive . . ." He laughed, and saw the human flinch. "I give you your life, Eirnin mac Flainn. For now. It is a gift I can take back any time I wish. Remember that, Eirnin mac Flainn. You live only because I let you live."

With the human nearly hysterical with superstitious dread, it was not at all difficult for Ardagh to cast the illusion that he'd stepped into shadow and simply vanished, rather than left by the door. Delighted with the ease with which even that admittedly small illusion-spell had worked, delighted, too, with his revenge on Eirnin mac Flainn, the prince went his way. Every word he'd told the man was quite true: it *was* more amusing to keep an enemy alive and most thoroughly, most satisfactorily, demoralized.

That night, he slept quite tranquilly, and smiled in his sleep.

Ardagh stood hidden in shadow in the royal keep this afternoon, quietly watching and waiting. Queen Eithne was there in her sunny little grianan, her women's house, but to the prince's annoyance, she was not alone. The queen sat embroidering a tunic; another woman sat beside her, working on her own project. The two of them made a pretty sight, the sunlight turning their hair to rich gold or blazing red and their needlework to stitched rainbows of color, and at first glance they were the very image of domesticity.

But they were speaking of war.

"With the winter coming, we're surely safe for now. But once the warm weather is here again, the danger is sure to come as well," Eithne mused.

"Once the northern sea ice has fully melted," the other woman agreed: it was Sorcha ni Fothad, Ardagh realized with a slight start, her eyes bright and fierce as those of a hawk. "Enough so that ships can put to sea. When a war leader has been cooped up all the long, dark winter with restless warriors, what better time to take ship and let off all that pent-up energy in some nice, fast raids?"

With a sudden burst of energy, Sorcha sprang to her feet, letting her needlework drop to her chair, and began to pace, restless as those warriors herself. "The only question is: where are those raids going to be? Where are they going to strike?"

"Eriu," Eithne said flatly. "That much seems clear. They've already discovered that there are riches to be found in these lands. The only real question is: whose kingdom will be struck first? Aedh has been debating—Sorcha, do stop that pacing."

"Och, I'm sorry. I didn't even realize I was doing it. It's just . . ."

"I know. The waiting is maddening."

Sorcha flinched as if she'd been slapped and turned sharply to face the queen. "More so for women. We're not supposed to do anything, not even plan our men's strategy!"

"Sorcha."

"I know, I know, that's the way things are. It doesn't mean I have to be happy with them. But can't King Aedh—"

"Do what? There's a limit to even the High King's reach and the span of his armies. To predict exactly where the raids will come would require more than normal means."

For a startled moment, seeing the odd flicker of light in Eithne's eyes, Ardagh was sure she was about to confess to using magic to aid her husband. But all at once the queen pretended to become totally involved in her needlework instead.

Not so Sorcha. "If only there was something we could do. If only there was something I could do!"

Eithne glanced up with a laugh. "What do you mean? Take up the sword?"

"Why not? Our mothers' mothers did!"

"These aren't the olden days."

Sorcha's sigh held a world of frustration. "No. And so I must wield a pen instead of a blade."

"Father Seadna claims the pen is a mightier weapon than any blade," Eithne said gently.

"Tell that to the Lochlannach," Sorcha retorted, then stiffened with a little cry of dismay. "A pen, yes! I nearly forgot. Queen Eithne, please excuse me." Her face was scarlet with embarrassment. "I promised to transcribe some of his poetry for my father before the day is out."

"A promise is a promise," Eithne agreed, amused. "Off with you, my dear."

As Sorcha hurried past him, so close Ardagh could have touched her sleeve, he thought, *It's true: she would have made a fine warrior-maid.* And, rather to his surprise, found himself adding in sympathy, *No wonder she is as prickly as she is, a falcon trapped in a pigeon's role.*

But now Queen Eithne was alone, and alone she might not be again, so Ardagh slipped silently into the grianan. As he expected, she was instantly aware of him, glancing sharply up. Also as he'd expected, she made no outcry, only hissed, "You shouldn't be in here!"

"Doubtlessly not."

"You don't understand! If anyone finds you here—"

"They won't. Nor," he added, "did anyone see me enter. Nor will they see me leave."

She blinked. "You look somehow . . . different."

"I *am* different. I found a new source of Power to restore me." *At least up to a point.*

Her eyes widened slightly in alarm, but she said only a sarcastic, "How nice for you. But why are you here?"

"What better chance to speak with you alone?"

Eithne froze, suddenly aware of: "You've killed someone. Recently."

"Yesterday. Didn't your husband tell you?"

"Och, of course. The bandit. I'm glad you weren't hurt, but you shouldn't have been—"

"It wasn't a bandit."

"What!"

"Simply put: I was attacked. I slew the attacker, and gave a warning to the one who'd sent him. There's the end of it."

"How can you be so calm?"

Ardagh shrugged. "Because it isn't important any longer."

"You tell me that someone tried to kill you, then you say that it isn't important? Prince Ardagh, you can't just—"

"The matter," Ardagh said firmly, "is settled."

Eithne stared. "You *aren't* human, are you?"

Ardagh ignored that obvious point. "Queen Eithne, what happened is past. What we need to discuss now is magic."

Her hands clenched on the needlework. "No."

"Magic, and the dark cloud menacing your husband."

The needlework slipped to the floor in a bright cascade of color. "I told you, if I could have put a name to it—"

"I can't, either. But together, ah, together, who knows what we might be able to learn?"

She started to speak, stopped, tried again. "You're asking me to risk everything."

"You've done it before. Queen Eithne, neither one of us can afford to see your husband threatened."

She winced. "No. All right, then. Let us see what we can do."

Ardagh looked about the small, secret chamber and sighed faintly. Eithne glanced at him. "What?"

"Nothing. Merely a touch of regret that magic should be something feared and forbidden in this Realm."

"That is as it is."

"I'm not mocking you," Ardagh told her softly, "nor condemning."

"Och, I know. It's only that I've had to hide my—my abilities for so long. Not," she added with a quick glance his way, "that they're such grand ones. Not like anything your folk could—"

"Eithne, I cannot teach you anything of our spells. While all my people have innate Power, a prince of the Sidhe is taught only as many spells as might be of use to him, and frankly, they're nothing a human could work, certainly not in this Power-weak Realm."

"I . . . hadn't expected anything else."

That was as blatant a lie as he'd heard from a human, but Ardagh kept silent, watching with sharp curiosity as Eithne drew a circle in chalk about them and set candles at the cardinal points, listening to her murmured benedictions as she lit each candle.

I trust this room has some ventilation? Ardagh thought, nose wrinkling fastidiously at the heavy scent of burning wax. *Ah yes, there, near the ceiling. What a primitive form of Setting Wards this is—but it's amazing that a human can set them at all.* "We can't use a mirror," Eithne said suddenly. "Not without moonlight to shine upon it."

Ardagh shrugged. "Mirrors are overrated. Water or earth or even the blade of a dagger will do as well. Actually," he added thoughtfully, drawing his own knife, "since we're almost certainly dealing with threats of a militant nature, a blade might be the most effective." *Particularly one that has already taken a life.*

"That's not iron," Eithne began, then gave a self-impatient little, "Tchah. Of course it wouldn't be iron. What is it, some manner of silver alloy?"

"Alloyed with metals not found in your Realm. But now, since silver can symbolize the moon, the mystic connection can only help."

"Yes . . . hold the blade so the candle flames hit it squarely and make it shine."

"Wait." Ardagh moved behind Eithne, encircling her with his arms before she could pull away, the knife before them both. The startled woman made one abortive attempt to break free, then froze, hissing, "What are you doing?"

"Hush, now. I'm hardly after your honor, or however that foolish human phrase goes."

That forced a nervous little giggle from her. "Hardly," she agreed. "You'd never be so foolish. But what—"

"Hush. If we are to use both our strengths, we must be in contact. Now, let us both stare into the blade. . . ."

Dimly he heard her murmuring her own divination spell, the words plainly improvised to fit the new situation:

"Mirror of silver,
Mirror of light,
Grant to us the gift of sight.
Clear the mists and let us see.
As we will, so let it be."

Feeble poetry, he thought with a touch of Sidhe disdain,
then blocked that from his mind as the Power began to rise,
a strange, uncomfortable mix of familiar Sidhe magic and
unfamiliar human, and he saw . . . he saw what? Vague
images . . .

. . . a face, two faces . . . a man and woman, tall and golden-
haired, crowned, the man in particular marred by a psychic stain of guilt and fear . . .

. . . a dragon fiercely looming up out of water . . .

. . . a dark cloud so heavy with menace the coldness made
him shudder, a dark cloud cut by a cross . . .

Ardagh came back to himself with a gasp, releasing the
equally shaken Eithne. "I saw something," he told her,
sheathing his knife, "but I'm not sure what any of it meant.
What about you?"

She shook her head. "I'm not sure. I *think* I saw a man
and woman."

"So did I." Quickly he described them, and Eithne stiffened. "I know those two!" she snapped. "They can only be
King Donnchadh and his Queen Derval. And that taint of
shame and fear," Eithne added with increasing rage, "surely
means they *were* behind the attempt to slay Aedh, the curse
of the crows on them!" At Ardagh's puzzled look, she added
impatiently, "That means . . . och, that they never enjoy
the fruit of their foul work."

Eithne broke off to snuff the candles carefully, working
from west to east, murmuring words of dismissal as she went.
She erased the chalked circle with equal care, then looked
up at Ardagh. "It was Derval's doing, surely," she told him,
brushing stray strands of hair back from her face. "That
woman is as close to being a snake—ha, yes, Donnchadh
is ambitious, but he'd never have acted without her pushing him, for her glory and that of their precious son."

Ardagh frowned. "I thought their son was here. I've met him, Breasal."

"Yes, the poor sickly creature. He wanders about like a ghost with his sad, sad eyes, as though the first breeze would blow him away. Och, well, no wonder he's sad. Derval has never once sent a message of love to him, neither she nor her husband."

"So the boy told me. That is one thing I cannot understand. No matter how disappointed they may be in him, the poor youngster, he is still their child!"

Eithne was silent for a moment, busy putting the candles carefully away in their storage chest. "I can see where that might be puzzling to you, you being what you are. Unfortunately, humans aren't quite so careful about their young. Donnchadh and Derval have, as the merchants might put it, written Breasal off as a loss."

"But how could they dare risk—ah, of course. There's a second son."

"A second, *healthy* son. Unfortunately, Aedh can hardly hold this second-born child as hostage as well. And so, he has no real hold over those two."

Stunned by this glimpse of human cruelty, of the casual casting aside of a precious child, Ardagh hid behind a rigidly controlled mask of calm. "What a pity this is all totally useless."

"Useless!" Eithne exploded. "They tried to kill my husband!"

"You and I know that, but there's not one scrap of non-magical evidence you can offer King Aedh to prove it."

"But—they—curse them, no. There isn't. But at least they were terrified enough by their failure not to dare try again. For now, at least."

"There's more we need to discuss," Ardagh said. "I saw other visions than that one. Tell me, when we stared into the blade's gleaming, did you see the dragon as well?"

The queen shuddered, anger fading. "Not clearly. But that omen is far too clear. A dragon can only signify the Lochlannach; their ships bear dragon figureheads. I don't suppose you saw where the thing was coming ashore?"

"Unfortunately, no." Ardagh paused, studying the woman,

then continued warily, "But neither King Donnchadh and his queen nor the dragon were the worst menace I sensed. There was . . . I can only call it Darkness. Did you see it or sense it?"

"I thought your people could see in the dark. Why would you be afraid of—"

"It wasn't a natural darkness; of course my people have no fear of that. No, this was a Darkness," he emphasized the word, "a Darkness of spirit chill enough to make me shiver. And . . . there seemed to be a cross cutting through it."

Eithne shook her head, frowning in confusion. "Your magic is far stronger than mine. I didn't see or sense anything like that. And I have not the faintest idea what it might mean. Though now that I think about it, there *are* two possible explanations," she added slowly. "One is that the—the Darkness is something that can be dispelled by the Church. The other . . ."

She broke off, eyes full of sudden alarm, and Ardagh finished for her, "The other is that the peril comes to us from the Church itself." He rubbed a hand over eyes that all at once felt painfully weary.

"Prince Ardagh?"

"I'm sorry. The ritual has drained my strength more than I'd expected." That one little respite in the forest had very plainly not been long enough. "Eithne, I must disappear into the forest yet again, this time for a longer span, to thoroughly . . . well, call it replenishing my magical self. Drawing Power from the land. But I shall return, I promise that. You will not have to face this Darkness alone."

"So the Church can burn us together," Eithne murmured. "That really gives me comfort." She stopped short. "Och, no, I'm sorry, I didn't mean that. It's just . . . I wish I could tell Aedh the truth."

"I know."

"But," Eithne continued with a shrug, "I can't. Go do what you must, Prince Ardagh." The corners of her mouth tilted up in a wry little smile. "If it has any courtesy at all, the Darkness will wait till you return."

THE KING OF
THE WOODLAND

CHAPTER 12

King Aedh stared at his guest as if he thought the prince had gone mad. "You wish to go *where?*"

Ardagh stifled a sigh and repeated, "I need to return to the forest. Alone."

"Are you *insane?* The last time you were out there alone, you almost got yourself killed!"

"That will not happen again."

"Oh no, of course not. You've spoken to every bandit in the forest and made them promise not to touch you."

"The man who attacked me wasn't a bandit. And the matter is settled. So if you will just give me the permission to—"

"Wait, now," the king said sharply. "Back up a little. What do you mean, 'The man wasn't a bandit'?"

Ah. This wasn't Eithne, more interested in matters magical than political. "He wasn't," Ardagh began in a sleek rush, "but I assure you that I have made certain his master will not bother me again and—"

"Stop trying to race past me with those smooth words of yours. Name me this master who sent out an assassin."

"I would rather not."

"I don't care about your would-nots. Who was it? Who would be harboring so powerful a grudge against you? Unless you've been making enemies behind my back there shouldn't be any . . . Eirnin!" Aedh realized suddenly. "It was Eirnin mac Flainn, wasn't it? Ha, yes, that's just the sort of cowardly attack he'd favor."

"Whether or not it was he," Ardagh said evasively, "I assure you, the one who was responsible for the attack has been made too thoroughly terrified of me to act again."

Aedh smacked his hand against his forehead. "Of course! How foolish of me not to have thought of such a tactic. The next time someone tries to kill me, I'll just shout 'Boo!' at him, and that's the end of it."

"Please. We both know Eirnin mac Flainn—yes, yes, it was he, I admit it—Eirnin is full of wild superstitions. It was no difficult thing to play to those fears the way I did in the court of law. He will not dare to bother me again."

Aedh started to speak, stopped, started again, "I suppose I should just be thankful you didn't kill the man."

Ardagh blinked. "There was no need."

" 'No need,' he says, as casually as though he was talking about ending a game of *fidchel*. God, I can't even begin to guess what politics are like in your homeland."

That struck Ardagh as unexpectedly funny. With a laugh, he admitted, "They are sometimes very strange. Even to us. If you permit it, I would like to attend some of your political sessions."

"Ha. You'd find them dull by comparison."

But he hadn't actually forbidden it, so Ardagh pushed on. "King Aedh, I really do need to return to the forest."

"But *why?* Och, no, man, don't bridle. I'm not questioning your religious beliefs or—or whatever it is that we're discussing here. But I cannot let a guest in my holding go wandering off into the wilderness alone! No, never mind the bandit-who-wasn't-a-bandit; I'll take you at your word that the matter's settled. I'm talking about prohibitions—questions of honor—you are a prince!"

These humans have more rules about what is and is not proper than even the Sidhe! "Your concern does you great credit, King Aedh," Ardagh said with careful formality. "But you need not worry, I promise you. No dishonor will be brought to you by my actions. Nor, for that matter, have I any intention of losing any of my own honor. I will not wander far from Fremainn, nor will I wind up lost in the wilderness like a strayed child." *I can't; I've magically set the location of Fremainn in my mind.* "And I am not," he added sardonically, "going off to worship dark gods or sacrifice furry little animals."

That roused a reluctant little laugh from the king, and Ardagh continued with a slight smile, "I merely need to be apart from others for a time. Focus my thoughts. Clear my mind." *Restore my magic.* "It is a custom." *Of some people, if not mine.*

Aedh all at once threw up his hands in surrender. "I won't pretend to understand what you're talking about or what's going on behind that fair face of yours, but I would not have it said I held a guest prisoner. Go if you must. Return when you will."

And don't get yourself lost or disgrace anyone, Ardagh added silently for him, *or you're on your own. Understood.*

Someone was following him. Ardagh rode on as though he wasn't at all aware of the subtle tracker, then smiled to himself. One of King Aedh's mercenaries, no doubt of it. No doubt, either, why he'd been sent: *I'd be wondering what my guest was doing, too, were I the king. Sorry to disappoint you, Aedh.*

Ardagh slipped from his horse, leaving the animal as safe as a whispered Sidhe Warding Spell that hopefully had worked could make it, and moved silently through the forest, shedding the merely human follower with ease. The prince moved easily as a wild thing past oak and ash, trying to avoid places touched by humanity. Overhead, some of the trees were already losing their leaves, but the underbrush, more sheltered from the changing season, grew progressively more tangled as he went along, a good sign that no humans had come this way. Ardagh slid through the tangle without trouble, glorying in the sweet, sharp green scents and the life all around him.

Ah, here was a site that fit what he sought almost exactly,

a quiet little glade with no trace of humanity in it at all. Yes, and bisected by a sleek stream as well: Earth and Water combined. Doubly Powerful, Ardagh thought with a pleased nod, with the earth just bare enough so there would be no interference from the lesser lives of plants.

The prince stretched himself out by the side of the stream, facedown, making himself as comfortable as possible so his body wouldn't distract him with complaints before he had sunk sufficiently deeply into trance. He let one hand touch the water, and dug the fingers of his other hand into the earth. Slowly, in contact with two Elements at once, Ardagh silently recited disciplines that caused his mind to relax . . . relax . . . relax . . . feeling the strength of Earth and Water seeping into him . . . feeling conscious thought sliding away into tranquility . . .

And for a time there *was* no time.

The renewed Power surging throughout his being brought Ardagh back to himself with a start. He rolled over onto his back, blinking up at a world gone dim blue with twilight. The chill of coming night was rising from the earth, and he shivered suddenly, curling up reflexively, hugging the numb fingers of the hand that had trailed in the water, massaging life back into them. His whole body ached dully, stiff but not unbearably so.

All at once Ardagh yawned and unfolded again, stretching like a cat. Mind and body snapped back together, fully reunited, and the prince sat up, listening to the forest stirring around him, all the hundred little lives chirping or whirring or rustling with the coming of night, Sidhe vision as sharp in the darkness as theirs.

Ae, but now he was truly aware of sitting on chill earth and breathing chill air, and Ardagh scrambled to his feet, pulling his woolen *brat* tightly about himself, glad of its warmth. Summer or autumn, this land never seemed to get genuinely hot or dry or even reliably warm.

But cold or no, the prince thought with a rush of joy, he felt most wondrously whole at last.

How foolish of me to have believed my first little touching of the earth the other day would have been sufficient. Oh, granted, no matter how long he tried, he never would be able to rouse enough Power to work High Magic in this Realm; Ardagh had already accepted that handicap. *But this time what Power I've absorbed should stay with me for far longer than a day; this time I can actually use whatever magics there are available to me. This time I can actually be a true Sidhe, not a poor imitation of a human.*

But he still needed the humans, Ardagh reminded himself. And he had best return to Fremainn before Aedh thought him eaten by wild beasts. Or in league with demons.

Besides, the prince realized with a shock of surprise, while this forest solitude was wondrously restoring, he rather missed the bright bustle of life at Fremainn. By now, all those cheerful, busy human lives would be sitting down to their communal dinner, laughing and quarrelling (sometimes both at the same time), including strong, clever Aedh and his equally strong and clever wife, and Sorcha—

Now why, of all those folk, Ardagh wondered with a bemused little frown, *should I think of Sorcha?*

Time enough to consider that when he was back inside the fortress. Ardagh shrugged, and set out for Fremainn.

Only to stop short, every sense at once painfully alert. Ae, Powers, Powers, could it be . . . ?

"Sidhe," he breathed, not yet daring to hope. Heart racing, the prince followed the elusive psychic trace he had so suddenly *felt*, terrified that it would vanish before he could find—

"That's quite far enough," said a voice, and Ardagh nearly cried out, for the words had been in the High Sidhe language.

A figure stood leaning against a tree with studied ease; only another Sidhe would have spotted him at all, or sensed the dangerous alertness behind the apparently lazy pose. He was clearly of noble blood, the high-cheekboned face refined of line, the tall, slender figure elegantly clad in tunic and hose of midnight blue silk shot through with gold thread: *spidersilk*, Ardagh thought, with a pang of nostalgia. The other's hair was a thick fall of gold so fair it was nearly silver, far smoother and finer than any human hair, and his eyes were the true cool green slanted eyes of the Sidhe.

"And what name might be given to you and claimed by you and known to your family?" he asked Ardagh lightly, only the barest touch of warning in his voice.

There was no possible answer to that intricate, carefully worded statement other than the truth. "I am Ardagh Lithanial," the prince said, thinking that at least he need not include his regal title.

For what good that did. "Lithanial," the other mused. "Now I do believe that Lithanial is the name of a royal house, though one whose holdings lie quite far from my own lands."

"Your lands."

The other Sidhe pushed off from the tree with easy grace, making it seem only chance that as he now was standing, he blocked Ardagh's path completely. "Why, yes, stranger. And only a stranger to this Realm would not know me. I am Finvarra, or so the humans name me: Fair Hair, more or less." He shook his shining mane with a laugh. "It rather suits me, does it not? I am," he added, almost as an after-thought, "king of the lands that brush against these mortal ones. And even though this is not quite my domain on which we stand, I still would like to know what a prince of the Lithanial house does here."

The Sidhe tongue sounded so wonderful to one who had never thought to hear it again that Ardagh almost failed to catch the unvoiced question. "Your pardon," he said hast-ily. "I have no desire to trespass or intention of doing so. But I also have no choice about being in this Realm."

"So, now. What might that mean?"

"That means," Ardagh said, too bitter to even try for Sidhe evasiveness, "that I have been most falsely accused of treason by my royal brother and sent to exile in this human land."

Finvarra's fair eyebrows shot up. "Indeed! And you are still Sidhe enough to have no ability to lie, that much I sense plainly."

"I do not lie," Ardagh agreed.

"Which means that you can only be telling a true tale— or at least one you honestly believe to be true."

"It *is* true. I made the exceedingly foolish mistake of underestimating certain nobles."

A fair, slanted brow lifted slightly. "Ambitious ones, I take it."

"Very."

"And your brother, I also assume, never quite trusted you."

"How could he? I am his closest kin."

"And therefore his potential rival, whether or not you meant to be such."

"I did not."

"Ah." It was a politely neutral sound. "Even so, being what you were, I imagine that he was eager to believe the worst of you."

"I never wanted his throne," Ardagh said flatly. "I still do not. I have never conspired against him alone or in any alliance. This I swear by earth and sky and Power."

Finvarra's face showed not the slightest trace of emotion at that potent oath: this was, Ardagh thought, a true Sidhe, no doubt of it. "And so you are falsely exiled, eh?" No emotion showed in Finvarra's voice, either. "And with no means of return?"

Sudden hope blazed through Ardagh so fiercely his legs nearly lost their strength. "Y-you can help me," he gasped, stammering in his haste. "Yours is a Sidhe Realm. If you will but give me passage through it, that will surely break my brother's spell and let me find my way back into my homeland. Will you do this thing?" *Powers, Powers, say yes!*

Finvarra hesitated a maddeningly long while, eyeing Ardagh speculatively. "Why?" he asked at last. "Are you likely to take the crown from your brother? No, you have already sworn not to do that. Why should I risk helping you, then, exiled prince who could never become a useful ally? I would not become involved in Lithanial feuds."

"You would not!" Ardagh cried. "Only let me pass through your lands, and I swear you will have no further involvement."

"Not from you. But can you swear for your brother as well? Prince Ardagh, I have had feuds enough with others of the Sidhe; we both know how those games are played.

And while wars can at times be entertaining, they do tend to be annoyingly destructive, both to my own lands and to the human lands they touch."

Ardagh blinked in confusion. "You . . . care about humans?"

Finvarra shrugged. "I take a human use-name, don't I?"

"But *why?*"

"Why? I like them! For all their mortal limitations, the men make fine gaming and hunting partners, and the women . . ." He smiled reminiscently. "Ah, yes. All in all, they are an entertaining lot, these humans, and not without their kindnesses."

"Yes," Ardagh cut in helplessly, "but—"

"You haven't learned that yet? Listen, now, once I was being chased—and by what and by whom is not the issue. Say only that I was on a Sidhe steed shod properly in silver, and eager to reach a safe Doorway home. But my horse threw a shoe, and the moment the poor beast's bare hoof came in contact with mortal soil, the animal stumbled and could no longer run. I would have been in a foul fix, indeed, for the sun was close to rising, and I'm sure you know the limits sunlight places on our kind."

He paused for a moment, for all the world like a bard building suspense. Ardagh, recognizing a classic Sidhe technique of delaying a decision through distraction and nearly wild with impatience for the story to be done, prodded, "What then?"

"Why, then, by sheerest chance I came upon the forge of a human blacksmith. He must surely have known the horse was no earthly horse and the rider no earthly man, but he saw only my desperate need, and shod that horse safely with silver so we could escape pursuit." Finvarra showed his ready grin. "Oh, I saw that blacksmith richly rewarded, I assure you! He found a nice treasure of coins blowing in on the morning wind."

"I see."

"No, Prince Ardagh, I don't think you do, not really. But then, to be fair, few of our kind have the patience to deal with humankind. A pity."

"King Finvarra, please. Will you let me pass?"

The king's slanted gaze slid evasively away. "Perhaps. But the true question is: will my *land* let you pass?" Something that might almost have been a most unSidhe-like flash of pity crossed Finvarra's face. "Come, let us see."

He led Ardagh to a small hill, far too smooth and regularly shaped to have been natural. "The humans think we dwell in burial mounds," Finvarra said over his shoulder. "Sometimes I think they confuse us with the ghosts of their ancient dead. But the confusion serves me well: I can hide Doorways in plain sight and not have any human dare tamper with them."

Unless that human is a grave robber seeking human treasure, Ardagh thought but didn't say. "And this—"

"Is a Doorway, yes, a minor one. Watch."

Finvarra murmured a series of intricate Words of Power, and a Doorway opened itself in the side of the mound. Ardagh caught a sudden sharp glimpse of clear Sidhe light, blazing Sidhe color, and cried out in an agony of longing.

"Wait," Finvarra said gently. "Wait."

The king slipped lightly from the human world into his Realm, disappearing as though he'd passed through a tangible veil. Ardagh, standing tensely in the human night, on the very brink of Otherness denied him, heard more Words of Power drift back to him, distorted by the barrier between the Realms, and dimly *felt* magic swirling in that Sidhe Otherness. *Please, oh please . . .*

But then Finvarra was climbing back into the human world, and his step was weary. "I'm sorry," he said softly. "I am sorry."

"What happened?"

"Nothing. Literally nothing. Prince Ardagh, your brother set his spell far too well. No matter how I sought to cajole it, the land just will not let you pass. Ah, wait, wait, all is not terrible. I will send along whatever message you please; that, I can do."

A message. *To whom?* Ardagh wondered bitterly. *Who would care what befalls me?* "Yes," he said, struggling to keep his voice steady. "If you would, King Finvarra, send a message to my brother. Tell him I live. Tell him I live and thrive and will yet return. Tell him that, if you would."

Finvarra shrugged. "Not the most tactful of messages. But yes, it shall be sent to him." Poised on the edge of his kingdom, the Sidhe king paused. "Prince Ardagh," he added, his voice almost gentle, "the human world is not such a terrible place. Surely you know that already. There is much enjoyment to be found here. Ae, but you don't want to hear condolences. Farewell, Prince Ardagh. It may be that we shall meet again; I am, as you've gathered, often in the human Realm. Whatever happens, may the Powers guide you."

"May they, indeed," Ardagh murmured, watching Finvarra disappear into his Realm. "May they, indeed."

Ardagh rode wearily back up the hill to the fortress of Fremainn, the morning bright about him. No matter what complications his absence might have caused, he could not have returned before this; he could not have borne being among those cheerful humans.

But what is, is. And what is set, he added fiercely, *can be cancelled. There has never yet been an enchantment that could not be broken, Eirithan's banishment spell among them. And till I find the way to break that spell, why, till then I shall live as fine a life as this Realm shall allow.*

To Ardagh's surprise (and slightly damaged pride), no one seemed to have even noticed his overnight absence. Instead, as the prince re-entered Fremainn and dismounted, he found himself in the midst of a wild swirl of excitement. Catching a servant by the arm before the man could scuttle past, Ardagh asked, "What is happening?"

"Don't you know, Prince Ardagh? We have received an important visitor this morning, a very important visitor indeed! Please, I must finish my duties."

As the human scurried off, Ardagh, frowning slightly, sighted a familiar face and called out, "Cadwal. A moment, if you would."

The mercenary stopped short, his face harried. "Prince Ardagh, I'm afraid I must go serve the king. And his guest."

Ardagh fought not to shout with impatience. "Who is his guest?"

"Och, that's right, you couldn't have heard or seen; you weren't here. As of this morning, we are hosting a bishop and all his retinue. The holy man has come all the way from Rome to see us." To Ardagh's surprise, he heard sharp sarcasm in Cadwal's voice. "Trying to make sure we haven't gone sliding back into pagan ways, begging your royal pardon," the mercenary added. "Ha, there he is, standing with King Aedh." He gave Ardagh a quick, speculative glance. "I guess you'll be wanting to meet the man."

Not particularly. Ardagh had caught the faint edge of hostility towards the Roman Church in Father Seadna's words often enough, and had no desire to get involved in human religious quarrels. But the prince could hardly refuse, not without some more tactful reason than that, so he followed Cadwal to where the bishop, with his retinue trailing behind him, and King Aedh, with *his* retinue grouped behind him, stood together in the open field before the royal keep.

Neutral territory, Ardagh thought, and wondered a bit at the military thought.

The Roman bishop was every bit as tall as King Aedh, and as strongly built as a warrior, but lean almost to the point of gauntness, as if his faith or some other driving force had consumed all spare flesh. He had pushed back his hooded travelling cloak, revealing robes that hung in intricate folds, white and green, patterned in gold with the signs of the Church. His eyes, Ardagh noticed warily, were cold.

"Ah, Prince Ardagh!" Aedh cried with the enthusiasm of someone thankful for the interruption. "I am glad to see you here. I wish you to meet our holy visitor. This is Bishop Gervinus, who has made the long journey all the way from Rome to see to our salvation."

Ardagh caught the ever-so-slight hostility behind the smooth words and wasn't really surprised; a king could hardly enjoy welcoming anyone who might challenge his power. But Aedh continued, the very image of urbanity, "And this, My Lord Bishop, is Ardagh Lithanial, Prince of Cathay."

"Indeed." The bishop smiled—with mouth, not eyes—and held out a hand, making it very clear he intended the prince to kneel, or perhaps even to kiss that hand or possibly the ring glinting there.

I kneel to no one, least of all to a human.

Ignoring the bishop's gesture, Ardagh dipped his head in politic courtesy instead, and saw Bishop Gervinus frown slightly.

But what Gervinus thought of his manners meant nothing. For in that moment, in a sudden surge of Sidhe Power, Ardagh knew as surely as if the newcomer had sworn it, *This bishop is the Darkness Eithne feared. The Darkness has come upon this land.*

STRANGENESS
IN THE NIGHT

CHAPTER 13

Stunned by what he had just sensed, Ardagh couldn't do anything at first but stare, thinking in a rush, *No magic to this one, no innate Power at all, but Darkness clings to him regardless: why? how? who is he?*, struggling to keep his face from showing the shock he felt, and hunt for something safe and neutral to say.

The bishop was under no such handicap. "Prince Ardagh," he said smoothly. "You remind me of my proper humility." His accent was heavy, but he spoke the language well enough. "Here I dared think I had suffered hardship journeying here from Rome. Yet you've travelled all the way from Cathay! You must have suffered far worse privation than ever I could have dreamed, coming to Eriu from so much farther away."

"Farther than any could dream," Ardagh agreed truthfully.

"How poetic." Gervinus's smile was quite charming and manifestly false.

King Aedh could only have been aware of the sudden tension between his two visitors. And even though Ardagh knew the king was no more pleased about the bishop's presence than was he, not a trace of anything but urbanity showed on Aedh's face and in his voice. "Your Grace, pray forgive us," he said, moving subtly between prince and bishop. "It is most rude of us to keep you standing while your retinue has already begun settling into their quarters. Come, Bishop Gervinus, if you would. I will have you shown to your guest house."

One that's not too near mine, I hope, Ardagh thought. *No, on second thought, the closer you are placed, the easier it will be for me to keep watch on you, Bishop Gervinus of Rome.*

The easier it will be to learn what you really are and why you are really here.

As Arnulf shooed the king's servants out of the guest house and began unpacking the bishop's belongings and his own, Gervinus sat unheeding, lost in his musings. Only when the acolyte picked up the chest containing the precious grimoire did the bishop come to himself and snap, "Not that! Leave that box alone."

Gervinus's lips tightened at Arnulf's guilty start. The idiot really had been about to try getting his hands on the grimoire yet again. *You never learn, do you? You think you can steal my sorcery. I am going to have to do something about you, Arnulf. But not quite yet.*

He glanced about the guest house indifferently, noting the well-made bed of this main chamber, the pallet for Arnulf, the finely tooled chests and chairs. The central fireplace would probably provide sufficient heat, but if the smoke hole in the roof didn't draw efficiently, it was going to provide a good deal of smoke as well. The outer room, meant for his servants, was even simpler. Still, his quarters back in the Vatican had been more spartan. And everything here was, rather surprisingly for barbarians, spotlessly clean. Since Aedh would hardly want to insult a bishop—and through the bishop, the Church itself—Gervinus doubted that there was any place better in the fortress.

Except, perhaps, for whichever hut the foreign prince inhabits.

Ah yes, the prince . . . what is he, I wonder? The men of Cathay were said to be dark of hair and slanted of eye, and that, Prince Ardagh most certainly was. But his were particularly odd eyes, almost uncannily green, clear and opaque in one. They revealed absolutely nothing of the thoughts behind their surface, and that, Gervinus mused, he trusted not at all. *I think I must learn more about him. Tonight, perhaps . . . yes,* the bishop decided, and put the mysterious prince temporarily from his thoughts. There were, after all, much more important matters to consider.

The first of which was that, just as with that tiny port city, no one here had been expecting his arrival. No messenger from Rome had ever arrived, or so the High King swore. Granted, it was a long, perilous journey that not everyone survived, but Gervinus, ignoring his little stab of insulted pride, had to wonder yet again if any messenger had ever been sent at all.

Could that be? Could they really have sent me off into nowhere? If so—ah, they really do wish to be rid of me, don't they?

Surprising that such a thought should hurt. It wasn't as though he cared what others thought of him, and he was long years from being the boy who'd been rejected by father and family. After all, one could only trust one's self, one's will.

As he trusted his own. What those bureaucratic fools of the Curiate didn't realize was that their contempt had actually done him a favor. Without interference from Rome, Gervinus told himself, he was free to act as he would. Do what he would.

But it may not be quite as simple as I'd first thought to win control in this land. This King Aedh is far from being the naive barbarian I had expected. No, indeed. There had been a firm will glinting in those grey eyes that had warned his would not be an easy mind to overwhelm.

Deus vult, Gervinus thought with mocking piety, *God wills it.* Before he could do anything at all, he must first learn everything he could about the king, about his court, about all his people.

And as for the Prince of Cathay, if he attempts to stand in my way . . . for all his oddness, he is only one man. And one man can so easily meet with a tragic accident.

Queen Derval of Clonach sat in a perfect imitation of calmness in her husband's keep, hands folded neatly in her lap, eyes downcast, watching from under the sweep of golden eyelashes as her husband and son raged at each other. They were such handsome creatures, the two of them, the father ruddy, the son golden. What a pity one of them at least was such a fool.

"It's been nearly two months since you sent out your men!" young Fearghal stormed. "Two months since that stupid, bungled attack, and we have done *nothing* to rid ourselves of the tyrant!"

" 'We?' " Donnchadh roared. "What is this 'we,' boy? Yes, I do say *boy,* you young idiot! A boy is what you are, Fearghal, all wild words and mindless bluster—do you think this is nothing but a hunting trip, something to be easily planned and executed?"

"I'm not—"

"It is the overthrow of a king, curse you, not the slaying of a deer! A king, Fearghal, the Ard Ri himself—"

"I know that, Father! But why aren't we planning something right now? Why aren't we doing anything at all?" Savagely, the boy continued, a wolf cub, Derval thought, challenging a wolf, "Is something bothering you, perhaps? Can it be, oh Father, that you are *afraid?* Afraid to—"

Donnchadh's savage slap sent him slamming back into a wall. Derval unfolded her hands and said coldly, "Enough."

"But he—" Fearghal gasped at the same time as his father's furious, "He *dared*—"

"Look at you." The queen made no attempt to keep the scorn from her voice. "Just look at you, brawling like two drunken peasants. And isn't *this* the way to win a throne? Don't you make fine leaders of the people, you two who can't even keep the peace between yourselves?"

Donnchadh opened his mouth, and for one wild moment Derval was sure he was going to whine a childish, "He started it!" But the King of Clonach only snarled, "Get out of here, Fearghal. Get out! Your mother and I have words to discuss."

Fearghal, Derval saw with a little prickle of pleasure, looked her way first for approval. She nodded, ignoring Donnchadh's glower, and the boy stormed his angry way out. "Close the door after you," Derval said tranquilly, and refused to wince at the slam that followed. "Oh, do sit down, Donnchadh. My neck is sore from staring up at you."

"That boy needs to have some manners knocked into his thick head!"

"He is but young. He will learn. And, like it or not, Donnchadh, our son has raised a good point. What *are* we to do about Aedh?"

"Are you accusing me, too?" the man cried. "I cannot risk another open attack on him!"

"Don't be foolish. We both agreed to that."

Donnchadh studied her, frowning. "What is it? You've already found a plan, haven't you? What?"

She permitted herself a small smile. "What better way to undermine a fortress than by boring from within? Not all who are part of Aedh's court are truly loyal to him."

"Of course not. But—"

"But," Derval cut in smoothly, "just as we are of the Ui Neill sept, so are others there. Odran mac Daire for one."

Donnchadh snorted. "That cold-blooded creature! I doubt he has the fire for ambition."

"No?" It was a purr. "Cold cunning is far more enduring than mere flame."

"Ha. Even if he did ever dream of rebellion, he'd dream of a crown as well."

"Why, let him dream. With secret promises of our aid to sweeten his slumber."

"I am *not* going to aid another to the throne!"

Derval bit back an impatient snarl at her husband's slowness. "Of course you aren't." *Idiot.* "We will offer him our aid, husband, make an alliance with our distant Ui Neill cousin—but after he's done our work for him, who's to say we ever made that offer?"

Donnchadh stared, then laughed, then stared again. "Sweet Jesus and all the saints, I'm glad you're on my side, Derval."

"As well you should be," she said without a trace of warmth. "As well you should be."

Bishop Gervinus glanced about the small audience hall, the "conversation house," as it was apparently named, aware that three pairs of alert eyes were watching his every move, their owners being King Aedh and, flanking him, Father Seadna, the monk who was apparently Aedh's personal priest, and Fothad mac Ailin, who was, if Gervinus understood him correctly, both Chief Poet and Chief Minister to the king, the one title being seemingly as important to these barbaric people as the other.

"You need have no fear," Gervinus told them in his most urbane voice, but saw no change in those wary stares. "Yes, I have been sent here by the Curiate of Rome, but I assure you that my mission is not one of condemnation. It is merely that, as you must surely admit, your land of Eriu lies very far away from the parent Church. So far, indeed, that it has been virtually out of touch with Rome for many years."

"And so," King Aedh said without a touch of expression, "you have been sent to be sure we still are good children of Mother Church."

Gervinus frowned slightly at the unvoiced cynicism. Oh yes, this king, barbarian or no, was no fool. "I am sure you and your people both are quite faithful, King Aedh. But . . ." He raised a helpless hand. "I have my orders. You do understand."

"Of course," the king agreed. "Be welcome to my realm, Bishop Gervinus." His voice was still carefully empty of any emotion. "If there is anything I or any of my people may do to make your visit here more pleasant, please do not hesitate to ask."

What if I told you that what I want is your throne? Gervinus thought with a flash of dark humor. "I'm sure my visit will be pleasant, indeed." *And profitable, oh yes. Quite profitable.*

By chance or design, Ardagh found himself seated beside Bishop Gervinus at dinner—a dinner, the prince thought, that was rapidly turning into a most uncomfortable affair, with everyone on edge about the ecclesiastical stranger in their midst, not sure what to say or do. Father Seadna, for one, was far more reserved even than his usual quiet self.

You don't like having someone from the Roman Church here, do you? the prince mused. *Particularly not one whose rank is so much higher, king's priest though you are, than yours.*

Queen Eithne, too, said virtually nothing, save for the occasional polite murmur. She, Ardagh didn't doubt, was as uneasy about Bishop Gervinus as he, her slight magic stirring in response to his aura, though of course she could hardly mention it. Only King Aedh and Fothad mac Ailin did their best to pretend nothing at all was unusual, keeping up a witty, entertaining banter that didn't quite sound true.

Gervinus didn't seem to notice the uneasiness surrounding him, or if he did notice, to mind. "Prince Ardagh," he murmured, "I'm sure you know that the Church has its believers in Cathay."

"Indeed." *I know it now.*

Watching him closely, the bishop continued, "But those believers, alas, are in the minority."

"That is as it is."

Gervinus frowned at that carefully bland statement. "Can it be, then, that you are not a Christian, Prince Ardagh?"

Both King Aedh and Father Seadna stirred uneasily; they'd been tiptoeing around that awkward fact since his arrival. Ardagh merely smiled. "Would my answer trouble you?"

"Why, only if you told me you were, indeed, not of the faith, for then I would worry for the state and safety of your immortal soul."

"Your concern seems most kind." *Even if it's false.* "But I assure you that you need have no fear. My soul is quite safe where it is."

Aedh's face was rigidly controlled, but Ardagh could have sworn the king was enjoying this verbal duel, letting the prince, the nonbeliever outsider, spar with the bishop as Aedh could not. Almost reluctantly the king finally

interrupted with, "Your pardon, Bishop Gervinus. I wouldn't
dream of correcting you. But you cannot know our ways,
coming from so far away as you do. Here we follow our
ancient Laws of Hospitality. A guest among us need not
answer personal questions if he does not wish it."

The bishop raised an eyebrow. "Surely the question of
paganism is no matter to be kept secret. Particularly when
your own land does, indeed, harbor pagans."

Aedh's face hardened. "There may, even as you say, be
corners of Eriu where folk still follow older ways. But my
people, no matter what they may believe or not believe,
are my people."

"Oh, of course! I would not dream of trying to undermine your authority."

And the sky, Ardagh added silently, *is made of blue enamel.
If you're trying to win control over King Aedh, Bishop
Gervinus, you've made a mistake. And if you're trying to
control me, that mistake might well prove fatal.*

*But why, oh why, do you carry that haze of Darkness
about you? If you were a creature of true magic, I'd feel it
in a moment. I'd understand you. Who are you, Bishop
Gervinus—and what?*

Still mulling over the problem of the mysterious bishop,
Ardagh prowled restlessly through the quiet twilight, nodding absently to this servant or that guard, not really seeing any of them. As the twilight deepened into night and
the chill of evening grew, the humans disappeared one by
one into their various houses, leaving only the prince, easily avoiding remaining patrols, to wander alone, wrapped
tightly in his woolen *brat*.

He wasn't quite alone at that. Jarred out of his reverie
by the sudden *feel* of another, Ardagh stalked silently forward. Ah no, it wasn't someone spying on him. It was Breasal
mac Donnchadh, the sad, sickly youngster, quite unaware
of him. A practice sword lay in the dirt where he had
apparently let it fall, and the boy sat beside it, huddled in
misery.

For a moment, Ardagh stood where he was, not wanting

to get involved in still another human matter, yet bemused
at the strength of the pull he felt to help even a child who
was nearly grown; knowing that the urge to aid any child
in need was a Sidhe instinct, a survival trait in a mostly
infertile race, didn't make it any easier to overcome.

Ah well. Yielding to what he was, Ardagh knelt at the
boy's side and said quietly, "There *are* other ways to fight."

Breasal turned with a gasp, hastily wiping at his face, not
quite before Ardagh's night-sighted eyes could catch the
trace of tears. "I . . . tried." Breasal's voice was barely more
than a whisper. "I thought if I did the exercises slowly, I
could . . . but m-my heart . . . I thought I was going to die
just now, and I-I . . . don't want to die, n-not yet."

"Who does?" Ardagh knelt quietly where he was, staring out at the night, allowing the boy a chance to regain
control. "I take it that the life of a scholar didn't appeal to
you. No, no, don't try to argue. I'd forgotten what a desperately proud thing it is to be a boy." *It's been long and
long since I've been that young, after all.* He extended his
senses, delicately probing. Yes. Breasal had recovered whatever strength was likely to be his. "It's too chilly to be sitting here. Come, now, up. Up, Breasal."

"What . . ?"

"You can't be a warrior like the others," the prince said
bluntly. "That path is closed to you. Face it. But that doesn't
mean you can't learn other ways to defend yourself. Ways
that may even make the other boys envious of you." *Ways
that won't put an undue strain on your heart.* "So now, are
you interested?"

Warily, Breasal nodded.

Very slowly, Ardagh led the boy through the moves of
Tarien'taklal, one Sidhe form of unarmed combat, a graceful,
flowing thing that looked deceptively like a dance but could
deliver smooth, elegant, deadly blows to a foe. Breasal could
hardly mimic Sidhe grace, but he imitated Ardagh surprisingly well, face fierce with concentration.

"It's not as easy as it looks," the boy admitted after a while.

"Few things are. No, no, your arm moves like this, slowly,
slowly—yes. You have it." But even this gentle form of

combat-dance could be tiring, so Ardagh added, "Enough for now. Go to bed, Breasal. We'll try another lesson another time. Oh, and no one else shall know of this meeting."

Relief flashed in the boy's eyes. "Thank you, Prince Ardagh. I—thank you." He bowed with the formal grace of the prince he was, then added another, "thank you," and hurried away. Ardagh watched him go, then shook his head. Gentle exercises like these could only help strengthen the boy's weak heart, but there was a limit to what could be done.

If only he was in a Sidhe Realm! The endless Power there could heal him in a moment. Here—ae, no. I have no such Power. And here I fear his life will be brief, indeed. Briefer even than the human norm—Powers, Powers, he thought in sudden pain, *I am among mayflies, here and gone while I—I will live on in this land alone.*

The night was turning very chill. Shivering, Ardagh headed back to his guest house.

Queen Eithne stood at the bedchamber window, staring out into the night, feeling painfully alone. Behind her, she could hear Aedh's gentle snoring, but there wasn't any other sign of life. In the utter darkness of the moonless night, it was very easy to start believing there wasn't any other life anywhere else in the world.

Was Prince Ardagh out there somewhere? If so, she couldn't see him, or sense him. But just then she longed to know that he, too, was awake, the only one in all Fremainn who would understand her fears. He would know whether or not there was a reason to be afraid.

I saw the way he looked at Bishop Gervinus and heard the easy, fearless way he fenced with the man. He would surely know if—if the bishop was secretly of . . . Darkness.

Och, ridiculous! This was a *bishop*, a holy man. He couldn't possibly be—

"Eithne?" Aedh muttered sleepily. "What're you doing out in the cold?" He patted the bed beside him. "Come back here where it's warm."

Overwhelmed with relief that she wasn't alone after all,

Eithne climbed back into bed. Her husband raised an arm, inviting her to cuddle up beside him, and she let her head rest on his chest, hearing his steady heartbeat, feeling his warmth.

"You're shivering," Aedh said, his voice more nearly awake now, and held her close. "What were you doing, standing there like that?"

"I . . . couldn't sleep."

"Eithne? What's wrong?"

What could she say? *I think Bishop Gervinus is a sorcerer. I think he's a servant of Darkness.* "I—I don't think I like Bishop Gervinus," she said at last, wincing at how lame that sounded.

"Huh, is that all? I don't much like the man, either, Cold creature, that, though for all we know the coldness is an act to test our fidelity to the faith. But like him or not, he's here, and we can hardly insult the Church by tossing him out like a— Hey, now, tears? What's this about, Eithne?"

Choking back her sudden unexpected sobs, she could only shake her head helplessly against his chest. Aedh held her even closer, silent for a while, then said knowingly, "Aha. The calendar."

For a moment Eithne wanted to hit him. Men were all too willing to blame any show of a woman's emotion on her monthly cycle. But then she added up the days in her mind and felt a reluctant little smile forming on her lips. He might be right, curse him for his smugness. Maybe all this wild panic over a stranger who was probably nothing worse than unfriendly *was* just a trick of the moon. Praying with all her heart that Aedh really was right, Eithne twisted about to suddenly throw her arms around as much of him as she could reach, and heard him chuckle.

"I love you, Aedh," she whispered fiercely. "I love you and our children and our whole kingdom."

And I will not, she added, but silently, *let anything happen to you. This I swear by all the gods who ever were and are.*

OPENING MANEUVERS

CHAPTER 14

Even the Sidhe sometimes slept as deeply as humans. That night, Ardagh's mind wandered vaguely through veils of dream landscapes, not quite focusing on memories of his home, not quite sure of the here and now. Forest . . . he was wandering through forest and quite at peace with . . .

The attack came. Too deeply asleep to understand more than *peril*, inner Sidhe defenses roused, sending the sleeping mind deeper, sealing it beneath a smooth psychic layer of *no one here, nothing here*, a layer of innocent blandness that left nothing on which an enemy could seize.

The attack slid past. As it faded, vanished, Ardagh moaned in his sleep, then suddenly woke, heart racing, every sense instantly alert to danger no longer present.

"What in the name of all the Powers . . . ?"

He rubbed a hand over his eyes. A dream? Had that been only a dream? Maybe. Magical beings did tend to dream of magic.

And yet . . . could someone have just sent out some sorcerous probe to study him? Ardagh sat sharply up in bed, questing with every psychic sense, for—for—

For nothing. Whatever that had been, not a trace of anything arcane lingered. Surely it *had* been a dream.

And yet . . .

No longer even slightly sleepy, Ardagh got to his feet,

slinging on the first clothes that came to hand, and stepped out into the night to see what he might find.

The air was very cold, the sky clear and blazing with stars. The bishop's guest house was as quiet as all the fortress of Fremainn, full of the *feel* of sleeping humanity, but to the prince's darkness-adjusted eyes the light of the one flickering candle glinting from behind the house's one leather-curtained window was bright as a beacon.

Now why, if all inside were asleep, did the bishop need a light? There was always the possibility that someone had forgotten to extinguish it or that one of the humans within feared the dark; some humans, Ardagh had already learned, did have such an odd terror. Something to do with their poor night vision, no doubt.

Somehow I doubt this is the case.

Very delicately, he expanded his Sidhe senses, probing gently, then just as gently drew back into himself. The bishop was indeed still awake, but lost to the point of psychic invisibility in study or prayer or whatever it was a human holy man might be doing at such an hour. There was not the slightest *feel* of magic to him, but that, unfortunately, was not surprising.

If only Gervinus bore innate Power, even such a tiny touch as Eithne possesses! It would be so easy to trap him then! Magic did, after all, call to magic; the bishop would never be able to hide such Talent from him. But of course Gervinus had no innate Power; he hadn't even been able to recognize that the prince was of the Sidhe.

But isn't there supposed to be another way for humans to manipulate Power? Less efficient, less clean, but still possible?

Father Seadna had reluctantly admitted in one of his discussions with the prince that such a thing existed. "Sorcery," the process was called, and it involved learning spells from books and reciting them by rote. According to the monk, sorcery was always an evil thing. Ardagh frowned in distaste. Of course it would be! How could something as unnatural as forcing Power where none belonged be anything *but* evil?

Such an ugliness would surely account for the Darkness I felt.

Ae, yes, but this didn't make sense. Gervinus, whatever else he might be, was still a prelate of the humans' Church, and as far as Ardagh could tell from Father Seadna's euphemistic words on the subject, that Church condemned any form of magic.

Or am I being naive? Humans are so easy with falsehood, after all. Maybe the bishop's seeming loyalty to his Church is a lie, too.

The prince let out his breath in a silent sigh of frustration. Maybe Gervinus really was doing nothing more suspicious than studying his prayers. As long as that candle proved someone was alert within, the prince couldn't very well slip into the guest house to find out. And without definite proof, with nothing stronger than a half-dream for evidence, he couldn't even be sure *anyone* had been working sorcery!

Some other time, Gervinus, Ardagh promised, and returned to his guest house, aching for the easy, mighty Power of his former Sidhe life, the Power that would have let him solve this ludicrous puzzle with one quick Word. Instead, helpless to do anything constructive, the prince sat awake and alert, hunting in vain for even the slightest trace of sorcery till at last the night brightened into day and the human world came awake.

Ae-yi, Ardagh thought, stretching wearily, *if I cannot prove sorcery, I can at least make every effort to keep the man from working any harm.*

I hope.

Gervinus sat hunched wearily over the grimoire set on the table before him, staring down at it by the uncertain light of the single candle as though the book had turned into something foreign.

That should not have happened. He had used the proper spell, the same one he had used a hundred times before to learn secrets about rivals, the one that had let him spy upon the Curiate when they'd decided his fate. He had spoken each word correctly and properly performed every one of the dozen seemingly meaningless gestures that were necessary to spark it into life. And yet—nothing! The mirror had remained only a mirror—nothing!

Stifling a yawn, the bishop leaned back, stretching stiff neck and shoulder muscles. Prince Ardagh hadn't warded off the spell; anything so strong would, according to everything he'd ever studied about sorcery, have set off psychic waves of shock. Instead, it had felt as though his spell were a stone that, rather than predictably sinking into the pool into which it had been hurled, had skipped smoothly across the surface, barely stirring a drop.

Fact: The spell could not have failed. Fact: It did. Fact: The prince used no magic to ward it off. Gervinus closed the grimoire with a snap. Three conflicting impossibilities-turned-truth should add up to something useful. *But what that useful thing may be, I have not the vaguest idea.*

The bishop fought back a second yawn. Every time he used the grimoire these days and felt that wondrous surge of Power, he also felt a strange, no longer to be denied *pull*, a craving to cast yet more and greater spells, even when sorcery wasn't truly required. Bizarre sensation, but it was nothing he couldn't control. Particularly now, when he was too weary to even think of further experiments. *Tomorrow night*, Gervinus decided. Tomorrow night he would try again, but aim his magic against King Aedh instead. *The spell*, he told himself, cannot *fail again*.

As Ardagh left his guest house, he started violently as a piercing little voice said, "I have a new toy."

He glanced down. "Ah, Princess Fainche!" Even after his bizarre night and the feeling that he hadn't quite gotten enough sleep, he had to smile. Even if she was, he was beginning to think, worse than a kitten for escaping where she should be. "What are you doing here, little one?"

"I have a new toy," she insisted, holding it out for his inspection.

"So you do." Ardagh obligingly crouched down to examine the toy, amused and a tiny bit flattered that she should have come all this way to show her new possession to him. It

was an intricate thing of willow twigs and ribbons that would
whirl out in colorful patterns when the toy was spun. It was
also, he saw, something else as well. "Very pretty. Your
mother is a clever woman to make such a toy."

Fainche nodded, not at all surprised that he would know
that her mother had made it. The thing could only have
come from Eithne's hand, Ardagh thought. There were half
a dozen little protection spells woven into it.

"Very pretty, indeed, Princess Fainche. But aren't you
supposed to be somewhere else right now?"

"She is, indeed," said a woman's voice, and Ardagh glanced
up to see Queen Eithne. She knelt beside her daughter,
urging, "Go on, Fainche. Go with my women."

The child hesitated, glancing doubtfully at Ardagh, then,
at his nod, scuttled off.

"She seems quite smitten by you," Eithne said with a smile.

"I like the young lady, too." Ardagh paused. "But this time
she wasn't wandering on her own, was she? You encour-
aged her to come here, didn't you?"

Eithne didn't even try to deny it. Pretending to be totally
involved in showing the prince yet another beribboned
trinket, she murmured, "It was the only way I could see
for us to exchange a few words in private."

Untangling two of the ribbons—red, to ward off evil
spirits—Ardagh frowned. "Bishop Gervinus."

"You feel it, too."

"Ae, yes. I woke from sleep sure that someone had tried
to probe my mind by sorcery."

She stared as blankly as though he'd told her the moon
had turned to milk. "Wait now, are you saying—sorcery—
are—are you accusing a bishop of—"

"Of nothing. Yet."

"I don't understand! You're one of the Sidhe; surely you
can tell whether or not someone is working spells."

"Not always. Not if the magic being used isn't natural
to the user."

"But . . ."

"Look you, I knew you bore Power as your birthright
almost from the moment I first saw you: I *felt* it. And you

sensed mine as well. But if the bishop is working spells simply
by reading the correct words and making the correct gestures,
without any inner magic being sparked to life, in that case
there isn't any *laithaie'al*, any . . . ae, I don't have the words
in your tongue . . . any magical aura, let's call it, to be sensed."

"Then how do you know he's working *any* spells? Prince
Ardagh, the man's a *bishop!*"

"Something that doesn't matter to either of us." The blunt
honesty made the queen wince, but Ardagh continued as if
he hadn't seen, "As to what he's doing, I'm not sure. Gervinus
might well have been using some sorcerous scroll or book
of spells, but I couldn't manage to steal into his guest house
to take a look." He frowned at her frown. "Don't give me that
horrified look: *I'm* not bound by your Laws of Hospitality.
If I could have worked my way in there, I would have done
so, but . . ." The prince shrugged. "Right now I can't prove
what Gervinus is or is not doing."

"I—I see. Well, we can hardly challenge a bishop—yes,
yes, I know, but he's an important man to the Christian folk—
we can't challenge him on such a terrible charge without very
real proof."

"Indeed not." Ardagh turned his attention back to the
toy, gently straightening the ribbons. "Eithne, do you know
how to work a . . ." He stopped, caught again by the barrier of a nonmagical people's nonmagical language. "There
isn't a human term for it. Call it a 'not here' spell, a small
charm that's just strong enough to let sorcerous intrusion
slide harmlessly off without leaving any traces. Can you work
something like that?"

She considered the problem for a moment, brow furrowed. "I think I know what you mean, yes. But what are
you saying? Prince Ardagh, please, are you telling me my
husband's in danger?"

"Or possibly you. Or possibly no one at all." Ardagh shook
his head in sudden impatience. "I'm not used to being so
uncertain. I don't mean to frighten you, either, but I can't
give you anything that says, 'Yes, here is the danger,' and
'yes, here is what you can do about it.' For all I know, we're
both overreacting to the fact that we've taken such a strong

dislike to the man. But . . . cast your spells tonight, Queen Eithne, just in case."

Gervinus clenched his teeth so hard his jaw ached. It could not have happened. The spell could not have failed him a second time, and in exactly the same way, skipping over King Aedh as smoothly as a stone over water. He pored over the grimoire, ignoring his aching head, ignoring the ache of failed magic that was echoing through all his being, hunting—even though he knew he was being ridiculous—for even the slightest trace that there had been tampering. But of course there was none. The intricate words and more intricate designs were just as they'd always been, calling to him, telling him to *try again, work a spell, work sorcery.* . . .

No! He was the master of the grimoire, not it he!

Just then, the candle, which Gervinus had absently noticed was nearly used up, gave one final flicker and burned out, leaving him blinking and tense in the sudden darkness. He could almost swear someone else had slipped into the room with him.

"Arnulf?"

No, you fool. Don't let whoever it is know exactly where you are! Smoothly, Gervinus slipped to his feet and moved to the window, then flung aside the leather curtain to let moonlight flood into the room—

The quite empty room.

"Jesu Christos." He ran a hand over his eyes. He was being almost as foolish as Arnulf, seeing specters where there were none. It was the spell's double failure weighing on his nerves, surely. But what could be causing that failure? What could—

Ah yes, of course. Foolish of him not to have realized it earlier: The grimoire had been bound and inscribed in distant Rome. Eriu itself, some foreignness of air or earth or aura peculiar to this land, must be behind the sorcerous interference he was encountering. Gervinus swore a very secular oath under his breath. He would need to work some experiments before he could work any sorcery at all, warily so no one would suspect what he was about, and learn what corrections must be made to the initial spells.

But not tonight, he added silently to the grimoire, this time not even trying to hide his yawn. Tonight he had done enough. If he was to do anything at all useful come morning, he needed sleep. Leaving a fresh candle burning to let prying eyes think someone was still awake, Gervinus sank to his bed and surrendered to exhaustion.

"Good morning to you, Bishop Gervinus."

It was the prince, the foreigner, strolling casually up to him as Gervinus left his guest house in the morning, followed by his retinue. Prince Ardagh looked so disgustingly cheerful that the bishop wanted to spit at him. Instead, Gervinus moved his hand in an abstract blessing, not at all surprised that the prince didn't kneel or even lower his head to receive it. "God give you a good morning, Prince Ardagh."

"It is a pleasant morning, isn't it? Not raining for once and nicely warm, and with that lovely blue sky." The prince stopped to study him, head to one side. "But what's this? You look so very weary, almost as if you lacked for sleep!"

"I could say the same about you."

The prince grinned. "It was too charming a night to waste in sleeping. I was up and about till fairly late. And you?"

His lighthearted chirping was beginning to grate. "I was up late as well," Gervinus snapped. "Studying the Holy Book. You would not know of such things."

"It would seem that such studying was fruitless," the prince replied with a charming smile. "You look most terribly dissatisfied."

"Hardly with the Holy Word!"

"Eriu, then? Can it be that Eriu does not agree with you?"

"You misread me, Prince Ardagh. The only dissatisfaction I feel concerns the number of pagans I have found in this land."

The prince's smile never faltered. "Perhaps those pagans are quite content with things the way they are. Perhaps they don't want someone intruding on their hearts and minds."

He knows, the bishop realized with a little shock of alarm. *He knows very well what I was doing—no, no, he couldn't know, he would have run straight to Aedh if that were so.*

Unless, of course, he wants something from me? Is this to be an attempt at blackmail? "This conversation is pointless, Prince Ardagh. Unless you have anything specific you wish to discuss?"

He stressed the word "specific." Prince Ardagh was silent just long enough to set Gervinus' nerves on edge. "Just a comment," the prince said at last. "Perhaps when you are studying in the dark, quiet hours of the night, it may comfort you to know that someone is watching."

"Is that some warped form of threat?"

"Now, did I say one threatening word?" Prince Ardagh gave him a new, dazzlingly bright smile. "Good day to you, Bishop Gervinus."

Still smiling slightly, Ardagh stood watching the bishop and his retinue until they had vanished around the bend of a narrow street.

The smile faded. Had he just moved a little too soon? He had been using an old Sidhe technique: when uncertain about a foe, attack without warning and transfer that uncertainty to the foe's shoulders. A Sidhe technique—but who knew how a human thought? Or how to predict a human's actions? Or, for that matter, a lack of action? Last night, Ardagh reflected, he had definitely felt *something*, the faintest of psychic disturbances, but it had been too slight an arcane trembling to prove anything. A failed Sidhe spell, with all its natural Power, would have left enough psychic residue to alert everyone in the area; one of these unnatural, book-learned sorcerous spells, it seemed, could only be detected without error if the cursed thing actually worked.

Someone, probably one of the servant women, had begun to sing at her work, one thin, clear thread of music, pure as the call of a bird, and Ardagh paused, a little shiver of delight racing through him, chasing away the anger. The game wasn't won or lost. And, lacking certainty, innuendo could be a most useful tool. Ah yes, and what an interesting reaction he'd roused from Gervinus!

Now, if I were he, I would be puzzling out what I wanted. And begin work on some means of destroying me. Well now,

*when it comes to matters magical, he's going to be as lim-
ited by this Realm as me. And if he actually does manage
to cast something as Powerful as a Spell of Attack at me,*
Ardagh thought with a fierce little grin, *I not only have my
proof, I have his death.*

The prince *couldn't* know anything, Gervinus decided,
striding along with a fierceness more suited to a warrior
than a cleric, his robes whipping about his legs. There wasn't
any way anyone here, not even that uncanny foreigner, could
know of his experiments in sorcery. Unless, of course, Prince
Ardagh was, himself, a—

Nonsense.

Gervinus stopped so suddenly his servants nearly crashed
into him. Absently waving away their stammered apologies,
he started forward again, more pensively this time. Now,
here was a useful thought: it didn't actually matter whether
or not the prince was a sorcerer. No, of course not. The
important thing was that the folk of Fremainn, most certainly King Aedh, come to believe he was.

Of course it was not going to be an easy thing to sway
the folk here against such a handsome creature; people
tended to believe that the beautiful must be good, never
once remembering that even Lucifer was known as the
Lightbearer.

Innuendo, the bishop told himself with a secret smile.
Innuendo would be far more useful than outright attack, at
least until he could find some tangible proof of wrongdoing.

But not yet. He didn't dare start any move so drastic as
attacking Prince Ardagh, not until he had learned more about
these people and put them at their ease. Not until he had
found the way to control them and the way they thought.
Not until he had found the way to truly rule this realm.
The fast-approaching winter would be an ideal time to settle
in. And after that . . .

*Guard your back, Prince Ardagh, for what good it will
do you. Guard it well.*

STRANGE POLITICS

CHAPTER 15

The hour was very late; the waning moon had set some time back, and the air held that chill silence that came between the human Realm's night and dawn. Ardagh, dark cloak wrapped tightly about him as he kept his usual vigil outside the bishop's guest house, mused that now was the time when humans were most likely to have their defenses down. *Even*, he added, staring at the guest house, *those of a bishop.*

Nearly a week had passed with not a sign of arcane or mundane danger from Gervinus; the bishop would know he was still too newly arrived in Eriu for anything of the latter, and judging from the man's increasingly tired face, the lack of the former had merely been because he'd been too weary from failed spells to try anything new.

He'd better try something new, and quickly, the prince thought with a flash of humor, *or I'm going to be too weary from watching him instead of sleeping to do anything about it!*

But in the past week, instead of working anything even remotely sorcerous, Gervinus had been doing his best to learn by more ordinary means everything he could about this fortress and the folks within it. He also, rather to Ardagh's surprise, hadn't issued so much as an innuendo against the prince.

Can a human possibly be as subtle as a Sidhe? And why,

I wonder, would a man who is almost certainly going to be called back to Rome want to know such detailed information about Eriu? He does intend to be called back, doesn't he?

Ha, look at this: the bishop's candle had just burned out. Ardagh waited patiently till he was sure it wasn't going to be relit, then delicately tested with Sidhe senses. Yes. The bishop had just fallen asleep.

At last! The prince smiled and moved silently forward. It was the easiest thing in the world to slip past the sleeping, snoring humans who littered the antechamber, and not much more difficult to enter the inner room, stepping delicately over the slumbering Arnulf who lay flat on a pallet just inside.

The prince paused, night-sighted eyes clearly picking out the bed and the bishop, who had collapsed across it, still fully clad, and was suddenly overwhelmed by a sense of the absurd. Ae, but this was ridiculous! Dear brother Eirithan would laugh till the tears came at the sight of a prince turned lowly thief.

I'm not a thief, Ardagh jibed at himself, *I'm a spy. A big difference, that.*

Whatever he was, this was hardly the time to stand and worry about it. Gervinus was genuinely asleep, but there was no way to ensure he would stay that way, not in this magic-poor Realm where sleep spells weren't guaranteed to work. Ardagh let his senses expand, delicately hunting, hunting . . .

Nothing. If a spellbook really was in this room, it gave off no more aura of magic than did the bishop. Where might it be, though . . . ? Anything so precious wouldn't be kept where prying eyes might see it, but the sparsely furnished room didn't allow many hiding places. The clothes chest, the prince quickly realized, held nothing more alarming than clothing, most of it clearly ecclesiastical (he warily refolded everything so no one would know they'd been disturbed), and there really didn't seem to be anywhere else that might—

Ah. The bed itself. Like that in his own guest house, it was a large, thick feather bed, ideal for hiding any number of small objects. Ardagh stole forward and looked warily down at the sleeping bishop, wondering if Gervinus kept the book under his pillow. Surely he wouldn't?

Surely he would. The corner of a plainly bound book extended slightly from under the pillow.

So, now. This isn't going to be easy.

Holding his breath, Ardagh softly started to pull the book out. He almost had it . . . a little more and . . .

Just then, Gervinus turned roughly over in bed. The prince started, his hand slipped—and something sharp as white-hot fire seared his fingers! Barely holding back a yell, Ardagh dropped the book with a crash, and saw the bishop's eyes flutter open. No time to do anything but dive for the door before the groggy Gervinus could recognize him, leaping over Arnulf even as he heard the bishop's first shout. Before the servants in the antechamber could stir, Ardagh was past them and out into the security of the night. Not quite night anymore, he realized with alarm. It was now light enough to be nearly dawn.

Keeping to what shadows remained, the prince hurried on till he was sure there wasn't going to be any pursuit. Then he fell back against a wall, clutching his scorched hand against his chest and gasping out oaths in the human tongue since the Sidhe language wasn't rough enough to relieve his feelings. Warily he stole a look down at his hand, half-expecting to find the fingertips charred.

No. There was no damage worse than blistering, but it certainly *felt* as though the flesh had been burned away. Ardagh warily attempted a healing spell, a small thing that surely wouldn't be restricted by the human Realm.

A small thing, unfortunately, that had never been intended to work against iron-burns, and certainly had no Power against them now.

Ae, damn it, *damn it,* how could he have been so stupid? Snatching at the book like some little boy after candy, never once thinking it might be guarded! Bah, he'd been among an iron-wielding folk so long without suffering much worse than an occasional bout of nausea that he'd let himself grow complacent. Maybe the lock binding the book had been of purer iron than the alloys used in Eriu, maybe foreign iron had more power, maybe there was some arcane ecclesiastical aura clinging to it, but the thing had burned him as surely as ever iron had scorched magical beings in the old tales.

Damn and damn again, I can't even be sure what type of book it was! For all I know, it's nothing more than a copy of the humans' Holy Book or one of those ornate prayerbooks they seem to favor. Some of those books were said to be so richly ornamented they were worth a regal ransom—reason enough to keep one of them locked to protect the precious contents.

He wasn't alone. Ardagh whirled with a snarl, wounded fingers hidden in the grip of his good hand, then relaxed marginally. "Lady Sorcha." He bit the words off angrily. "You are an early riser."

"Oh, I often—" She broke off with a frown. "You've hurt your hand." Before he could wave her away, Sorcha had caught it gently between her own, studying the scorching. "Now, how did you manage *this?*"

"By being stupid."

"Huh. It looks like you tried to pick up a coal that wasn't quite cool." She glanced up at him without expression. "Accidents happen. That's why most of the women here keep a good selection of salves. I have a nice one Queen Eithne concocted that should take the pain away. Wait, and I'll fetch it."

When she chose, she could move as swift as the Sidhe, it seemed, gone and back so quickly Ardagh didn't quite have time to reach his guest house. Blocking his path, Sorcha snapped, "I told you to wait. Now don't be such a heroic idiot and hold still."

The salve was cool and soothing, with a sharp, not unpleasant herbal scent, and removed the pain as quickly as the woman had promised. As Sorcha busied herself with binding his fingers with clean strips of cloth, Ardagh studied her, puzzled by the concern he saw on her face, so much at odds with her sharp tongue. The herbal scent surrounded her, mingling with her own faint, clean scent, making her seem at once very human yet part of something far older, far more basic than humanity, and the prince tensed, not quite sure in that confused moment whether he was feeling relief or gratitude or something much warmer, not sure whether he wanted to move towards her or away.

"That does it," Sorcha said suddenly, and Ardagh straightened guiltily. If the woman had been aware of his confusion, she didn't show any sign of it. "Here. There's enough of the salve in this vial for you to apply it once a day. Keep that hand cleanly bandaged and as dry as possible. If it doesn't seem to be healing after a day, send for me, but I doubt that you'll have any trouble; it's not such a bad burn. Just don't repeat . . . whatever it was you were doing to get it."

"I won't," Ardagh assured her dryly. "Thank you."

She raised an eyebrow, as if trying to read something more into the simple words, then muttered, "You're quite welcome," and hurried away.

Ardagh strode coolly up to the door of the High King's council hall. Even if, in the week since his aborted attempt at espionage, he hadn't been able to learn the contents of the bishop's mysterious book, the days had been calm and the nights totally untroubled, for both himself and the royal couple. His hand had healed quickly, leaving not even the smallest scar. Bishop Gervinus had never even tried to accuse him of attempted theft; the human had, after all, still been half-asleep and must have decided that the whole thing had been a dream sparked by the book's accidental fall.

Interesting. If Gervinus really had been trying any sorceries this past week, the bishop must be feeling thoroughly frustrated by now, because there hadn't been the slightest sign that even the smallest of spells had worked.

Not so frustrated that he hasn't been learning all he can about local politics. He is almost certainly going to make himself part of today's meeting of the royal council.

As am I.

"Stand aside," Ardagh told the guards, and they, nervous about refusing a princely order, obeyed. The prince, aware of the demands of drama, stood framed in the doorway just long enough for every head in the crowded room to turn in his direction.

Ah look, I was right: Bishop Gervinus has already intruded. And tsk, he looks so weary. Almost like a man who's been up all night conjuring in vain.

As the bishop gave him a decidedly hostile glare, Ardagh smiled. Then his glance locked with Aedh's quizzical gaze. The prince dipped his head in regal courtesy, receiving the king's nod in return. "Have I your permission to join this gathering?" Ardagh asked politely.

No matter how he might feel about having both Ardagh and Bishop Gervinus in the same council meeting, Aedh could hardly have refused. With a gracious wave of his hand, he indicated a spot to his left. Ardagh moved smoothly to the space, which put him next to Fothad, almost directly opposite the bishop, and sat absolutely still, waiting as a predator waits till the humans were no longer aware of him, listening until he was sure of the direction of discussion. He recognized every participant by now, from the somber, scrupulously honest Beinion mac Cuan, thin and grey-haired, to those idiots Diarmait mac Flann and Connall mac Lare, alike in their red-gold hair and foolish faces, who'd once had that quarrel over cattle.

The one I solved.

For a time there was nothing of particular note, just the accumulation of details that went into the smooth running of every land.

Ha, but what nonsense was starting up? Eriu was more or less at peace, internal squabbles notwithstanding. Why would these folks wish to stir up trouble where none existed? Ardagh knew by now that these were a quick-tempered people, swift to laugh or take offense, but even so, this seemed a bit extreme. He sat watching and listening carefully, and with a little shock realized exactly what was happening.

Why, you sly, subtle creature! he told the bishop. *You're doing it, aren't you? Yes . . . every time the discussion seems about to settle down, you stir it up again with a word or a look.* Beinion could hardly not react to a hint that his east-coast estates just might be imperiled, even if there was no proof behind the hint. And hot-blooded Diarmait, trying to argue with the bishop, was hardly going to be calmed by that gentle, pitying glance. And the others—oh, the bishop had been doing his research well. He knew exactly what would best touch each man's pride.

A masterful job, Gervinus, truly devious. And you're doing it so delicately that even Aedh doesn't see how he's being led.

But what was the point of all this—ah, of course. What better way to gain a foothold here than by causing dissention and stepping into the breach?

Clever human. But I'm not going to let you keep that foothold.

Ardagh cleared his throat suddenly, and had the satisfaction of seeing several of the men, who by now had forgotten all about him, start. The prince glanced about the crowded room, gaze passing lightly from this counsellor to the next. "Perhaps I'm not understanding this clearly." He kept his voice empty of all but apparently innocent interest, very much aware of Bishop Gervinus' suddenly alert stare. "It's autumn, nearly winter. Everyone is restless as so many stags, and as full of pent-up energy. And so, to let off that energy, you *want* to be at war."

"Of course we don't!" Fothad protested. "But we can't let enemies attack us."

"Ah, but which enemies? It would seem to me that there's only one active at the moment, though hardly likely to attack till spring. Everyone has told me how the Lochlannach, as I believe those sea-folk are named, have been raiding odd corners of Eriu."

Several men nodded.

"But the Cymraen folk have not."

"No," Aedh said, the barest hint of dry humor in his voice, as if he saw very clearly where Ardagh was going.

"So instead of attacking those who have attacked you," the prince continued delicately, looking around the room, "you wish to attack those who have not."

"We have to strike them before they strike us!" someone protested.

"Ah. Go to war against someone just in case he might someday happen to think of going to war against you. I see."

That roused some insulted rumblings. "There have always been attacks from Cymru!" a second man yelled, and another voice added, "Our lands have *never* been at peace!"

"Yet you and they are related."

"Distant kin," Fothad agreed.

"And the Lochlannach are not. I see. A family squabble. My, what fun." There were more disapproving growls at that, but the prince ignored them. "And while your two lands argue," he said, voice sharp, "the Lochlannach are free to strike as they will, knowing your two lands are too involved in squabbling to defend yourselves."

He sat back, face a cool mask, watching the excitement he'd created, thinking it all looked rather like a disturbed nest of ants.

Only Bishop Gervinus remained uninvolved. Eyes hard as winter ice, he sat regarding Ardagh with chill speculation. Ardagh stared right back, putting all his Sidhe will into the stare, and smiled inwardly to see the human flinch and look away.

"I find I must agree with the prince," Gervinus said unexpectedly. "It would seem to me, though I admit to being new to your situation, that attacking the people of Cymru would be a sinful thing. After all, are they not Christians? While these Lochlannach, these barbaric men of the North, most assuredly are not."

Oh, smoothly done, Gervinus! A neat shift of position. Now let us see what you do with it.

"Hardly," Aedh agreed with the bishop, and Gervinus gave him the thinnest of smiles.

"That is a fact of which you must be all too well aware, King Aedh. But I wonder if you realize just how painful the situation has become."

"Meaning?"

"I hesitate to mention this."

"Come, Bishop Gervinus, you may speak freely here."

"As the king wills. King Aedh, I fear it may be some of your own people who aid the raiders."

The room erupted into outraged shouts, even quiet Father Seadna adding his protests. As the storm raged, Ardagh sat back, studying the bishop, wondering.

King Aedh held up a hand for silence. "Bishop Gervinus," he began, voice tinged with barely controlled anger, "you are a man of the Church, not of the world, and so I cannot believe you quite realize what you've just said. You cannot possibly be accusing any of my people of the worst kind of treason."

Gervinus lowered his head as if overcome by reluctance. "Alas," he murmured, "I must. King Aedh, the Lochlannach warriors are pagans—and pagans, as you cannot deny, linger here in your own lands." He glanced pointedly up at Ardagh, then down again. "Surely you know, you all know, that they who have denied the Light have no love at all for those who have been shown the true path to salvation."

"But that's not how it is here!" Father Seadna burst out.

The look the bishop gave him was that of a lord to some insolent underling. "Indeed? In what way?"

"Och, I won't deny that I've seen the occasional offering: flowers left near a standing stone or ribbons tied over a well said to belong to the old gods. But the folk who leave such things are usually old, or women so desperate for children they'll try any superstition. Misguided folk, surely, but never evil."

Gervinus shook his head pityingly. "That is exactly what you, what we all, are meant to believe. What better way to attack Christendom than by lulling our suspicions—then striking at us through a godless alliance?"

"And yet," Ardagh cut in, "the Lochlannach, from all I've heard, do not discriminate pagans from Christians when they attack."

That earned him a grateful glance from the monk, and a new glare from the bishop, who snapped, "Their primary targets are monasteries!"

"Why, of course they are!" the prince said as though

humoring a not-too-bright child. "It's a matter not of religion but of sheer practicality. If you were a sea-raider who'd just made a perilous voyage, wouldn't you head straight for poorly defended prey? Monasteries are often set on rocky, isolated coasts and islands, am I not right? Sites that would be the first land the sea warriors would reach."

"Quite true," Father Seadna said sadly. "And every monastery has its treasury. It would be an easy thing for any Lochlannach raiders to learn this fact. And they would hardly care, followers of their dark gods that they are, that the gold they found in such a treasury was shaped into holy objects."

"Exactly!" Ardagh leaned forward, staring at the bishop. "Listen to the good monk. There isn't any need for any of your convoluted theories of conspiracy. What we have in the Lochlannach aren't the members of some diabolical plot, but *thieves,* nothing more than gold-hunting, seafaring *thieves.*" He straightened to look around the entire room, putting all his Sidhe will behind the stare. "And if you believe anything else, you risk tearing your land apart!"

This time the murmurs were all approving. Ardagh sat back again, watching the bishop glowering at him, and smiled.

This game is mine, Gervinus.

DISTURBANCES AND CONFRONTATIONS

CHAPTER 16

As the royal council filed out of the hall, Ardagh worked his way through the crowd until he was walking beside Bishop Gervinus. It was not where the prince would have chosen to be had things been different; this close to the bishop, he was once again very much aware of the sense of Darkness hovering over Gervinus.

Sorcerous Darkness? he thought with a burst of renewed frustration at not being able to learn the answer. *Or can I merely be sensing coldhearted, ruthless human ambition?*

Either way: "A word with you, if you would."

The bishop glanced at him, hostility in the cold eyes. "I assume you mean a private word."

"I think that might be best. If you would follow me?"

He led Gervinus to a quiet little triangle formed where the walls of two houses came together at an angle. "It is unlikely anyone can overhear us now."

"Speak."

"Bishop Gervinus, let us be frank. Neither of us is native to this land, so neither of us can claim anything more than an outsider's interest. But you will—I assume—eventually be returning to Rome, while I have chosen to make a home for myself here." *Even if the original choice was more or less made for me.*

Cold dislike still radiated from the bishop, but his face remained as emotionless as sharply cut stone. "Meaning?"

"Meaning," Ardagh said smoothly, "that I have a definite interest in seeing that the life of this land remains peaceful and happy."

"And I would not?"

"I'm not saying that." *Literally, if not figuratively.* "But since you are an outsider and so newly arrived you may not quite understand the situation here in Eriu."

"And you do."

"Up to a point, yes, and I must agree with Father Seadna."

"What, you?" There was a world of scorn in the simple words.

"I am not blind. I've been here long enough to see that these are an exuberant people, these folk of Eriu, quick to hate or love or laugh. Some of them may be pagan, indeed; I cannot speak for others' souls, nor am I worried about others' beliefs. But I think that there is little genuine evil in most of the folk, pagan or Christian."

Gervinus raised a skeptical eyebrow. "You are hardly in the position to judge good and evil."

Ardagh grinned without humor. "Because I am not of your faith? I assure you, I can still tell Light from Darkness. Not all," he added pointedly, "can."

"What are you trying to say, Prince Ardagh?"

That I suspect you of sorcery—no. Not yet. Nothing more on that subject, not till I can hold up the evidence in your face. "Why, nothing more than a simple statement of fact."

He met Gervinus' stare. And once again, it was the human who had to look away. "Do you seek to *lecture* me?" Gervinus snarled.

"Oh no. Just to comment that there's no point in rousing everyone about a danger that doesn't exist."

"The danger from Pagandom is very real!"

"Nonsense."

"Of course you would belittle it. If, indeed, that's all you're doing," the bishop added darkly. "I wonder, Prince Ardagh, just what role are you playing in all this?"

"I could ask the same thing about you. In fact, after this

council meeting, it seemed fairly obvious to me that you were deliberately trying to stir up dissention."

"That's ridiculous. What would be the point?"

"What, indeed? I speak no Latin, Bishop Gervinus, and I have never been to Rome. But Fothad mac Ailin is a learned man. He taught me one ancient Roman maxim—yes, from the pagan days—'Divide et impera.' That means, 'Divide and rule.' "

"I know what it means." The bishop's voice was very soft, very deadly. "Choose your words carefully, Prince Ardagh. Are you accusing me of harboring such ambition?"

"Should I?" the prince asked, the heart of innocence. "Is that what you mean to do?"

"Of course not! I am a man of God. I cannot and will not betray my vows."

"Whichever vows those might be."

"To the Church! To God!"

"Of course."

"Prince Ardagh, I am a high-ranking official of the Church. You, for all your beauty, are a pagan foreigner. If it comes down to a confrontation, which of us do you think is more likely to be believed?"

"Nicely put. But hardly conclusive."

"Enough clever words, Prince Ardagh. I will do as I will. Is that understood? I will not brook interference. Is *that* understood?"

"Why, Bishop Gervinus," Ardagh purred, "if you are truly doing the work of Light, there is no need at all for anyone's interference. And remember what I told you once before: it is very possible that someone will be watching to be sure that such remains the truth. Is *that* understood?"

If Bishop Gervinus had borne innate Power, Ardagh didn't doubt the human would have blasted him on the spot. Instead, the bishop muttered a furious, "I have finer things to do than banter words with an idler," and stalked away.

Ardagh stood watching. "Oh yes," the prince murmured in his native tongue, "I think we do, indeed, understand each other. And I shall, indeed, be watching."

This time, Cadwal thought with a bit of self-depreciating humor, he had actually managed to catch sight of the prince approaching him before the man could startle him. "Prince Ardagh. In mind of another duel?"

"With myself under better control, you mean?" Amusement glinted in the green eyes. "No, I'm not reading your mind. Yes, the thought was clear on your face."

"Ah."

"Don't be embarrassed. Or alarmed, for that matter. I will not lose control again. And no, I'm not looking for swordwork right now. Instead, I would like a lesson in knife-fighting."

Cadwal stared. "B-but that's not—it's not the sort of thing noble folk learn!"

"Which fact almost got me killed; I'm sure you've heard about my battle in the forest by now."

"You survived that nicely."

"Only because I was lucky enough to get in a telling blow, and that merely by chance. I don't wish to repeat the experience. Granted, it's unlikely that I'll find myself in a similar circumstance, but one never can tell what the future will bring. And so, will you teach me?"

Do you expect me to refuse a prince? The mercenary shrugged. "If that's what you want, why not? Besides, I . . . owe you something for turning the council away from attacking Cymru. No, I don't care why you did it, so don't give me those uncomfortable looks. It would not have been a good thing for me to have to choose between my people and the king who supports me. Och, well, enough of this. We'll go get ourselves a pair of wooden daggers—"

"Wood?"

"I am not," Cadwal told him, "going to risk myself to even blunted metal in the hands of a novice."

He saw the faintest color rush into the fair face. "Of course not. Let us, by all means, arm ourselves more suitably."

No need to rummage deeply in the armory. Cadwal quickly dug out the wooden practice daggers from a box near the door (noting once again how far from the entrance the prince stood) and tossed one to Prince Ardagh, satisfied to see the easy grace with which the man caught it, and caught it properly by the hilt.

"All right, now, if we use this corner of the practice field, away from most of the traffic, we shouldn't gather *too* big an audience. Ready? Good. First lesson: Knifework's not at all like handling a sword. You crouch like this, weight on the balls of your feet—ha, yes, you've got it right off."

"I learned in a hurry back in the forest," the prince reminded him.

"Mm. Right. Lucky you're a fast learner."

"Having someone trying to gut you is a wonderful incentive."

"Can't argue with that." But then Cadwal frowned. "Before we go any further, why aren't you protecting your arm?"

"Eh?"

"Your free arm! Didn't you wrap anything around it during the fight?"

"Ah, no."

"*Iesu Grist!* You're lucky you didn't get it cut to ribbons."

"I'm lucky I didn't get *me* cut to ribbons!"

"Well, we're going to try reducing that risk. Wrap the end of your *brat* around your arm like this. Right." Without warning, he lunged and the startled prince jumped back. Cadwal stopped short. "Is that what you're going to do? Dance with a foe?"

The green eyes blazed. "What am I supposed to do, then?"

"Block me, like this. We'll go through it slowly. As I come at you, *right,* block my knife arm with your free arm." He thought he saw a flicker of distaste cross the elegant face at the thought of such close, rough contact and grinned. "Told you it's not the sort of thing nobles learn. Up close and dirty fighting. You still want to continue?" At the prince's grim nod, Cadwal shrugged. "To work!"

Bishop Gervinus smiled a polite, politic smile, glancing subtly about the small "conversation house" to be certain he and the king really were alone. "It is very gracious of you to take this time to speak with me, King Aedh." *Even if you plainly hate the idea.*

"Could I be less than courteous to a guest?" Though his words were perfectly polite, not much warmth was in the king's voice. "Particularly such a guest? What would you discuss, Bishop Gervinus?"

"First, may I say what a charming land you rule?"

Aedh dipped his head politely. "I can hardly take credit for its beauty, of course. All I can do is try to keep everyone at peace. And though I do sponsor craftsmen and the like, it's the monasteries who do the work of spreading learning."

"And, of course, the faith."

"Of course. They've been sending out missionaries to Albion and other lands for centuries. But you'd know that. And I don't doubt you'll be making your own tour of the monasteries when you are done here."

"Indeed," Gervinus lied. *And you can't wait to see me out there and gone from Fremainn. You'll just have to be patient, Aedh.* The last thing he wanted to do was waste time with provincial abbots who would not wish their rigid little rule challenged.

"But this can hardly be what you wished to discuss," the king continued. "If you have some uncomfortable secret message from the Church, one you worried about sharing with my ministers, please have no fear about delivering it."

"Oh, no. It's nothing like that. King Aedh," Gervinus added in his smoothest voice, "as I already mentioned, I have not been sent to censure, but merely to observe, to see how matters go in Eriu."

"Observe as you will, good bishop. I doubt that you'll find anything outrageous."

"Oh, most aspects of life here do seem to be quite proper. Unfortunately, though, I've noticed one matter that I fear does need further investigation."

"Which is?"

Gervinus hesitated as though suddenly overcome by awkwardness. "This is most embarrassing."

"Come, speak."

"I know that your people hold the concept of hospitality as something sacred."

"We do," Aedh said flatly. "We have since the ancient days. What are you trying to say?"

"Oh dear. This *is* awkward."

"My Lord Bishop, I am afraid that I am a very busy man, and . . ."

"Of course. I will come to the point. King Aedh, what do you know about Prince Ardagh?"

The king frowned slightly. "That he is a prince, that he comes from Cathay, that he is in exile from his brother's reign to keep the peace of his land."

"Forgive me for doubting your word, but is there any proof of any of that?"

"Why—I—what else can he be?"

"I see," the bishop murmured. "No true proof, then."

Aedh's frown deepened. "Bishop Gervinus, I am well aware you dislike the idea of a non-Christian in our midst. But Prince Ardagh has . . . never given me any reason to regret his stay among us."

Gervinus heard that slightest of hesitations and pounced on it. "Even if he has not always followed your ways."

"What would you expect of the man? He *is* a foreigner, after all. Prince Ardagh has done a wondrous fine job of adapting once the laws were explained to him."

"Ah, then he has transgressed in the past."

"What he has or has not done is not a matter for discussion. The prince is not a criminal." Aedh's voice was now unmistakably cold. "Understand this: I owe Prince Ardagh my life. I would certainly have fallen to foes in an ambush if it hadn't been for him."

"Why, how fortunate that he happened to be there. And at just the right time, too."

"Very fortunate. Bishop Gervinus, I think we both know that this conversation is going nowhere."

Ah. Too overt. Gervinus feigned a contrite smile. "In that case, let us pretend that it never took place. My thanks again, and my sincere apologies for wasting your time."

But no apologies at all for allowing me the chance to plant the first small seeds of doubt in your mind.

❂   ❂   ❂

Prince Ardagh was proving to be almost an alarmingly fast learner, quick to strike, quick to react, graceful even in the most difficult of moves.

Isn't there anything he can't do? Cadwal wondered. Remembering his long, harsh days of mercenary schooling—the mud, the sweat, the aching muscles—he couldn't help but feel a little stab of envy, and drove his pupil harder and harder still.

And rather to his relief, Cadwal finally saw signs of weariness begin to show on the prince's face; God knew *he* was getting tired, but there was not a chance of him yielding before a novice gave up. Satisfied, the mercenary stepped back, letting his arms fall to his sides. "Enough."

He was panting, by God, and sweaty; so, he saw with a little shock of surprise, was the prince, though why he should be surprised that Prince Ardagh could get sweated up just like any other man . . . Cadwal shrugged. "A good day's work."

The prince saluted him with the wooden dagger. "A good teacher."

"Mmph. It helps to have an eager pupil. Don't go off thinking you know it all, though, not after only the one lesson."

"Of course not."

"You show promise, I'll tell you that. And with your skill with a sword, you'd make an excellent mercenary." *Iesu, man, why don't you just cut your own throat while you're at it?*

But to his relief, the prince only grinned. "I'll keep it in mind."

All at once he went very still, tense as a predator. Cadwal, turning to see what was alarming him, saw Bishop Gervinus strolling with Father Seadna. "Huh. You really don't like the man, do you?"

The prince never took his gaze from the bishop, but he retorted, "No more than do you."

"Och, well, it's not really my place to like or dislike."

That did earn him a quick, wry glance. "How politic."

"That's me. Politic. King Aedh pays the bills, and I'm politic. Now, go and get into dry clothes before your muscles start cramping up."

Bishop Gervinus smiled urbanely, a man seemingly totally at his ease, as he and Father Seadna walked together. *That's right, Prince Ardagh, watch me. Watch and worry.* "You need not look so alarmed, Father Seadna. I'm not about to make any official proclamations or condemnations. After all," he added, ever so delicately, "there are surely no reasons for any condemnations. No, I merely wished a chance to talk with you, away from the others."

"I see."

"I told you, there's no need for alarm. I merely wished to find out from a fellow cleric what life is truly like here and how you manage religious duties for your king."

The monk gave him an uneasy little sideways glance. "You understand that I cannot discuss matters King Aedh has told me in confidence."

"No, no, of course not! I would hardly expect you to violate your priestly vows. But what *is* it like to be a Churchman in this land?"

"What would you have me say? I doubt that religious life here is different from that practiced in any other God-loving land."

"Indeed? It seems to me, in my admittedly brief stay so far, that the people of Eriu are like no other."

"I'm afraid I don't understand what you wish to know."

Gervinus hesitated, as though uncertain how to broach an awkward subject, then shook his head. "I will be blunt. You know that those in Rome have begun to wonder if the folk of Eriu are genuinely still true to the faith."

"They are."

"What, no lost sheep? Not one straying member of the flock?"

"No more than is the norm."

"The norm!" the bishop said in genuine surprise.

"We *are* only human," Father Seadna reminded him gently. "We are all fallible at times, even you and I."

Could the monk possibly be as *good* a soul as he seemed? Pretending to be looking straight ahead, Gervinus glanced slyly sideways at Father Seadna, but instead of the naivete he expected to surprise after hearing such a docile statement, he saw a sharp intelligence in those quiet eyes. No matter how gentle, how moral, this Father Seadna might be, he, like his king, was not a fool.

Bah, how could he be a fool? He is the king's own priest, after all. "You must be a remarkably patient man."

Father Seadna frowned slightly, as if not at all sure where Gervinus was leading him. "With God's help, I try to be. And of course I don't have an overwhelming burden. There are other monks here in Fremainn to help minister to the flock."

"Of course," Gervinus agreed. "What I meant is that you show remarkable patience in dealing with those who have not yet accepted the Light."

Father Seadna stopped short, stung. "Of whom are we speaking? The folk of Eriu? Or can you mean Prince Ardagh?"

Gervinus spread his hands expressively. "He is most blatantly a pagan."

"I have spoken with him on religious matters on many occasions. While I haven't yet managed to convince him to convert, the prince has listened to me with interest and courtesy each time. And in the meantime," Father Seadna added, "he is as he is, a foreigner doing his best to make sense of what, for him, is a totally alien world. And he is doing a rather good job of that."

"No need to bristle! I have already assured you I am not condemning you. Even if," Gervinus added, seemingly casual but watching the monk for reaction, "you have not yet been totally successful in your mission." *There, now. That should nicely plant a seed or two of uncertainty with you, too.* "And as for Prince Ardagh adjusting to life here, so King Aedh has affirmed. So now," he said with a smile, "shall we stroll on?"

Still smiling slightly, Gervinus returned to his guest house. Arnulf was waiting, looking eagerly alert. The bishop glanced quickly around the room, hunting for signs that the acolyte had been searching for anything. Frustrating for Arnulf if he had; the precious grimoire was tucked into a fold of Gervinus' robes.

"Master?" Arnulf asked. "How did it go?"

"Well enough. An intriguing beginning." Neither King Aedh nor Father Seadna were going to be easy men to control, no doubt about that—but the royal counsellors were another matter. It had been almost ridiculously easy to have those hot-blooded idiots at each other's throats during that one meeting alone.

Or rather, he'd almost had them there. He would have, if it hadn't been for that princely intruder. "Prince Ardagh is likely to remain our biggest problem," the bishop said, as much to himself as to Arnulf. "And so he must be our first target. The man is just too clever, too quick, too alien—" and just possibly too knowledgeable—"to be left untouched."

"But he's a prince!" Arnulf protested. "How are we to be rid of him?"

"An excellent question."

"Well, prince or no," the acolyte began, "he's still only a man. Maybe a knife—"

"No, you idiot! The last thing we want to do is risk any unseemly involvement in violence. But the prince is a pagan, remember. There should be something useful to be done with that fact."

"Something, yes," Arnulf snapped, "but what?"

Gervinus glanced at the acolyte in disapproval. "Patience, boy. You must learn patience if ever you are to master the Art."

"The Art doesn't seem to be serving you too well," Arnulf muttered, then froze when he realized the bishop had overheard him. "I didn't mean—"

"A lesson for you, Arnulf. Sorcery is a tool. And like any other tool, it can sometimes fail. The only thing of which you can ever be truly sure is your will. Mine has never failed me, and never shall. Can you swear the same? Well?"

"No."

"Then don't be so swift to criticize. Now, leave me alone and—no, wait."

"Master?"

"I have a task for you, Arnulf. I wish you to wander about Fremainn. You can speak with common folk as I cannot; they are too wary of my rank."

"While I am nobody."

Gervinus ignored the petulant note in that. "Exactly. Listen. Learn. And if you hear anything against Prince Ardagh, anything at all, I wish you to note it down and report it to me exactly. Can you manage to do that, Arnulf?"

Gervinus saw resentment flash in the acolyte's eyes at his contemptuous tone, but of course Arnulf dared not argue. With a curt little nod that was just this side of being rude, the youngster left.

Time passed, spent by Gervinus in various tests of sorcerous discipline. His cool words to Arnulf notwithstanding, the investigatory little spells with which he'd been experimenting lately, carefully altered from those he had first sent out to study Prince Ardagh and then King Aedh, should not have failed. Even if there had been nothing spectacular to learn, he should have learned *something*.

Patience. Even as he had lectured Arnulf, patience was the thing. If a spell failed, it only meant there hadn't been anything overt for it to seize upon. There was still time to study, to experiment. He was doing well enough without sorcery, and—

The sudden return of his acolyte brought Gervinus back to the present with a start. "Well? What news?"

Arnulf shook his head. "Nothing. In the space of these few hours, I've been told that," he ticked the items off on his fingers, "Prince Ardagh is cold or gentle, well humored or arrogant, graceful as a dancer, exotically foreign, a wonderfully fine musician and a good storyteller. He also seems to like gathering stories from just about everyone as well."

"Stories."

Arnulf shrugged. "Fairy-tale things. In particular, he seems to be collecting tales of people opening gates into magical realms, has been for some time. He doesn't seem to be very happy with any of the ones he hears."

Gervinus waved that away. "What else? There must be something more than that the man likes fairy tales."

"Not really. Maybe not everybody likes the man, maybe he even makes some of them downright uneasy with those foreign ways and looks of his—particularly those men with pretty wives—but I couldn't find one person who had anything actively bad to say about him."

So, now. Either the prince was going out of his way to impress the common folk, or they were just too much in awe of his strangeness and beauty to be less than wary about discussing him. A pity. It was so much easier to start a flood of bad feeling by starting with the underclasses. "You can't have spoken to everyone. Go out there again, after dinner. Nightfall makes people more fearful, and more willing to mention their fears."

"But—"

"You will go," Gervinus told him, and turned his back on the acolyte.

But when Arnulf returned, late at night, it was with troubled eyes. "What?" the bishop asked.

"I . . . uh . . . have someone with me. Waiting outside to speak with you. A nobleman."

Gervinus refused to show even a hint of surprise. "About what?"

Arnulf shrugged. "He wouldn't say. He told me only that he really did need to speak with you. His eyes," the acolyte added judiciously, "looked haunted."

Haunted. Gervinus's lips tightened at the melodrama. This was probably nothing more than some idiot with sins to confess. Let him go to goodly Father Seadna. But no, he couldn't very well refuse the Church's mercy to anyone, believe in that mercy or no. "Very well. Send him in."

The man rushed in, young and florid, ignoring the wondering servants in the outer room, brushing past Arnulf so quickly the acolyte staggered, and fell to his knees before the bishop in melodramatic panic. Gervinus noticed with distaste the amulets that hung from about the man's neck and glinted from his fingers. *Superstitious fool.*

His terror was very real, though. "My lord, my lord, you must protect me!"

"Gently, my son," Gervinus purred, waving Arnulf out of the room. "First tell me who you are."

"Och, of course. I—I am Eirnin mac Flainn, cousin to the kings of Meath and courtier here at Fremainn."

"I see. And why have you come to me and not Father Seadna? What have you done that's so terrible, Eirnin mac Flainn?"

A hint of guilt flickered in the young man's eyes for an instant, but he insisted, "It's not what *I've* done, it—it's what's being done to me."

"And that is . . ?"

"I—I don't know how to—"

"Come now, I can hardly help you unless you tell me what troubles you. I promise you," Gervinus added with a great deal of forced patience, "no harm shall come to you."

But still Eirnin hesitated. Then, just before the bishop was about to call to Arnulf to have this idiot removed, the young man burst out, "It's the prince, Prince Ardagh."

Gervinus just barely kept from starting. "What of Prince Ardagh?"

"I know it sounds fantastic, but—he's a sorcerer, my lord, a foul, dark sorcerer, and he—he threatened to kill me by his magic. He hasn't done anything lately but—but *look* at me, as if he's playing with me. The way a cat plays with a mouse before it—before— Please, my lord, I don't dare go to Father Seadna; he's a good man, but he would never have the—the power to deal with sorcery."

Not by the slightest twitch of muscle did Gervinus reveal his thoughts. *Now, were I a true religious man, I would go down on my knees in praise. Here is* exactly *what I've been seeking.* "I see. Go on, my son. Tell me more, and I will do all that is within my power to help you. Tell me everything."

After Eirnin mac Flainn had gone on his way, wild with relief that the power of the Church was going to shield him from sorcery, Gervinus sat in thoughtful quiet. He had sworn Eirnin to silence about the entire issue, and the young idiot was just superstitious enough to keep that silence until the bishop chose for him to end it. But right now . . .

Arnulf poked a wary head into the room. "Master? Was that meeting helpful?"

The bishop snorted. "You tell me. You were almost certainly listening at the door." Ignoring Arnulf's too-indignant splutterings, Gervinus continued, "He is not the most useful of tools, discredited among his people as he is."

He paused, thinking back to what he knew of the *Lex Salica Karolina*, the law code of his Frankish ancestors that had recently been modernized by Charlemagne. It hardly applied to these uncivilized folk, but still . . . was a servant here considered free or slave?

Bah, it hardly mattered: the woman was a nobody either way. "Barbaric folk, these, to consider the rape of a common serving woman a crime at all, let alone one not solvable by simple payment of a fine, but there it is."

"But his story—"

Ah well, one did what one could with what one was given. "For what such a story from such a man is worth," the bishop mused aloud, "it was most certainly helpful."

"You don't *really* think the prince is a sorcerer, do you?"

Gervinus shook his head. "Just a very clever man. But what we believe isn't the issue; it's what the others believe. Now we must see that what is begun is nicely pushed on its way."

"But how—"

"By doing nothing."

"*What?*"

"Nothing for now. Boy, think before you try to interrupt. How long have we been here?"

The acolyte frowned in confusion. "Less than a month all told, but why—"

"Less than a month," Gervinus agreed. "Hardly long enough to become at home in this barbaric place. Certainly not long enough for people here to relax in my presence. Whereas they have plainly had more than sufficient time to quite accept Prince Ardagh. Do you see my point, Arnulf?"

"Well, yes. But we're from the Church! That has to count for something."

"That we are of Mother Church matters not at all at the moment. If we speak out against him now, we, the foreigners, the outsiders, with nothing more than the evidence from someone they consider a criminal, who here will believe us?"

"But—"

"No, Arnulf. For now we really can do nothing. Save wait. And be polite." Gervinus smiled thinly. "And in the process, most thoroughly ingratiate ourselves among these our far-flung . . . brethren of the Church."

That intense knifeplay session he'd had with Cadwal earlier in the day had burned off some of the frustration Ardagh had been feeling, but the basic fury remained. He was a Prince of the Sidhe, not some foolish human! Were things as they should be, he would not even need to *notice* such a creature as Gervinus. Or, if it pleased him to be aware of the bishop, he should have been able casually to humble the man with no more than a Word, a Gesture—bah, no, he would never have bothered sullying himself with such a task. He would have let a servant do the chore!

The prince let out his breath in a long sigh, head thrown back. Ae, this ranting was useless. Lovely though the image of Gervinus on his knees to him might be, it wasn't likely to happen, not in this Realm. And so—

He lowered his head, suddenly aware of being watched. "So now, Breasal."

The boy dipped his head politely. "I—I didn't mean to break into your thoughts."

"No matter. They weren't leading me anywhere. I assume you're interested in another lesson in *Tarien'taklal?*"

Breasal grinned. "I still can't pronounce it, but yes, if— if it pleases you."

Ardagh felt himself smile in spite of himself. At least this youngster wasn't trying to play any games of control over him! "Come, boy. Let's begin."

Breasal had come a fair way from his first lesson, though of course he never would be as graceful as a Sidhe child, and he did seem to be developing more stamina with each session, but Ardagh was still painfully aware of the boy's fragility. The prince watched carefully, and when Breasal seemed to be having difficulty breathing, called a halt. Predictably, the boy gasped out a protesting, "I'm not tired."

"Indeed," Ardagh said noncommittally. "Go change into warmer clothing before you take a chill."

But Breasal hesitated, hovering near him till the prince asked impatiently, "What?"

"I . . . uh . . ." The boy was plainly trying to find some way to thank him that wouldn't be insulting. "I know you like the old tales," Breasal said at last. "I remembered one you might not know, something my old nurse once told me."

Ardagh raised an eyebrow, hardly believing this boy could tell him anything of use. Foolish, though, to turn his back on even the faintest hope, so he told the boy, "Come in out of the chill," and led Breasal into his guest house. There the prince listened to yet another story of yet another human passing into a magical world. Nothing new, nothing useful—

Ardagh sat bolt upright in his chair. "Go back a bit. Repeat those words."

"What King Cormac said at the Hollow Hill? But those are just nonsense words!"

"Humor me."

Frowning slightly, Breasal repeated them.

"You're sure," Ardagh pressed. "Those are the exact words."

The boy eyed him uneasily. "Uh, yes. At least as exact as I remember them. They stuck in my mind, you see, since they rhyme so neatly." He shrugged. "Even if they don't make sense."

"Mm." Few pieces of that incantation held any Power at all. Most of them were, just as Breasal had said, pure nonsense. But when the nonsense was discarded, what was left just might be the remnant of a very real spell. If Ardagh combined it with the other bits of storied magic he'd gleaned and what little memory of Doorway spells was left to him . . .

Powers, oh Powers, could it be? Could it be enough to force open a Doorway home?

"Ah, Prince Ardagh?" Breasal asked nervously. "You did like the tale, then?"

Ardagh roused himself and smiled. "Oh yes. Believe me, Breasal mac Donnchadh, I liked it very much, indeed!"

THE SEASONS TURN

CHAPTER 17

Ardagh stood alone by night, ignoring the cold, dank winter and the sleeping fortress around him, his senses turned away from reality, focusing only on his will, his Power.

"As'raiathal," he whispered. "Open. *Lanta'ial na thanai*, I so call. *Saniathat li nathiel*, I say with all my will. In the name of the Directions I call, in the name of the Winds I call, in the name of Light and Dark I call. *As'raiaithal, as'raiathal . . .*"

He could see it, sense it. Heart pounding fiercely, Ardagh felt the shimmering form, felt the Doorway form, felt beyond it the first faint whisper of *home*—

It was gone, so suddenly that for a moment he was so stunned by grief he could not move. It was gone. Heedless of the chill rain beginning to fall, Ardagh fell to his knees, drained and hopeless, head in hands. Ae, no, no, it was useless. All his study, all his questioning of everyone in this keep, all the gathering of every tale they knew of magical Doorways—useless. The scrap of magic Breasal's tale had granted him had almost been enough.

Why did I heed Breasal's tale? Why did I dare to hope? There was magic, yes—but not enough, not quite enough. There's not enough Power in this whole forsaken Realm to break the spell of exile. I am trapped here, trapped forever!

The damp cold rising from the wet earth was beginning to seep into him, and at last Ardagh struggled back to his feet, swaying with exhaustion and shivering. This human land didn't even have a proper winter! Instead of the ermine-white snow and crystalline ice of the Sidhe realm, bright and pure in the radiant air, there seemed to be nothing here but this chill rain and eternally grey skies discouraging all but the hardiest of souls.

Ah, and the memories this sorry contrast of winters roused . . . the glittering, elegant royal Sidhe processions clad in flowing pale silks and paler fur, riding lightly through the snow on slender steeds whiter still than the snow around them, silver bells ringing sweetly from every ribbon woven through the horses' flowing manes—

No, Powers no, he would not think of this, he would not remember what was lost to him.

Not lost, curse it. Never lost. I will not despair.

Oh, easy to claim! Staggering with the weariness that could only be the magical backlash from a failed spell, Ardagh made his slow, painful way back to his guest house. He had one dizzy glimpse of the bed seeming to surge up towards him. And then he had fallen across it into deep, exhausted sleep.

Gervinus turned and twisted, seeing nothing on all sides, literally nothing, literally endless Emptiness. Emptiness all around him, pulling at him, telling him that this was the only truth, this endless nothingness into which he would be lost forever, no hope, no help, no escape, he would fall and fall forever and know he fell . . .

"Master? Master!"

Gervinus woke with a gasp, staring up in horror at—

Arnulf. Only Arnulf, and bright daylight behind him. "You were dreaming," the acolyte said, his face unreadable. "I, uh, thought I'd better wake you."

Idiot. And the idiot had seen him helpless and afraid. Gervinus stared coldly up at Arnulf. "I know I was dreaming. You did well to wake me. Now leave me."

"But—"

"Leave me!"

As Arnulf shut the door behind him, grumbling about

not having even been properly thanked, Gervinus sat up, rubbing his hands over his face. What a foul dream that had been. What a foul, foul dream—and it was made all the worse because he knew its cause. The urge to use sorcery without stop had been growing stronger with each day, with every time he even thought of casting a spell. Yet when he resisted the urge, refusing to be enslaved to anything, even this, the lack of sorcery pulled at his nerves, troubling his dreams. He had been resolutely denying himself the use of the grimoire lately, telling himself, truthfully enough, that there had been no real need for it. And so . . .

"Dreams," Gervinus muttered in self-contempt.

But then he realized his hand was creeping almost of its own accord for the grimoire, caressing its leather-bound surface. Gervinus angrily snatched his hand back, then paused. Even though right now he didn't need spells to help him insinuate himself into the High King's court, he didn't dare cut himself totally off from sorcery. One didn't stop practicing a weapon then expect to be proficient in its use.

So, now, Gervinus decided, he would experiment this day, cast the smallest of test spells. Such study needed to be done at any rate, particularly since those prior spells had failed, to be sure Eriu would permit them. And mild experiments would surely be enough to soothe his mind's craving. Surely.

Bah, of course they will.

The bishop got to his feet, this once refusing to call for servants, dressing himself. It wasn't until he was perfectly groomed and apparently absolutely calm that he called for Arnulf's return.

The acolyte entered warily. "Master?"

"I did appreciate your waking me from my dreams. But waking me could not be the only reason you entered here."

"Uh, no. I thought you'd want to know that the Cathayan prince has fallen ill."

Gervinus kept his face rigidly calm. "How so?"

"From what I've heard, his door was left half-open last night, and that's not like him; he's so careful of his privacy and all that he doesn't even have a body servant."

"I know that. Go on."

"Well, when servants did creep in to be sure he was all right, they found the prince so soundly asleep they couldn't wake him."

"No signs of injury or disease? None at all?" How bizarre! "It wasn't . . ."

"My doing?" That Arnulf had seen him helpless still rankled, and so Gervinus purred with sorcerous warning, "Now what do you think?" and watched the acolyte's sudden shudder. "You have delivered your message, boy," the bishop snapped. "Leave me."

After Arnulf had all but run out of the room, Gervinus sat in thoughtful silence for a time. So now, Prince Ardagh was ill. How very interesting. And surely there was something to be done to ensure that the prince never recover?

And here I thought I'd be working on nothing but mild experiments today!

Unlocking the grimoire, Gervinus began to read. Contrary to what the superstitious commons believed, there were few spells powerful enough to kill a man yet allow the sorcerer to go undetected. And all those lesser, nasty little wasting-away charms only worked when the victim was made aware of their presence. He had, in the interest of sorcerous research, tried a few against the prince, but they had been so mild they'd had no effect at all.

And I could hardly tell him, "I've bewitched you," or ask him why he'd been unaffected!

He continued to browse. The herbal spells were all quite intriguing, promising everything from madness to painful death for a foe—but, alas, it was unlikely that any of the suitable herbs would be available in the middle of winter.

Gervinus read on. The idea of saying the Mass for the Dead with Prince Ardagh's name inserted as the deceased amused him—but since the prince was hardly a member of the Church, such a spell would have absolutely no power over him. There must be something else. . . .

Ah, yes. Here was a nicely unpleasant little spell, involving trapping a strand of the victim's hair in a branch; since hair and self were psychically linked, the victim's mind would be dragged further and further from sanity as the tree grew around that hair.

Charming.

It really wasn't a very powerful spell for all its cunning, but put it together with the fact that Prince Ardagh was already ill, and it just might heighten the illness sufficiently. But the thing did require a lock of the prince's hair.

"So be it," Gervinus said aloud. Prince Ardagh, whether he wished it or not, was about to receive an ecclesiastical visit.

As the bishop had expected, the prince's guest house was crowded with royal physicians and servants, all of them looking both bewildered and worried. Also as he'd expected, they all moved out of his way, letting him approach the bedside.

He stood looking down for a moment, coldly admiring the elegant lines of the prince's sleeping face. *A shame to destroy such beauty, but that's the way of things.* The bishop let his hand rest on Prince Ardagh's head as if in benediction, and in the process managed to snag a few long black hairs in his fingers. With a quick, subtle jerk of his hand, he pulled them free. *You are mine,* he told the prince, and smiled.

Ardagh woke at the tug on his hair, instantly aware of the *feel* of Darkness that meant the bishop. It was Gervinus, surely, who'd just taken that sample, and the prince had to fight to keep from reacting. Judging from the number of humans he sensed all around, they must surely have thought he'd fallen mysteriously ill. The prince was *not* going to reveal that he had come so suddenly awake and have Gervinus claim a miracle! And he certainly couldn't tell everyone that what had struck him hadn't been disease but magical backlash.

In fact, I can't do anything at all but wait till they leave.

Wait he did with cool Sidhe patience, until the bishop was gone and a good many of the servants with him. At last Ardagh dared open his eyes and was engulfed, as he'd expected, in a storm of excitement from those who'd remained.

"I'm all right, truly," he tried to convince them. "Truly! Come, stand back. Give me room enough to at least sit up." Ae, dizzy! "How long was I asleep?"

"Two days," a respectful servant told him.

So! He'd been fortunate. Some backlashes killed outright. Others were strong enough to keep the magician asleep for a week or more—and in this Realm, with its lack of magical knowledge, so long a sleep would have meant death by starvation.

Again, it's nothing I can tell these folk.

"Ah, Prince Ardagh?" It was one of the royal physicians. "If we may?"

He sat politely still for a time while they checked pulse and heartbeat, then said, "Enough. I'm quite healthy. In fact," Ardagh added as his energy-starved body began complaining, "there's only one thing I truly need right now— and that's food."

Much to his relief, that sent most of the humans scurrying out of his house. The rest hovered around him as servants returned with a quickly assembled meal, all set to watch him eat until he waved them all away. In the midst of enthusiastically devouring his food in the sudden wonderful solitude, Ardagh paused, remembering:

Ah, Gervinus. It might have been an accident, that snatching of hair; the heavy rings the bishop wore might well have snagged a strand or two. And then again . . .

Pushing aside what was left of his hasty meal, the prince went in search of his ecclesiastical quarry. But before he'd taken a dozen steps, a new wave of weariness overcame him, not so much physical as psychic weakness. That heartbreaking failure to find the way home had drained most of his forest-won Power.

What of it? Ardagh scolded himself. *You haven't been turned into an invalid! You have just as much innate Power as when you first entered this Realm. You'll survive. And there will be time enough to return to the forest.*

Not just yet, though. Ardagh glared up at the heavy grey

skies. Regardless of what the humans thought, he seemed to be immune to their various illnesses—but that didn't mean he could survive a night exposed to the winter wilderness.

I'm not too happy at the thought of leaving myself helpless in trance with Gervinus about, either.

Ardagh started resolutely forward again, and found the bishop standing in a niche between two houses where he must have thought no one could see him, examining something small and dark, then busily stuffing it into his pouch.

My hair, Ardagh thought, stealing silently up behind him. "It won't work," the prince murmured, and smiled to see Gervinus start.

"Ah, Prince Ardagh." The bishop concealed his surprise nicely. "Should you really be up and about so soon?"

"It won't work," Ardagh repeated.

"What *are* you saying?"

"I felt you tug some hair from my head. I'm sorry to disappoint you, but you won't be able to do anything with it."

"Are you sure you're not feverish? Granted, I might have caught some of your hair on my ring when I said a benediction over you, but I assure you that was an accident."

"Fortunate. Because it is impossible to work spells over my people's hair." The prince smiled. "But of course you would have no reason to even think about such a matter. And a benediction would have been a very kind thing. If such had, indeed, been delivered. Good day, Bishop Gervinus."

As he returned to his guest house, Ardagh felt eyes upon him. Turning, he found young Prince Niall watching him solemnly. "Well?" Ardagh asked.

"Fainche was scared." The boy made it sound like an accusation.

The prince raised a surprised eyebrow. "What, for me?"

Niall nodded, then admitted gruffly, "I was, too, a little."

"I see." Ardagh bowed politely. "Thank you. But there was no reason to be afraid."

"I thought—uh, *Fainche* thought you weren't going to wake up."

"Ae no, Niall, I was in no danger from that. I was tired, that's all, very tired. Haven't you ever done anything that made you so weary you simply had to sleep? And sleep for a longer time than usual?"

Niall nodded warily. But he wasn't satisfied, that much was clear from the way he wasn't meeting the prince's gaze. "What is it?" Ardagh asked gently. "What truly worries you?"

"I saw Prince Breasal faint once," Niall said, barely audibly. "I thought he wasn't going to wake up again, either. And I heard the physicians talking to my mother once. They told her someday he—he might not wake."

"I see," Ardagh repeated helplessly, wondering what he could possibly say to set the boy's mind at ease. "Niall," he said at last, "Breasal mac Donnchadh is a sickly young man, you know that. I'm not sickly at all, nor in any danger ill health might cause. I promise you this. And you know I never lie."

That did it. Sudden relief flickered in the boy's eyes. "I'm glad," Niall murmured.

All at once clearly embarrassed by his own concern, the boy gave Ardagh a most formal bow, then hurried away, leaving the Sidhe staring after the human in genuine bewilderment. How astonishing! How very astonishing that the child should actually have been worrying about him! And did that mean that others cared about what happened to him, too?

I never will understand these people, but for once there was not the slightest trace of bitterness in the thought.

But days passed, and there was nothing for the bitterness to do but return. Winter, Ardagh thought, must surely be the slowest-paced of mortal seasons. And the most wearying. He could not have been feeling this lassitude for longer than his awakening from magic's backlash, but it felt as though he'd been carrying about this—this darkness of mind and spirit for all time. The brief, chill days, the leaden skies, the sodden earth, and the weariness, the endless weariness . . .

It will pass, Ardagh told himself, *surely it will pass. All I need do is wait, outlast the winter, return to the forest.*

But what good would that do? A brief restoration of

strength, but he would still be trapped here, trapped in an alien world, trapped—

No, curse it, no! He would not, could not, give in to the season. He could not let himself begin to doubt.

Ah well, the humans weren't managing these dark, dull, rain-swept days any better. King Aedh, left with little to do but oversee courtiers' petty squabbles or the occasional hunt for boar or wolf, fairly burned with the impatience of a clever man with no target for his cleverness. Fothad spent most of his time barricaded in his quarters, struggling with poem after poem, and Cadwal and his men were out each day, regardless of weather, practicing their skills with the desperation of highly trained men with nothing much to do. And then there was—

"Prince Ardagh."

He turned. "Lady Sorcha." She was so bundled in the folds of her heavy woolen *brat* that only the hint of a face was visible, but there was no mistaking those sharp eyes.

That sharp voice. "I thought you'd fallen asleep on your feet."

"Hardly. I was merely thinking."

"Chilly place for meditation." But a hint of understanding glinted in her eyes, and a hint of softness tempered her voice. "The winter gets to all of us. You aren't the first to be weighed down by the shortness of daylight."

"I wasn't—" But Sidhe truthfulness stopped the lie before it could be formed. "I was," he admitted.

Sorcha studied him warily. "You *are* recovered, aren't you? From that long, mysterious sleep?"

"Quite."

"And there's no other illness troubling you? No? Well then," she snapped with sudden force, "there's no reason for you to be moping about like a lonely hound!"

He glared. "If I'm a hound, lady, then you, most certainly, are a gadfly!"

That only provoked a quick grin. "Ha, he does still have emotion! I was beginning to wonder."

Ardagh, about to snap back at her, stopped in midbreath, frowning slightly. "Why are you doing this? Why help me?"

"Ah God, why, indeed? Maybe because I've seen this darkness claim others. Maybe," she added painfully, "because I remember poor Meallan. Granted, in his case it was the drink as like as not causing the depression, but . . . I've often wondered if . . . if that night he wandered out to die . . . if it hadn't been the inner darkness driving him to—"

"Sorcha," Ardagh said very gently, "I am not Meallan. Despair has been a close companion these days, I admit it, but I have not surrendered to it. Nor shall I."

"Huh."

"I shall not. But why *are* you doing this? Why me? There must be other folks suffering from the same malaise—"

"Other folks," she said shortly, "aren't in exile. They don't have to bear that extra burden."

"Cadwal—"

"Has his men's well-being to concern him. He doesn't have time to brood. Prince Ardagh," she added after an awkward moment, "this may sound hopelessly saintly, and a saint I most certainly am not, but . . . well . . . whenever the darkness seems the heaviest, remember that you can always talk to me. I can't promise you a soothing answer; I do tend to be, as you so gently put it, a gadfly. But I will listen."

"Thank you. I—"

But with a curt dip of the head, Sorcha walked away, leaving a very confused Ardagh behind her.

Now, what was that all about? Really about? Was she simply being kind? Or was there something more?

Such as what? This isn't some soft, simpering little girl! Besides, I—ae, what do I think of that gadfly-turned-human? I . . . don't know, Ardagh realized in astonishment. *I really don't know.*

Nonsense. She was human, only that. This stupid, endless winter was affecting him, nothing more. Ardagh determinedly turned his mind from thoughts of that sharp, clever face (that most intriguing face—no, that all too human face) and forced it instead to consider Gervinus.

Ah, yes, Gervinus! How stunned the bishop must have felt when he'd opened his pouch and found it empty! But then, what Ardagh had told him had been the literal truth. Spells could not be worked on Sidhe hair—not when a spark of Sidhe will had charred them to ash in a heartbeat.

But, disconcertingly, Gervinus had never showed the slightest sign that he'd noticed anything odd. In fact, Ardagh mused, in these days when everyone else was battling despair or simple boredom, the bishop had been the only one forever cheerful, without even the smallest hint of menace.

And as the season slowly turned toward the winter solstice—and, Ardagh learned, to one of these folk's most vital religious days, the celebration of their deity's birth—Gervinus continued to be disconcerting, to smile and be polite to everyone. He officiated at Mass and all the other rituals that were a part of human religion as though he truly were a holy man, saying smooth words to noble and commoner alike.

Clever man, clever man. Whether or not they like him, Ardagh thought, *they already want to trust him, by virtue of his rank. Bah, he almost has me believing he's undergone some sudden reformation.*

Almost.

As the season turned slowly to spring, Ardagh made sure he was everywhere Gervinus turned, made sure he was always urbane, always smiling. There was no reason for Gervinus to complain—and yet Ardagh was careful never to let the bishop go anywhere without his company, never let the bishop do any but the most innocent acts. He could feel the fury growing in Gervinus at this constant, gentle, almost friendly surveillance—but what could the human do? Complain that Ardagh was being too nicely polite? Protest his unfailing good manners?

Am I frustrating you, Gervinus? Have I discouraged you? I doubt that. Much more likely: have I turned you quite completely and irrevocably into my enemy? I rather hope so. It's so much more honest!

As he entered the council hall, Ardagh sensed King Aedh's tension as strongly as if it were something tangible. The king waited in silence till all were seated, then glanced about the room, his eyes fierce with pain. "I won't keep you waiting. Some of you might have seen the messenger arriving from the monastery of Saint Beinean. He brought me sorry news."

Father Seadna stiffened in alarm. "Not another Lochlannach raid?"

"Unfortunately, yes. A small one: only one ship, a quick attack and away. The monks were . . . relatively fortunate." Aedh's voice was rigidly controlled. "Only five dead, and only part of the treasury stolen."

Father Seadna instantly began murmuring prayers for the slain, his pain a very real thing, his voice all but drowned out by the militant shouting of the other counsellors. It was the shouting, Ardagh realized, of frustrated men. "There's no way to foretell where these raiders will land?" he asked over the turmoil.

Aedh shot him a savage glance. "How? They come out of the night like so many battlecrows, and are away again before even the swiftest of messengers can reach us. I have sent an emissary to the monastery, offering what aid I can. But by now there's little that can be done but help bury the dead."

The prince fell silent, stunned anew at how defenseless these folk could be: no magical barriers, no magical beacons, dependent for information only on how swiftly a horse could run.

King Aedh glanced around the room again, his smile bitterly ironic. "At least we now know one thing. The winter ice has melted, even in the northern lands. Welcome to springtime, everyone."

Gervinus had heard and disregarded the tale of the Lochlannach raid. The deaths of a few unfortunate monks were hardly important save to their fellows, nor was the theft of a few treasures meaningful. Time enough, he thought, returning to his guest house, to worry about actually stopping those pagan raiders when he was in control of the throne. Right now, they were more useful as they were, as was anything that undermined Aedh's credentials.

Sorcery, whispered his mind without warning, *sorcery would speed the process and*— No! He had managed all this winter without once resorting to the grimoire . . . surely those small experiments here and there hardly counted . . . of course not. He had resisted, and he would continue to resist!

But one special irritant remained in the way. "He's doing it on purpose," Gervinus muttered. "That cursed creature is *trying* to drive me mad. Watching me, following me, always there, always smiling so innocently—damn him!"

The watching Arnulf blinked in confusion. "Who, the prince?"

"Of course the prince, you idiot!"

"I thought we were going to get rid of him."

"We are!"

"Uh, how? You already ruled out violence, and you said that the testimony of someone like that whatever-his-name-is can't be of much use to—"

"His name is Eirnin mac Flainn. Now, hush. Let me think."

Ignoring the acolyte, Gervinus let his thoughts roam further and further from the present, hunting this plan and that. *Sorcery*, his mind whispered, *sorcery. Just the smallest, smallest of spells, just enough to steal control from one who could not resist* . . . "Yes," the bishop said so suddenly that Arnulf started. "Oh yes. Two goals gained in one: the saving of one royal life *and* the condemnation of another." He broke off, frowning at Arnulf. "Stop staring like that, boy. It makes you look stupid." *More stupid than you already are.* As the acolyte straightened guiltily and tried to look properly conspiratorial, Gervinus told him, "Tomorrow I wish you to go out among the folk yet again."

"But—"

"No, wait, hear me out. This time I don't want simple gossip. This time you are to find me someone of noble birth, someone who is weak of body or mind. Someone who would never be suspected. Most certainly not," the bishop added with a smile, "of treason most terrible."

THE ASSASSIN

CHAPTER 18

" 'Find me someone of noble birth,' " Arnulf muttered to himself, stalking out into the still chill spring air. " 'Find me someone who is weak of body or mind,' " he added, and snorted. Easy enough for the Master to command. But who was it who got stuck with the actual work? Not his High and Mightiness, that was sure!

I've risked my hope of salvation, maybe my very soul—for what? He keeps promising to teach me true magic, but what have I learned so far? Nothing!

Well, almost nothing. Arnulf admitted that he could light a candle with a muttered incantation (even if the process left him with a headache and flint-and-steel was easier), work a few other minor spells, and sometimes almost see far-off events appear in the Master's little bronze mirror.

Right. He gives me crumbs of magic, then sends me off to do whatever pleases him, as if I was nothing but a—a common errand boy!

But those crumbs *were* magic, just enough to tantalize, just enough to keep him loyal, hoping, silent.

Arnulf glanced about, wondering if anyone had seen him arguing with himself, and shuddered faintly. This was such a—a foreign place! Bad enough to have been trapped on that miserable excuse of a ship on that endless journey (his stomach lurched at the memory), but to end up *here*—Arnulf

218

thought with longing of the tranquil marble halls and gilded columns of Rome.

" 'Find me someone who is weak of body or mind.' "

How was he going to do that? All the folk here looked healthy as horses, and as far as he was concerned, they were *all* weak of wit.

All save one. That foreign prince, now, there was an eerie fellow, with his too-green eyes and his inhumanly beautiful face, like an angel off one of the churches back home— no, no, there was nothing angelic about the man. He was almost as uncanny as one of the Master's conjurings. Mm, yes. Maybe he really was as sorcerous as that idiot Ernan or Eirnin, or whatever his name was, insisted. Maybe—

"Good day."

Arnulf yelped, for a crazy moment sure the prince really *had* been conjured up. "P-prince Ardagh."

"And you would be . . . Arnulf, is it not? The acolyte to Bishop Gervinus?"

The green stare was so compelling that Arnulf could only nod and gasp out, "Yes."

"And of course you do your master's bidding."

"Y-yes."

To his horror, Arnulf realized that he was on the verge of volunteering something about that most forbidden of subjects, sorcery. He could feel the word forcing its way to his lips, no matter how hard he struggled. In another moment he was going to blurt out all the truth—

"Prince Ardagh. A word with you, if you please."

At the sound of that new voice, the prince turned away from Arnulf with a small sound of anger. With the weight of that green stare suddenly gone, the acolyte nearly crumpled in relief. It was the High King, but all Arnulf cared about was the fact that for the moment neither King Aedh nor Prince Ardagh were paying any attention to him. Before they could remember him, he scurried off. Right now, hunting up someone weak of body or mind seemed the most desirable task in the world.

Ardagh waited for King Aedh as he, in courtesy, must,

aware of his prey scuttling out of his grasp, hiding his frustration behind a mask of Sidhe calm.

Darkness take it, I almost had him. I almost had him confessing to his master's sorceries. Now the chance won't come again; the boy will almost certainly be warded when I next see him.

No help for it now. He could only hope the acolyte was off on some totally innocuous errand. "King Aedh. You would speak with me?"

"Just a word or two. I thought you might like to help me judge a new mare I'm thinking of purchasing. We can best watch her gaits from a distance."

"In other words," Ardagh said as the stocky dun mare was led across the practice field at a brisk trot by a panting handler, the mare snorting and prancing in the chilly air, "you wish us to exchange a few words in private."

Aedh chuckled. "You *are* learning our ways. And our ways are what we need to discuss."

"Are they? Which?"

"Look you, I'll admit in confidence—and deny in public I ever said it—that I don't like Bishop Gervinus any more than you do. It may be his Frankish background, it may be his own particular style, it may be just the way he's decided to test us, but yes, he is an unfriendly lot even when he's being at his most charming. But even if he was the coldest, harshest man in the world, you cannot continue to bait him like this."

The mare was fighting her handler, tossing her shaggy head, trying to break into a canter. Watching the struggle, Ardagh asked mildly, "Is that what you think I was doing?"

"And stop playing games with words! Bishop Gervinus is a man of the Church, and you cannot, you *must not* interfere with Church business."

"I'm not. There now, look, the mare has calmed a bit. She's a pretty thing, isn't she?"

"Och, man, listen to me! A bishop's business *is* Church business."

"Is it? Then it's the Church that is doing its best to cause dissention here."

"Don't be ridiculous."

Ardagh turned to study the king. "Surely I'm not the only one who's seen what Gervinus has been attempting in the council meetings."

Aedh met his steady gaze for a moment, then shook his head. "I don't know *what* he's doing. Testing us, perhaps, the way I said. Testing our wisdom or our faith."

"Testing your weaknesses."

"Oh, come! For what possible purpose?"

Ardagh shrugged slightly. "It seems uncomfortably obvious to me."

"Conquest, you mean?" The king laughed sharply. "Prince Ardagh, you don't understand our faith at all if you believe that."

"Perhaps the bishop doesn't quite understand it, either."

"Enough." Aedh's voice was suddenly totally without humor. "Do you have proof that he has stepped one step beyond propriety?"

Proof of propriety? I wish I had proof of his sorcery! "No."

"Then kindly drop the subject. What Bishop Gervinus is or is not is not the issue: he *is* an officer of the Church. I've already had my full share of fights with the monasteries. I cannot afford a feud with Rome as well." Aedh paused, glaring. "Do you understand what I'm saying? I have troubles enough as High King; I don't need you adding to them. And I am already risking a great deal by giving sanctuary to a non-Christian."

Very carefully, Ardagh asked, "Do you wish me gone from here?"

To his relief, the king never hesitated. "No, of course not. You've earned your place here from the day you saved my life, and you continue to earn it. I hold my breath every time I let you step in to solve court issues—I never will figure out your convoluted Cathayan logic—but somehow you do manage to solve them every time. And save me from some awkward situations."

The prince bowed sarcastically, knowing that Aedh meant he, the uninvolved foreigner, was free to act when the king could not and say what the king could not, and Aedh grinned without humor. "I didn't think I'd have to explain that." The king's voice softened slightly. "And I've seen the work you've been doing with Breasal mac Donnchadh."

Ardagh frowned, embarrassed. "I haven't been doing that for personal gain."

"I know that. Which makes the kindness speak out in your behalf all the more strongly. Besides," Aedh added with a reluctant little grin, "the women of Fremainn, including my little Fainche, would never forgive me if I threw you out."

A chuckle escaped Ardagh before he could stop it, and Aedh's quick grin flashed anew. "Let's be blunt, shall we? I don't really care what you do or don't believe, Prince Ardagh. I haven't got time for religious fanaticism. There's nothing of Evil about you, I could almost swear to that, and that's the main thing." He paused, glance suddenly speculative. "I . . . ah . . . don't suppose you could *pretend* to convert? Just for as long as the bishop is here? No? Och, well, that truthfulness of yours can be a nuisance at times. But you will behave yourself, won't you?"

"Indeed," Ardagh agreed after a moment. "As long as it does not interfere with honor or justice, I shall, as you put it, behave myself."

Aedh threw up his hands in relief. "That's all I can ask. Now, what *do* you think of the mare?"

Gervinus, hand resting lightly on his grimoire, glanced up as Arnulf entered. "Well? Did you find the one I seek?"

"I . . . think so. There's a boy here, one of the—the royal hostages, I think. His name's Breasal mac Something-or-Other, and there's nothing wrong with his mind; at least I don't think there is. But he looks like he's sickly enough to collapse at anything that's even the slightest bit too taxing."

"Ah, Breasal mac Donnchadh! Of course. I've seen the boy in the company of Prince Ardagh rather often." The bishop paused, considering, absently caressing the book's cover, then smiled. "How perfectly convenient. Come, Arnulf, you must have seen him at closer range than did I. How old would you say the boy is?"

Arnulf shrugged. "Who can say how old any of these barbarians are?"

Gervinus held up a hand in warning. "Open contempt is as much a weakness as open fear or impatience. Do not show it to me again. Is that understood?"

"Uh . . . yes."

"Very well. Now, once again, how old would you say the boy is?"

Arnulf's eyes glinted with fear and resentment, but the acolyte answered strongly enough, "Anywhere from maybe fifteen to eighteen. He's so scrawny it's difficult to tell."

"Perfect." The bishop got to his feet, slipping the grimoire back into the folds of his robes. "I think this Breasal mac Donnchadh is in dire need of spiritual counselling."

"Uh . . . Master? May I ask what this is about?"

Gervinus hesitated, studying Arnulf's face for any trace of potential treason. But nothing was to be read there now but utter confusion, and the bishop smiled slightly and said to himself, "Why not?"

Quickly he told the acolyte his plan, and saw dismay flash in the youngster's eyes.

"B-but—your pardon, Master, but that's not going to work. It can't!"

"Exactly. I don't *want* it to work."

"And Breasal—he won't—he can't—the strain is going to kill him!"

"Quite probably," Gervinus agreed without expression. "If so, that would be all the more useful to us." He paused, still studying the acolyte. "Well, Arnulf? Do you disapprove? Are you going to run screaming to the king about this?"

"And be seized as a madman?" the acolyte retorted. "Or maybe burned as a witch?"

Gervinus let the faintest of new smiles touch his lips. "So, now. You see the perils as well as the rewards of linking your fate with mine, don't you? Good. Come, Arnulf. We must see to young Breasal."

He followed Arnulf out to where a slender young man sat sadly by himself while other youngsters played some manner of boisterous game. "Ah yes," Gervinus breathed, taking in the too-pale skin, the too-thin face, "perfect," and moved in on his prey.

Fothad mac Ailin smiled ingenuously. "Ah, my Lord Odran! Just the man I wished to see."

Odran mac Daire, son of the Ui Neill sept and distant kin to Kings Aedh and Donnchadh both, determinedly kept his face to its usual cold lines. "Am I, now? About what, might I ask?"

"So brusque, my lord, and on such a fine day! Why, such a day makes a man long to be out and doing . . . oh, I don't know. Something heroic. But for now, will you not take the air with me, my lord?"

Odran frowned slightly. Fothad was quite capable of acting the dreamy-eyed poet interested only in the next rhyme, but only a fool forgot that he was also the High King's Chief Minister. "Of course."

As they walked, apparently at random, Fothad suddenly stopped short, pointing up to the sky. "Would you look at that? A fine eagle, that one, flying so freely. They say the eagle flies so high, its feathers are scorched by the sun and lives so long it is nearly immortal." Humor glinted in the poet's eyes. "They say. But the eagle flies on regardless of tales, not a thought in its head, surely, save where it shall next hunt. Never a worry for any of the things that trouble we poor humans. Such as a lust for power. For conspiracy."

That had been slipped into the man's chatter so smoothly Odran almost missed it. He stopped short. "Am I being accused? Of what?"

Fothad blinked innocently. "Why, of nothing! Surely we are merely discussing the customs of birds. Unless, of course, you'd wish to discuss something else. The receiving of messages from other, lesser kings, perhaps."

"I don't—"

"Of course you don't. For receiving such messages without the High King's knowledge would be treason." Fothad dropped a parchment into Odran's hands. "Good day to you, my lord."

Alone in his chambers, Odran mac Daire strolled casually about, seemingly at his ease, checking corners and doorways, any place a spy might be hidden to watch or overhear. Only then did he unroll the parchment Fothad had given him, noting without surprise that the seal had already been broken; the Chief Minister had as good as told him the message had been read. Inside, Odran found an innocent enough message, friendly clan-greetings that were just detailed enough not to look suspiciously innocuous.

Derval of Clonach, he thought. *It must be she. Donnchadh would never be so cunning.*

Cunning, indeed. There between the lines, for those who knew the code, was a clear enough message. The man smiled without humor, wondering if Donnchadh knew what his wife was about—or that she had already been in secret communication with Odran before this.

With me, and with who knows how many other discontented Ui Neill folk? He had some men loyal to him even now when he was an enforced guest of the High King, but even if he had been free to call them to him, there were hardly enough of them to accomplish anything as final as a dethronement. Each discontented lord could say the same. What it all came down to if any of them were to succeed was unity; strength of arms and unity. *We are all after the same thing, my sly Derval, and so you would try to unite us. Well enough. But only one can sit the High King's throne. And which of us that shall be—there we differ, dear Derval. There we really do differ.*

" . . . and so," King Aedh continued to his wife and Ardagh as they strolled towards the dining hall in the fading red light of late afternoon, "the ambassador turned about as red as that cloak and said—

"Why now, Breasal, where are you headed?"

The boy was wandering towards them, face set in a grim mask, eyes wide and staring. Almost, Ardagh thought uneasily, as though he was fighting some silent battle with himself—or just possibly with another. Sorcery?

Even as the prince was about to voice his growing alarm, Eithne asked, "Breasal, what are you—"

With a cry of anguish, the boy drew a knife and lunged at Aedh. Ardagh sprang forward with Sidhe speed, catching Breasal's thin wrist in a grip firm enough to send the knife clattering to the ground.

"No," Breasal gasped, fighting him weakly, "you can't— I must—don't want to—must—I—no, no, I won't . . ."

The boy's eyes rolled up in his head, and he followed the knife to the ground. Ardagh dropped to his knees at Breasal's side, the *feel* of the boy's laboring heart pulling at him. Blocking the shouting and commotion from his mind, the prince concentrated only on willing a more regular rhythm into Breasal's heart, on willing life to stay in the weakened body.

Suddenly he sensed Darkness looming over him. Ardagh glanced quickly up, to find himself facing Bishop Gervinus, surprising a look of cold triumph in the bishop's eyes. Now, what . . ?

But Ardagh didn't dare let himself be distracted from the boy he was trying to save. Shutting the bishop from his thoughts with Sidhe thoroughness, he turned all his attention back to Breasal, *feeling* the weakened heart gradually slow to a bearable rhythm under the force of his will.

But will it stay this way? I'm not sure.

Still, he wasn't a healer; there wasn't anything more he could do, even if he had the full use of Sidhe magic. He could only hope that—

Surprisingly, Eithne was suddenly at his side, even more surprisingly, she was . . . sniffing the boy's face, like some hound seeking an elusive scent. Catching Ardagh's puzzled glance, she shook her head slightly, then called out to uneasy servants, "Take Breasal to his bed. Keep him quiet and warm. Go!"

As Ardagh scrambled back to his feet, watching the boy being carried away in wary arms, Eithne following closely, he became aware for the first time of the storm of worry surrounding the king. Ha, and listen to Gervinus, adding to the noise as if he really cared what happened to the man.

And doesn't he? Ardagh wondered. *Isn't it Aedh he seeks to rule?*

"Yes, yes, I'm all right," Aedh was insisting, waving everyone back. "The blade didn't even touch me. I'm all right, I tell you! You don't have to say any prayers for me, Bishop Gervinus. Save them for the . . ." His voice wavered. "For the would-be assassin."

"The would-be assassin," Gervinus echoed, his voice ringing out with sudden evangelical fervor, "was surely *not* that poor boy."

"Oh come, we all saw—"

"Your pardon, King Aedh, but you saw only what you were intended to see." Gervinus glanced about as though suddenly overcome by caution. "I don't think the rest of what I need to say is suitable for all ears. But speak I must."

Aedh hesitated a moment, then snapped out, "So be it. Come." His sweep of the hand included Ardagh, Fothad and several of the ministers. "We will discuss this in private."

Ardagh watched King Aedh gaze sharply about the audience hall at those whom he had ordered here, wondering at the man's complete self-possession. Save for the anger below the surface, Aedh looked totally unruffled, as in control of his emotions as any Sidhe.

"Be seated, all of you," the king ordered. "Now, Bishop Gervinus, you may speak freely."

Gervinus' glance flicked to Ardagh, then away. "That does not make what I must say any easier. King Aedh, you cannot believe that poor boy plotted on his own to slay you. He has neither a reason nor the strength of body to commit such a crime."

"Who do you accuse?" Aedh's voice was ice.

"God forgive me for what I am about to say, but justice must be done. And so I can accuse none other than that man!"

His hand stabbed straight at Ardagh. Hit by a hot wave of shock and fury, the prince only just fought down the urge to lunge for the bishop's throat. Instead, raising his voice over the sudden uproar, he said, "Now that is ridiculous!"

"Is it? King Aedh, I hereby state that this man who calls himself Prince Ardagh, who claims to come from far-off Cathay, who has eaten of your food and partaken of your hospitality—I say this man is nothing but the worst, foulest of traitors!"

"Words come cheaply." Using every bit of Sidhe self-control, Ardagh managed to keep his voice cold and level and deadly, his face from showing anything of the fury racing through him. "Now let us hear some proof."

"Why, even as I've said, it is impossible to accept that the boy could have willingly, sanely, attacked the king who had, with all Christian charity, given him a home."

"Agreed," Aedh growled. " 'Sanely.' The boy who attacked me was hardly that."

"No, he was not," Ardagh cut in, "because someone had most foully overcome his will!"

Gervinus whirled. "You accuse yourself out of your own mouth!" Turning hastily back to the king, he continued, "Have we not all heard this man's smooth words? Have we not all been charmed by them? Beguiled by them?"

"Your pardon, Bishop Gervinus," Fothad interrupted, "but where is your point?"

"My point is simply this: If grown men cannot resist his charm, how, then, could an innocent boy be expected to resist?"

"What's this?" Ardagh asked incredulously. "Are you accusing me of *seducing* him?" If the man claimed he had abused a child, Gervinus was dead, bishop or no.

Something of that threat must have been clear in the prince's voice and eyes. "Of seducing him to treason," Gervinus corrected smoothly. "Were not the two of you often alone together?"

"I was teaching him ways of self-defense!"

"What, such a sickly lad? All here could swear that he was unable to so much as wield a sword—"

"There are other ways than brute force to fight. As we both know quite well. Go on, Bishop Gervinus. I am waiting with fascination to hear what monstrous deeds I've worked."

"Why, what can I say? While you two were alone, with none to overhear—who knows what words might have passed between you?"

"Oh, clever! 'Might have'—who can argue against something so vague?"

"Vague, indeed," Aedh said. "Bishop Gervinus, if you have no better proof than this . . ."

The bishop sighed. "Your pardon, King Aedh, but I never would make such a charge without proof. I hated to bring this into the discussion, since the man in question has been discredited, but Eirnin mac Flainn came to me in terror the other night. I break no confidences when I tell you the reason for his terror: sorcery, worked by the man who sits here before you."

"Eirnin!" Ardagh exploded. "Is *that* your prize witness? What, did he claim I bewitched him? Worked dark magic on him? Ha! You all saw the 'magic' I worked on him in the court of law—mere trickery, nothing more."

"It was not trickery that had him in such a panic," Gervinus countered. "Nor was it trickery that so worked on a sickly boy's mind he was turned to an assassin. What could have done such a thing *but* sorcery?"

A new storm of excitement burst out. But a woman's peal of scornful laughter cut through the shouting.

"Eithne!" Aedh exclaimed as she came striding into the hall, chestnut hair and blue cloak streaming out behind her. "This is not fit!"

"Forgive me, husband. I would never dream of intruding on men's affairs. But I could not stand aside and watch harm be worked against a guest. Sorcery! Your pardon, My Lord Bishop, but surely you *cannot* expect us to believe such nonsense. It would make just as much sense to accuse me of being a—a pagan witch!"

Oh, cleverly played, Eithne! Ardagh thought. *The truth makes a wonderful weapon.*

Ardagh saw Gervinus' startled stare shoot from him to Eithne to Aedh as the latter let out a humorless bark of a laugh. "This has gone far enough," the king said. "My Lord Bishop, Eirnin mac Flainn can hardly be accepted as a credible witness, not after Prince Ardagh helped us prove him guilty of rape. And to accuse the prince of something as outrageous as sorcery—as my wife says, as soon accuse her of the same!"

"But—the boy!" Gervinus protested. "He had no conceivable reason to attack, not without outside provocation."

"Which," Eithne said firmly, "he had. And there was nothing of treason about it! My lords, Breasal mac Donnchadh often has need of strengthening potions. Some of them contain such herbs as wolfsbane or hellebore, herbs powerful enough to warrant that doses be measured with care. Think of yourselves as boys his age. Think of his pride, his impatience with his body's flagging energy."

"He took too large a dose," Aedh breathed. "Of course."

Eithne nodded. "When he collapsed, the scent of wolfsbane was strong on his breath. A dose strong enough to be scented would easily have been strong enough to distort his senses to the point where he might see enemies where there were none." She held up her hands. "No sorcery was involved, my lords, no dark plot. There was nothing here more terrible than a boy's foolishness. Your pardon, my lord bishop, but now you see why I could not keep silent."

"Indeed!" Such horror was on the bishop's face that Ardagh could almost believe it real. "I can only thank Our Lord that you had the courage to speak out, good woman." The gaze he turned to King Aedh was heavy with remorse. "I know not how I can possibly make amends for such a wrongful charge. The only excuse I can possibly offer in my behalf is that my fear for your safety overcame all common sense. I let myself be swayed by the prince's foreign looks and mysterious ways."

"It's not my pardon you should be asking."

"True, quite true." Gervinus turned to Ardagh, his face, now that only the prince could see it, a mask, his eyes like stone. His voice, though, was a model of humility. "I have most gravely wronged you, Prince Ardagh. But Our Lord did preach forgiveness for one's foes. Can you find it within your heart to forgive me?"

Damn you. What can I possibly answer to that? I will not lie, most certainly not for your sake. Yet if I tell the truth and refuse you, I become an enemy of your faith—and leave the seeds of doubt still in everyone's minds.

"What is done, is done," Ardagh said at last, and let the humans make of that what they would. But as they left the audience hall, the prince murmured to Eithne, "There was no scent of medicine on Breasal's breath."

"I know that," she whispered back. "I couldn't think of anything else to say. It *was* sorcery?"

"Sorcery. Nothing provable." Even if Breasal recovered fully, it was doubtful his mind would ever be clear on what had happened to him. And obviously neither Ardagh nor Eithne could accuse the bishop, not without admitting to and proving the existence of their own Power.

And so, Ardagh added to himself, *we are left in a worse position than before.* Glancing back over his shoulder, he nearly choked. *Ae, look at Gervinus!* The man was virtually abasing himself before Aedh. Yes, and look at how Aedh and the others were smiling and offering him sympathetic words, almost as though *he'd* been the one falsely accused!

Humility, Ardagh thought. Proper Christian humility, as Father Seadna would put it. And through apparent humility, Bishop Gervinus had just endeared himself to these Christian folk. The prince remembered Gervinus' scornful warning: "I am a high-ranking official of the Church. You are a pagan foreigner. If it comes to a confrontation, which of us do you think is more likely to be believed?"

Which, indeed? Curse him, he's won this encounter. Now he's free to work whatever harm he will. And if I act against him without proof even a lump of earth could see—he, the good man of the Church—why, then I am the villain.

Powers, now we will never be rid of him.

CHALLENGES
AND RESCUES

CHAPTER 19

She was with him again, his Gwen, his sweet Gwenith, laughing as she walked beside him. No fine lady, she, but lithe and tanned and graceful, her hair bleached nearly white by the summer sun, her skin turned to rich dark gold, her eyes in that strong, tanned face blue as the cloudless sky. She was his and he was hers, and even if neither of them were the stock figures out of the barddi's tales, it never mattered. They were together, they were together, and nothing more mattered in all the world. . . .

Cadwal woke with a start, calling out "Gwenith," stunned to find himself alone in the darkness. Alone . . . ah dear God, yes, alone here in a foreign land surrounded by foreigners, and Gwenith was gone, never more his, never more in all this world his.

He swore under his breath. It was over ten years since . . . since his exile. The old pain had no right to revive itself after so long, sneaking up on him in his sleep like this, reminding him—

Pw, his face was wet. Fortunate that his rank as leader of the High King's mercenaries entitled him to these small private chambers in the barracks and so no one had heard his shout; ridiculous for his men to catch him weeping at

232

his age, mourning for what couldn't be like some fool of a grieving boy.

But the echo of that grief clung with him no matter how fiercely he mocked himself, and at last Cadwal surrendered to the weight of it. Maybe a breath of clean night air would clear his mind and lighten his soul a touch. Dressing more by touch than sight, not wanting to risk waking anyone by lighting a candle, the mercenary stole out into the night.

Och, chill out here, and damp. The hour wasn't very late; the moon, when the shifting clouds let him see it, was still almost directly overhead. Odd effect, those sudden cold rays of silver light come beaming down without warning, like something a magician might conjure.

Cadwal froze, for a wild moment sure he really was seeing a conjuration—no. The eerie figure suddenly revealed by the blaze of moonlight was no one more alarming than Prince Ardagh, practicing the moves of knife fighting by himself with silent vehemence. Cadwal watched for a while, appreciating the man's quick grace: if it came to a fight, he decided with professional interest, the prince would probably be able to make up in swiftness what he lacked in down-and-dirty experience.

But there was a fierce edge to the way the prince was practicing, as if this was a man brimful of angry frustration, and letting out that frustration in the only safe way he could.

Sooner or later, though, he was going to realize he was being watched. Rather than being caught spying, Cadwal stepped boldly out of hiding. "Keep the knife a little lower when you follow through."

The prince froze, his face gone suddenly very cold and still, his eyes so chill and flat a green in the uncertain moonlight that a little shiver raced through Cadwal. Inhuman . . .

But in the next moment, the frozen pose melted into life, and Cadwal thought with a touch of relief, *Not inhuman. Just a man who's embarrassed at having been caught off-guard like this—and one, I think, who's feeling a bit of despair under the embarrassment.* "We're both having a bad night, aren't we?" the mercenary asked softly, and wasn't really surprised to see the prince nod slightly in agreement. "Not a good night to be out, either," Cadwal continued, making conversation, not sure how to end this. "Too damp and chilly. A better time for being inside somewhere, maybe sharing a bottle."

He'd only half meant it as an invitation, sure he would be refused: a prince and a mercenary drink together? But then he was struck utterly still with astonishment, for Prince Ardagh said thoughtfully, "I think that might be a wise idea."

"Oh . . . uh . . . you sure?" *Come on, man, you sound like an idiot!* "I mean, I have a couple of bottles all right, but they're in my rooms. Not exactly a regal setting, you understand. Royal kitchen or dining hall aren't going to be open this time of night."

The prince shrugged. "Your rooms will do."

He's as lonely as me, Cadwal realized with a new shock, *as lonely—and as reluctant to admit it.*

Much to his relief, his chambers were clean. But of course they were, Cadwal railed at himself, they always were. He insisted his men—and he—keep their quarters as spotless and well tended as their weapons. A mercenary had little enough, after all, save his personal standards, and the minute he started to let those standards slip, despair had a chance to destroy him.

As it tried to get me this night.

"Don't have much in the way of furniture, you see, but that's the most comfortable chair." There were only the two, and the one plain table in this outer room. Cadwal, rummaging in a supply chest and pulling out two earthenware bottles, glanced back over his shoulder to see the prince carefully seating himself, looking incredibly elegant and exotic against the simple setting. "You . . . sure you want to do this?" the mercenary asked.

"Are you planning to poison me?"

"Hell no—uh, that is, I mean I—"

"I was joking," Prince Ardagh said gently.

"Sure! I knew that." Dammit, the man had him babbling like an idiot. Yes, this was a prince, but he sweat just like anyone else and got tired just like anyone else, and presumably enjoyed a drink as much as the next man. *And stop dithering and give him that drink!* "Be careful with this," Cadwal warned, filling an earthenware cup (trying to be casual about the fact it wasn't fancier glass or metal) and passing it over.

Prince Ardagh eyed the golden liquid warily. "Mead?"

"Sort of. Homebrew." He watched, holding his breath, as the prince took a wary sip. One slanted brow shot up, but all Prince Ardagh said after a moment was, "Interesting."

Cadwal chuckled. "Strong, too, a lot stronger than what they serve at court, so like I say, be careful." He filled his own cup and took a good swallow, feeling the hot gold burning its welcome way down, taking away some of the inner chill. "I don't usually drink by myself, if that's what you're thinking. Drunken mercenaries don't last very long. I keep this here for . . . well, for emergencies."

"Such as this," the prince murmured, and sipped his mead; he even, Cadwal noted, did *that* gracefully.

"Right. Like this." Cadwal swallowed again, then hazarded, "Heard about what happened today. Between you and the bishop, I mean."

"Have you?"

"You surprised? I should think a prince would be used to everyone at court knowing his business."

"That's why I don't . . . why I didn't . . . live at court."

Cadwal saw the sudden pain shadowing the green gaze and changed the subject hastily. "Look, man, I don't think you're a sorcerer, and I don't blame you for being mad as hell at the accusation. But . . ." He shrugged. "Can't blame the bishop for being a bishop. Hunting out evil and all that."

"Is that what he's doing?"

Another dangerous subject. Cadwal frantically changed it again. "You've got the basic knife-fighting moves down right. Keep practicing them, of course, and we'll go over some more advanced ones tomorrow." That sounded alarmingly like a command, and he amended quickly, "If you'd like."

"Yes." The prince sipped again. "I still am not sure which skills I might need in this land."

"Ha! I've been here ten years now, and *I'm* still not sure." Cadwal reached out to refill the prince's goblet, then refilled his own as well. "Not easy adjusting, is it?"

"No." Prince Ardagh made a great deal of brushing his long black hair back from his face with a hand, then added very softly, "You never do quite stop longing for home, do you?"

Cadwal let out his breath in a slow sigh. "No," he admitted, and took a new drink. "No, you don't. Ah hell, let's not get maudlin! Too easy to let self-pity drag you down."

"I've noticed."

"Mm. You can't be used to this sort of thing, drinking like a commoner, I mean."

"Hardly." A hint of amusement touched the prince's voice.

"Huh. Should take you to a tavern sometime. Show you how to really—" He broke off, feeling his face redden. "*Iesu.* I keep putting my foot in it, don't I?"

"Because I am a prince? Right now I am weary of worrying about titles." Prince Ardagh leaned forward, face grave but eyes amused. "Tell me, how does one drink properly in a tavern?"

Cadwal chuckled in spite of himself. "Depends on what you're looking for."

"Eh?"

"Mercenaries, no matter what folks say about us, don't go hunting trouble: Our only source of livelihood's our fighting skills, after all, and we can't afford to risk them unless we get paid. That means we avoid taverns where the place is old but the furniture's too new—means they have to keep replacing it thanks to the customers—or where there are a lot of stupid young hot-bloods just looking to start something."

"Sensible. And once you've found your tavern?"

"Then the first thing you do, you make sure the drink doesn't have something more or less than you paid for, if you get my meaning. The same goes for the . . . ah . . . the women who serve it." Damn, he was reddening again! Cadwal added, "Got to pace yourself. Relax."

"Easy to relax with this." The prince held up his cup in wry admiration. "Most pleasantly soothing after the initial shock, isn't it?"

"Sure is."

"I think I would like to visit a hu—a tavern sometime."

Cadwal could almost have sworn the prince had been about to say "a human tavern." Och, impossible; the mead was starting to confuse his ears or Prince Ardagh's mouth. "No, you wouldn't," the mercenary said. "They're dark, smelly places. Not romantic as the bards make them out to be, not at all."

"I see. This is much more tranquil. And," the prince added, saluting Cadwal, "cleaner."

They went on making small talk, talk that grew increasingly less wary as time went by and the level in the bottle lowered. They finished that one, by mutual agreement went on to the second. And somewhere along the way, Cadwal realized they'd reached the point of the prince asking him the forbidden question: how he'd become a mercenary. But such genuine concern seemed to be in Ardagh's voice by now that Cadwal found himself saying: "I loved. Loved a woman named Gwenith. Ahh, yes . . ."

Seeing her in his memory, the mercenary added softly, "We were happy, like two youngsters in the first flush of life, so happy . . ." He started to shake his head, changed his mind when his senses swam, and refilled his cup instead. "Now I'm the one getting maudlin."

"If you would rather not—"

"Look you, what happened was a lord, a *brynthi sgum* of a lord. I worked for him, I'd sworn fealty to him. He wanted my Gwenith. She didn't want him." Cadwal shrugged. "Goes against all our laws, man taking a woman who doesn't want him. But he was a lord, as I say. Thought he could do anything. He sent me away on some stupid errand, and while I was away . . . She cut him, my Gwenith, cut him in self-defense. And . . . well . . . she got the *bastart* right where a man least wants to get cut."

"Ah. Good for her."

"No! Not good! Not at all! You see, he lived. He had her condemned as—as a witch. And he . . . she . . . I got there one hour too late, one little, little hour too late."

He could not go on. Cadwal drank deeply, fighting back

memory with all his might. If Ardagh said one word of pity, he would shatter, he knew, shatter like glass. But the prince said nothing, only sat where he was, his very stillness somehow more soothing than any easy words of comfort. And after a time Cadwal was able to finish, "I went after him, of course. Killed him. Killed my liege lord. And that's why I'm here."

"What you did is not a crime, not to my people."

"Huh."

The slanted green eyes were very bright. "Listen to me. He had already forfeited his right to your oath by his actions. And what he did to an innocent woman—in my Realm such a man would most legally have been condemned to death."

"Fine, but we're not in your Realm, are we?"

He saw Ardagh wince slightly. "No. We are not."

"Och, well," Cadwal blustered, sorry for himself, sorry for his drinking partner as well, "the past is just that. Look you, there's little enough left in this bottle. What d'you say we put the poor thing out of its misery? Give it an honorable funeral and bury our memories with it?"

The prince saluted him with his empty cup. "An excellent idea, good Cadwal. An excellent idea, indeed."

There were times, Sorcha ni Fothad thought, when it was most annoying to be an early riser. Particularly now, when the morning was so overcast it was difficult to tell whether or not it was no longer night. Or at least not *quite* night.

At any rate, like it or hate it, she was most disgustingly and thoroughly wide awake, and likely to stay that way, and there wasn't much else to do at this ridiculous hour but dress and go for a quiet walk outside. Although propriety nagged that she should really have a woman in attendance, it was safe enough here for a noblewoman alone; no one would so much as raise a finger against her, not within the walls of Fremainn.

Clutching her cloak about her against the damp, Sorcha stood leaning on the wooden balustrade rimming the ramparts, looking out over the earthen rings of the fortification to where the forest loomed as a dark gray-green mass in the dim light.

"A gloomy view," said a voice beside her, and Sorcha started, "but not unattractive in its solemn way."

"Prince Ardagh! I didn't hear you approach and—" She stopped, studying him, then added warily, "This time, you *are* drunk."

He considered that carefully, elegant brow furrowed. "Why, yes," the prince said at last, clearly surprised, "I believe I am, a bit. How very bizarre."

He plainly wasn't at the stage of unpleasantness or stupidity; Sorcha, all too well acquainted with her late husband's ways, had long ago learned how to accurately judge the level of a man's intoxication. Bemused at his surprise, she asked, "Haven't you ever been this way before?"

"No. I have never dared lose even the smallest edge of my control. Not with my brother as he is."

The prince turned sharply away, staring with fierce, blank eyes out over the land. Stung by sudden pity, Sorcha asked softly, "You miss your homeland, don't you?"

"How should I not?"

"I'm sorry. That was a foolish question."

But he, leaning on the balustrade, continued, so quietly that she had to strain to hear, "It is so very beautiful, my land. No garish sunlight as there is in this Realm, but ah, a radiance shimmers in the very air, and the color of leaf or bird or sky is so clear it seems newly born. There are wonders in my land, Sorcha ni Fothad, wonders enough to make you laugh or weep or sit wide-eyed as a child."

"And I," he added, in so matter-of-fact a voice it made her heart ache, "shall never see it again."

"Surely you will!" she protested. "You aren't a criminal. There must be *some* way to lift your exile!"

He turned to her, the faintest sad smile touching his lips. "Fierce Sorcha, kindhearted Sorcha, I wish there were. But . . . Still, I am learning that there are compensations in this land." The prince paused, studying her, his eyes for once quite readable, and bewildered. "Truly, there are."

"Prince Ardagh . . ."

"Shh." He bent and, before she quite realized what he meant to do, kissed her. And she—och, Meallan, for all his faults, had been a gentle lover, but it had been long and long since he had—since they had— The prince was strong and gentle in one, fierce and tender, and if his breath was touched with mead, Sorcha thought wildly, it only sweetened the kiss. She tried for one proper moment to resist, then told herself, *Idiot!* and threw herself wholeheartedly into returning that kiss with all the pent-up passion within her.

And are you going to let him have you? a dry inner voice wanted to know. *Right here on the ramparts?*

God, yes—

No!

Gasping, shaken, Sorcha struggled her way free, wondering what she was going to do if the prince tried to grab her again.

But he only stared, looking every bit as confused as she, then asked softly, "Was that . . . was that kiss of your will, too?"

It was the drink talking, nothing more. Astonished at the disappointment she felt, Sorcha bit back the hot *what the hell do you think?* that first came to mind and stammered, "It—it was an accident. We both—"

But he held up a hand for silence, and if drink had been confusing him just a moment ago, its influence seemed to have vanished as abruptly as though he'd banished its effect by magic. Eyes now their eerie, unreadable norm, the prince stood alert as a hunter for an instant, then cried, "Breasal!" and raced off.

Breasal? Had something happened to the boy? How could Ardagh possibly have known? Bewildered, Sorcha gathered up her skirts and followed, almost managing to keep pace with him by running full out. Ahead of her, the prince stopped so sharply, dropping to his knees, that she nearly fell over him.

"Breasal!"

Prince Ardagh was already gathering the fallen boy into his arms, voice fierce with worry. "Where did you think you were going?"

"Don't know . . ." The boy's voice was a strained whisper, his young face grey and twisted with pain. "Didn't want . . . just didn't want . . . to die indoors . . ."

Oh dear God. Sorcha fell to her knees beside the prince, whispering, "I think we'd better call for Father Seadna."

Prince Ardagh glared at her. "No!"

"He's *dying!* Do you want him to pass unshriven?"

"He is not to die. I will not let Gervinus have his death."

"Wh-what—"

"He is not to die!" The green eyes were so terrifyingly sharp that for a moment Sorcha could almost believe he really was going to win out.

"No man can hold back death!" she protested. "I'm going for Father—"

"No! He *won't* die, I tell you. Sorcha, I don't have time to argue. Help me or stand aside!"

He struggled to his feet, the boy sagging against him, and scanned the sky fiercely. "Still dark . . . dark enough, I hope. Help me, Sorcha. I must get Breasal as far from human dwellings as possible."

He's mad, Sorcha thought, *he must be mad,* but she found herself saying, "We'll never get out of Fremainn; the guards will stop us."

"I know. The larger practice field will have to serve. Help me!"

Together, they half-carried, half-dragged the semiconscious Breasal to the open area. Ardagh gently settled the boy to the grass, then glanced up at Sorcha, commanding, "You are to ward off any guards who might come this way."

"But how—"

"I don't care how! Do it!"

She might have retorted, might have complained or argued or said *something,* but now the prince was on his feet again, his eyes blazing, and the words he spoke were . . . alien. Incredibly fierce, incredibly beautiful, like no other language she'd ever heard, they seemed to gleam in the air, calling, summoning, pleading, over and over again. . . .

Finvarra? Sorcha picked that name out of the strangeness. *King Finvarra? But—but he's myth! Isn't he?*

She staggered back, tripping over her own feet, landing with a thump on the ground, staring at the sudden shimmering in the air, at—at—

No. Oh no. I don't—he isn't—that can't be—

He was beautiful and terrible as an angel must be, this new being who stood in the midst of the shimmering as casually as a man might stand in a doorway. His hair was a shining mass of gold, his slanted eyes a clear, frightening green—

Ardagh's eyes, dear God, Ardagh's elegant, fierce beauty! They were of the same race, these two . . . beings, they must be, even if Ardagh's hair was gleaming black, not gold, and he was dressed like any other man of Fremainn, while the golden-haired one wore shimmering robes that changed color with every move, now green, now blue, now no shade she could name, they were of the same race, even if that race was most surely not human—

Aware that she was slipping over the edge of hysteria, Sorcha bit down on her lower lip, *hard,* reminding herself that she was the daughter of a scholar-poet, forcing herself to observe as keenly as he would. Finvarra . . . this was Finvarra, the King of the Sidhe of Eriu, and Ardagh had called him here.

The king wasn't happy about it. That much was clear from his angry tone, even if she couldn't understand his words. But then Ardagh stood aside and let him see Breasal, lying in a miserable little heap, and Finvarra gave the softest cry of dismay and stepped out of the shimmering onto mortal soil.

He saw her. The chill green gaze softened slightly, and Sorcha reminded herself that Finvarra, or so the stories said, tended to be kindly disposed to humans. Particularly to human women. When the whim struck him. She could hardly do him a proper courtesy, not sitting on the ground like this, but she bowed nearly double and received his polite little dip of the head in return.

But the king's attention had already turned back to Breasal. Gently he and Ardagh coaxed the boy back to his feet. As he sagged helplessly against Finvarra, barely breathing, Sorcha saw the king's arm go about the boy in so tender a curve that her heart skipped a beat for sudden sharp, irrational hope. Together, Finvarra and Breasal moved through the shimmering—and suddenly and undeniably were gone.

"Oh." It was all Sorcha could manage. "Oh."

Ardagh turned to her, and she shrank back in spite of herself, because for all that he looked weary enough to sleep where he stood, Otherness still blazed from his eyes. "Go on," he said softly, the very faintest edge of warning in his voice. "Say what you are burning to say."

"That was Finvarra. *The* Finvarra. The Sidhe King of Eriu."

"It was."

"He—you—you two look alike. Of the same race, I mean. But he—that means—you aren't human, are you?"

She saw something flicker in the eerie eyes: danger? desperation? "No. I am not."

To her utter amazement, Sorcha heard herself laugh. "Why, this is wonderful, this is amazing!"

It was hardly what he'd been expecting, either. Staring at her as though she'd just gone mad, he asked warily, "What?"

"All along I thought that the Sidhe were myth and that magic had vanished from the world, and now I see I was very, very mistaken and—och, I'm sorry to babble, but this is so very exciting—"

"Is it?"

This time there was definite warning behind the words, but with it, more than a hint of that same desperation. *He needs this sanctuary,* Sorcha realized. *He really is in exile, and if he thinks I might endanger his stay among humans . . .*

She dared not hesitate. Sorcha snapped, "Don't glare at me like that! I'm not going to tell anyone."

The unvoiced menace remained unshaken. "Humans lie."

"Yes, of course we do," she retorted, "but I don't, not here, not now." He wasn't believing her. He must already have seen too many examples of casual human falsehood, and that chill hint of peril still shadowed him, alien, inhuman—God, yes, inhuman, and in God's name, how was she going to convince him he was safe?

"Look you," Sorcha cried in sudden inspiration, "do you know what it meant to be a bard in this land? It meant bearing the whole history of the clan in your head. It meant learning and studying and never, ever changing the truth. It meant giving one's word, knowing that word was sacred. I'm the daughter of a poet, yes, but a poet is the modern equivalent of a bard—and when I give my word, I keep that word! You have sworn to do us no harm, and so I will keep your secret, *I* so swear!"

There was a moment of tense silence. Then, to her surprise, the prince began to laugh, very softly and wearily. "Nicely said, most nicely said. And I believe you, mostly because I have no other choice."

Sorcha scrambled to her feet. "What about Breasal? King Finvarra took him to—to the Sidhe Realm, didn't he? To heal him?"

"Powers grant, yes. And give the boy a happy life. We do not harm or cast away children, any children."

"I know that," she said gently. "You just proved it."

"Eh?"

"You were willing to cast away your safe harbor without a second thought, all to protect poor Breasal."

"I did what I must."

Without another word, Prince Ardagh started to walk away, plainly embarrassed, but Sorcha hurried after him. He glanced at her, glanced away, then added quietly, "I'm sorry if I frightened you just now. As you guessed, I saw my refuge crumbling under me."

Sorcha glanced about. Fortunate the hour was only now turning to full day; only Sidhe and human idiots would have been up this early, she jibed at herself. Not another soul had seen what had happened out here. "Does no one else know the truth about you?"

"One other. One I will not mention and who has reasons for keeping silent. And now, Lady Sorcha, it has been a very long night and morning, and I really must rest."

"Och, of course. But . . . what happens when no one can find Breasal?"

He shrugged. "Finvarra has left a log."

For a moment she stared blankly, then cried, "Ah, the way the old stories have it!"

"Magicked to look like Breasal's body, yes. The illusion will hold long enough for burial, or so Finvarra has assured me." He paused at the doorway of his guest house and gave her a deep, formal bow. "Thank you for your assistance. Forgive me for any . . . indiscretions I might have said or done while the mead controlled my tongue and a fair portion of my will. And now, Lady Sorcha, good night—or rather," he added as an early ray of sunlight cut through the clouds and caught him in the face, "good day."

DEATH OF A LOG

CHAPTER 20

Queen Derval of Clonach sat alone in her solitary bed, absently braiding and rebraiding her long golden hair. The queen had long ago insisted on separate sleeping chambers, and if Donnchadh had agreed with an enthusiasm that meant he had his light women on the side, it was worth the chance to have an occasional respite from his company.

Particularly now, when she wished to be alone with her thoughts. Derval had been uneasy for days after sending that parchment message to Odran mac Daire in Fremainn, knowing that of course it had been read by other eyes, worrying that the code had been a touch too clever, too obvious. But today had proven her worries false.

Tossing back her half-finished braids, Derval drew a small clay charm out from under her pillow and studied it yet again by the flickering light of her bedside candle. There was nothing at all unusual about the charm; it was the type meant as a general warding-off-of-evil trinket, borne by just about anyone who was at all superstitious.

But what the charm was intended to do was not by any means as important as what it signified. It had come to her from Odran mac Daire, there in Fremainn, as part of their agreed-upon code. A small thing, this charm, easy to smuggle out of a royal fortress with no one suspecting. That it had come to her at all meant the man was interested in her plans.

Derval turned the charm over in her hand, counting once

again the tiny lines scratched as if by accident into the clay. Five. That meant Odran was telling her he could gather fifty warriors to him were he free of Fremainn.

"Not enough," she whispered. "Not nearly enough." But Muirgheas mac Art, who was *not* in Fremainn, also had his fifty, and Cronan mac Deaglan, who, like she, was willing to sacrifice his firstborn, hostage, child if need be, had his seventy, and there were yet others to be contacted, others discontented with the current rule for no other reason than ambition.

It was at least a start, Derval decided, and smiled. If only she could arrange—

"Derval."

She started, hastily closing her hand about the little charm. What was this? Her women had orders not to let anyone enter without her permission, not even: "Donnchadh. What is it, husband? Mad with lust for me?"

He didn't even try to react to the jibe. Wild-eyed, hair a bright, tangled mass about his head, Donnchadh said hoarsely, "The dream."

"The . . . dream."

Before she could do more than slip the charm safely back under her pillow, he came rushing into the room, nearly throwing himself on top of her, like a child in desperate need of comfort. *So Breasal had once thrown himself, terrified of his nightmares,* an unwanted flash of memory reminded her, *and you cast him aside, telling him that only weaklings were afraid of bad dreams.* The memory made her say sharply, "What nonsense is this?"

Face hidden against her breast, Donnchadh merely shook his head. Derval caught a double handful of his hair and pulled his head back. "What *is* the matter with you?"

He pulled away, turning to sit on the side of the bed, shivering. "The dream. I've had it several nights running."

Derval tensed. Donnchadh had never shown any talent at all for things oracular, but everyone knew there were such things as prophetic dreams that could come to almost anyone. Even to one such as he.

"Tell me," she snapped. "Describe it."

"I—I am at court, walking down the length of a huge royal audience hall."

"Not the one here in Clonach?"

"I don't know. In the dream I can't tell if it's my own or that at Fremainn. Beside me walks a man in a hooded cloak, and even though I never do see his face, he—he gives off such a feeling of evil that I want to run. But I don't, and we walk on together to where Aedh stands smiling at me. The man in the hooded cloak hands me a dagger and says, 'Strike'—and I do, I strike Aedh down!"

What, and is this *what terrifies you?* Derval thought in disgust. *Then we might as well stay at home like meek little mice!* But she fought back the urge to snap that out, forcing herself to say soothingly instead, "Why, husband! This is not so very terrible. After all, haven't we been plotting just such a thing?"

"Not like this! Not cold-blooded murder!"

"That's just your sleeping mind's way of making it all seem wildly dramatic." She ran a hand through his tangled hair in feigned affection. "Forget this dream, Donnchadh; it means nothing more than ambition yet unfilled."

"You don't understand." He glanced back over his shoulder at her, his eyes wide with horror. "If that were all to the dream, I could ignore it. But when I bend over Aedh to be sure he's dead—I see not his but our own son's face instead! I wake knowing I've killed our son!"

Derval's caressing hand closed reflexively on Donnchadh's hair. "Fearghal?" she asked, barely breathing. Oh God, the ill omen of that—

"No." Donnchadh twisted free of her grasp, still shuddering. "Breasal. It is Breasal, it is my firstborn son, who lies dead by my hand."

An unexpected lance of pain stabbed at her. Hiding it as best she could, forcing a smile, Derval murmured, "This, too, means nothing. We both know the boy is sickly, husband; we both have lived with the fact that he is unlikely to reach manhood. You have merely let it weigh too heavily on your mind. Come, Donnchadh, think. This dream of yours is not an evil thing."

He turned to glare at her. "How not?"

"Why, you are still feeling guilt over having sent our son as hostage. And so your sleeping mind cut him free."

"By killing him!"

Oh, you great fool! "It is the king you kill," Derval said with forced patience. "That he wears Breasal's face is mere dream-illusion, meaningless."

"What of the hooded man? What of him?"

Who knows what that means to your sleeping self? Who cares? "He is the burden of guilt you have carried," Derval quickly improvised. "But in the dream, your mind cast that guilt from you, into a separate man whom you can ignore. And that you kill the king means that even though the dream has frightened you now, you will still triumph!" *I should have been a bard,* she told herself sardonically. *That was as foolish a tale as ever a bard might sing.*

But it served its purpose. "Yes!" Donnchadh cried eagerly, and caught his wife in a tight embrace. "Och, my clever wife, my clever, clever wife, you're right. I shall, indeed, triumph!"

Yes, my husband, Derval corrected while she feigned interest in his sudden burst of passion, *there shall be a triumph. But it is not you but we who shall enjoy it.*

Arnulf paused in the middle of helping his master dress, a thong dangling from his hand, a ray of early morning sunlight crossing his slight body with bright gold. "I still don't understand. We lost, but we won?"

Gervinus snatched the thong from the acolyte's hand and finished tying it himself. "Most certainly. Oh yes, it would have been most gratifying to see the foreign prince go up in smoke and flame, or however it is that these barbarians dispose of their pagan witches, but since we may not have that pleasure—yet—let us bask instead in the reflected glory the king has granted us."

"But . . ."

"Come now, Arnulf. Think. By so tenderly abasing myself before him, I have proven myself a most properly humble Christian, a gentle soul under my crisp official shell. One who can work his way into places a colder man could not and—" He broke off with a frown. "Now, what is that clamor? Go out there and find out."

In only a few moments, Arnulf came hurrying back inside. "There's been a death. The—the boy."

"What boy? Breasal? Yes? Ah, the poor sickly lad! His tragic end is not at all surprising. Of course," Gervinus added, the note of false pity leaving his voice, "it would have been more useful to us had it happened yesterday, but since it has not . . . come, Arnulf, we must prepare to mourn."

He most definitely had not, Ardagh thought blearily, gotten enough sleep. Not more than three of the humans' hours could have passed before someone discovered "Breasal's" log-body and raised such an outcry that there wasn't a chance of sleeping any longer. Dunking his head in a basin of cold water helped a tiny bit, but now he had the problem of a headful of long, wet hair. Wringing the heavy black mass out as best he could, Ardagh mused that it really was getting too long. But the thought of having even a trusted human so near his neck with an iron blade . . . he should only be glad the Sidhe didn't grow any such animalistic beards as humans seemed to favor. . . .

Ae, this wasn't working. His mind was trying to slide back into sleep. Ardagh splashed his face once more, and succeeded only in wetting his hair all over again. With a sigh, the prince tried summoning a precious bit of magic to dry it.

And failed. For a moment he sat in confusion, then bowed his head resignedly. The small amount of useable Power remaining after his aborted attempt to return home had nearly been extinguished by that desperate call across Realms to Finvarra. And right now he was just too weary to make use of what little innate magic was left. *At least*, the prince thought wryly, *I should be grateful I'm not . . . what's that elegant human term . . . ? 'hung over' as well.*

Ae-ye. What this meant was that weather or not, he couldn't wait much longer to return to the forest. But that certainly couldn't happen until he was fully awake. Right now, Ardagh decided vaguely, what he needed most was clothing. Here was a cloth thick enough to pat some of the dampness out of his hair, but he needed something to actually wear—ha, yes, there was a fresh tunic in the chest where clean clothes were supposed to be, and he could easily shake out the creases in his *brat*.

As he dressed, Ardagh could not fight off a pang of nostalgia, remembering his own estate, where at a word from him quiet servant-beings would lay out whatever clothing he wished and a new outfit could be formed with a few easy flashes of magic. Right now Breasal was probably enjoying just such magical pleasures. Ironic that a human should be so easily allowed to pass into the Sidhe Realms while he, a prince of royal Sidhe blood was left standing locked outside.

Ae, no. Self-pity was far too easy right now, groggy as he was, and after having survived the winter, he wasn't going to let himself lapse into such foolishness. Think only of today, Ardagh decided. That was more practical. Less perilous, too. Servants, now. Someone usually crept in here when he was out to tidy things up and leave him clean clothing, but maybe he should surrender after all to the way a prince was supposed to live in this Realm and actually keep a servant or two, the way everyone kept insisting. But that would mean sharing the only privacy he had, that within this small building, with a human, and he still wasn't ready to—

Someone was knocking shyly at his door. "Please, Prince Ardagh."

Ardagh's sigh turned into a yawn. Combing his still damp hair hastily into place with his fingers, he called out, "Enter."

A servant stood in the doorway, wringing his hands. "King Aedh would see you."

Of course he would. "Lead on," Ardagh said in resignation, and followed the man to the royal conversation house.

"Prince Ardagh." Aedh's face was very solemn, his eyes deeply shadowed. "I fear I have some sad news for you." The king hesitated, plainly struggling for composure, and Ardagh waited patiently, already sure of what he was going to hear. At last Aedh continued, "Sometime during the night, Breasal mac Donnchadh . . . left this mortal world."

It wasn't *quite* the wording he'd expected. Ardagh almost strangled trying not to give what would be the most awkward laugh, hoping it would look as though he was struggling with shock instead. Left this mortal world, indeed! Powers, Powers, what an accurate summation! "So I have already learned," he managed to say with reasonable sobriety.

"One thing I will ask you to share with no one else," Aedh continued. "We both knew the boy was sickly, but . . . I am afraid he was more sickly than we dreamed. We must hold the burial with unseemly haste, because the body is showing some clear signs of . . . of disease."

What disease? Ardagh's mind gibbered. *Root rot?* Ae, Powers, no, he was *not* going to laugh! The lack of sleep was making him giddy. It wasn't disease the humans had seen, of course it wasn't disease, it was only Finvarra's logspell starting to dissolve under the weight of mortal sunlight—though he couldn't tell the king *that!* Voice quavering a little with the strain, the prince said, "I am sure there is no contagion to harm your people." *Except maybe for wood lice—stop that!*

"I pray you're right. But I still don't dare wait. Even though a hasty burial is always going to give rise to rumors of dark deeds, I can't risk—"

"Nonsense," Ardagh said hastily. "Everyone in Fremainn knows how near to death the boy was every day."

"True, but—"

"Look you, if you like, I will handle the body myself, prove to everyone there is no danger from it." *Except from splinters—No!*

"I would not inflict such an ordeal on you, but thank you." Aedh paused. "I have already sent word of their son's death to King Donnchadh and his wife."

That cut short any urge to laugh. "I doubt it will matter much to them," Ardagh said. "Any more than did his life."

His frankness plainly shocked the king, but Aedh didn't try to disagree with him. "That is another reason why I have

decided the burial must take place within Fremainn, where
the poor boy can at least rest among those who cared for
him." The king paused again. "Which brings up another
point. I thought that since you were friendly with poor
Breasal, God rest him, you would wish to participate in the
funeral."

The funeral of a log—no, no, don't think of that! "I don't
know if I . . . ah . . . could manage that."

"Look you, I'm well aware that our faith is foreign to you,
but surely some matters reach across cultures."

"Indeed." Ardagh realized with sudden half-hysterical
certainty that Aedh was going to ask him to speak over
the grave. Speak over the grave of a log—ae, no, no, he
would never be able to get through that without laughing! Besides, how could he possibly deliver any manner
of eulogy? He would not lie, yet he certainly couldn't admit
the truth! Desperately evasive, Ardagh said, "I will do what
I may."

The day was suitably gloomy for a funeral, the sky totally
overcast now and a drizzle seeping down from the sky. But
when Ardagh saw who was to perform the ceremony, he
nearly choked all over again.

*Bishop Gervinus. A false holy man for a false funeral.
How very fitting. Particularly since it was he who almost
caused the boy's death. And what would you say, Gervinus,
if I told you that your victim has escaped you, and showed
you just what it is you bury?*

The prince kept a determinedly stolid face throughout
the ritual, though it was almost more than even a Sidhe's
will could endure to hear Gervinus solemnly praise the
"dead" Breasal and call down the blessing of Heaven on a
log. All around Ardagh, folk were weeping, save for Sorcha,
who was doing her best to hide her lack of tears with a shawl
pulled over almost her whole face. Ardagh didn't dare look
at her; he was sure that it would be the final strain on his
self-control and he really would break out laughing. Aedh
and Father Seadna were eyeing him suspiciously enough
as it was.

Oh Powers, he was being called forward. *Ae-ye, the truth is becoming a very difficult thing, indeed!*

"I . . . knew Breasal mac Donnchadh for only a relatively brief time," he began, improvising desperately. *So far, so true.* "But in that time, I found him a brave, good-hearted youngster." *Still true.* "I . . . know he could not help but resent the sickly body that kept him from . . . ah . . . from doing what he wished. But he bore up under his restrictions as courageously as any hero." *Indeed.* "I am sure he will be missed." Powers, why was he thinking of that—that log again? That beautifully decorated, sadly deteriorating piece of wood being honored by everyone, including himself—ae, no, he would *not* laugh, he would not! Struggling for composure, Ardagh hastily concluded, "B-but I am convinced that however he may have struggled in this world, Breasal mac Donnchadh is now happy and healthy in—in a far finer world than this."

He didn't dare attempt another word. With a curt bow, Ardagh turned and walked away, keeping himself rigidly under control, hoping the humans would think he was battling with grief.

He made it as far as the back wall of the royal keep, a blank, windowless expanse of wood, where no one could see him. And there Ardagh finally collapsed into gusts of helpless laughter.

Ae, no, someone was coming. The prince straightened, struggling mightily for control, then relaxed again with a sigh of relief. "Sorcha!"

She was hurrying along, shawl over her mouth, making suspicious little noises that didn't exactly sound like weeping. "You, too!" Ardagh exclaimed, and she turned to him, giggles bursting from her, setting him to laughing anew.

"Th-this is ridiculous!" she gasped.

"Quite."

"We shouldn't—people are mourning, yet we're—"

"Mourning a-a log!"

"I know, but—but—I can't help it! It's wrong, but—but—when you gave that eulogy, I c-couldn't even look at you. And that line about a-a fairer, finer world—"

She burst into a new torrent of glee, and the two of them laughed helplessly together till they were brought up short by lack of breath.

"Oh. Oh dear." Sorcha wiped her eyes dry with a corner of her shawl. "That really was ridiculous."

"It was." Ardagh took a deep, steadying breath. "I don't usually have fits like that."

"Me, neither."

He could feel the idiotic laughter still quivering within him, waiting to erupt anew. "I think," Ardagh said firmly, "a stroll about Fremainn is needed."

"Calm us down," she agreed. "Clear our heads. And if anyone sees us, they'll think we're mourning together."

"Mourning a log."

"Stop that!"

Not daring to look at each other, they walked on. "I . . ." Sorcha began, then stopped.

"You have a question," Ardagh said. "What?"

"It's not exactly a question. It's just . . . I didn't know that your people laughed."

He looked at her in indignation. "Do you think us made of stone? Of course we laugh. Not necessarily at what you humans might think funny."

"Except for logs."

"Except for logs." *And when was the last time I laughed like this? So freely and with such silly abandon? Not at my brother's court, that's for certain. No, it was . . . however long ago, when I was in my garden with small Ninet, and she was doing that silly, happy little prance because it was a bright day and she was feeling full of joy. Ae, Powers, Ninet, I hope you're safe and happy. . . .* Shaking off the past, Ardagh added, "And thank you, by the way. The temptation to tell what you knew to soothe everyone's grief must have been very strong."

"It was, a bit—but who would have believed me? Besides," the woman added sharply, "I did give my word, if you'll recall."

"So you did. Thank you anyhow."

She glanced at him, eyes bright with sudden daring. "You can reward me, if you'd like."

"Eh?"

"Not with treasure, I didn't mean anything like that. But . . . may I ask you questions? About—about your homeland?"

He looked at her eager face, thinking, *a scholar-poet's daughter, indeed.* It occurred to him with a little start that Queen Eithne, the only other human who knew his true race, had never once asked a question about him or his people. It wasn't, surely, that she lacked curiosity. No, Ardagh realized, the woman was interested only in her family and its safety; her life surrounded them. But Sorcha—study her as he would, Ardagh could not find a scrap of anything but honest, friendly curiosity in her eyes. And a wistful little voice in his mind whispered, *It would be so very good to be able to talk freely to someone, to have someone with whom I didn't have to forever pretend.* "You may ask," Ardagh said at last. "Though of course there is always the possibility that I may not choose to answer."

"Fair enough."

"And remember this: I do not give you permission to share any information I might give with anyone else."

"Of course not," she agreed quickly. "I'm just curious about your land for *me.*"

He frowned slightly. "Why?"

"Why? Because—because I want something that is *mine*, something that has a purpose for *me.*"

"I don't understand. You are the daughter of the High King's own Chief Minister. Surely you can—"

"Surely I can do nothing." Her quiet voice was so much more believable than any melodramatic ranting. "Prince Ardagh, I am a childless widow, which cuts me off from my late husband's people. I am my father's only heir, which means I am probably not going to be wed off again. There is nothing for me to be here in Fremainn *but* Father's heir, nothing for me to do save copy out his manuscripts. And get into quarrels with visiting princes I mistake for drunkards."

"Ae, just when I think I have finally begun to understand this realm, these people, I realize I know nothing! You are yourself, a separate, sentient being. You are not enslaved to anyone, are you? No? Then why in the name of all the Powers can't you do as you will?"

Sorcha sighed. "Because I was born female."

"What has that to do with anything?"

"Please. You saw what happened in the law court when I tried to defend my poor serving woman. If you hadn't stepped in to help, the case would have been thrown away and I would have been whispered over as the foolish woman who thought herself the equal of—" Sorcha cut herself off in midsentence. "I hate whiners. Life is as it is, at least in this human land." Staring up at him, she added, "Don't you see? That's exactly why I was so delighted to realize who and what you were! My physical world may have narrow boundaries, but that doesn't mean my mind needs to be restricted, too."

Blinking fiercely, Sorcha turned sharply away. "I'm sorry. I must sound like a child."

"No. Or rather, yes." That made her start. As the woman looked back over her shoulder, Ardagh added, teasing gently, "You remind me of little Fainche fascinated by a new toy."

To his delight, she chuckled. "Unlike Fainche," Sorcha retorted with a defiant little grin, "I can promise you this, Prince Ardagh: you are one toy I will not break!"

She scurried off before he could retort.

IN MOURNING

CHAPTER 21

Father Seadna sat in blissful solitude in the keep's herb garden, the mix of sweet and sharp scents pleasant in his nostrils, the buzz of bees the only sound as he studied his prayers.

"Father Seadna. A word with you if I might."

The monk started, prayerbook flying from his hand. A tall, graceful form retrieved it before it could touch the ground, returning it to Father Seadna's hand in one smooth movement. "Forgive me. I didn't mean to startle you. But might I have that word with you?"

"Ah. Prince Ardagh." *I'm not the first who's been startled by him, and I'd swear he doesn't do it on purpose; God has given the man the silent grace of a cat!* "Of course, my son. Come, sit beside me."

For all that grace, the prince looked very weary, like a man, Father Seadna thought, who's used up most of his strength in some great endeavor and hasn't yet had a chance to replenish it. "How are you enduring?" the monk asked gently.

That earned him a startled glance. "Well enough. Ah, you mean regarding Breasal."

"Of course. I saw how greatly you were affected during the funeral."

Was that a stifled *laugh?* Oh, surely not. More likely some spasm of remembered grief. "Father Seadna," the prince said gently, "I'm aware that your concern is kindly meant.

258

But be assured I'm not running mad with sorrow. I know as surely as you know the sun will rise that Breasal mac Donnchadh is far happier where he is now than ever he was before."

Father Seadna shook his head in amazement. "Your faith is a wonder to see, Prince Ardagh. I only wish . . ."

"That it was *your* faith?"

"That, too, of course; I'll not lie about it. But what I meant was that I wished others might see that there are those who, outside the Church though they are, are yet not totally lost souls."

"Others," the prince echoed with a dry little laugh. "We both know exactly which 'other' you mean. No, you need not give me that look of alarm. I'm not asking you to name names."

He fell into that sudden intense stillness that seemed quite a natural part of him but always put the monk in mind of some peaceful predator. Possibly one waiting to see what prey might approach, Father Seadna mused, and asked, "Of what did you wish to speak, Prince Ardagh?"

"I was wondering about a matter. Idle speculation, some might call it, perhaps, or simple curiosity."

The monk chuckled. "There is nothing simple about your curiosity, my son, we both know that by now."

He was rewarded with a quick, charmingly rueful smile. "I admit it."

"Och, well, better a lively curiosity than a mind closed to wonder. What is it you would ask?"

The prince hesitated. Plucking a sprig of early mint, he twirled it idly between his fingers for a moment, then tossed it aside. "I know the Church frowns on such things as this 'sorcery' of which you've spoken. I have good reason to know," he added sardonically.

"Prince Ardagh, no one here ever truly believed you a sorcerer, least of all me. Surely you realize that."

"I know you never did, and thank you for it. As for the others, ae, who can say? But am I right in guessing that by extension the Church ban on sorcery falls upon all things magical as well?"

Father Seadna frowned slightly. There was never any telling what was truly going on behind that elegant face. "My son, I must ask you this, knowing that you will not lie to me: are you planning to dabble in forbidden arts?"

"Do I look a fool?"

"Hardly. Do I?"

"Ae, no. Of course not. And you do deserve a complete answer. No, Father Seadna, I am not planning to dabble in any sort of forbidden arts. Now, may I have an answer to my question as well?"

"Yes, Prince Ardagh, generally speaking, the Church does frown on the use of magic, save in the hands of those such as the saints, who were inspired by the Will of God."

"I see."

That was definitely the glint of a predator in those green eyes. "This is hardly an idle question," Father Seadna said in warning. "My son, if you have anything you feel you should share, please remember that whatever you tell me will be kept in strictest confidence."

"No," the prince said, getting smoothly to his feet. "Thank you, but I am not ready to burden you with anything."

With the usual intricate little salute that meant that as far as Prince Ardagh was concerned, his side of the discussion was ended, he left.

Now what, Father Seadna wondered, *was that about? Sorcery, magic . . . he* can't *be planning to work some revenge on Bishop Gervinus for that charge of sorcery, can he? Arrange matters so the bishop, not he, looks like the guilty party?*

Oh, most surely not. For by now the monk knew that Prince Ardagh, even as he'd stated, never lied. And to foster so terrible a charge, all to gain some petty revenge— that would be the most flagrant form of falsehood.

Queen Derval looked sharply up from her needlework, staring out the window of her grianan at the messenger on a lathered horse who was riding into the courtyard below. Letting her needlework fall, hardly noting the maidservant who scrambled to her knees to catch it before it could touch the floor, Derval went down to see what news might have arrived.

The horse, trembling with exhaustion and breathing so hard it seemed about to fall, had just been led away. The messenger, looking nearly as weary as his mount, was trying to brush off his travel-stained clothing when he caught sight of Derval and went down on one knee. "Queen Derval."

"I see that you clutch a scroll. What news have you brought?"

"It . . . uh . . . it is for the king's eyes, my queen."

"The king is out riding his lands. Come, give it to me." When the messenger hesitated, she added, a touch more sternly, "I am his authority in his absence. Would you challenge that authority?"

Head bowed, the messenger handed over the scroll. A sudden pang of alarm shot through Derval as she saw that it was fastened with the royal seal. Breaking the seal with not quite steady hands, the queen read the message twice through to be sure, amazed at the genuine pain she felt. But there was stronger than pain as well: there was triumph, cold, bitter triumph.

Throwing back her head with theatrical grandeur, Derval, Queen of Clonach, began to keen with grief.

She was still keening, now within her chambers, voice hoarser but still thick with anguish, when Donnchadh returned. Practically hurling himself from his horse, he raced to her side. "Derval! What is it? I could hear you from the courtyard. What's happened?"

"My son! He's killed my son!"

"Fearghal," Donnchadh breathed. "Dear God, has anything happened to—"

"Not Fearghal, husband, Breasal! Our firstborn son is dead, dead, dead!"

Abashed at the surge of relief he felt, Donnchadh said in as conciliatory a tone as he could manage, "Now, Derval, you knew this day might come."

"Not like this! Never like this!"

"Hush, now. The boy was sickly from the day he first drew breath." Her constant shrilling was setting his nerves on edge—particularly since he suspected that it was almost totally an act. "Derval, *please!*"

She glared at him. "You dare speak, you who never suckled a child at your breast!"

"Bah, neither did you. You were all too eager to give our children over to a wetnurse. Derval, *Derval!* Breasal was my son, too."

Derval's wailing stopped suddenly as though he'd slapped her. "Then avenge him."

Donnchadh stared. "Avenge him? Against *whom?*" He straightened slowly. "Oh no. You can't believe that Aedh killed him."

"No? Then why was our son so quickly, so shamefully buried?"

"Sickness—"

"Poison! Husband, our son, our firstborn son, your heir, was murdered!"

Ambition. Derval's regal ambition, just waiting for her child to die so she could use him . . . Feeling like a wild thing being forced into a snare, Donnchadh said, "No. Och, no. Even if that was true, what would I possibly do about it? I do not have enough men to take on the High King in combat and survive."

"Not alone, no."

"Now what does that mean? Derval, what have you been doing? What plots have you been working behind my back?"

"What have I been doing?" she snapped. "What you should have been doing all along. Look! Here are promises from Odran mac Daire, from Cronan mac Deaglan, from Muirgheas mac Art—"

"Derval—"

"—promises of aid," she continued, unheeding, "pledges of warriors to back your cause. They will—"

"Derval!"

"What? What brave words are you about to say, husband?"

"I—you—how *dare* you?"

"How dare I what? How dare I take a step forward

when you stood rooted in place? How dare I try to act when you want to huddle in fear? *How dare I wish to avenge my son?*"

"You don't understand," Donnchadh countered. "You're a woman, you can't understand—this isn't *fidchel*, Derval, this isn't some game from which you can walk away with no harm taken!" Seeing the fury blazing up in her eyes, Donnchadh hurried on before she could attack, "One can't risk moving too quickly, making one wrong decision. Every move has to be considered before any action is taken. . . ."

"Every move has to be considered before any action is taken. . . ."

Fearghal mac Donnchadh, now only son and heir to the throne of Clonach, stood with his ear pressed up against the door, listening with all his might, and nearly spat in disgust at what he heard. How could his father, his own father, be so *weak?* " 'Every move has to be considered,' " the boy mimicked in a savage whisper. "And so, *no* action is taken!"

No action by Donnchadh, maybe. But damned if he was going to sit around and—and mope! The crown of Clonach was all well and good, but Clonach was such a tiny, boring little place. *Maybe Father wants to grow old and die here and never even try for anything more, but I was meant for better things, I know it!*

With any luck at all and the courage his father seemed to lack, who knew how far he could rise? Fearghal's hand closed about the hilt of an imaginary sword, lunging at an imaginary foe, seeing that foe fall. Ha, yes, who knew? He could rise all the way to the throne of all Eriu!

Yes, right, but how was he to do it? Donnchadh clearly wasn't going to be of any help. But what if he, himself, took a hand? Got into Fremainn somehow . . .

And then what?

Fearghal glossed over that little inconvenience. He'd figure out a plan once he was inside the royal fortress. And getting inside, he realized with a grin, he could do. He really could do it—and it would be so easy! The messenger would be returning to his royal master soon enough, and with sufficient coins he would surely agree to take an eager young serving boy with him to see the fine sights. Yes, oh yes, it would work! Where Donnchadh had failed, Fearghal mac Donnchadh would succeed!

Gervinus walked alone amid the buildings of Fremainn, seemingly lost in prayer but actually deep in secular thought. He had ingratiated himself with King Aedh as thoroughly as seemed plausible; he was *not*, the bishop told himself, going to act the fawning fool. But ingratiation could only go so far, particularly since he'd had to overcome that sly interference from Prince Ardagh.

No. He would not think about the prince now. That, Gervinus told himself with cold honesty, had been his mistake from the first. He had surely been on the right trail with that pseudo-assassin, that much was clear after the fact. But he never should have let personal prejudice, personal dislike for Prince Ardagh, stand in his way. He should never have let the lure of sorcery, no matter how tempting, affect his judgement. Difficult, dangerous though the prince might be, his obliteration was *not* the main goal.

And yet, Gervinus mused, there really was something useful about the idea of a pseudo-assassin . . . one who was not really expected to succeed yet could produce a credible attack. An attack that would look quite thoroughly convincing, not like the weak attempt made by the late Breasal.

It would be risky. Controlling Breasal's mind had been fairly easy; although that mind had been quick and supple, the boy had lacked the strength of body to resist. But any new "assassin" would have to be normal both in mind and body if he or she was to be believable.

Ah yes, believable. Gervinus pursed his lips thoughtfully. He would have only the one chance at this, and the plan certainly wasn't going to work if he picked the wrong tool. A good many people in Fremainn probably held grudges against the king. But whichever one he finally chose must have a good and convincing reason to take such a final, perilous step as regicide.

And who could that possibly be? Who at court could be harboring such intense hatred he'd be believable as an assassin?

A *bizarre problem,* Gervinus mused. But one that definitely needed to be solved.

Donnchadh hurried to where Derval was waiting, her face impassive but her hands fiercely clenched. She wasn't doing all that much better than he, the king thought, in hiding her panic. Panic that his news wasn't going to soothe. "They haven't seen him, either. None of my servants or guards or *anyone* has seen Fearghal."

"That's impossible. He's not a—a spy, able to fade into his surroundings, he's a boy, only a boy. Someone has to have seen where he's gone."

Donnchadh held up a helpless hand. "His horse is still in the stables, but that doesn't mean he couldn't have taken some other mount. So many people are always coming and going—it's impossible to tell. Damn the boy for a fool, for all I know the Lochlannach have him!"

"No. We'd both know it were those heathen on our shores. But a horse, now . . ." Derval mused. "A horse and hounds . . ."

"What—"

"Ah, husband, wait, I think I have it. Didn't you give Fearghal a new hunting hound not a day ago? And wasn't he eager to test out the beast?"

"Hunting." Donnchadh spat out the word. "Of course. Fearghal has gone hunting. By himself—I'll have the hide from him for that stupidity!"

"By himself," Derval echoed softly. "Would he be quite that foolish?"

"Bah, of course. Boys are impulsive, you must know that by now." He stopped at her sharply indrawn breath. "What is it?"

"Impulsive, yes. Just how impulsive?"

"Derval, please, no word games. What are you—"

Face pale, Derval asked, "What if he was impulsive enough to try what you haven't dared do? What if Fearghal was impulsive enough to go all the way to Fremainn?"

"By himself? But that's ridiculous! He would never . . . dear God. He would."

"The little idiot!" Derval hissed. "He could upset everything!" She caught at Donnchadh's arm. "We've got to get him back. You have to send men—"

"No, no, there isn't any need for that," Donnchadh cut in. "Send a spy instead. Don't give me that wonderstruck glance; I know you have them. Send one of your spies to make sure that's where Fearghal really has gone. And don't look so terrified, either. We both know Aedh is soft where youngsters are concerned. Look at the good care he took of Breasal. Saints rest the boy," Donnchadh added in belated piousness.

"The good care! He *killed* our son! We can't let him take another!"

"Derval, hush. Hush! What good is it to go rushing off and attack a king who's better armed, better fortified—and trap our son in his fortress in the process? No. Send your spies out first."

He caught the oddest glint in her eyes. Almost, Donnchadh thought uncomfortably, as though that was exactly what she'd wanted him to say. Almost as though all this was merely part of some strange, ambitious game she was playing.

"He could upset everything." Now, what does that mean?

Well, whatever game it might be, Donnchadh added to himself, it was one *he* meant to win.

I will not stare, Fearghal mac Donnchadh scolded himself as he trudged into Fremainn behind the messenger. *I will not.*

He hadn't expected the messenger to take him so literally. But the man had insisted that Fearghal dismount some distance away from the royal keep and come into the fortress on foot like the nobody he was pretending to be.

Right, Fearghal thought. *You just wanted the chance to sell my horse.*

He had been grumbling about it for some time, muttering to himself that he'd never had to walk a day in his life, that a proper prince *rode* everywhere. But Fearghal had to admit that by now he was dusty and weary and bedraggled enough to really look the shabby part.

And if he was a nobody, the boy told himself defiantly, there wasn't any good reason he couldn't gawk. Besides, there was so much worth gawking at! Fremainn was just so *big*, so crowded with people and buildings. Fearghal had always thought of Clonach as a grand place, but now he realized with a shock that was his world rearranging itself that Clonach had been nothing more than a shabby little nowhere.

How could Father ever have been content to rule over nothing more than that?

Well, *he* wasn't content, not now, not after seeing all this. Maybe the sheer size and bustle of Fremainn was a little alarming, but it was also exciting enough to make his heart pound wildly. And this was all, Fearghal vowed as he trudged along in the messenger's wake, this was all going to someday be his!

Ardagh sat in the royal conversation house with King Aedh, Fothad and Father Seadna, and struggled to look properly alert and aware of what the others were discussing.

It wasn't easy. The warm, close air wasn't helping him at all. *This is ridiculous. I feel even more—more* languid *than I did before I took Power from the forest.*

Focus. He must focus on what Aedh was saying.

" . . . but so far there hasn't been so much as a word out of Clonach."

Clonach? Ah, yes. The home of Breasal's cold-blooded parents. The prince roused himself enough to note, "It seems a bit odd."

"Now there's an understatement!" Father Seadna snapped, then half-raised a hand in apology. "It *was* their son who died, may he rest in peace. No matter how King Donnchadh and his queen ignored the poor boy during his life, they can hardly be ignoring his death as well."

Fothad shrugged. "Who can say?"

The king shook his head ruefully. "Who, indeed, with that

pair? Lucky we are that Donnchadh is such an indecisive fellow—the last thing I want is rebellion on the part of Clonach."

"A bad time for rebellion," Ardagh remarked. "Is Clonach not a seacoast kingdom? Yes? Then it must be difficult enough to raise crops on rocky, salt-washed land without taking away farming folk from spring planting to be soldiers."

"Och, yes," Fothad agreed. "Besides, Donnchadh certainly can't rebel, not with his land lying under threat from the Lochlannach."

Aedh laughed shortly. "Never thought to be grateful to those Godless heathens for anything—your pardon, Prince Ardagh. But while we're discussing Clonach, let us not forget Queen Derval! That cold-blooded creature is as ruthless and ambitious as anyone, and twice the thinker of her husband. Who knows what acts she may be able to pressure Donnchadh to commit?"

"I doubt she can make him overcome his worry about the Lochlannach or—" Fothad broke off, frowning. "Prince Ardagh, what's wrong? Are you ill?"

It would have been pleasant just to let himself drift off into a doze, but Ardagh forced himself back to awareness yet again. "Not at all. I'm quite well." *Only feeling the lack of Power, not that I can admit such a thing to you.* "But I will take some fresh air, if you will excuse me."

Aedh nodded, and Ardagh thankfully stepped outside. The air out here was still damp and chilly, but at least it was refreshing enough to keep him awake. More or less. Sinking to a low wall, the prince leaned back against the side of the conversation house and closed his eyes.

"Prince Ardagh?"

He opened them again with a start. "Ah, Lady Sorcha."

"Never mind the formalities. We've spoken together often enough by now to forgo them. Are you ill?"

Ardagh sighed. "No. I am not ill, merely weary." Remembering how much she knew by now of who and what he was, he added honestly, "Weary from the lack of Power in this Realm. Ae, don't look so worried! I'm not about to die for lack of magic. At least," the prince continued with dark Sidhe humor, "I don't *think* I am."

"That's not very funny."

The fire in her eyes sparked an unexpected little twinge of guilt within him. "Granted," Ardagh muttered.

Sorcha sat down beside him, still staring. "You never would admit this to me, but that's why you collapsed early in the winter, isn't it?"

"Eh?"

"The time when no one could wake you—that had something to do with the lack of—of magic, didn't it?"

"Something. I had tried to open a Doorway that night. And failed."

"A Doorway?" Sorcha echoed, then froze. "A Doorway home, you mean. Och, Ardagh . . . I'm so sorry."

"So," he said, "am I."

"B-but isn't there anything you can do? Our Realm can't be totally without magic!"

Ardagh turned to say something, but instantly forgot whatever it had been. Ah, the warmth in her eyes, the concern . . . lovely eyes, even if they lacked the Sidhe slant . . . why hadn't he ever stopped to truly notice that before? And they were set in such an intriguing face. . . .

A human face, the prince reminded himself sharply. A mortal face. One that would age when his would not. And, ae, the unexpected pain of that thought! Trying for cold Sidhe objectivity, Ardagh told himself he'd clearly been away from his own kind for far too long if he was beginning to even consider—

"Ardagh?"

"No," the prince said sharply, "your Realm is not without some magic. What I need to do is spend some time out in the forest; there's a good deal of Power to be gained from that wild life-force."

"Then why aren't you—"

"Doing what? Camping out in the wilderness? The process isn't exactly a holiday: I need to spend a fair amount of that time in contact with the earth itself. And I can hardly do anything like that till the weather stabilizes." At Sorcha's startled glance, he added, "What?"

"Och, I don't know. Worrying about the weather just seems so *mundane!*"

Ardagh snorted. "Mundane subject or not, I am *not* invulnerable to cold and damp."

"Then the weather doesn't get like this in—in your land?"

The prince glanced at her in sudden amusement. "We never have discussed that, have we? And what, pray tell, do you think the weather is like in the Sidhe Realms?"

"Why, ah, I don't know. Soft as springtime, the stories all say, but without the dampness. Never the cold or sleet, either or, for that matter, the heat of summer. Och, and the stories say that in the Sidhe lands it is always twilight."

Ardagh laughed. "Hardly that. Hardly any of that! It's true that we have no sun—you have no idea how astonished my first sight of this one was!—but our very air holds its own clear light. Our days are bright enough! And yes, we do have both day and night, just as does the mortal Realm, but our night . . . ah, our night . . . so very different . . ."

For a moment, remembering with painful intensity, he quite forgot he sat in very mortal Eriu, staring blankly into space. For a moment he saw only the Sidhe night, dimly hearing himself murmur, "It has a sky full of stars, brighter, more wondrously colorful than any you know here; it has a moon glowing by its own clear light, a clear, bright, silver moon without a stain."

Sorcha made a wordless little sound that could have meant either longing or human pity. Startled from memory, Ardagh turned to her, seeing her face so gentle, her lips slightly parted and . . . and what if he repeated that kiss now that his mind was clear of drink? Tentatively, wondering, Ardagh leaned forward.

But Sorcha quickly turned away. "And seasons?" she asked, a little too earnestly. "What of those?"

Who cares about the cursed seasons?

But she was human, he snapped at himself once more, she was mortal, there could never be anything between folk of two such different worlds. "We have our seasons, too," he said with forced calm. "And don't look so surprised! How else, even in our magical Realm, would farmers be able to grow food? We *do* need to eat and drink, truly we do! And we have rain as well, though nothing like this steady, chilly drizzle, and snow, pure as silver, we have fruit and flower sometimes on the same tree—yes, I've heard that song, too— and oh, it is all more beautiful than any of my words can possibly tell."

"I wish I could see it," Sorcha murmured. "More to the point," she added more sharply, "I wish *you* could see it."

Ardagh sagged back against the wall. "So do I, lady. So do I."

"You *are* ill!"

"No. Just weary, as I told you. Very weary." No matter the weather, he realized he dared wait no longer to return to the forest. "I will ask this favor of you if I may."

"I won't know what to answer," she retorted with something of her normal fire, "till you tell me what you want."

"I . . . there is one in Fremainn I do not wish to know what I am doing, where I am going. I can't tell you any more than that, and I will not name that one. But . . . I am going into the forest tomorrow. If I am not back by the following morning, I would greatly appreciate your sending someone into the forest in search of me."

Her eyes widened. But she could not have missed the urgency behind the words. And all Sorcha said was a quiet, "It shall be done."

THE STORM

CHAPTER 22

King Aedh glared at his Chief Minister. "Go ahead. I brought us into the conversation house so we could have privacy. Speak."

Fothad glanced down at the parchments in his hand. "The news isn't as bad as all that."

"But it's not very good, either, I take it. What is it, yet another of those cursed Lochlannach raids?"

"No. And the restoration work is well begun at Saint Beinian."

"Just as it is at Hi-Coluim-Cille and all the other sites those brigands have attacked. That doesn't give me any more help in stopping them. Fothad, I frankly don't know what to do next! You know as well as I that I simply don't have the men to ring round all of Eriu; no king could. And even if I kept a troop on constant readiness, I couldn't possibly get them there in time to stop one of those lightning-quick raids."

"No one's blaming you."

"*I'm* blaming me! This is *my* land, *my* people, and I can't do anything to help them! And maybe nobody is out-and-out blaming me," Aedh continued dourly, "but these raids certainly aren't helping my prestige. More, they're giving a lovely excuse to certain rulers to consider rebellion."

"Certain rulers including Finsneachta of Leinster."

"Oh yes, Leinster. That *is* what you wanted to discuss, I

take it? Yes? I'm going to have to march against Finsneachta
sooner or later—ha, no, sooner rather than later—before
that sorry excuse for a king can muster enough support
against me. Now that spring is here," Aedh added thoughtfully, "and the roads are passable—"

"Now? Are you sure the time is right?"

"Is the time ever right? Lochlannach on one front,
Leinster on the other—what would you have me do, Fothad?
If I strike against one of the hounds, the other bites. But
if I don't strike against either, they both bite." He grinned
without humor. "At least I know where to *find* Finsneachta!
Those Lochlannach—you're a poet, Fothad. Go into a poetic
trance like the bards of old and see if you can't conjure me
up a vision of when and where those sea thieves will strike
next."

"You . . . are joking, aren't you?"

"Och, man, what do you think? If anyone was going to
summon up visions, I'd expect it to be our uncanny Prince
Ardagh, with those uncanny eyes and those mystic trips off
into the forest."

Fothad's eyes widened. "He's gone again?"

"Going, at any rate." Aedh shrugged. "Who can say what
that one's about? I had someone follow him once, find out
what he's doing out there. Not that I think our guest is up
to anything dangerous, you understand," he continued with
a grin. "I admit to merely being curious. But he lost my
man quickly enough."

"Not surprising, the way he moves."

Aedh shook his head. "A prince of Cathay who practices
mysterious rites. A bishop from Rome watching everything
we do. Leinster on one hand and Lochlannach on the other.
Life certainly can be interesting, can't it?"

"Most," Fothad agreed dryly.

"Where are you going?"

Ardagh turned, barely biting back a sigh. At any other
time he would have enjoyed talking with little Princess
Fainche—but not now, not when he had finally coaxed
permission to ride down into the forest from King Aedh

and was eager to be gone. Of course, the prince added honestly to himself, this time it hadn't been too difficult a struggle; Aedh had put up nothing more than a token protest over his guest's departure.

Hardly surprising: the king has too many other issues on his mind to worry about me.

Besides, Ardagh acknowledged with a faint smile, by this time Aedh wasn't about to be surprised by any new eccentricities on the part of his guest.

"Where are you *going?*" Fainche insisted.

"Hush, child. It's not polite to shout."

"But where—"

"Into the forest, little one. To . . . think." *Among other things.*

"You can think here."

"No, I can't. Not deeply. There are too many distracting people in Fremainn. Too many people asking me what I'm doing or where," he tapped her lightly on the nose with a forefinger, "I'm going."

"I don't want you to go."

"Whyever not?"

She only shrugged, kicking at a pebble.

"Ae, Fainche," Ardagh said helplessly, not at all sure how one calmed such a young child's fears. "I'll come back, I promise." *Barring the unforeseen.* "Is that what frightens you, that I'll just—run away? The way a certain princess was going to do when her brother teased her?"

That roused a reluctant little giggle. Ardagh smiled. "I will come back," he repeated. "But now, my dear young lady, if I am ever to return, I really must leave."

Odran mac Daire, courtier and noble, Odran of the Ui Neil sept—Odran, he thought with a touch of dour humor, the secret ally of Derval, Queen of Clonach—stood watching Prince Ardagh and little Princess Fainche talking together. A charming picture, the two of them, the tall, exotic prince and the tiny, pretty child. Like a bright-feathered bird, that little one, always flitting about. A good target for a plot—

No. She was a girl, just that, which gave her limited value

on the political scene no matter how much her father seemed to prize her. How much more effective a bargaining counter would be the little one's brother, royal heir Prince Niall himself! Oh yes, Odran thought. If only there was a way to steal that one . . .

Ha. Far better to puzzle out a way to steal *himself* out of here! His hands were tightening into fists, and with an effort, Odran forced them to relax. "Courtier." A polite word for "hostage." He was held here as surely as one of the underkings' children. Yes, and how wonderfully satisfying it would be to hold a royal hostage of his own!

As soon dream of holding the moon. But thoughts of young Prince Niall were bringing to mind another royal heir: Fearghal mac Donnchadh, Derval's son. Or rather, Odran corrected silently, Derval's lost son. All messages that came to him here were watched, Chief Minister Fothad had made that quite clear, but even so there were still ways information could be conveyed: a quick word, a swift gesture, a scrap of parchment with secret, seemingly innocuous markings on it. Derval's spy had been here this very day, telling Odran of her son's disappearance, and probable destination.

As if I remember what the brat looked like. I only saw him the once, and that, several years ago. As if I care what happens to a boy who can only be an obstacle to me.

Still, there was this: if he could pick out Fearghal from all the others who swarmed through the fortress, what a nice tool the boy could prove. Almost as useful a hostage as Prince Niall mac Aedh himself.

Interesting idea, Odran mused, and smiled slightly. *Most interesting.*

Fearghal, normally heir to the kingdom of Clonach but right now a ragged nobody, crouched in shadow, staring in amazement at the tall, elegant man with the long black hair and the slanted green eyes. He had *never* seen anyone like that! How many more strangenesses could this fortress contain? How could he ever manage to survive here? And why oh why had he ever been stupid enough to think he could do anything to win a throne all by himself?

No, no, wait. Maybe he could still get close to King Aedh, close enough to—

To what? Assassinate the king? Where was the honor in that? Besides, Fearghal thought, glancing down at himself with a flash of honesty, who was ever going to permit such a ragged, filthy creature anywhere near a king?

"You, boy!" a haughty voice snapped, and Fearghal jumped. "Stop skulking about like an idiot! There's work to be done."

Wonderful, just wonderful. His servant's disguise was so good that now he was going to have to *act* like a servant!

I'll get out of this. Somehow. And do what? Return to Clonach? Return in disgrace? No! *I will* not *slink home like a—a guilty little boy!* Fearghal vowed. *I won't go back at all till I can return as a hero!*

Though how he was going to accomplish that, he hadn't the vaguest idea. For now there wasn't anything else to do but pretend to be as much a nobody as he looked. Gritting his teeth, Fearghal mac Donnchadh, heir to the throne of Clonach, dutifully followed the other servants and hoisted a bundle that felt heavy enough to contain rocks onto his back. Sharp-edged rocks, he amended, staggering along under the weight. Sharp as his frustration. Or, though he hated to admit it, his fear.

Arnulf frowned. He had been following the boy for some time, puzzled. There was nothing to separate this servant from all the others in the line of burden-bearers, and yet . . . what little magic Gervinus had granted him was tickling his mind, telling him, *Look. Study. Learn.*

Learn what? Arnulf's frown deepened with frustration. Maybe Gervinus would know at a glance why this servant boy should be worthy of study, but he hadn't deigned to share that much of his abilities with his acolyte.

Ha, but what was this? No magic needed to see that the servant was ever so subtly slowing down, dropping back place after place till he was last in line. Arnulf grinned as he saw the boy glance warily about, then throw down his burden and scuttle off.

Now where can you be going? Let's see, shall we?

He followed, staying just far enough back to keep the boy from seeing him. At last his quarry stopped, hiding against a wall, back to Arnulf. The acolyte came up behind him and murmured, "Rough life, isn't it?"

Instead of the gasp of fright, the surge of guilt he'd expected, what Arnulf got was a startled but clearly aristocratic glare and a fumbling for a weapon—a sword?—that wasn't there. A sword? the acolyte wondered. *Just who is he?*

No servant, that was for sure. In the next moment, the boy had managed a credibly coarse, "Yeah. Rough." But it was so blatantly an act that Arnulf, testing, said, "Everyone's always after you, 'Do this, do that!'"

"They are!" It was said with heartfelt enthusiasm—and without noticing that he'd let the rough accent slip. "You, too?"

"Me, too." Pretending gruff friendliness, Arnulf shook the other's hand before the boy could pull away. *Soft! Soft as the hand of a noble!* "I've only got the one master ordering me around," the acolyte continued warily. Then, realizing with a sudden shock that the boy had no idea who he meant, Arnulf added, "One master, but he's worse than a dozen of them. I go here, there, do this, that, whatever he wants, with never a word of thanks from him."

"That's right. They never do thank you, do they? Not the way it was when I—when I was in the other place."

Aha. "And that was . . . ?"

The boy shrugged, eyes gone wary. "Doesn't matter. I'm here now."

"Right. Here. Where they work you like a slave. They do, you know. Work you till you drop. And don't even try to think of escaping," Arnulf added, watching the boy closely. "They'll hunt you down for that, yes, and maybe brand you."

"They wouldn't *dare!*"

"Why not? You're nothing but a servant, right? They can do whatever they want: brand you, flog you, maybe even kill you—"

"That's barbaric!" the boy snapped. "In Clonach my father would never allow—"

He clamped his mouth shut. Arnulf, pretending he hadn't heard a thing, told him, "Well, do your work and you won't get hurt. Good talking to you, but I have my own job to do."

With a wave of his hand, the acolyte left, his thoughts racing. Clonach? "My father would never allow"? This boy was no common soul, not at all! And his hands were far too soft to ever be mistaken for those of a servant.

"My father," eh? Arnulf wondered. *Could it be?* Oh no, that was too improbable!

And yet, Gervinus had proved to him over and over again that the strangest things, the most improbable things, could prove possible. Could the father of this soft-handed, well-spoken boy actually be none other than the King of Clonach?

A prince hiding out as a servant. Arnulf shook his head in disgust. *Sounds like something out of an old tale, a tale that's been told almost to death.* If it hadn't been for the evidence of that voice, those hands, yes, and those not-quite-covered-up slips of the tongue—the evidence was there, the acolyte realized with reluctant acceptance. The boy really was a runaway prince.

I'd better go tell Gervinus. Never can tell what he'll find useful.

But then Arnulf slowed to a stop, considering. He really should tell Gervinus—

No. With a little thrill of alarm, Arnulf realized that he wasn't going to do it. Frightening, this sudden decision to keep information from the Master, and totally illogical. And yet, here it was. He was not going to tell Gervinus about the boy. This once he was going to have a secret Gervinus did not know. This once, petty though it might be, he was going to hold on to at least a shred of power!

As Ardagh rode down from the fortress of Fremainn, he fought the urge to glance back over his shoulder. Gervinus was watching, he was as sure of it as if the bishop had called his name.

Look all you will. You cannot stop me.

That wasn't the real issue. It was what might happen once he'd entered trance.

You aren't that Powerful, Gervinus. At least I hope you are not.

Ah well, he'd taken what small precautions this Realm permitted. Before he had left, Ardagh had taken Cadwal aside and murmured, as he had to Sorcha, "If I am not back by morning, kindly send someone into the forest in search of me."

A puzzled Cadwal had nodded warily. Faint security, Ardagh knew, but better than none. And it was hardly likely the bishop or any of his retinue would follow.

It's not human followers that concern me, the prince thought with dark humor, *not that I can do anything about it now,* and rode on into the forest.

Ah, and what a lovely change! Though the trees and bushes were still mostly bare, each twig was tipped with a bud waiting to burst into new green leaves, and the wakening life-force of the woodland was so strong it nearly staggered him as he dismounted. Tying his horse, Ardagh wandered on into the rapidly darkening twilight, smiling, the dim light no barrier to his Sidhe vision, glorying in his solitude.

And then, with a suddenness that saw him springing back with a gasp, the air shimmered with the opening of a Doorway. *Finvarra? Can it be—* "Breasal!" Ardagh cried.

The boy stood framed by the magical shimmering, clad in a Sidhe tunic of grass-green spidersilk, his hair held back by a thin copper band. And oh, what a wonderful change in him! No longer wan or sickly, he stood straight as a slender young tree, his skin pale from the sunless Sidhe sky but radiant with health. "Prince Ardagh, I—"

"No! Don't step out of the Doorway! Setting foot on mortal soil will undo all that's been done for you."

Breasal froze as though turned to stone. But then, being still the boy he was, he had to explode into words: "Och, but I have to thank you! You saved my life—you brought me here, to this wonderful place, and—and I can do anything I want now without pain or worrying that I'm going to—to— And the king's so kind to me, everyone's so kind, he's given me a place at his court. I'm one of his squires now, King Finvarra's, and he's given me tutors in so many exciting things, even magic!"

By now he had to stop for breath. Before he could start up again, Ardagh, smiling, told him, "I'm glad for you, boy, truly glad."

A shadow passed over the boy's happy face. "But it's not right," he said plaintively. "I mean, I'm in the Sidhe Realm but you're not."

"Believe me, Breasal, if I could do anything to alter that fact, I would. Ae, don't worry, boy. I'm delighted to see you healthy and happy. I'll find a way home someday. And then you and I can visit together like the royal folk we are. The Doorway's not going to stay open much longer. Give Finvarra my regards if you would."

The Doorway was, indeed, closing. With a final wave of his hand, Breasal vanished, leaving the forest lonelier for his going. With a grimace, Ardagh settled back into his search for the site in which he could regain what little Power was in this mortal place.

Ah, but now he had once more gone beyond the touch of humanity. *Here,* Ardagh thought, and cast himself to the ground. Ignoring the chill, the prince cast open his mind, his senses, his very essence, and drank in the wondrous, wondrous Power of the forest's life.

It was, Gervinus thought with a cold little inner smile, turning out to be quite a useful day. First that fool of a woman had come to him, begging him to bless her sickly baby. Yes, she'd been nothing but a commoner, but the fact remained that she had come to *him,* not Father Seadna or any other local prelate. Even if relations with King Aedh or Chief Minister Fothad remained as cool as ever, this blessing was the first indication of acceptance by the folk. And when the commons insisted, wise royalty acquiesced.

Ah, and if that had not been fine enough, there went Prince Ardagh, riding out of the safety of Fremainn without the slightest bit of caution—riding out into the wilderness.

Gervinus shook his head in disbelief. Who knew what pagan rites the prince planned to perform? Who, to be quite honest, cared? With any luck at all, bandits or beasts or simple bad weather would get the man and that would be that!

And yet . . . and yet . . . *why risk his return?* a voice deep in his mind whispered. *Why not be sure it never happens? You'll never have a better chance.*

Through sorcery? No! That would be too perilous.

There will never be a better chance to be rid of Prince Ardagh, his mind insisted. *Assassins and the like are so risky, the chance of failure so high. But sorcery . . . ah, sorcery will leave no awkward traces.* "No," Gervinus snapped. But his mind continued, unbidden, *Sorcery will rid you of the prince and yet leave you looking utterly, utterly innocent.*

He had returned to his bedchamber without realizing it. Gervinus drew out his grimoire from his robes with hands that were not quite steady, and stood for a long, silent while, staring down at the book almost in terror.

Nonsense! He was master of the sorcery, not it, him! And it did make sense to use that sorcery in one quick, untraceable attack.

He would do this, Gervinus decided. All he need hope was that the prince not return too soon. Or rather, he corrected himself wryly, all he need hope was that the prince never return.

Flinging open the door, the bishop told his servants coldly, "I wish to be left undisturbed. Undisturbed, is that clear?"

He watched them bow in submission, then turned back into the chamber. Let the idiots think he wished to spend some time alone in prayer!

Even so, Gervinus warily barred the door to his bedchamber behind him. *"Trust no one, fear no one."* He filled a basin with water, then stood for a moment in silence, gradually clearing his mind of extraneous thought and firming his resolve.

Yes. Now.

He cast open his grimoire with a little gasp of joy and began to read aloud, even as he had that day aboard the

ship to Eriu, adding to his summons the restriction that the
demon arrive quietly, *quietly*. The last thing he wanted was
for Arridu to alarm everyone in Fremainn!

And Arridu, much to the bishop's relief, obeyed, appearing
as a shimmering Something, hanging like a veil of dark water
in the air. But this time Gervinus felt an eerie amusement
radiating from the demon. And he suspected uneasily that
this polite compliance was being performed merely because
it amused Arridu to comply.

For the moment.

"What would you, human?" The chill voice sounded
equally amused.

Refusing to let himself be cowed, Gervinus forced himself to reply as calmly as if he was merely discussing the
weather (oh, apt choice of words, that, the bishop thought,
considering Arridu's power), "A small task. One that may
even entertain you."

*"Ah, I see. You have tired of living and wish me to assist
you out of life."*

Demonic humor. "Hear me out," Gervinus commanded.
"And, by the ring I wear, the ring that bears your name,
do not interrupt me again." He waited a tense second, then,
when Arridu said nothing, continued, "In the nearby forest there is a man—tall, fair of skin, his hair long and black,
his eyes slanted green."

"And what would you have me do with such a one?"

Gervinus smiled. "Why, kill him. That is all I ask. Kill
him in whatever way most pleases you, then depart this
Realm in peace, taking no other life. Is that agreed?"

*"One life? Only one? It barely seems worth the effort. But
. . . agreed,"* hissed the demonic voice. And this time the sense
of amusement was very strong, indeed. With a rush of chill
air, Arridu was gone, leaving Gervinus breathless and shaken.

The bishop roused himself with an effort. The grimoire
still lay open as though begging him to read it. Gervinus
picked it up, but by chance found he was looking at a page
dealing with ensorcelled daggers. Interesting, but he was
hardly going to go hunting for black cats to sacrifice or dig
up various organs from human corpses.

He straightened in sudden inspiration. The blade itself didn't need to be ensorcelled. Poisoned weapons were common enough in Rome—but what if the salve smeared on the knife wasn't a poison, not exactly?

Full of suddenly renewed energy, Gervinus sank to a chair, leafing eagerly through the grimoire for the section dealing with potions. Yes . . . ah, yes . . . he had wolfsbane already, and the other ingredients should be easy enough to find. No one would think to question his raiding of Fremainn's herb gardens. He would gather the ingredients now, mix the potion, say the binding spells over it while sorcery still raced through his mind; sweet, so sweet.

Ah yes, yes, this was a most useful day, indeed!

Ardagh awoke with a shock, mind torn between the wondrous surge of Power returned and the sudden sharp awareness that he was in peril. He struggled to his feet, dizzy from the abrupt return to reality, wondering what—

Something attacked. Ardagh staggered back, nearly tripping over a protruding root, frantically trying to ward off whatever it was and gather his dazed senses at the same time. The Something lunged, a great dark mass swirling through a hundred shapes at once. No time for defense: the prince threw himself aside, feeling branches lash at him and thorns catch at his clothes. He landed with Sidhe lightness, rolling, scrambling up again, never taking his gaze from the Other, realizing in that moment *demon* and desperately hunting through his mind for a combat spell. Nothing! There was nothing that would work in this Realm that was strong enough!

"Ae!" The demon's sudden swipe with suddenly grown talons just barely missed slashing him open. The talons lashed out again, and Ardagh abandoned bravado and ran, twisting, wriggling, struggling his way through the tangled forest. He burst out into a clearing, gasping—only to find the demon facing him as if it had been there all along, radiating such sadistic joy it sickened him. No combat magic, no sword . . .

What can I do? Ardagh thought wildly. *Throw rocks at it?*

Despairing, he drew his dagger. As the demon came plunging down over him, he lunged up at it with all his might, feeling the blade cut into something that felt nothing like flesh.

And the demon screamed. To Ardagh's astonishment, it screamed as though he'd mortally wounded it.

Faerie metal! he thought wildly. The magic innate in Faerie metal must be alien to a demon!

Very probably. For before Ardagh could take a new breath, the demon swirled up like some great storm cloud impossibly soaring back *up* into the sky, and in the next instant was gone. The prince stood gasping and shaken in its wake, hardly believing what had just happened, hardly believing the danger was over.

Was it? A tickling on one forearm made him glance down. For a moment Ardagh stared blankly at the slight trickle of blood, thinking that a twig or thorn must have—

No. No pain at all, a slash neat as one from a physician's blade, the edges of the small slash white and lifeless . . . it could only mean one thing: a demon-wound. The—quite literally—damned creature must have caught his arm with a talon before it had fled. That was the way of such seemingly trivial wounds: the lack of pain lulled the victim into not noticing the injury until it was too late, until demon essence had seeped into every vein from even that slight cut with deadly venom.

Powers . . .

There was a cure, Ardagh's memory insisted. He dared not wait, dared not wonder if the cure would work in this Power-weak Realm, or if he could find the correct herb. Instead, Ardagh hunted fiercely till he'd found—ah, thank you, Powers, yes!—a stalk of homey garlic. Close enough to what he'd have found in Sidhe Realms, close enough in physical healing strength.

Pulling the plant from the earth, the prince crushed the bulb against the wound, wincing at the sting, and rushed out the Words of Healing, Words of Exorcism that added magical strength to physical. To his relief, Power rose and swirled about him, but it wasn't as strong as it should be, not nearly as strong. No hope, though, but to continue, praying it would be enough.

As the last Word locked into place, Ardagh fell in sudden total exhaustion, dragging himself into the shelter of a bush. His last waking thought was that either this had worked, and he would awaken, or it hadn't, and he wouldn't. Either way, there was nothing more that could be done, except surrender to sleep.

Gervinus looked down at the dagger in his hand with weary satisfaction. Mixing the potion had been simple enough, but imbuing it with sufficient sorcerous Power had been another matter, and joining potion and blade so that not a hint of stain marred the metal had been almost more than he could manage. But it was done. The weapon was ready. All he needed now was the hand to wield it.

And sleep. *Deus*, yes, Gervinus thought, sinking gladly to his bed, sleep . . .

But just as he drifted gently off into oblivion, the world seemed to explode into horrifying noise and white-hot flashes of light. The very walls of his house shaking around him, Gervinus sat bolt upright, gasping, knowing instantly, *No normal storm—Arridu!* Arridu enraged and recoiling in demonic fury as such beings did when their purpose was blocked back on the summoner—

"No!" Gervinus shouted in panic, scrambling to his feet, his voice drowned out by the roar of thunder all around him. The walls were cracking, the roof shaking—in another moment the whole thing was going to come crashing down on his head! He threw up both arms in desperate command, shouting, "I hold your ring. I hold your name!"

No response.

"You cannot attack me!" Gervinus roared, now as much furious as afraid. "Demon, hear me! Obey me! You must obey!"

"You cheated me!" The demonic voice was barely discernable from the turmoil of the storm.

"I? I sent you out to kill; you accepted with glee. Have you failed me?"

"You have failed me!"

"No!"

"Yes! You sent me after one who bore metal never forged in mortal lands!"

"I never—"

"You let me be touched, be cut, be hurt by Shachshakax *metal!"*

For one instant, Gervinus lost his concentration completely, startled by the ugly, demonic word, thinking in confusion, *What metal can that possibly be?* And for that instant he lost his hold on the demon, and staggered under the renewed lash of the storm, hearing the house begin to crumble about him, the stench of ozone sharp in his nostrils.

But then Gervinus gathered every bit of his will, forcing himself back under control, shutting out the danger about him. Clenching the ring savagely in his hand, he shouted, "Come what may, you will obey me, Arridu! You must! I hold your name, Arridu, and if you do not obey, you shall be tortured by eternal flame! I hold your name, I hold your will, and I command you now—*begone!*"

Would he be obeyed? Would he? His heart was racing so fiercely it seemed about to tear free from him, his ears rang with the surging of blood, and in another moment his will was going to shatter. If Arridu refused to obey him, there would be nothing he could do but die.

But with a suddenness that left Gervinus gasping, the demon was gone, and only an abruptly tranquil night remained.

A PRINCE ENSORCELLED

CHAPTER 23

Someone was touching him, shaking him. Someone was calling his name. Ardagh forced himself up through layers of sleep, thinking with groggy Sidhe humor, *It would seem that the magic worked after all.* But who was this trying to wake him? The prince blinked, vision focusing slowly.

"Lady Sorcha." His voice sounded rusty. "What are you doing here?"

"It's morning!" she said sharply. As Ardagh pushed himself up on one elbow, looking up at the sunlight filtering down through the leaves, Sorcha added, a touch more gently, "You said that if you weren't back by now, I should send someone after you. And so I did." Her gesture took in the two soldiers, mercenaries from Cadwal's band, who stood on either side of her.

The worry behind the sharpness touched him. "You came, too. That, I did not expect."

She shrugged with blatantly feigned unconcern. "I thought you might need help. Particularly after the storm."

"Storm?" Ardagh got carefully to his feet, swaying a bit, and glanced down at his forearm: a thin, clean line crossed it, the mark of an old, well-healed wound. *But the demon has a token sample of my blood. Hopefully, not enough to let it work any harm.* "What storm?"

"You . . . didn't notice it?"

"Obviously not. Presumably," he added, glancing about at the undamaged forest, "it missed striking here at all."

"Och, well, it did sweep down on Fremainn seemingly from nowhere." Sorcha shook her head. "And a more savage storm I can't remember. It didn't do as much damage as it might, God be praised, but it tore right through the outer palisade, ripped apart some of the less secure roofs, and—and completely smashed the guest hut of Bishop Gervinus."

"Did it, now?" Ardagh murmured, beginning to suspect what had happened. A demon left with an unfulfilled mission was as dangerous as the recoiling backlash of an unsuccessful spell. As dangerous, that was, to the one who had summoned that demon. "And," he asked delicately, "was the bishop harmed?"

His tone hadn't been quite innocuous enough. Sorcha's glance was suspicious, though she answered without comment, "No. Several members of his retinue suffered injuries, though, and a few of them died, God rest their souls."

"I see."

"The bishop was badly shaken, anyone could see that. But he did what he could for the injured and the dead."

"I'm sure he did." Even though Gervinus had been the one responsible for their harming, he could hardly break the image of caring holy man he'd been so carefully cultivating. "There is nothing more for me to do here," Ardagh said. "Come, let us return to Fremainn."

Gervinus knelt by the side of one of his fallen aides; the man would probably recover, but a collapsing wall had caught him a stunning blow, and now, half-awake, he had clutched at the hem of the bishop's robe in entreaty.

My work, Gervinus thought sardonically. *Helping these idiots cope. As if I could actually make injuries vanish through prayer. My work, yes. Comforting them all.* Were he not still at heart the Frankish noble trained to a harsh school, he might almost be begging someone to comfort *him.*

Bah, what nonsense! The demon had, after all, obeyed.

It was far from here, in whatever hellish place it called home, and he would never need to put himself in its path again because he simply would never call on it again. And—

Gervinus nearly started as a shadow fell across his face. Before he could move, Prince Ardagh had dropped to his knees beside him as if joining him in prayer, long-fingered hand almost touching his own.

"You know and I know," the prince murmured almost conversationally, "that the storm was no storm."

"What are you—"

"You know and I know that it was, instead, a demon sent to slay me. You know and I know who it was sent it, and upon whom it recoiled in fury."

Gervinus stared at him in feigned outrage, mind racing, and saw the green eyes go so completely cold, so completely, inhumanly cruel that he was left wordless. "And you know and I know," the prince continued softly, his voice all the more chilling for never losing its conversational tone, "what will happen to the one who dares try sending it against me again."

Prince Ardagh was back on his feet in one smooth motion, face totally without expression. "See to your men," he said. "Such a master must surely be touched by their plight."

He was gone before Gervinus could utter a word.

Damn him. Damn him! There isn't a thing I can say, nothing that won't make me look either an idiot or a monster. And those eyes . . . I could almost believe the man as demonic as Arridu.

Oh, what foolishness! Just because someone could let his eyes go so very cold, that didn't make him other than human. Besides, cold eyes or no, if the prince had possessed any genuine proof of clerical sorcery, he wouldn't have been wasting time on threats. No, no, he would already have gone rushing off with that proof to King Aedh.

And isn't it odd, Gervinus mused, *that he was able to recognize a demon for what it was—and was able to repel it?*

What had Arridu claimed he bore? Some bizarre demonic blade? Had Gervinus, ironically, been correct all along with

his accusations, and was Prince Ardagh genuinely a rival
sorcerer?

Jesu Christus! If that was so, Gervinus thought, he'd need
to gain control over Aedh as quickly as possible.

*The assassin, I must find my assassin-tool. But how?
Where? Who is he, dammit? Who is he?*

The servant groaned under Gervinus' hand. With an
unvoiced oath, the bishop turned his mind back to pretended
piety. At least Aedh was seeing to it that his house would
be swiftly repaired. Glancing up, Gervinus noted that already
there were laborers enough to have—

He stared. Odd . . . there was something about that boy,
the one with the sullen, fine-featured face, the one who
looked far too finely made for such rough work. . . .

"Arnulf," he called over his shoulder.

"Master?"

"Arnulf, who is that boy?"

Was that the barest hesitation? "A servant. Nothing more."

"Only a servant?" Gervinus turned in sudden sharp suspicion, surprising a hint of uneasiness on the acolyte's face.
"Who is he, Arnulf? Tell me."

"I . . . uh . . ."

"Tell me!"

Reluctantly, head down, Arnulf muttered, "I was going
to tell you, really. But the storm and all—"

"I am reaching the edge of patience, Arnulf. Who is the
boy?"

"I'm not sure. I think he's royalty." As though the words
were being torn from him, the acolyte continued reluctantly,
"Hands are too soft for a servant. Words are too educated.
And the way he talked . . . I think he's the son of the King
of Clonach."

"What!" Gervinus' mind raced, *But he's—no, this would
be the* second *son.* Now that the truth had been pointed
out to him, it seemed impossible that he ever could have
missed seeing the telltale elegance beneath the dirt. *This
is the second son of Clonach come to avenge his poor,
murdered brother. How stupidly heroic!*

And how very useful. Gervinus snaked out a hand,

snagging Arnulf by the arm and dragging the boy back into what was left of his private chamber. "How long have you known?" the bishop growled.

The acolyte squirmed, trying to pull free, then hung limply in Gervinus' grip. "I . . . uh . . ."

Gervinus shook him. "How long have you known and not thought to tell me?"

"I *was* going to tell you, honest! Just didn't get the chance, the storm and all that, and—"

"Liar." The bishop threw Arnulf from him, watching coldly as the acolyte landed flat on his back then scrabbled frantically away, ending up cornered against a wall.

"I w-would have told you," Arnulf whimpered, "I swear it!"

"And are you adding perjury to your other sins?"

As he stared at the helpless, sniveling creature, Gervinus all at once lost control of his pent-up fury and fear and sheer frustration. Even knowing he was blaming Arnulf for everything that had gone wrong, it still felt wonderfully satisfying to send blow after sorcerous blow raining down on Arnulf, enjoying the acolyte's cries, blow after blow till at last, drained and gasping, the bishop straightened. If he didn't stop now, he was going to kill Arnulf.

No great loss. But it would be difficult to explain such a death. "Get up," Gervinus snapped. "Get out." He stood coldly, ignoring the bitter, hating glances the still snivelling acolyte cast his way. "Send the prince of Clonach to me," the bishop added. "I wish to speak with him, alone."

The boy who entered *almost* had the proper servile manner. Almost.

"You sent for me, my lord, ah, bishop?"

And his voice certainly wasn't that of a servant, either. Gervinus smiled. "I wished to welcome you to Fremainn, prince of Clonach."

He sat back in dark amusement to watch the boy's storm of confusion, fear, alarm. And then, still smiling, the bishop moved in to take possession of his prize. "I know of your sad loss," he purred. "And, if you will allow me, I mean to help you assuage your sorrow. Come, child," the bishop added, reaching out one arm, "let me touch you. Let me give you my blessing."

Aedh glanced at Fothad and Father Seadna, who had just entered the conversation house. "Come, sit. Fothad, I am not thrilled with what's being done to repair the outer palisade."

Fothad frowned slightly. "The men are working as quickly as they can."

"Not quickly enough."

"It's not as if we were left without any protection," the poet said, almost defensively. "The storm didn't do any damage to the earthenwork defenses."

"I know that," Aedh snapped. "But I don't like the idea of Fremainn having to go without that palisade. Particularly now. I have some information that I'm sure is just what you both wanted to hear." He made no attempt to hide his sarcasm. "The reason we haven't heard anything out of Clonach is that they've been too busy hunting for the heir to the throne."

Father Seadna frowned. "The boy's disappeared? Why should we need to—" He stopped short. "Och. Don't tell me."

Aedh nodded. "So it seems. Fearghal mac Donnchadh, as far as any spies could tell me, is now somewhere within Fremainn."

"But why—how—"

"The 'how' is easy enough," Fothad murmured. "Fremainn is full of all manner of servants. All the boy would need to do was dress the part. Who'd notice him?"

"The 'why' is easy enough, as well," Aedh added. "He's just at the right age to be properly heroic and stupid. Probably has some wild idea that he's going to avenge his brother." The king snorted. "Don't give me those stares, you two. Do you really think I'm in any danger from an untried boy?"

"Accidents," Fothad said, "happen."

Aedh shrugged that off. "More pressing than any threat from him is that we find Fearghal as soon as possible. If we've figured out he's here, so has Donnchadh. I've Leinster on one flank and the Lochlannach on another and a fortress with damaged walls and roofs; I don't need Clonach nagging me as well. Find me someone who can recognize Fearghal," he ordered Fothad, "and recognize him under whatever the boy's disguise may be. Catch me our royal runaway so we can ship him right back to his father."

Our royal idiot, Aedh added to himself. But then, most boys were idiots at that age. *Indeed. And I can hardly wait till my Niall reaches it. Amazing the human race survives.* "Come. Let us go see how the rebuilding's proceeding. Maybe the sight of their king watching will goad the workers a bit."

"Indeed," Fothad said without the slightest trace of irony in his voice. "Oh, indeed."

It felt wonderful to finally be *doing* something, Fearghal thought, touching the dagger hidden in his sleeve for maybe the hundredth time. He wasn't sure exactly what that something was going to be, or who had suggested it to him; he couldn't quite seem to remember much of anything. Except for this one thing, this one certainty: he knew without a doubt that if only he kept going, hunting for King Aedh, everything would work out most splendidly. He would, at last, be a true hero.

"You came back."

Ardagh paused on his way to his guest house, glancing down at solemn little Fainche with a smile. "I told you I would."

"You didn't get wet. Why not?"

"There wasn't any rain in the forest. I trust," he added with amused courtesy, "that you didn't get wet, either?"

She shook her head. "I was inside. Everyone was scared of the storm. Except me," she added proudly. "I wasn't scared at all."

"Good for you. I—" Ardagh froze, all at once *feeling* the faintest prickle of warning, wondering, *Now, what . . . ?* "Excuse me, little one," he said, trying to keep the sudden alarm out of his voice. "There is something I must investigate."

Queen Eithne sat in her grianan, studying the intricate embroidery knotwork she'd nearly completed. Nicely done, if she did say so herself, and the combination of blue, green and red on the interlacing was working out much more harmoniously than she'd expected.

"You see, Sorcha?"

The young woman glanced up from her own work with a bored nod. "Pretty. Not like my own tangle." Sorcha shook her head. "I'm better with a quill than a needle."

Eithne smiled. "My poor, impatient Sorcha. There are, no matter what you might think, pleasures to be taken in the slow, careful art of needlework, and I only wish you could—"

She started to her feet, embroidery sliding from her lap, all at once alert and terrified.

"Queen Eithne?" Sorcha asked uneasily. "What—"

"Aedh," the queen whispered and, heedless of Sorcha's stare and her bewildered ladies' cries, hurried from the grianan.

Gervinus, bent over his grimoire in a sardonic and very conscious parody of a man lost in prayer, watched Fearghal's progress in his mind's eye. It had been so ridiculously easy to overcome the boy's will: Fearghal had already been fairly burning with his childish, single-minded ambition. It had been a little more difficult to surround the boy with an avoidance spell, a tiny, fragile thing that should be just enough to let an apparent servant near the royal presence without challenge, but he'd succeeded. It grated on the nerves to once more have to depend on a boy to do his work, but there it was.

And now, ah now, if only Fearghal did his job, and did it right!

Colm mac Colm—which wasn't his true name, though good enough for an ordinary-looking, easily forgettable spy— was thoroughly sick of hunting for the missing Prince Fearghal, and rather wishing he could sit down somewhere (maybe, he thought dryly, with the royal counterparts) with a pleasant drink. But of course he couldn't give up a mission midway, not if he meant to go on living. And he certainly didn't intend to go back to Queen Derval and say, "Sorry. Just couldn't find him." No, the cursed boy had to be somewhere here in Fremainn. And sooner or later he would do something to reveal himself, and then—

Colm stopped short, blinking in sheer astonishment. Och, it couldn't be so easy. That dirty, bedraggled creature couldn't possibly be Prince Fearghal. But it most surely was, even in that unlikely garb; Colm had seen the boy at close range often enough to be sure of it. But, dammit, there were too many people here. He couldn't just go up to the prince and carry him off!

All he could do was what a spy did best: follow, wait and watch.

" . . . and if there aren't any Lochlannach raids within the next month," Aedh glanced from the half-rebuilt palisade to his Chief Minister as he spoke and continued in the same tone, "I vote we fly to the moon."

Father Seadna, standing on the king's other side, nearly choked on a startled laugh. Fothad blinked, reddened and said, "I beg your pardon?"

Aedh grinned. "Welcome back, Fothad. I trust it was an entertaining mental voyage."

He hadn't thought it was possible for the poet to redden any further, but so Fothad did. "I *am* sorry," he said contritely. "I didn't mean to wander—I just—"

"What is it, man? What's bothering you?"

"Och, nothing to worry the land." Fothad's voice was just a touch too light. "Personal matters."

"Sorcha," Father Seadna murmured.

"Well, yes," the poet admitted with a wry smile. "I confess it: discussing the wandering Fearghal mac Donnchadh brought out the parent in me."

Aedh chuckled. "You can hardly be comparing your daughter to a hotheaded fool of a boy! You've raised quite a sensible young woman, you know."

Fothad groaned. "But that's just it. She *is* a woman."

Aedh stared blankly, then suddenly grinned. "Ah, I think I understand. Sorcha *has* been spending a fair amount of time with our Cathayan prince, hasn't she?" He added teasingly, "Why, Fothad, what's the matter? He's a fine catch, royal blood and all."

"He's a *cu glas*," the poet snapped. "I will not have my daughter involved with an exile."

Father Seadna held up a hand in protest. "You're making too much of it. Whatever else Prince Ardagh may be, he is a man of honor. If he has sworn to do no harm to you or yours, he will keep that vow. Besides, we both know there hasn't been a bit of scandal about their meetings. All he's been doing is telling her about his homeland."

And she, of course, isn't at all interested in his handsome face, oh no, Aedh thought with an inner laugh. "Fothad, I don't think there's much you can do about it. She's a grown woman, a widow, not some green girl."

"Well, yes, but . . ."

"Sooner or later, you're going to have to think about letting her wed again," Father Seadna said.

"Not to a *cu glas!*"

Aedh shook his head. "Glad am I my Fainche's only five! I have some little time yet before I need worry about her betrothal or—" He turned with a frown. "Hey now, boy, you're not supposed to be here."

Fothad had gone alert as a hunting hound. "How did you get past the guards? Who are you?"

Aedh, studying the boy, said, "Oh, I think we can puzzle that out. You're Fearghal mac Donnchadh, aren't you?"

Eithne could have screamed her frustration. Every lady in her service seemed determined to ask her questions, block her path, delay her. "I can't stop now!" she repeated frantically. "We'll discuss it later. Please, I haven't the time right now!"

Aedh, och, Aedh . . . the sense of danger was burning at her, more fiercely with every second.

"Get out of my way!" Queen Eithne screamed, and raced on. She would never reach Aedh in time, never!

❦ ❦ ❦

Ardagh bit back a shout of pure fury. The *feel* of sorcery was growing stronger with every step he took, but there were just too many humans in his path, servants, guards, every one of them seemingly determined to get in his way, slow him down, keep him from the king. Abandoning courtesy, the prince fiercely pushed and shoved his way along. He was never going to reach Aedh in time, never!

"He has a knife!" Fothad hissed. "The guards, where are—"

Aedh waved him to silence, his attention all on the wide-eyed, white-faced boy. The last thing he wanted was for some overzealous guard to injure the crown prince of Clonach.

"I'm not going to hurt you, Fearghal," the king crooned, stalking forward as slowly and carefully as though he was trying to catch a wild creature. "And you don't want to hurt me, either. We both know that. I didn't kill your brother, Fearghal. The poor boy died of illness. It was God's will, Fearghal, and you're not going to challenge that, are you? No. You're going to let that knife drop, and neither of us will need to mention it again."

He made one incautiously quick step. With a cry, the boy lunged. Aedh lunged, too, catching the wiry young body in his arms. Someone had done a fine job of teaching the prince warrior tactics, because the boy, kicking and twisting fiercely, almost managed to escape. He tore his knife hand free before Aedh could grab it. The blade glinted in the light, and a woman screamed. Aedh realized *Eithne*, and in that half-second's inattention nearly lost his hold altogether. He gasped, more in surprise than pain, as the knife nicked his arm.

But Fearghal hadn't a chance of escaping the strength of a grown man, and Aedh slowly, trying not to break the boy's wrist, twisted the knife from his grip and held him, helpless as a baby in its mother's arms, till at last the king felt all resistance ebb. He shook the boy, just hard enough to make the point *I have your life in my hands*, then asked, "Can I release you? Will you act like an honorable warrior?"

Of course the boy couldn't argue with that. As Aedh warily released him, he stood sullenly still.

No. Not sullen. Frightened, certainly—he'd be an inhuman youngster if he wasn't—and . . . confused? How could he possibly be confused? A moment ago Fearghal had definitely acted as though he'd known what he was doing, and . . . and . . .

Aedh frowned. Odd . . . his mind didn't seem to be functioning as clearly as it should . . . it didn't seem to be functioning . . . very well at all . . . and his legs weren't doing their job of holding him up. . . .

As Aedh sagged, he felt strong arms catch him—Fothad on one side and, rather to his surprise, a somewhat breathless Prince Ardagh on the other. "Poison," he got out. "Knife . . . little bastard . . . poisoned me . . ."

It was the last clear thought, other than a despairing, *Eithne,* he was able to frame.

ENEMIES REVEALED

CHAPTER 24

Aedh found himself helplessly looking back over the years, caught in this strange half-dreaming state that insisted he see himself, see his life till now. . . .

And how very exhausting it seemed. Since he'd taken the throne, his life had been one continuous juggling act, playing this king against that, supporting this noble over that, fighting—

Ha, yes, fighting. Always that, whether he wished it or not. He had just managed that tenuous peace in Meath by splitting the land between the princely brothers, though it was just a matter of time before one of them massacred the other (and then he would probably have to battle the winner; such was life). And next he would most surely be taking arms against Leinster to put down *that* potential threat before it grew into something too large to be easily controlled.

Bah, we don't need the Lochlannach, he thought with wry, weary humor. *We do enough fighting among ourselves!*

"And do you want this?" a voice suddenly murmured, soothing and warm. *"Are you not weary of warfare, weary of the endless, endless struggles on the battlefield and in the council chamber?"*

Och, yes, Aedh thought. There were times when he was weary, indeed. But who was questioning him? He tried to ask, "Who are you? How do you know what I—"

No words would come. It didn't seem to matter. His thoughts weren't clear enough to let him worry about such things. Far easier just to listen to the voice whisper, "*Do you not long for rest? Imagine. Imagine peace, quiet, a chance to sit with your wife and watch your children grow.*"

Yes. It would be pleasant. Pleasant to relax and just be a man with a wife and a family—

No! Aedh struggled against the soft thoughts wrapping his mind round like some warm, suffocating blanket. What nonsense was this? He was no weak little man, he was High King of Eriu! He was fully aware and accepting of all the strain that title meant; the throne was his by right and strength of arm.

And I will hold that throne for as long as God wills it.

But even that small defiance seemed more wearying than anything he could endure. "*And does your arm never grow tired?*" the warm voice coaxed. "*Think, ah yes. Think. Wouldn't it be so wonderful, so very wonderful, to give over fighting? To let someone else help you, ease your way, make the difficult, difficult decisions over which you agonize?*"

Yes. It would be so wonderful to let someone else help him, to make his decisions—

No, dammit! He would not. He must not. He was king, and while any ruler must delegate, he must never, ever, deal away his power, and . . . and . . .

He couldn't think clearly. The voice wouldn't let him think, gently prodding and prodding at him, urging him softly, *surrender, surrender* till he couldn't think at all or resist or—

"*No,*" said a new voice, cold and clear as the edge of a blade, cutting sharply through the haze of confusion. "*You must not surrender.*"

He didn't want to yield, he certainly didn't, but he just couldn't . . . he couldn't . . .

"*A drug holds your mind,*" the cold voice snapped, as sharply as a palm slapping his face. "*You must not let it win.*"

But he was so weary, and the first voice continued to coax softly, "*Don't try to fight. You don't want to fight. Rest. Surrender. Surrender to me. . . .*"

"*You must not! You must fight back!*"

He should recognize this cold, fierce voice, surely. He should recognize the soothing voice as well. But his mind couldn't seem to hold on to memory and . . .

. . . and suddenly his mind was flooded with new, cold strength, with the cold, clear will telling him, *You are not alone. I will help you, King of Eriu. Fight! The drug must not win!*

"Yes," Aedh said, "I will not let it win."

With that other's strength behind him, he could tear free of the smothering softness and—

—just as suddenly find himself standing on a barren reddish plain beneath a barren reddish sky: reddish earth, reddish sky and nothing to break the emptiness, nothing to give him any hint of distance. This wasn't any real place: his mind had clearly been insisting on putting him *somewhere,* and without any outside clues, had compromised with this.

Boring of it, he thought. *Fothad would probably have landscaped the place as splendidly as some magical Sidhe Realm.*

All I get is—emptiness.

Emptiness, and hot still air. Feverish air. He knew fever dreams; he'd suffered enough of them due to wounds, nearly died in one once when a wound had gone bad. . . .

Ah, no. That soft, so-tempting voice just on the edge of perception had begun crooning to him once more, soothing him, telling him, *surrender, surrender* . . . it was the softest, most soothing sound in all the world . . . so very soothing . . . telling him *surrender self, surrender will, surrender* . . . it would be so easy to let go, surrender thought, mind, will . . .

No! He had never yet surrendered to anyone. Never would. A king who surrendered, who lost his battle, lost his crown as well, lost his very life. Aedh fought back with all his mind and will, swearing silently, *I will not surrender, damn you!* But it wasn't quite enough; the poison, the drug, whatever had been on that cursed dagger was still weakening him, and that damnable croon was continuing, *surrender, surrender* . . . and it was growing more and more difficult to resist. . . .

Then Aedh felt his nonmaterial hand clasped in a firm, cool, steady grip that seemed very real. *"He sought to lose me in the labyrinth of thought,"* the cold voice said. *"I will not be so easily lost."* And Aedh felt that cold, clear mind against his own once more, willing new strength into him, telling him, *resist, resist!* If he turned his head and stared with all his might, he could almost see . . .

Dream reality shifted. Without warning, he *could* see who stood beside him: Prince Ardagh. And in this Otherly place his beauty seemed strange and alien, fiercely sharp as the edge of a knife, almost alarmingly inhuman. The prince's long black hair snapped out behind him like a war banner though there was no wind, and his eyes blazed a wild, glowing green as they stared at the enemy. Suddenly Aedh could see him, too, this figure shrouded in a dark cloak, this figure clutching a leather-bound book that reminded him very much of the odd prayerbook Bishop Gervinus was never without.

Bishop Gervinus? The dark cloak parted, revealing hints of ecclesiastical splendor. "No," Aedh said. "No. That's impossible."

And, "Yes," Prince Ardagh said. "It *is* possible. It is true."

His, Aedh realized, and wondered that he hadn't recognized it before, was the cold voice that had helped him pull free from the entrapping softness, the voice that was sharp and clear and utterly without pity or sentiment.

Utterly without deceit.

The prince had never yet lied; he could not, Aedh knew without thought, be lying now.

"You cannot believe this man," the bishop began, "this foul, pagan sorcerer."

But Aedh hardly heard the words. He had, he suspected, never been meant to see or hear so truly. No, of course he hadn't! The drug had been intended to confuse as well as weaken him till he had become a willing slave. If it hadn't been for Prince Ardagh, he would probably already have sunk into quiet, helpless submission.

But the prince had saved him, cleared his thoughts. And now, no matter what accusations the bishop made, no matter how he tried to cloak himself in piety or kindness in this feverish otherness, the way he did in reality, here there could be no such earthly deception. No matter what he said, he could not hide his voice, his inner voice that had wrapped Aedh in softness, nearly lulled him into surrendering power, life—

"I do believe Prince Ardagh!" Aedh snapped, cutting through the bishop's words. "I believe him and I defy you! Bishop or whatever you really are, I am king, I will remain king, *and I will not surrender!*"

He awoke as suddenly as that, still blazing with righteous anger—and found himself in his own bed, Eithne, nearly sobbing with relief, at his side.

"You're alive, you're healed!" she gasped, and threw herself into his arms, burying her head against his chest, her hair and clothes sweet with the residue of what he guessed had been one of her healing potions.

But the dregs of the enemy drug, whatever it had been, were still in him, just enough to make him feel as though he'd drunk far, far too much mead the night before. "Gently, love," he said, "Och, gently. I'm all right, truly." Aside from a head that ached and a stomach that was not at all happy. "Eithne! You've seen me ride off into battle often enough and never acted like this, yes, and seen me come home hurt as well."

"And agonized over it every time!" she retorted, pulling back so that she could stare at him. "But that's the way things are when one is wife to a king, and I live with them as best I can. This, this was different! This was *sorcery,* husband, the blackest of sorcery used against you. It was meant to break and—and enslave your mind."

"You learned all that from one drug-smeared knife?"

Eithne gave an inarticulate little sound of impatience. "What was on that knife, as far as I could tell, was a weird mix of herbs, each one intended to confuse the senses. Put together, they would have been enough to thoroughly overthrow your will, making you the puppet of whomever had the skill to snare you."

That was enough to chill the heart. "At least," Aedh said,

struggling for the bright side of it, "it *was* a drug and not out-and-out poison. You could do something to counter it." He felt her flinch. "It *was* your doing?"

"I could counter the drug's effect, yes. But not . . . not . . . the mind behind its use." Her quick, tear-slicked glance was full of . . . what? Jealousy? Jealousy that another could help where she could not? "Prince Ardagh," the king said suddenly.

Eithne pointed. Carefully, Aedh turned to see the prince lying crumpled at the side of his bed (graceful, an irreverent part of his mind noted, even in that ungainly pose). Aedh sat up in alarm, then groaned, forgetting Prince Ardagh for the moment in the struggle not to be ill. Eithne hurriedly slipped from the bed and returned with a goblet of something that smelled minty.

"Here. This should help."

Aedh's stomach lurched in defiance, but he managed to drink the whole thing down without stopping. He waited, eyes shut, testing, and at last opened them again and said, "Yes," in relief. "It does. Och, but Prince Ardagh—"

"I . . . think he's asleep."

As though the words had been a cue, the prince started and came suddenly awake, staring up at Aedh, the fine-boned, elegant face dazed as though he'd come from an exhausting trial. Seeing him so weary, Aedh breathed, "It really happened, didn't it? You really were there—wherever *there* was—with me."

"In a manner of speaking." It was little more than a whisper.

"But—how?" Aedh pressed, knowing that right now the prince was still too dazed to evade the truth. "How did you do it? Who—*what*—are you?" And then, hardly sure he wanted to hear the answer, "*Are* you a sorcerer?"

That struck a spark. Life flashed back into the green eyes and the prince sat bolt upright. "Not that." His voice was contemptuous. "Never that." He was back on his feet in one sudden, fluid movement, and if his face was still pale, his glance was disconcertingly steady. "Ask that of Bishop Gervinus. See what answer you get of him."

"Yes," Aedh snapped. He wanted nothing so much as to stay in bed and sleep the last traces of the drug out of his system, but of course he couldn't indulge himself like that. His people had to be shown that he was still alive and well. The king struggled to his feet, very well aware of how clumsy he seemed compared to the infernally graceful prince. The touch of envy he couldn't quite repress made him say, "And we both know you didn't save me out of altruism. Och, no, you didn't want to see your sanctuary vanish."

For an instant he thought the prince was going to turn on him in anger, for an instant he wondered, *What if he does? What, then?* But to Aedh's amazement, Prince Ardagh instead treated him to one of those charmingly open smiles of his. "Precisely. Now, ask your question of Bishop Gervinus."

Gervinus, indeed. But first, his people's reassurance. The mystery of exactly how Prince Ardagh had saved him would have to wait as well—presuming that he ever could get the whole truth out of that slippery fellow. Still, at least the prince was very clearly on his side. Far better to have a friendly mystery than a mysterious enemy!

No one, the king realized, had wasted precious time undressing him before getting him to bed. Good. No need to waste precious time now, either. He shouted for servants to give him a hurried grooming, then stepped, mostly steadily, out into the open, Eithne on one side, Prince Ardagh on the other.

Mm, look at this. All along he'd thought that comparison of a confused scene to a disturbed anthill had been badly overused by poets. But a disturbed anthill was exactly what Fremainn resembled: a wild, panicky roiling of people who weren't exactly sure where they were going or what they were doing. He must have been trapped by the drug for quite a while; judging from the early afternoon slant of the sun, he'd lost about a day. No wonder everyone was in such a panic!

"I am alive!" he shouted into the turmoil, in the regal voice trained to carry over the noisiest of crowds. "I am unhurt!"

He saw startled faces turn to him (like so many flowers turning towards the sun, that irreverent bit of his mind jibed), saw eyes widen and smiles appear. There were gasps, murmurs, and at last a ragged roar of cheers. Gratifying, the enthusiasm there, even if most of it was out of plain relief that there was still someone in charge rather than personal concern.

Ha, here was Cadwal, his weather-beaten face impassive as always, but his eyes showing an agony of frustration and alarm over having been unable to protect the man who'd hired him. *Not your fault,* Aedh thought, *not if sorcery really was involved.*

But he wasn't going to let Cadwal off so easily. "Bring Bishop Gervinus to me, now!" Aedh commanded. "And bring me that boy . . . Fearghal. Bring them both to me!"

Cadwal, clearly glad to be doing *something,* snapped out orders to his men, who hurried off into the still-milling crowd. One of the men returned almost at once, dragging a desperately proud, definitely frightened Fearghal with him. The others took longer to return, and returned empty-handed, their faces grim.

"Where is he?" Aedh demanded. "Where is Bishop Gervinus?"

Before they could answer, Prince Ardagh cut in, "Gone, of course." As Aedh turned to him with a frown, the prince continued calmly, his eyes cool, "No, I'm not using that sorcery of which he accused me, only logic. If you were he, and your treasonous plan had gone so very wrong, would *you* linger for punishment?"

"Prince Ardagh is right," one of the guards said hesitantly. "The bishop is gone as though he'd never been here."

Damn. And it wouldn't have taken sorcery to escape amid all that turmoil, either. *Knew we weren't getting that palisade repaired quickly enough.* "What about his retinue?"

"They're all still here, looking confused as lost sheep. And we found his acolyte hiding in a corner of the guest house."

"So. Bring *him* to me. And you, Fearghal, the time has come for answers. Why did you attack me?"

Silence.

"Well? You must have had a reason! Come, boy, speak up."

The young prince stiffened. "I would if I had something to answer!"

"How nice to see the pup has fangs," Aedh drawled. "But that is *not* a satisfactory reply. Why did you attack?"

He knew, and suspected Prince Ardagh knew (since the man had made it plain often enough that he would not tolerate the harming of a child) that he wasn't going to do anything to Fearghal. But Fearghal didn't know it. White-faced and proud as a king going to execution, he told Aedh, "One thing's true. I did come to Fremainn of my own free will."

"To try your hand at assassination?"

"No! I mean, I-I-didn't know what I was going to do when I got here. I didn't know Fremainn was so . . . *big*. But then the bishop spoke to me. He wanted to . . . I think he said he wanted to bless me. He put a hand on my head, I-I think he did, anyhow. But I don't remember anything else, not a thing."

"Do you expect us to believe that nonsense?"

Sheer terror flashed in the boy's eyes—the look, Aedh thought, of a prisoner under torment who has told all he knows and is terrified that it's not enough. "You must!" Fearghal pleaded. "You have to! I-I can't tell you anything else, I don't *know* anything else!"

"Indeed."

"It's true! I swear it! I swear it on—on my father's crown!"

Aedh glanced once more at Prince Ardagh. The green eyes said, clear as words, *you see?* Right. *And what*, Aedh returned silently, *am I supposed to do about it without an ecclesiastical prisoner as proof?*

Smooth over the whole thing as best he could, that was what. It would be easier to keep peace with the monasteries that way, too; they wouldn't have taken kindly to him holding even a Roman cleric captive. "Och, well," the king said with false relief, raising his voice so all could hear him, "it's plain we were all deceived. That was no true bishop, no matter how it seemed, but a cunning villain in a most cunningly wrought disguise." Never such a thing as too much melodrama when speaking to a crowd. "What vile plots he was concocting, we may never know, but he's gone now. And we are well rid of him."

"We are not rid of him." It was the softest of growls from the prince.

"For now we are," the king muttered to him, "and that's enough. Ah, and here's our fine young acolyte, what's his name, Arnulf."

Arnulf, shivering, refusing to meet anyone's eyes, had just gotten fully into a snivelling, sorry tale of abuse and betrayal, swearing on all the saints that ever were that he'd known nothing of Gervinus' true nature or of his treachery, when Aedh saw Prince Ardagh go sharply alert, staring at a sudden upheaval in the crowd.

God, now what?

A woman was pushing her frantic way through: "Sorcha!" Aedh exclaimed. "What's happened to you?"

Her dress was torn, her hair disheveled, and a bruise was purpling one side of her face. Eithne cried out and raced to her side, putting an arm about her, but Sorcha pulled free, staring at Aedh. "Never mind me, I-I'm just bruised a bit. It's Odran mac Daire—I—he—" She stopped short, eyes wild, glancing from Aedh to Eithne, then took a deep breath and began again. "He's taken advantage of the confusion to commit a terrible act of treason, King Aedh.

"Odran mac Daire has stolen away your son!"

ATTACKS AND COUNTERATTACKS

CHAPTER 25

Ardagh heard Eithne give one little, heartrending cry, then fall silent, but he couldn't take his gaze from Sorcha, seeing the dazed eyes, seeing the bruised face, feeling a new, hot anger against the one who'd hurt her, realizing, almost in despair, *I did not want this. A human woman—ae, I did not want this,* knowing it was too late to resist.

"Go on," Aedh murmured to Sorcha, but she was swaying on her feet. Ardagh raced to her side, catching her in his arms, sure she was about to faint, but she painfully continued, "It happened . . . happened during the confusion . . . after you had collapsed and . . . and none of us knew if you still lived. Found myself shoved over to the edge of the palisade . . . you know, the . . . the spaces where it is still under construction." Her voice strengthened slightly. "And I saw Odran mac Daire seize Prince Niall." Ardagh felt a shudder run through her. "I *should* have screamed," she said, "but I didn't think . . . instead, I tried . . . tried to stop him. That's when I got this." She touched her bruised cheek gingerly. "Don't know . . . don't know what happened next. Head hurts so much . . . don't know how long I was . . . out . . . but Odran's gone, Prince Niall's gone. . . ."

This time she did go limp in Ardagh's arms. He looked

309

in panic at Eithne, but she, for all that she radiated terror over her missing son, shook her head slightly, telling him clearly, *This, my magic can heal.*

As she vanished into the royal keep with her servants and the half-conscious Sorcha, Ardagh reluctantly turned his attention back to Aedh. "You can't send soldiers."

"I know that!" the king snapped. "If the traitor sees an army coming after him, he might panic." *And kill his hostage.* The unspoken words hung heavily in the air. "Cadwal! Put together a small group of your best. Odran can't have gotten very far."

"I will be one of the hunters," Ardagh cut in. "Ae, don't look at me in such surprise! Do you think I'd let a child come to harm, least of all a child who's befriended me as the little prince has?" *Besides, I—I cannot bear staying here to worry about Sorcha and What Might Be.*

He received no argument from Aedh. "Go out there," he said. "Go out there, and bring my son back to me."

He'd nearly killed three horses getting here, and now that he'd finally made it back to Clonach, Colm mac Colm, sometimes merchant and sometimes spy, had to wonder if it had been worth the rush and risk. "It's true," he insisted, keeping just out of King Donnchadh's not inconsiderable reach where the king sat brooding beside his cold-eyed queen. "Your son, Prince Fearghal, really *is* in Fremainn. I saw him there. There can be no mistake."

Donnchadh sprang up, towering menacingly over the much shorter Colm. The spy refused to let himself reveal alarm in either glance or movement—you never attracted a predator's attention to you—but continued as levelly as he could, "Wait. There is more yet to tell. Remember," he added warily, glancing from King Donnchadh to Queen Derval, who, though she had never moved, seemed far more perilous than her easily angered husband, and back again, "that I am but the bringer of news, not its cause."

"Yes, yes," Donnchadh snapped, "you're safe. But only if you stop this hesitating!"

"Go on," murmured Derval. "What more is there to tell?"

There was still no expression on her lovely face, but Colm found himself fighting back the urge to lick suddenly dry lips. "Simply this: Prince Fearghal tried to kill the Ard Ri."

"*What!*" That was close to a shriek from Donnchadh.

"Tried to stab him, yes. He failed," *of course he failed, that fool of a boy couldn't stab a rabbit correctly,* "but there must have been something odd on the blade, because when I left, King Aedh had collapsed, and I have no idea if he will ever recover."

"And my son?" Derval asked, still quietly. "What of my son?"

"Och, the Ard Ri's men have him—remember your vow," the spy added in alarm to Donnchadh as the king's arm shot up, suddenly drawn knife glinting in his hand. For one endless moment, Colm was sure he was a dead man.

But then Derval said quietly, "Donnchadh."

As though suddenly realizing where he was, the king lowered his arm again, slamming the knife back into its sheath, his eyes wild with unspent fury. "I must get him out of Fremainn. Derval, I can't wait any longer. They'll kill my boy. I don't care the cost: I have to get him out!"

One of Cadwal's men laughed as they rode through the darkening forest. "Look at that. Bastard left us a track a child could follow."

Ardagh exchanged a quick glance with Cadwal. "You thinking the same as me?" the mercenary asked.

"That it's just too blatant a trail? Exactly. He's in a hurry, but he can't be a complete fool. Send most of your men after it, yes?"

He received a nod and a sharp grin in response. As the majority of the mercenaries crashed on down the too-clearly-marked trail, Ardagh, Cadwal and the remaining men slipped from their horses and began tracking on foot.

"Got to hurry before it gets too dark to see," Cadwal muttered.

Ardagh wisely said nothing, though his thoughts were tinged with contempt at human night-blindness. But then, if Cadwal couldn't see where he was going, neither could Odran. "There." The prince pointed out a freshly broken branch. "And there."

Cadwal nodded. "Prince Niall's leaving us a nice clear trail. Clever boy."

"Or Odran's making it look that way."

The mercenary's eyes glinted in the darkness. "Suspicious, aren't you?"

"Just wary." Ardagh dropped his voice even more. "Go on, keep following the trail. I'm going to cut off to one side and try to cut off Odran's retreat."

"You can't get through that underbrush without sounding like a herd of cattle!"

Ardagh grinned. "No? Watch."

He melted into the forest, very much aware of Cadwal's amazement. These humans were fair trackers, but they moved so maddeningly slowly! Besides, now that he was away from them, he could use his full abilities and not have to explain anything to anyone. He moved with Sidhe ease and silence through the underbrush and the ever-deepening gloom, hunting with more than the physical senses, *feeling* the unmistakable sense of *human*, trying to narrow it into the *feel* of the specific ones he sought—

Yes. Ae, yes.

If he had been silent before, Ardagh was twice as silent now, prowling with slow care through the bushes, stepping with delicate wariness so no twig or dry leaves would betray him.

Ahh, yes, indeed. There in the dim light sat Prince Niall, tousled but apparently unharmed, radiating a mixture of quite understandable fear and a regal rage that rather delighted Ardagh; the boy was very much his father's son. Niall was bound hand and foot with makeshift strips of cloth—Odran, then, hadn't actually planned to steal him when he did, hadn't brought rope or presumably anything else of use, but was merely taking advantage of the moment. The man must have some plan, though; nobody fled into wilderness at random. He must be plotting to meet up with others, probably his own men.

Or could he mean to meet with just one other? Gervinus, perhaps?

But where is Odran? Too near, surely, for me to be able to just carry Niall away. The man can't have gone far; he wouldn't dare leave his prize unattended or—ah, yes. Here he is. Gone was the coldly elegant courtier. Odran's *brat* was smeared with dirt, showing where he'd fallen several times in the darkness, and his fine linen shirt was ripped and rumpled. Gold still glinted incongruously from about his neck and from the clasp holding his *brat,* all the more incongruous since he was holding an awkward armload of branches. *Tsk, look at the fool, building a fire as though he hadn't a care.* But then, a nobleman could hardly be expected to have any woodcraft at all; used to the bustle of the court, he would be unnerved by the forest darkness and want the comfort of light even if it might betray his position. Yes, now he had managed to get a fire burning, dazzling Ardagh's night-vision. *And it's surely going to bring Cadwal running.*

And endanger Niall in the process. Ardagh smiled a thin little humorless Sidhe smile. Here he was, surrounded by forest Power; let him use it against this child-stealer. Delicately, enjoying himself, the prince spoke soft, magical Words, sent out waves of Strangeness to Odran, chill whispers of *danger all around you, danger-without-a-name, Darkness prowling after you, stalking you, Darkness about to engulf you, Darkness just behind you.*

Ha, yes, look at Odran glancing nervously around! No sign of the sophisticated courtier now at all. Good! Let him feel something of the fear he'd caused the boy. A little more persuasion, Ardagh *felt,* and the man would break into open panic. A little more again, and he would flee or simply collapse. Either way—

"What's the matter?" Niall said suddenly. "Scared?"

No! Ardagh thought. *Be quiet, Niall, let me work.*

And, "Be quiet," Odran hissed.

"Scared the forest's going to get you?"

"Be quiet, boy!"

Stop it, Niall! I can't concentrate on magic and *you. You're shattering my spell!*

But of course the boy couldn't hear him. "Better hope the forest does get you," Niall taunted his captor, "because whatever it can do is going to be nicer than what my father does when he catches you—"

"I said, be quiet!"

The shout was punctuated by the sound of a slap and Niall's sharp little cry of pain. Wild fury blazed up in Ardagh at that cry. Abandoning his broken spell, he sprang at Odran. He and the man went crashing to the forest floor, rolling, grappling, struggling to free weapons. Odran was even less used to brawling than the prince, but that didn't stop him from trying to bite and kick and gouge.

Quick learner, curse him. But I can still—

Something white-hot seared his arm. The prince gasped in startled pain, lost his grip on Odran, and felt the man wriggle free. Both of them scrambled towards Niall: Ardagh got there first, finally managing to draw his dagger, and whirled with a snarl to face Odran.

Who has his sword drawn. Wonderful. This isn't a throwing knife. How do I—

With superb timing, Cadwal and his men chose that moment to come roaring through the underbrush. Odran turned and fled. Ardagh made one desperate lunge to stop him, only to hit his already scorched arm against a tree and recoil in helpless pain. When the mercenaries would have started after Odran, Cadwal shouted, "No! Our first job's to get the prince back safely."

Ardagh, gasping for breath, slashed Niall's bonds. "Are . . . are you all right?" he asked the boy, and the wide-eyed Niall nodded.

"I knew someone would come for me," he said bravely, then stopped. "Och, but your arm! Are *you* all right?"

"Good question," Cadwal said. "Here, let me see." His hands on Ardagh's arm were surprisingly gentle. "Mm. Nasty scorch. Doesn't look dangerous, though. What did you do, land on the fire?"

Ardagh touched the scorched spot gingerly. "It feels that way." *But it's most surely an iron-burn, just like the one I received from Gervinus' not-prayerbook.* Not a bad one, as Cadwal had noted, though it certainly hurt as fiercely as had that first burn. *And does that mean Odran is carrying some token given to him by the bishop? Is he actively in alliance with Gervinus?*

There was no way he could tell the humans his suspicions. Ardagh glanced at Cadwal and frowned. "What?"

Cadwal was very plainly holding back amusement. "Nothing. Just that you let Odran get away and got hurt in the process."

"I hardly see the amusement in that!"

"Och, man—ah, Prince Ardagh, that is, I'm not laughing at you. Wouldn't be that rude. Or stupid. It's just," he added with a sly sideways glance at the prince, "marvelously comforting to see that even you aren't perfect!"

"I never claimed to be perfect. Come, back to Fremainn."

Panting, stumbling over rocks and roots, snagging his clothing on branches and thorns, tripping over his sword and his own tired feet, Odran staggered desperately through the forest. Damn, ah, damn, who would have thought things would fall apart so quickly? His snatching of the boy had been an impulse, a stupid thing. Had he really expected to get far enough away to escape?

Yes, of course I did. I thought I could get all the way back to my own holdings. And now here I am in the middle of nowhere, no horse, no hostage, no—

"At last. I was wondering where you were."

Odran stopped so sharply he nearly fell. There in an open glade stood a dark-robed figure, holding two horses, one of which he recognized as his own runaway. "Who . . . ah." The figure had pushed back the hood of his robe. "Bishop Gervinus. What are you doing out here, my lord bishop?"

"The same as you, my lord Odran. Fleeing Fremainn."

"But—why?"

"Why? You experienced something of that 'why,' I think. You felt something of the Darkness surrounding the High King."

"I don't . . ." But Odran remembered the strangeness that had seized his mind just before, the terrifying sense

·that *something* was coming for him, *something* was stalking him. He stiffened. Such fancies belonged to a fool of a poet, not him! And yet . . . the terror had felt very real indeed. "Sorcery . . . ?" he asked doubtfully.

"Oh yes, sorcery. Sorcery in so dark and tangled a web that even King Aedh himself is snared. Think of it, my lord. I know you have no love for him, but think: have there not been signs all along? Suspicions on his part, actions that seemed too swift, hatreds that seemed too sharp to be true?"

A small, sane part of Odran knew such occasional lapses or bits of illogic were true of any man, without any sorcery being involved, but he couldn't seem to find the words to say that. And the bishop continued, turning fact into fantasy, fantasy into fact, citing strange example after example till they no longer seemed strange.

"I am but one man, bishop though I be. I could no longer bear to stay in that foulness." Gervinus' smile glinted in the darkness. "Neither, it would seem, can you. What are you planning, my lord Odran? Where are you going?"

It was so soft and soothing a croon Odran couldn't seem to find anything to say. All he could do was listen helplessly as Gervinus continued, feeling the smooth words wash over him, stealing into his mind, his heart.

"Where are you going, my lord Odran? Back to your holdings? Back to raise your men against the king who has betrayed your trust. Back to join others who feel the same way. Back to those who will raise arms against the wrongness. Those who will rid Eriu of evil, cleanse it, replace the corruption with a true king, a king worthy in the sight of God and man. Is that your goal, my lord Odran? Is it? Is that your goal, my lord?"

Odran, drowning beneath the tide of words, seeing only a bright, bright future, and himself with a crown set on his brow, gasped out, "Yes! I am your man!"

"Of course you are," the bishop said, and smiled anew. "Now come, there is much to be done."

"Arnulf. Arnulf!"

The acolyte sat bolt upright, staring wildly into the

darkness. Had he actually heard that—that voice tickling at his mind? Here he was, still alive and unhurt; the High King seemed to be believing his story of innocence betrayed and total ignorance of any wrong done by Gervinus, so far, anyhow. And it was so good, for the moment, not to have to worry about anything. But . . . but . . . he wasn't sure what he wanted. Even while half of him longed to be no more than ordinary, half of him still longed for sorcery. And now:

"Arnulf! I know you can hear me."

The acolyte looked nervously about. "Master . . . ? Is that . . . you?"

"Of course it is! And no, I am not anywhere near you, so stop that ridiculous staring about and listen."

God, the bishop was scrying him as well as using mind-speech! That meant, Arnulf thought, that he was still important to Gervinus, he was still *somebody*. Terrified and elated at the thought, Arnulf sat perfectly still and said, "Uh . . . yes. I'm listening."

"I'm sure you've been feeling sorry for yourself, abandoned like that. But you haven't been abandoned, Arnulf. I left you there for a reason. Can you guess what it is?"

Arnulf chewed his lower lip. "To be your spy?"

"Ah, the boy does have wits! Yes, Arnulf. Yours will be a very risky position. You must be my eyes and ears in Fremainn. Can you do this for me? Can you, Arnulf?"

Could he? "Y-yes," Arnulf said, and then, more strongly, "yes. Of course I can."

There might have been a hint of doubt in Gervinus' mind-voice, but what he said was simply, *"Good. You are to tell me whatever new thing happens."*

"But how can I—what shall I—"

"Come now, I've taught you something of scrying! And even you should have enough skill with magic by now to know what to do!"

"But—"

"Don't argue with me. If you see something important, you are to do what you must. Is that understood? You are to do what you must!

"I understand."

"Very good. I will speak with you again. For now, my loyal apprentice, good night."

With that, the contact was broken, leaving Arnulf shaking and confused and elated. He had not been abandoned. "You will know what to do," he said softly. Oh yes, oh yes, he did.

Breathless, Arnulf sat staring at a new, exciting future. Come what may, he would survive. Come what may, sorcery would still be his. And if the occasion arose, he would use that sorcery and show Gervinus just how Powerful this small, despised apprentice could be!

Ardagh stood to one side just outside the royal keep, watching as Aedh and Eithne, hair turned to flame by the torchlight, faces brighter than the flame with joy, enfolded their son in their joint embrace. In that moment, he thought, they were no more than parents welcoming back a child they'd feared lost forever. To the prince's eyes, Eithne looked very weary, weary with more than a mother's worry, and he wondered with a little pang of alarm about Sorcha.

As Niall, now sagging with exhaustion, was hurried off to bed, Aedh glanced about at Ardagh, Cadwal, the gathered mercenaries. "What can I say that won't sound trite? I do thank you, both as a father and your king, I thank you with all the gratitude that can be in one man's heart."

"And I," Eithne added, "I add my blessings on all of you."

Aedh turned to enter the keep. Eithne started with him, but Ardagh said softly to her, "I burned my arm in the struggle. It is but a slight scorch but very uncomfortable." True enough. "Would you have some salve for it?"

"Of course. Come with me." But as she applied the salve, which, from the herbal scent of it, was the same that Sorcha had once used on his hand, Eithne murmured, "You're being a bit transparent, Prince Ardagh."

"I don't—"

"The injury to her head was not severe. I cast a healing spell over Sorcha, and she will be fine."

Before he could thank her, or say anything at all, Eithne had hurried away. Ardagh stood looking after her, part of him wanting to follow, to go to Sorcha, part of him shouting, *Fool! She is but human!*

Powers. Too much was happening too quickly—the disappearance of Gervinus, the escape of Odran and the near-stealing of Prince Niall. The spell he'd thrown over Odran hadn't been fully cast; he was feeling the shadow of backlash from that as well. And the air hung heavy with the promise of more trials to come. Did the humans feel it too, this ever-growing tension?

All at once too worn for further thought, Ardagh returned to his guest house. What would happen, would, he told himself pragmatically, and collapsed into deep, dreamless sleep.

THE DUEL

CHAPTER 26

The morning was early enough to still be chill and grey, and a faint mist filled the air. Ardagh shivered and drew the folds of his *brat* more tightly about himself. Every now and again this Realm reminded him just how alien it was. How alien its people were . . .

I cannot let myself love her. I cannot let her love me. It would only lead to pain.

Easy to think! More difficult to accept. Ardagh shivered again. This Realm . . . yes, this Realm was changing him, softening him. It must be, or such thoughts as love for a human woman would never even have occurred to him.

And yet, there was something so intriguing about this one woman, this Sorcha ni Fothad, human or no, something so intriguing about her fierce spirit and delight in learning, something about her quick, clever mind and—

No! He would hurt her by never aging, she would hurt him by aging far, far too swiftly, leaving him alone. Powers, so they all would, down to cheerful little Fainche, they would all, with their so-brief mortal lives, age and die and leave him so painfully alone—

With a great effort, Ardagh turned his mind from the aching fear trying to overwhelm him to safer memories of his homeland, of the magic gleaming in air and earth, fire and water, of his tranquil, lovely estate filled with flowers, and little Ninet softly picking out a melody on her harp. . . .

Enough of this, too. And surely it was only mist making his face damp. Ardagh roughly rubbed it dry and swore a harsh human oath under his breath. Wouldn't he make a fine sight, all soft-eyed and miserable, for this early morning council King Aedh had called?

"Prince Ardagh."

The prince turned sharply, forcing his face back into its usual mask of cool self-control. "Ah, my lord Fothad." Keeping his voice as casual as possible, he asked, "How does your daughter?"

"My daughter, praise God and Queen Eithne's healing skills, does well. The queen insists she stay in bed one day more, but assures her that she'll be perfectly fine after a little rest."

"I am truly glad to hear it." *Now, there's a fine understatement.* "But you obviously want to talk with me alone."

"Yes." Fothad's gaze was suddenly uncertain, like that of a man about to broach a subject he didn't really want to discuss. "And it's a good thing you've brought up the subject of my daughter, because it's of my daughter we must speak."

"Must we."

"Prince Ardagh, please. I thought now, before the meeting, as good a time as any."

"For what?" the prince asked in sudden impatience. "Come, man, what are you trying to say?"

"This isn't easy. But . . . Prince Ardagh, I have no complaints as to your rank; the good Lord knows it's more noble than mine."

"How kind of you to notice."

"Please. I—well now, if you were anyone else but who you are—"

Ah. "*What* I am, you mean. *Cu glas.*"

Fothad winced. "You put it bluntly. But since you do: yes, that's exactly the problem. You *are* a foreign exile. One with no true legal standing in Eriu. I don't know how you truly feel about my daughter. . . ."

Ae, Powers, neither do I. But Ardagh remained firmly silent, and after an awkward moment, Fothad repeated, "I don't know how you feel about her, but as a man of honor, surely you see that—that—och, I'm saying this badly, and I a poet—that there can never be anything of honor between you."

Misery was rapidly giving way to anger. Voice cold with the force of his barely supressed emotion, Ardagh said, "And there will never be anything dishonorable between us, either, if that's your fear. I've already given you my vow about that, if you recall."

"Of course. I didn't mean—"

"I am quite well aware of my precarious standing in this land. And believe me, I have no intention of involving myself in anything that cannot be satisfactorily settled." *A masterpiece of vagueness, that,* the prince jibed at himself, but Fothad, after studying him fiercely as if to puzzle out what he truly meant, held up a hand in resignation.

"I will accept that. For now."

Ardagh raised an eyebrow. " 'For now'? Why, my lord! Are you threatening me?"

"There's no need for that, is there?" But then Fothad's fierce gaze fell. "Look you, I confess it: I've been suffering guilt all along over wedding Sorcha off to a drunkard. My only excuse is that Meallan cast a good image in public; none of us guessed the truth about him. I don't want to see my daughter hurt again."

"Do you think I do?" But then Ardagh sighed. "You do love your daughter."

That got him a surprised glance. "Of course I do!"

"You don't understand. In my brother's realm, true love, love without some sly ulterior motive, some purpose of politics or alliance, is far too rare. I'm . . . not sure I've ever dared feel it." *Most certainly not now.*

Fothad blinked. "Och, well," he said carefully, "I've heard it's like that in some royal courts. All the more reason, then, for you to appreciate my wanting to protect Sorcha."

"I . . ." Ardagh shook his head. "I will not stand for a lecture. Not even from you, my sometime teacher. And no man," he added in quiet warning, "may tell me what I can and cannot do. I have sworn to do your daughter no harm.

More than that—" He glanced up, very glad for the interruption. "Come, man, we are being summoned to council."

Aedh looked about the council chamber. " . . . and so we have a bishop who is not a bishop somewhere out there, Odran mac Daire also loose and presumably making for his homelands, and a whole retinue of very bewildered church servants on our hands. We also have one equally bewildered Prince of Clonach who may or may not have been ensorcelled and who made an attempt on my life. We won't mention Leinster, Meath, or the Lochlannach right now, but I think that sums up the situation to date. Any suggestions?"

"We cannot," Ardagh said, "allow Gervinus to go free."

Father Seadna frowned slightly. "What harm can the man possibly work now? Alone in a strange land with no one to aid or befriend him—I think we may safely leave it to Our Lord to punish him."

"Alone, yes," Ardagh argued, "but hardly without defenses. You know something of what I mean," he added with a sharp glance at Aedh.

Who evaded it neatly. "I'm sorry, Prince Ardagh, but I must side with Father Seadna. Yes, the man definitely intended harm to me—"

"Ha!"

"—but what happened could just as easily have been explained away as an effect of the drug as anything else."

"No! I—" Ardagh resolutely cut himself off in midsentence. *Keep arguing like this, and you're going to have them believing you're a sorcerer as well.* "So be it. I yield to Father Seadna." *For now.*

"As for the retinue," the monk said, "I can only suggest that they be returned to Rome. There is no place for them here."

Ah well, one more try. "What of Arnulf? Does anyone here truly believe him innocent?"

Father Seadna frowned at him. "Is there any reason to believe him to be otherwise?"

"He was the personal servant of Gervinus. Granted, he

doesn't seem to be the keenest of wits, but he would have to have been incredibly stupid not to have known at least something of the man's plans."

"Precisely," Aedh said. "And that's exactly why he's not going anywhere. Yes, we'll send the others back to Rome or wherever else they wish to go. But Arnulf, I think, stays here where we can keep an eye on him."

"Yes," the prince began, "but what if—"

But the rest of what he wanted to say was drowned out in the sudden blare of horns.

"Well now, a messenger's arriving." Aedh sat back in his chair, fingers steepled. "Wish to wager with me, anyone, that his message concerns Donnchadh of Clonach?"

"No takers," Fothad said.

The panting messenger was ushered in. Struggling to catch his breath after what had plainly been a frantic ride, he told the king that Donnchadh of Clonach was already on the march and nearly halfway to Fremainn.

"So now." Aedh's smile was sly. "It would be rude to make him come all the way here." He got to his feet, and the others hastily followed suit. "We must make preparations to meet him. While we can yet pick the ground."

"Wait, now." Fothad blocked his path. "You can't be meaning to battle him."

"Him. Not his men. No need for that. Come now, Fothad, as a poet you surely have heard of *fir fer.*"

"The challenge of single combat? Of course I have, but—"

"Well, then."

Ardagh frowned, trying to puzzle out Aedh's strategy. "If I'm not mistaken, a duel counts as true combat in the law. If you duel him and lose, that law says you lose your crown as well."

"I have no intention of losing. I've seen how Donnchadh handles a sword: all passion and force but little finesse."

"Passion can crush finesse," Fothad began, but Aedh cut in, "Nothing's without *some* risk."

"But if Donnchadh loses," Ardagh said, "then it's his crown that's forfeit. You don't really want him deposed, do you?"

Aedh grinned. "Clever Prince Ardagh! No, indeed. Far

better the nuisance I know, with the Lochlannach threat to keep him mostly in check, than some stranger on the throne of Clonach."

Ardagh gave a sudden sharp laugh. "Clever King Aedh, rather! I see the point of your little game. But it's going to be a tricky one to win *and* lose."

"Och, yes," Aedh agreed. "But where's the fun in a game that has no challenge at all?"

Queen Derval of Clonach, thinking herself securely alone in her grianan, looked up in shock from her scroll at the stranger who so suddenly stood before her, wrapped in a dark, concealing cloak.

Not quite concealing. She could have sworn she caught glimpses of what could only be ecclesiastical garb underneath it: sadly bedraggled and stained with mud, perhaps, but ecclesiastical nevertheless. Astonished curiosity kept her from shouting for guards. Instead, Derval asked, "Who are you? How did you get in here?"

"You need have no fear of me."

"I'm not afraid of you," Derval retorted with contempt. "One shout is all I need to be rid of you. I just wish to know how you got past the guards."

She thought she heard the softest of chuckles. " 'All things are lawful for me—' "

" '—but not all things are expedient.' I can quote Scripture, too. I repeat, who are you?"

He bowed ever so slightly, then pushed back the hood of his cloak to reveal a lean, strong-featured face, cold, intelligent eyes holding a hint of—of what? Madness? Or power beyond anything she'd yet seen? "Bishop Gervinus," he told her smoothly, "late of Rome."

Derval's eyes narrowed. "My husband's spies are failing him, it seems. I was told that you were in Fremainn."

"So I was. Till I could remain there no longer."

"Ah? The High King is hardly one to wantonly banish a Churchman."

"Oh, I assure you, I left voluntarily."

"If in haste?"

He smiled. "Queen Derval, I think I'm not mistaken if I say that you and I are both realists. Leave the softer thoughts of 'honor,' 'loyalty,' 'it has always been so,' to others. You and I know that 'honor' and 'loyalty' are very relative concepts, indeed. And that there is nothing set for those with sufficient clear sight, nothing that cannot be changed by those with sufficient daring. And something must very much be changed in Eriu. May I sit?"

She gestured brusquely at a chair. As he seated himself, Derval said, "Your Grace, those are very pretty words. Quite stirring, in fact. What are you implying with them, I wonder? Treason, perhaps?"

"Treason," he murmured, "can only be committed against a worthy lord. Queen Derval, please. I know exactly what you've been doing, the alliances you've been making."

Her heart gave a great, terrified leap. "You could not," Derval began, then cut off the words in fury, realizing that she'd just been tricked into a confession. "How did you know?"

"I knew."

"Bishop Gervinus, I am not a child to be satisfied with easy words! And here is another quote for you: 'Beware of false prophets.' "

He smiled at that and held out his arms. "A hit, a true hit. But I am not a prophet; I make no claims to know the future. Unless, of course, you and I might form an alliance of our own. Then I might foretell quite an intriguing future for us both."

Derval frowned. There was nothing of normal human lust in those icy eyes, nothing but that cold, impersonal, political interest. "What do you want of us, Your Grace? My husband on the throne? And yourself, perhaps, behind him?"

"Ah, I applaud you, Queen Derval! It's so rare in this land to meet someone to whom everything need not be explained a hundred times over."

"Answer me, Your Grace. Why should my husband and I ally ourselves with you? Why should we exchange one overlord for another?"

"Because, Queen Derval, I don't think you have much

of a choice." He stood, seeming suddenly to loom over her like a great mass of darkness. "I suspected you might resist, though I admit I never expected so marvelously cold and controlled an intellect."

"What are you—"

"A pity you are quite so clever. I wish that alliance, Queen Derval. I wish the names of your fellow conspirators. And I shall have them."

Such melodramatic words. But Derval couldn't mock them. His eyes . . . there was nothing in them, nothing at all but endless, endless emptiness. Held helpless, Derval fought to move, to scream, to fight back, but there was nothing . . . nothing.

Nothing.

Ardagh stood peacefully under a tree at the edge of the open meadow Aedh had chosen, waiting with cool Sidhe patience, amusing himself by watching the humans waiting. Cadwal and his mercenaries showed little outward strain, save for the occasional clenching of a fist on a sword hilt; they had been through this type of thing who knew how many times before. Aedh's own men looked less steady. *There's the danger,* Ardagh mused, *their hot blood.* If they broke ranks or gave in to tension, Aedh might well have a full-fledged battle on his hands.

The king knew it. "A lovely day for a duel, isn't it?" he commented to no one in particular. "And a duel, one to one, is all it is to be, regardless of outcome. Is that understood?"

There were reluctant grunts and nods.

"Good. Because disobedience of a royal command is as treasonous as— Ah, here they come now."

So this is Donnchadh of Clonach, Ardagh thought, eying the tall, mail-clad figure at the procession's head. *He looks splendid as a hero out of one of Fothad's poems—and about as foolish as his son, riding openly in the lead like that, with no one guarding his flank.* If Aedh were a shade less honorable—or less clever—he could have cut Donnchadh down with one cast of a spear.

But Aedh only stood waiting, looking deceptively lazy

despite his own mail-clad self as he leaned on his sword. "Welcome, Donnchadh of Clonach." His voice was deceptively lazy, too. "And what brings you here all the way from your own lands? And with armed men, too."

"You know why," Donnchadh said without ceremony. "Give me back my son."

"I'm afraid I can't do that. No, don't give me that alarmed stare; the boy's not hurt. But you see, there's the little matter of his having tried to kill me."

Ardagh saw Donnchadh's ever-so-slight wince, and smiled. Point one to Aedh.

"He is but a boy!" Donnchadh protested. "Boys are impulsive."

Aedh feigned surprise very nicely. "I'd call attempted assassination a bit more than impulsive."

"I have come," Donnchadh said, biting off the words, "for my son. I do not intend to leave without him."

"Well, then," Aedh retorted, smiling, "there's only one thing to be done about it." He raised his sword with a quick, easy grace that pleased Ardagh's Sidhe sensibilities. "Since I am the injured party, and since you are, after all, the boy's father, I say we keep this a personal matter, one to one. I propose that we duel, just you and I, and the winner keeps the boy."

Donnchadh could only have known what defeat would mean to him under the law, but with the rashness Ardagh had expected from him, he cried, "So be it!"

Sword drawn, he leaped from his horse and sprang to the attack, blade smashing against Aedh's quickly lifted sword. No ordinary duel, this! The king of Clonach meant to kill his opponent, and Ardagh wondered suddenly if Aedh knew what he was doing. Although the High King seemed in excellent physical condition, he wasn't exactly a young man, not by human standards.

But then, Donnchadh was no boy, either. He was taller than the solidly muscled Aedh by about a head, but their reach seemed about equal. And Aedh had been right, Ardagh noted after the first few moments of the duel: Donnchadh's swordplay really did lack finesse.

But it certainly makes up for that lack in sheer ferocity!

And what, the prince wondered in sudden uneasiness, happened if ferocity won out over skill? What if the High King was injured to the point of losing the fight or was outright slain? Of course, a human as unsubtle as Donnchadh would be incredibly easy for anyone stronger of will to control; it would not be difficult to win an influential place at his court. But rather to his surprise, Ardagh realized that he didn't want that. Aside from the utter chaos into which Eriu would be thrown—a chaos that would affect him, as well—he had, the prince admitted to himself, become too fond of these folk to see them hurt, human though they were, fond of Aedh and his Eithne, of Fothad and Cadwal—

And Sorcha. Ardagh's mind flinched away from that last name.

Aedh didn't seem at all perturbed by Donnchadh's fury. If anything he seemed to be feeding it, almost as though he was amused by the whole thing, calmly countering this slash, neatly dodging that, his powerful frame moving with steady, easy grace. The prince found himself smiling slightly despite his uneasiness, pleased by the artistry of the performance, aware that Aedh was deliberately never inflicting more than scratches on Donnchadh, never letting Donnchadh inflict more than scratches on him.

A pretty dance. But Aedh seems to be keeping only to the defensive. A dangerous tactic, that! *When is he going to take the offensive? Or maybe,* the prince realized suddenly, *he doesn't* mean *to take it.*

Cadwal didn't see the point. "What does he think he's doing?" the mercenary muttered. "What the *hell* does he think he's doing? Look at that!" he snapped at Ardagh. "Look! King Aedh had a clear opening at Donnchadh's neck, right above the line of that mail shirt, but he didn't even try to take it. Ha, and he could have gotten Donnchadh right across the swordarm, but he didn't even try that, either!"

Ardagh glanced at the mercenary with a sharp grin. "Don't you see? What he's doing is tiring Donnchadh out. That's what all this is about. He's tiring Donnchadh to the point

where Aedh can safely call their battle a draw with no winner
or loser, and be believed."

That tactic wasn't helping Donnchadh's temper. While
he didn't make any wild demands that the coolly dodging
and parrying Aedh stand still and fight, ever-increasing anger
and frustration blazed in his eyes.

"Careful," Cadwal murmured as though Aedh could hear
him, "careful. Can't tell what a man driven mad by rage
will do."

Without warning, Aedh staggered slightly, stumbled back
a step, his grace suddenly gone. Cadwal and Ardagh
gasped—but for different reasons.

Sorcery! Ardagh knew. *Ineptly cast, but sorcery cast at
Aedh!* Not Gervinus; nothing that one did would ever be
so awkward. *Then who?*

No time to worry about it, or any elegant response. Ardagh
cast a wall of raw will about Aedh to block the spell. And
in the next instant wondered, could he hold it? It should
be so easy, one of the most basic, near-mindless forms of
defense. Instead, the impact of spell against spell shivered
along every nerve, forcing him to gasp for air, struggling
like the newest of novices to hold the wall in place. This
cursedly magic-weak Realm!

But if that thrice-cursed amateur sorcerer could cast a
spell (though doubtlessly with the concrete aid of magical
tools), a prince of the Sidhe could counter it! The strain
sent Ardagh to his knees—let the humans make of that what
they would—but he was winning, he was winning—

Yes! The spell broke so suddenly he nearly fell forward.
Brushing wet strands of hair back from his eyes, the prince
realized, *Arnulf, that's who it was. It could only have been
he.* Breaking the spell had probably knocked Arnulf senseless
if it hadn't killed him outright. Ardagh gave a mental shrug;
the acolyte wasn't quite young enough to spark Sidhe
instincts of child-protection. *He shouldn't have meddled.
Magic's not a game for beginners.*

Aedh might or might not have realized what had nearly
happened to him. His fatigue might or might not have been
real—Ardagh, struggling to catch his own breath, rather

thought not—but there was no doubt at all that Donnchadh of Clonach was at the point of staggering. Aedh could have taken him easily—if that had been Aedh's intention.

Instead, the High King drew back and laughed, the shaky laugh of a truly weary man, and lowered his sword.

"I think we may have a problem here, Donnchadh. I don't really want to go another dance-round; do you?"

Donnchadh, clearly trying not to pant, managed only a snarl.

"I'll take that for a no." Aedh shook his head. "No winner, no loser. Tell you what, Donnchadh. Neither one of us can afford winding up dangerously weakened. Rather than we continue and risk that, let us declare our match a draw. Since you didn't lose to me, take back your son and welcome to him."

Donnchadh could only have been aware of the subterfuge Aedh had just worked, but with his son's life at stake, he was in no position to argue. All he could do was brusquely order, "Get on your horse," to the very subdued Fearghal, hurl himself onto his own horse, and just as brusquely ride away, his men trailing after.

As soon as it was clear there was not going to be any further threat from Clonach, the High King's own men relaxed, hands leaving sword hilts or spear shafts. They rushed in, ringing Aedh round, congratulating him, loud in their relief. But Ardagh, caught in the crush, heard Cadwal note to the king, "You've made an enemy there."

Wiping his sweaty face with a scrap of cloth, Aedh only shrugged. Seen up this close, his fatigue was evident, though he was clearly nowhere as weary as Donnchadh had been; small streaks of blood here and there showed that he hadn't been totally untouched by Donnchadh's sword, though there didn't seem to be any injuries worse than scratches. "Made an enemy?" he said with a sardonic grin. "You think Donnchadh of Clonach's ever been a friend? Never could prove it wasn't he that set that ambush for me, back when we first met up with you, Prince Ardagh—hey now, what's the matter, man? You look as drained as I feel."

Ardagh shook his head impatiently. If Aedh hadn't been

aware of the sorcery, the prince wasn't going to waste time enlightening him. "We must return to Fremainn, and quickly. There is someone there who must be questioned."

The prince didn't stop for the others' baffled remarks, but threw himself onto his horse and rode headlong for Fremainn. Let them follow or not as they would. Tired or not, he must reach Arnulf—and reach him before Gervinus did.

But returning to Fremainn meant returning to a new swarm of chaos, excited folk running in from all sides, eager to greet their returning, victorious king. Ardagh fought his way through the throng, glad that their excitement over Aedh was keeping their attention from him (seeing Eithne flinging herself into Aedh's arms, seeing Sorcha standing to one side, grimly refusing to let either distract him), and hurried to what had been the bishop's guest house. Guards stood watch—a useless watch where sorcery was involved—but they stepped hastily aside at Ardagh's brusque wave of a hand. The prince rushed into what had been Gervinus' bedchamber, then stopped short.

There Arnulf lay, still breathing but limp as a tossed-aside doll. Beside him, a bowl of clear water and various bits and pieces of odd substances screamed *sorcery* at the prince's senses. But it wasn't going to be proof enough for the humans. Ardagh bent to the acolyte's side and set about returning him to consciousness.

At last Arnulf groaned and stirred. His eyelids fluttered open, his eyes focused, and he froze, staring up at Ardagh in horror.

"That's right," the prince said, "fear me. You have every reason to fear me, you would-be assassin."

"I d-didn't—I'm not—"

"Don't even attempt falsehood. We both know exactly what you tried to do. And failed. It will be far, far easier for you, Arnulf, if you confess here and now."

"I didn't—"

"Confess, Arnulf." The prince fixed him with as cold a Sidhe glare as he could summon. "Confess." He had him now; Arnulf's never very strong nerve was about to shatter. "Confess."

But suddenly the acolyte was squirming away, staring up in new horror at nothing. Nothing tangible, that was, Ardagh thought, *feeling* the softest prickle of new magics.

"I didn't do anything wrong!" Arnulf whined. "You *told* me I was to do what I must. No, no, I didn't know it, I didn't mean to misunderstand!"

He's talking to Gervinus! Ardagh realized with a shock. *It's no trick, no hallucination. Gervinus is scrying him, I can* feel *it—and there isn't a thing I can do about it, not without a channel back to wherever the man's scrying from.*

Aware that others had begun crowding into the room behind him, the prince caught Arnulf by the shoulders. "Now's your chance to be free of him," he hissed. "Hurry, confess what you've done, then tell me where to find—"

But in a sudden fierce spasm of pain, the acolyte tore free. His voice shrilled up into an anguished scream. "You never said I wasn't to use sorcery!" he shrieked, then screamed even more fiercely, this time clearly past the point of words. Hands shooting to his chest, Arnulf gave one last, terrible cry—then fell lifeless to the floor.

VISIONS

CHAPTER 27

Ardagh glared about at the humans in ever-growing frustration. He had to search this room, find something, anything, a hair, a scrap of cloth that had belonged to Gervinus. He had to scry for the bishop while Gervinus was still too drained from the long-range murder of his acolyte to Shield himself—and Shield himself anyone who could have managed that murder would surely know how to do—but these well-meaning idiots wouldn't let him! Instead, since he'd been the one who had actually seen Arnulf die, they all insisted on going over that death again and again, trying to make it fit neatly into some mundane category. Trying, too, to give him comfort he neither needed nor wanted.

Just leave me alone, that's all I ask! "No," the prince snapped for what seemed the hundredth time, "it wasn't his heart that gave out—ae, yes, it was, but not from any natural causes! Arnulf was working sorcery!"

"Of course he was," Father Seadna said sadly. "The evidence is all about the room. Poor, foolish, misguided young man. We'll never know what took him away from the Light and down the dark path that killed him, but—"

"We *do* know—" Ardagh began, then cut himself off sharply before he revealed information a magickless man couldn't possibly have. Trying a slightly safer path, the prince told them all, "It's Gervinus we want. Don't you see? Gervinus *had* to have known what his acolyte was doing!"

Father Seadna gave him an infuriatingly patronizing smile. "Prince Ardagh, I know the death of this poor young man virtually in your arms must have been a terrible shock for you. And we all know how strongly you dislike the—ah—bishop. But you're seeing perils where they don't exist."

"I—"

"Be assured King Aedh did send out men to find Bishop Gervinus. They failed."

Ardagh just barely held back a shout of sheer impatience. "I know that." He could hear his voice starting to shake with anger, and with a great effort forced himself back to Sidhe calm. "But we cannot let it go at that. Arnulf was nothing more than an inept apprentice. He had to have had a mentor. And who else could that mentor have been? Gervinus is an ambitious man wielding who knows what Power. He represents a very real threat. And we must find him!"

"We will," Father Seadna soothed. "Prince Ardagh, please. Even if what you claim is true, even if Bishop Gervinus is practicing some manner of—of the Dark Arts—you have just seen for yourself the wages of such studies."

What I've seen was murder! But Ardagh couldn't tell the humans that. He couldn't tell them much of anything and keep his true self a secret. Cursing the need for that secrecy, cursing this entire all but magickless Realm, he gave up on courtesy and patience. There were ways to scry out a person without any tangible clues as aids, not as effective, perhaps, but those methods would have to serve, because if he waited till this house was safely empty, it would be far, far too late to do anything. With a curt bow, Ardagh pushed his way through the throng, not much caring what they thought of him, and left the humans to do with the late Arnulf as they would.

Out in the clean air, the prince stood for a frantic second glancing sharply about, trying to focus his thoughts. What bothered him most was: how was it that Gervinus had been able to successfully work such a spell as had slain Arnulf, and at such a distance?

Ae, of course. Maddening to think that in this Realm a human, one born without a scrap of Power, might still have more sorcery at his command than a prince of the Sidhe—all because of that cursed spellbook lending him artificial aid, the spellbook with its charms that, unlike Sidhe magic, were attuned to this human Realm.

Too much time already wasted; even with the book to strengthen him, Gervinus would still be weary after his spell-casting, but was almost certainly already in the process of Shielding himself from magical spying. Without any tangible clues to help him, not the smallest scrap of cloth or lock of bishopic hair, Ardagh knew he must have a human to ground the search—use a human to find a human, he thought wildly. And that could only mean Queen Eithne.

But Eithne was closeted with her husband. That left only one other who knew what he was and could be trusted not to reveal what she knew:

"Sorcha." It came out as a startled squawk as they nearly collided with each other. "Look you, lady, I don't have time to explain, but I need your aid. You know what I am; you're the only one I dare trust. I must work a scrying spell, *now*."

"I'm glad to see you, too!" she exclaimed as he virtually dragged her into his guest house. But as he released her and began frantically hunting what he would need—water, curse it, clean water, wasn't there any . . . yes here, but he didn't have a ritual blade—ah, never mind, his dagger would do, murder reflected in a killing blade, yes—Sorcha, clearly struck by his urgency, asked only, "What do you want me to do?"

"Stand there, just like that. Don't move or speak unless I ask it. And don't fear: nothing will harm you."

She shivered when he lit the three carefully placed candles (they should properly have been of wax specially wrought at the full of the Faerie moon, but these Earthly things would have to serve), shivered again when he placed the bowl of water (clean water but not, alas, that from a pure spring sited true north) precisely in the center of the triangle formed by the candles. But Sorcha wasn't totally afraid; out of the corner of his eye, Ardagh noted her scholar's intent interest, particularly when he began to whisper the initial Words of Scrying over the water.

Now. Ardagh caught Sorcha's hand in his own, refusing to let himself note how soft and humanly warm it was. He drew his dagger with his free hand, touched the blade's point first to her arm, not quite drawing blood, symbolically grounding his search for a human with human essence, then touched the point to the water, the scrying mirror, sending his search outward, chanting, chanting . . . *feeling* Power growing, ever so frustratingly slowly . . . growing . . . growing . . .

The water was shimmering now, glittering, turning smooth and sleek as silver. Sorcha gasped softly in wonder, but Ardagh refused to hear her, refused to see her, refused to see anything but the water, the mirror, the image he must see, the image he would see, *Gervinus, Gervinus* . . . he could see the man, almost see the man and—and—

Ae, Powers, he couldn't hold it! He couldn't hold the magic, and—

Pain slashed through his mind like white-hot flame. Before he could so much as scream, Ardagh was hurled away into darkness.

Something was tickling his face. Vaguely aware, Ardagh woke slowly, only gradually realizing he was lying on the floor. Yes, and his head was pillowed on a woman's soft lap, and it was the ends of her long braids that were tickling him. Opening his eyes, he found that the lap belonged to Sorcha, bending over him. And for a long moment he could do nothing but look up into her eyes, their depths for once gentle and worried. And just then, Ardagh realized, he wouldn't have minded if Time itself had ended so that he could go on lying there like this.

Sorcha had started when his eyes opened, but for a long, long moment after that, she didn't move. Then she asked warily, "Are you all right?"

"Yes."

"Good!" She stood up so suddenly Ardagh nearly cracked his head on the floor. "Don't you ever dare do something like that to me again! Telling me this wasn't anything dangerous, then collapsing like that—dammit, I thought you were d-dead!"

He blinked up at her, astonished but too dizzy to speak, and Sorcha cried contritely, "Och, I'm sorry," and knelt by his side again. "Are you sure you're all right?"

"Quite." He managed to raise himself up on one elbow, staring. "But next time kindly warn me before dropping me like that."

"But what happened? One moment you were casting your spell, in the next, you just—fell over. I . . . really did think you were dead."

"That would have mattered so much to you?" he said, and regretted the banality even as he said it.

That brought her back to her usual sharp self. "What do you think? I take it that the spell failed?"

"It failed. What you saw was a magical backlash, unspent Power recoiling, fortunately not seriously, on me."

"Ah, like the one that struck you down a few months back! When you slept for two days."

"Indeed. This Realm is wonderful for such mishaps." He sat all the way up, then winced as a new surge of dizziness swept through him, and rested head in hands. He felt Sorcha's hand rest lightly on his shoulder for a moment.

"You're sure you're all right?"

"Yes." Carefully, Ardagh straightened. For a moment his face and hers were almost touching, so close he could feel the warmth of her breath on his cheek. But then Sorcha scrambled hastily back to her feet. Ardagh tried to smile up at her, felt it turn into a grimace instead.

"It's my fault the thing failed. I was in too great a hurry; I didn't want to accept that such a specific scrying spell couldn't quite work in this Realm."

"And Arnulf?" Sorcha asked suddenly. "Was it a magical backlash that killed him?"

"No. That," Ardagh said, "was most certainly murder."

"Murder!"

"Gervinus killed him from afar to keep him from confessing." The prince got slowly to his feet. "I don't hear you arguing."

"I can't."

"Then you alone of all the humans here are unique." He

stopped short, studying her, not sure if what he was feeling was joy or anguish, then added softly, "You are unique, aren't you?"

He saw the color rush into her face. "Och, I . . ."

"Sorcha, I can't lie, even to myself. This is a foolish time and place for it, but—we can't deny that there's something happening between us."

For a moment he was sure she *was* going to deny it. But then Sorcha murmured, "No. I suppose we can't. Ridiculous!"

He stiffened, stung. "Ridiculous?"

"Who and what we are, I mean. You, a prince of the Sidhe, so handsome it stops my breath in my throat—"

"Is that all you see?" Ardagh cut in indignantly. "*Beauty*?"

"Of course not," she returned just as indignantly. "Do you think I'm that shallow? I also know that I'm *not* a beauty, and most definitely *not* of the Sidhe. No," Sorcha said more softly. "No. It would never work between us."

"I . . ." But he couldn't finish, knowing that there was no way to avoid the painful truth: no, indeed.

"How old are you?" Sorcha asked without warning.

Ardagh blinked in surprise. "I don't really know," he admitted after a moment. "Younger than my brother, certainly, but as to more specific years . . . my people don't really need to keep track of such things."

"Exactly." Her voice was just a little too controlled. "Time doesn't matter to the Sidhe, does it? You'll stay just as you are, youthful, beautiful, no matter how many years pass, but I—I'm only human. I would quickly age and grow ugly in your eyes, and—and then I would—" She waved a wild hand. "Besides, if—*when* you find your way back home, off you'll whisk—not that I blame you for that—and here I'd be, left discarded."

"Sorcha . . ." he began, then tried again, more resolutely, "I agree with you. Ae, not about the discarding; I could never be so cruel to you. But there would be too many problems if we let emotion come between us. We cannot let this continue."

"Certainly not."

"I would never want to cause you pain."

"And I—" With a strangled little cry, Sorcha threw herself into his arms. She gave him a quick kiss so fiery it left Ardagh breathless, then tore herself free, running hastily away. And his keen Sidhe ears heard the sound of soft, despairing sobs. Struggling to catch his breath, aching to run after her, he forced himself to stay where he was, although it took every scrap of Sidhe will to keep mind and body both under control.

I'm sorry. Powers, Sorcha, I am sorry.

He was still too worn from the effects of the backlash and the events of the day to think about it further. Suddenly too weary even to go on standing, Ardagh walked slowly back into his house and sank to the bed, sitting lost in hopeless, hopeless thought.

Ardagh woke suddenly, finding himself sagging sideways on the bed, astonished to learn he actually had slipped from musings into sleep. It hadn't been a deep or very long one, and he had no idea what had awakened him. The prince straightened slowly, stretching to work the stiffness out of his muscles, then went to take care of a nagging body's needs. It took only a few moments more to straighten clothing and smooth down hair, then he stepped back out into the fading day.

Nothing odd out here, just the usual quiet that came over a human dwelling place as the night came on. He must have completely missed dinner, but he wasn't particularly hungry. Instead, Ardagh headed towards the ruin that had been Gervinus' guest house. There probably wasn't much point in going here now, so long after the murder, and yet . . . he shrugged.

No one was within; no need to guard an empty building. Arnulf's body had, of course, been removed, and Gervinus' retinue were elsewhere, maybe even started on the long journey back to Rome. Ardagh moved silently through what had been the bishop's bedchamber, looking for something useable, something Gervinus had handled.

No. The man had known enough to snatch away anything

that might be linked to him. Disappointing. But, Ardagh mused, since Gervinus had occupied the room for a fair amount of time, his aura couldn't yet have quite faded. He shrugged again. Worth a try. The prince sat quietly in the center of the room, eyes closed, letting his mind relax . . . relax . . . he could almost see Gervinus now, yes, almost feel the man's thoughts . . . feel the coldness, the ambition, the anger . . . anger, yes . . . hatred . . .

Ardagh opened his eyes with a sigh. There was nothing more than this: Gervinus bore him a sharp personal hatred—mutual, the prince thought and hardly a surprise—a hatred sharp enough for the echoes to still linger in this room, and had been furious at him and everyone else in Fremainn about having to flee like a thief. But there had also been an undertone of plotting, of alliances to be made. . . .

Ae, useless. All this told him was what he had already guessed. Gervinus was indeed out there searching out the malcontents, trying to weld them into one strong army against Aedh.

And how am I supposed to prove it?

Ardagh scrambled to his feet and went out into the night again, not sure exactly what he was hunting. All he needed now to make things perfect was to run into Fothad accusing him of dishonoring his daughter—

Ae, curse it all to the Lowest Pits of Darkness! He did *not* want to be involved in all these human plots. He did *not* want to have to worry about any of them. And he most surely, most thoroughly, heartily, definitely, did *not* want to think, act, or even live like a human! He should up and flee Fremainn himself, set out on his own, free and—and unencumbered!

Of course. Free to go where? Do what? What else was there for him in this Realm?

Wonderful. See me feel sorry for myself. Just like a human.

And wouldn't dear brother Eirithan enjoy this sight?

"That for you, Eirithan," Ardagh said with a very rude hand gesture he'd seen Cadwal make, and laughed in spite of himself. There were *some* useful things to be learned from humans! Spirits unexpectedly restored, he started back to his guest house.

And this time he did run into Fothad. The poet was wandering slowly in the darkness, very plainly a man lost in thought, but he stopped short when he saw Ardagh. The prince hesitated at the sight of the man's troubled eyes and asked, "We're not going to feud, are we?"

"Is there need?" Fothad returned. But then he added more softly, "Forgive me. I don't mean to attack you."

"And I certainly don't want to attack you."

"Prince Ardagh, I . . . will you walk with me?"

"If you wish."

They went on together in silence for a time. Then Fothad murmured, "I can see why you like to stroll about at night. It's so wonderfully peaceful out here with no one but the occasional guard about. Of course," he added with a sideways glance at Ardagh, "it must be particularly easy for you to get about."

"Eh?"

"I would guess that you have incredibly keen night vision. Your eyes fairly glow in the dark."

"A trait of my people," Ardagh said without expression, and was glad when Fothad left it at that. "My lord, you didn't join me to comment on my vision. What would you?"

Fothad was silent for a time, then burst out, "She's an old man's child, my Sorcha. That's part of it. I have no other chick; I tend to forget this one's a woman grown."

Ardagh glanced at him, glanced away, uncomfortable. "You don't have to say this."

"I do. I all but accused you of dishonorable deeds earlier this day. It wasn't just. I know you're an honest man. Incredibly honest." Fothad's eyes glinted in the darkness, as human eyes did when damp. "I also had no right hurting you about your exile."

"It is as it is."

"No. I see the pain of it in those eerie eyes of yours even now, even in the darkness."

Ardagh rather doubted that; there were limits to human vision, and this was, after all, a poet used to hyperbole. But the kindness behind the exaggerated words kept him from commenting. Fothad continued, "Prince Ardagh, I know you've come to love my daughter—don't flinch; you know it's true. I suspect she loves you, too. And I truly wish I could give you both my blessing! But . . . you are as you are, and the law is as it is."

Do you think it's your silly human laws that worry me?
"Look you," Ardagh said, "I know anything between your daughter and myself is impossible. It's more impossible than you could ever believe. And I would just as soon not discuss the matter any longer."

"As you wish." But Fothad was watching him closely. "What are you?" the poet wondered. "A prince of Cathay? Or can you be someone else? Maybe even . . . something . . . else?"

Trust a poet to see below the surface. Even if it had taken him this long for that insight. "I am a prince of my people," Ardagh said evasively. "And I—" He froze, thinking, *Ae, no. Not here. Not now.*

Too late. A Doorway was forming, he could *feel* it. A Doorway *had* opened, shimmering clearly against the darkness, and young Breasal, dressed in silken Sidhe robes, stood within it.

"No . . ." Fothad breathed in awe. "I don't believe it. . . ."

He thinks it's a heavenly vision, Ardagh realized. *Of course. Being of these people and their beliefs, what else can he think?*

Breasal realized it, too. He gave Ardagh one quick glance of pure panic, then hastily straightened into what he presumably hoped looked like an angelic pose. And he proclaimed in a voice that sounded a little too melodramatically pure and sweet to Ardagh, "I come from—from the one who has given me shelter. I come in return for the kindness shown me."

That meant, Ardagh translated silently, that Finvarra was letting the boy return this one last time with a message in thanks for sending Breasal to his kingdom. Nice to know the boy was being so well received. But what message could be so important that—

"I come with a warning!" Breasal exclaimed, and all at once he wasn't being theatrical at all. "The Lochlannach—they are sailing even now and will be making landfall within the week."

Ardagh heard Fothad's sharply indrawn breath. "Where?" the poet asked. "Breasal, if ever we treated you with kindness in life, tell us now: where are they to land?"

The embarrassed color came into the boy's face at that "in life," but he answered without hesitation, "Kilfenora. Two ships will land near to the monastery of Kilfenora." Now the color was definitely sharp in Breasal's face: that monastery lay not too far from his father's lands. But with good presence of mind, the boy managed to add, in a beautifully Otherworldly tone he could only have learned from Finvarra, "Seek them there, oh you who stand here. Seek them there and stop them!"

With a sweep of his arms so melodramatic that Ardagh nearly choked on unexpected laughter—the boy really *was* learning from the flamboyant Finvarra!—Beasal stepped back into Faerie and was gone as the Doorway vanished.

Fothad turned to Ardagh, face alight with reverence. "You saw it too."

"Yes." Still smitten by Breasal's imitation of Finvarra, the prince didn't dare say more; the last thing he wanted to do was burst into misplaced laughter.

Fothad must have taken his struggle not to laugh for dazed wonder. "We have been granted a heavenly vision, Prince Ardagh. I never dreamed such a thing might come to pass, not to me; I am no holy man." *I'm certainly not!* Ardagh thought, but didn't dare say. "And yet," the poet continued, "we *have* been granted a vision."

But then Fothad's awestruck face hardened. "And we must make sure that heaven's warning isn't in vain." His trained voice was suddenly cold and clear as a war trumpet. "Aedh will be most glad to hear this news. This once, och, this once we shall stop those sea thieves before they strike!"

LOCHLANNACH
AND OTHERS

CHAPTER 28

There was emptiness all around him, terrible, endless emptiness, and he was falling into it, endlessly aware, endlessly falling, endlessly . . .

Gervinus woke with a gasp, drenched in perspiration, for one horrifying moment, surrounded by darkness as he was, sure that it hadn't been a dream at all or, even more terrible, that the dream had followed him into reality.

Impossible. Grimly he willed his pulse to slow, his heart to cease its wild pounding. It *had* been only a dream, only that. And even if he had been having more and more of the dark kind lately, more than ever he'd endured as a child, that still gave the things no real power over him.

And yet, and yet . . . almost before he realized it, Gervinus found his hand reaching for the grimoire, found himself clutching it to him as another man might clutch a holy charm. Only its sorceries seemed to give him true comfort in these troubled days; only when casting the spells held within it did he feel any true relief from the inner chill tormenting him.

Nonsense. Nonsense, indeed. There was no reason to be feeling this foolish darkness, not now when things were going so well, so suddenly, wondrously well, after that disastrous last day in Fremainn. Oh, true, it was unfortunate

that he had needed to kill Arnulf. But then, who would
have expected that the little idiot would ever have become adept enough to try working true sorcery on his
own? Up until that last inconvenient moment the acolyte, for all his flaws, had been of some use. But betrayal
could not be permitted. And, those inept attempts at sorcery
or no, betrayal it would have been the moment that Arnulf
had been questioned. As questioned he would, without a
doubt, have been.

Besides, Arnulf's death by sorcery, Gervinus thought with
a touch of dour humor, and sorcery cast from afar at that,
had definitely impressed these new allies. Never mind that
the strain of it had nearly killed him. No, no, they were
perfectly willing to believe what they wanted to see: that
Gervinus had struck Arnulf down with the aid of Divine
intervention. Therefore, they were also blatantly going to
be willing to believe that any other magics he might need
to display were not sorcery but the gift of Heaven.

Of course they believed. What else could be expected
of these uneducated fools? Gervinus glanced about his
decidedly rural surroundings at the sleeping warriors lying
all around, and shrugged. Sleeping on bare ground and eating
definitely inferior rations for a few days wouldn't hurt him;
they reminded him of the discipline every Frankish noble's
son endured. The enforced company of so many uneducated minds was another matter. A pity that he could not
have partaken of the hospitality of Queen Derval of Clonach
instead.

Ah yes, Derval . . . now, there was a fascinating woman,
coldhearted and ruthless as any man, with a love of the devious that was equal nearly to his own. What an amazing
network of conspirators she had managed to assemble, all
on her own!

But she was, unfortunately, what she was, wife to King
Donnchadh. And Donnchadh, equally unfortunately, was
Fearghal's father. Even if Gervinus had managed to successfully banish from Derval's mind the memory of the
information he'd forced from her, there was always the
danger that when Donnchadh came riding home with his

son in tow, that son would recognize the one who had ensorcelled him.

Ah well. It had been no easy thing to convince Derval to give up her precious list, not even with the grimoire's aid; in fact, it had taken every bit of sorcerous persuasion he could summon to overwhelm that bitter, stubborn will. But in the end, it had been worth the trouble. Each of these hastily assembled allies believed—or acted as though they believed, which amounted to the same thing—that Gervinus was on a holy mission. What that mission might be, other than to rid them of King Aedh, no one seemed to care. Oh no, they were far too ambitious for such fribbles, seeing any excuse as good enough, each man thinking that *he* would be the one to end up sitting the High King's throne. It hardly mattered which one won out. God knew they bickered so much among themselves already it was amazing no one had been slain! There was such a thing as being *too* independent: these volatile folk would never agree long enough to make one united land.

Ah well, *Deus volunt*. Not one of these braggarts was the equal in cunning and strength of will of King Aedh, and whichever one of them finally managed to kill off the others and take the throne—why then, Gervinus would most easily rule the ruler.

But first, he thought, *we must be rid of King Aedh*.

There hadn't been any time for a grand farewell, Ardagh thought, just a hasty gathering of men and weapons, and some frantic scurryings-about by women trying not to look worried.

One of those women was Queen Eithne. Ardagh watched, surprised by a pang almost of envy as she ran to her husband for one last fierce embrace. What, he wondered uncertainly, must it be like to have someone so very worried about you?

Some Sidhe sense made him turn sharply to find Sorcha staring at him. For an instant he wondered if she meant to imitate Eithne. But no, the prince realized, she and he had already just barely skirted impropriety by being alone together in his guest house, no matter why; she could hardly risk rashness now.

Couldn't she? Catching him by two strong fistfuls of hair, she pulled his head down and gave him a kiss fierce enough to almost be a declaration of war. As he straightened, stunned, she glared at him.

"Bring yourself back, Prince Ardagh." It was an order. "We are *not* leaving this matter unsettled."

He bowed. "As you will it, my commander."

That forced a reluctant half-smile from her. It vanished just as quickly. "Bring yourself back," she repeated, and marched off into the crowd. Ardagh, very much aware of Fothad's stare on him, watched her go, hearing Cadwal's chuckle in his ear.

"Should send that one after the Lochlannach," the mercenary murmured. "She'd have them back in their frozen homeland with one flash of those sharp eyes. You have yourself a fine, strong lady there, Prince Ardagh."

"She's not my—"

But Aedh had already given the signal for them to ride out, and there was nothing to do but follow.

After the strains of their rapid ride, Ardagh thought, they should have been rewarded with some dramatic vista, something worthy of the struggle. Instead, the monastery of Kilfenora looked more like an assemblage of toy buildings set down near the rocky seashore than any place where people might actually live or be in any sort of peril: neat stone walls, neat thatched roofs, neat patches of garden with not a leaf misplaced. The monks probably thought such perfection tranquil. Undistracting.

Boring.

It was also nearly as defenseless as a toy. No earthenwork rings, no palisade, only the one pretty stone wall that looked solid enough—and the less than sturdy wooden gate that any truly determined raider could cave in. But then, the prince thought with only the slightest touch of irony, the monks, trusting in their isolation, would have believed themselves perfectly safe.

Which they had been, till now. But they would still be defended, assuming that this lean old eagle of an Abbot Cuana would ever believe what King Aedh was telling him. The abbot listened without a flicker of reaction to the tale of Breasal's miraculous appearance and the warning of approaching peril, studying Ardagh all the while as though he expected to see horns and cloven hoofs.

"Do you, then," the abbot said directly to Ardagh, "claim to be a holy man to receive such a vision?"

"Hardly that. But the boy and I were friendly while he was still . . . in this world. And," the prince continued blandly, "I have no reason to doubt anything he says to me now."

The sarcasm not quite hidden behind the innocent words made Abbot Cuana stare in disapproval, but Aedh cut in impatiently, "The vision was seen by my Chief Minister as well. I have no reason to doubt *him*. Yes, the whole thing sounds bizarre. But this will be the first chance anyone has had of stopping the Lochlannach in their tracks, and I don't intend to waste it. Like it or not, my lord abbot, we are staying."

Ardagh glanced down at Kilfenora from the headland on which he, King Aedh and Cadwal sat their horses in the near-darkness of early morning. Or what, he guessed, was near-darkness to the humans; he could see quite clearly. The constant rush of waves drifted up to him, cut again and again by the shrill shrieks of waking seabirds, and the clean, sharp scent of the ocean filled his nostrils, rousing bits of memory of the seas in his own Realm, of one long summer's night spent idly sailing a silver boat under a moon-silver sky. . . .

But, Ardagh told himself resolutely, this sea had its beauty, too, smashing itself into wild white froth against the rocks or swirling in endless patterns against the narrow beach. The prince realized with a sudden sharp stab of curiosity that he had never yet had a chance to see much more of Eriu than the heavily forested lands around Fremainn. Yet traders' tales spoke of odder regions, of barren, rocky places like the Giants' Causeway, said to have been built by supernatural forces (that, he doubted!) or long, rolling stretches of mountains like so many great Hollow Hills. Maybe when all this excitement with Lochlannach and stray bishops was settled, he would go see these things for himself and—

Ardagh cut off that thought. It was the thinking of someone who had decided that this land was his home.

And Eriu can never be that. Never.

From here, the monastery looked even more like a collection of toy buildings, with no clues at all to the men living within the confines of that neat wall.

"I don't understand them," he said softly, and saw Aedh's eyes glint as the king glanced his way.

"The monks, you mean?"

Ardagh nodded, then remembered that the human probably couldn't see that and added, "Yes. Even after these past two days of waiting, with nothing much to do but clean weapons and talk to the monks, I still have no idea what drives a man to such isolation."

Aedh shrugged. "God, they say. Who knows? They seem to be content enough."

Some were, Ardagh thought, as tranquil as their setting, but others were quarrelsome as courtiers or restless as warriors. And not a woman to be found anywhere. In short, the prince decided dryly, Kilfenora was, with all its contradictions, a very human place.

An imperiled one. Ardagh straightened, staring out to sea. "Look."

The morning was already promising to be unexpectedly fair. Perfect weather for a fight, as no doubt the humans would say. The two approaching Lochlannach ships, still far off but sailing the tides lightly into land, were graceful as a pair of seabirds against the stark, midnight blue of the ocean and the slowly brightening sky, their square sails brilliant red. So beautifully made were those ships from the sweep of carven prows (were those stylized beasts meant to be dragons?) to the equally perfectly curved sterns that the sight of them nearly left him breathless. How could anyone as barbaric as the Lochlannach were said to be have built such ships? Surely these weren't—

"I see them." King Aedh sat leaning his arms comfortably on his saddle's pommel, looking as tranquil as a man watching the waves: the raiders were still too far away to be accurately counted.

"At last," Cadwal muttered. "Abbot Cuana's thoroughly sick of us after these two days of nothing much. Particularly since we've been eating our way through his monastery's supplies."

Ardagh grinned at that and Aedh laughed outright. "He'd be more sickened by those visitors out there," the king said, "and so would his whole monastery. Looks like it really was a heavenly vision you and Fothad were granted," he added, glancing quickly at Ardagh. "An accurate one, at any rate."

"Did you doubt that?"

Aedh shrugged. "I gambled my honor on it, didn't I?" He turned back to the ocean, peering out at the distant raiders. "Two ships, maybe . . . can't really tell in this dim light. What do you make it, Cadwal?"

"Two ships, definitely, no more than that. Must have been planning a quick raid and away. How many men are those ships carrying, though . . . fifty, maybe?"

"Sixty," Ardagh said without thinking, and both humans stared at him.

"Fothad's right," Aedh exclaimed, "you *do* have extraordinary night vision. Sixty men, then."

"Gives us a bit of a numerical edge," Cadwal muttered. "Plus, of course, the element of surprise, particularly if we hit them hard from the start. They'll be expecting nothing more than defenseless monks. Certainly won't be expecting anyone able to fight back."

"Indeed they won't," the king agreed and grinned. "Heyho, my children, back to Kilfenora. We have a welcome to prepare."

Ardagh glanced about. King Aedh had hidden his men behind Kilfenora's wall, aligning them in a wedge pointed towards the relatively fragile wooden gate, opened a crack so the raiders could be tracked. As Cadwal and Ardagh waited, thrown together by chance, Cadwal looked at the prince and shook his head. "Still wish you weren't so fussy about not wearing mail. Getting spitted by one of those louts would be a stupid way to go."

I'm not delighted by the idea, either. But the thought of being closely encircled by iron is even more unpleasant. "Mail would slow me down," Ardagh said, truthfully enough, glancing down at his old Sidhe hunting leathers. "These will serve. And I don't intend to let those louts spit me."

Cadwal's shrug said volumes. "Got some good blades on them, if rumor's true."

King Aedh heard that. His grin was a predator's silent snarl. "We'll see how many of those blades we can claim, eh? Nice for our smiths to study. Och, but it would be rude of us not to greet our guests, nor give them proper hospitality." His sword whipped free of its scabbard with a high *skree* of metal. "Wait, now. Wait. We want them all off those ships and caught between two lines of swords." He waited as calmly as though turned to rock. "There, now," Aedh said at last. "That's the last of them. And here they come. Shall we?"

The Lochlannach came charging in like so many howling wolves, tall, fair-haired, weather-beaten men smelling of too many days at sea, bearing swords and small shields and clad in mail (*Good,* Ardagh thought about that last, *that will slow them down,* then amended that to *bad, it doesn't seem to be slowing them down at all*).

No time to ponder it. With sudden savage roars of their own, Aedh and his men came sweeping out through the gate at the Lochlannach, the wedge splitting open to encircle them, and Ardagh, without much choice in the matter, was swept along with them.

For a few fiery moments, the men of Eriu had the easy advantage of surprise, trapping the raiders between their two wings, cutting down those who were too startled to react in time—but the advantage lasted only for those few moments. Caught off-guard though they were, the Lochlannach were damnably quick to recover and savagely hungry for a fight. Ardagh saw a tall, broad-shouldered warrior who was clearly their leader, heard him shouting what was

certainly a command that they break off the attack on
Kilfenora and concentrate on fighting their way free of the
trap. And Cadwal had been right: those were splendid blades
the raiders wielded.

Splendid *iron* blades, Ardagh corrected silently. Iron mail.
Iron helmets—Powers curse him for an idiot, what was he
doing here? Trying to prove himself a thrice-cursed hero?
His body was protesting the nearness of all that perilous
metal, threatening to weaken him, sicken him, but caught
in the middle of things as he was, any weakness would kill
him! Battle frenzy, now, if only he could open himself up
to battle frenzy, let it seize him the way it had on that long-
ago day when he'd first seen King Aedh . . . but it wasn't
working; his mind was remaining stubbornly clear. Dodging a dying man—of Eriu or Lochlannach, he didn't have
time to see—Ardagh caught a blade against his own, staggering back under the impact; the raider was his height but
far wider in the shoulders.

Like an ox. The prince heard himself grunt as the raider's
sword came down on his again. *A powerful one.* Rather than
let himself be driven helplessly, Ardagh leaped back like a
cat to give himself some room to maneuver, then lunged.
Ha, yes! The Lochlannach blades were finely wrought but,
like the blades of Eriu, meant only for cutting; they lacked
true points.

His did not. As the Lochlannach drove his sword whistling
down at Ardagh's head, Ardagh lunged, deliberately high. His
sword *skreed* against the upper edge of the shield and took
the startled raider in the throat, efficiently and messily.

The prince just barely managed to pull his blade free from
his choking, crumpling foe before another man closed with
him. He ducked right under the raider's upraised swordarm,
whirled, got in a backhanded slash across the man's legs,
felling him, whirled again to face a new attacker, stabbed,
dodged, thrust, sometimes hitting mail, sometimes shield,
sometimes flesh. This was the only way he was going to
escape unhurt, by sheer speed of reflex: a Sidhe could react
far faster than any human, even a Sidhe half-sick from the
presence of too much iron.

All around him, men continued to fight, to fall, to die. The air was sharp with shouts and screams and the clash of blade on blade, sharper with the stench of blood and worse. *The abbot is not going to be pleased with having his sanctuary so desecrated. Not that there's a choice about it.*

Ardagh caught a glimpse of King Aedh, neatly flanked by his mercenaries, a savage grin on his face: it must have felt wonderfully satisfying to finally be doing something about Eriu's tormentors. The prince caught a quicker glimpse of Cadwal, efficient as some machine. No sign of enjoyment on the mercenary's face; this was pure business to him. Ardagh lithely dodged a blow from an ax (his mind all the time gibbering, *a weapon Aedh's men don't use; I'll wager that changes after today*) that would have split him, lunged again, slashing someone's arm, twisting aside just in time as someone else's blade scored his hunting leathers and very nearly him—

And found himself staring at a boy in armor, a boy who couldn't possibly be all that much older than Prince Niall.

Powers! What idiot takes a child into battle? But then, there wasn't supposed to be a battle, just a raid. Just enough to train a boy in the raiders' way.

What happened next happened far too swiftly. Ardagh saw the javelin fly, heard himself shout uselessly, "No!" He dove forward, hoping without hope to pull the boy aside, but even Sidhe reflexes were not quite that swift. The javelin pierced the boy, and Ardagh fell to his knees, catching the crumpling child in his arms, seeing bewildered shock and pain in the young eyes, knowing, aching with horror, that there was nothing he could do to help, nothing but take away that pain as best he could, sending his will into the boy's mind, soothing, soothing. . . .

He heard the softest of relieved sighs, then felt the child go limp and lifeless in his arms. Gasping and drained, Ardagh stared wildly up and found himself locking stares with a Lochlannach warrior—no, a chieftain, the leader of the raid, the tall, broad-shouldered, rough-faced man with the aura of command—

And grief. This was the boy's father, Ardagh knew it in a

flash of insight. For what seemed a long, long while the prince knelt, frozen, the dead boy in his arms, his gaze still locked with that of the Lochlannach chieftain.

The chieftain blinked. Ardagh sensed rather than saw a sword come whirring down from behind. *No chance to move—*

But the blade was stopped with a clang of iron by a second sword. Ardagh let the boy's body fall and scrambled back to his feet, the sheer will to live fueling a desperate new surge of energy. "Cadwal!"

Before he could thank the man for the rescue, the mercenary glared at him, muttering something under his breath about "Damn fools who don't watch their backs," and returned to the fight.

Which was rapidly changing to a rout. The Lochlannach leader snatched up his son's body, shouting at what was left of his men, clearly ordering them back to the ships.

"Let them go!" Aedh's roar rose over the shouting. "Let them go, I say! I *want* them to go home and warn the others. Let them tell everyone in their cursed cold northern lands what they've learned this day: they will find no easy victims here!"

Unless, Ardagh thought, almost too weary with shock and battle and iron-sickness to stand, *unless the next time that they come, they come in greater numbers.*

It was not over. They had bought themselves some time this day. But it was far from over. And Ardagh suspected that Aedh, beneath the wildness of his battle-glory, knew it, too.

BESIEGED

CHAPTER 29

The men of Eriu watched, some standing alone, some leaning weakly on others, cheering wearily as the Lochlannach ships caught the wind and sailed away.

"Hardly enough left on board to sail them!" someone yelled, and roused a new round of cheers.

"Bet the first storm they hit sinks them!"

"Bet the first big *wave* sinks them!"

But despite the banter, there was a fierce alertness to Aedh and Cadwal and many of the warriors; Ardagh guessed why, and murmured, "They won't be back. At least not this time."

The king glanced his way. "How can you be so sure?"

All at once the words wouldn't come easily. "His son," Ardagh managed. "That was his son who . . ."

"The boy who was killed?" Cadwal asked sharply. "The one who almost got *you* killed? That was the chieftain's son?" At Ardagh's nod, the mercenary spat out, "Damn! If I'd known, we could have held the boy for ransom. Too late now."

"Is that all the child meant to you?" Ardagh asked, almost in wonder. "A prize to be won?"

"Hell, man—Prince Ardagh, that is—I'm no more glad about a boy getting killed than you are, even a son of one of those sea thieves, but that's the way things go. Father had no business putting a youngster like that into danger anyhow. And let's save our worrying for our own living and wounded, yes?"

Stunned anew at the casual way humans could throw away their young, Ardagh turned sharply from Cadwal before he could say anything he'd regret, then stopped short, staring, realizing only now that the battle was over how costly the victory had been. What had been a peaceful, grassy shore was now a torn-up, bloodied field, and a good many of the bodies lying there were those of Eriu.

Aedh had already begun moving through the ranks of the fallen, counting the dead, giving what comfort he could to the wounded, such sincere concern on his face that a pang of almost-regret shot through Ardagh. *This* was what a ruler should be, not merely a warrior or politician, but someone who truly cared for land and people.

You should see this, my brother, Ardagh thought, then wondered at himself. The prince of the Sidhe Realm he'd been had never much worried about others, either. A shudder raced through him, and suddenly he couldn't seem to stop shivering.

Cadwal shot him a quick glance. "You hurt?" When he shook his head, the mercenary shrugged and muttered, "Damned lucky," and went searching for his own dead. After a time, Ardagh gained enough control over himself to follow. There wasn't much he could do, no great spells he could work, certainly not in this Realm, but he could at least try to ease pain.

And that thought astonished him as well.

It had, indeed, been an expensive victory: although some thirty of the Lochlannach had been slain, a full twenty men of Eriu had died as well, and another ten had been too badly injured to be moved. Ardagh, riding through forest with King Aedh and his party, headed back towards Fremainn, remembered the look of mingled horror and grief that had filled Abbot Cuana's face at the sight of the battlefield. The abbot had vowed that the injured would receive the best of care, and the prince, seeing the compassion in Cuana's eyes, had believed him. As, of course, had the men of Eriu.

The Lochlannach wounded, on the other hand, had been summarily dispatched—no false sentimentality there, Ardagh thought with Sidhe approval—and the dead disposed of in a mass pyre. *Sanitary.* A nice insurance, too, whether the humans knew it or not, against any Lochlannach spirits walking. *Assuming human spirits really do walk.*

He glanced at Cadwal as they rode. Five of the dead had been the mercenary's own men, but not a sign of emotion showed on the leathery face. Ardagh wondered how many times Cadwal had gone through this? How many times had he lost men he'd eaten with, drunk with? Men who'd grown close as brothers?

No, Ardagh thought. Poor choice of words, that "brothers." Unlikely that either he or Eirithan would ever feel the smallest twinge of grief at the other's death. And why should that honest fact fill him with such bitterness? Such . . . regret? He shuddered anew.

Powers, let me leave this Realm. I don't know who I am anymore. I'm not even sure what I am. Powers, Powers, let me go home.

Ae, ridiculous. He was weary, that was all, and still suffering the shock of having been surrounded by too much iron. If only they could have spent one night more at Kilfenora he would have had a chance to recover, if he could only have had one more stretch of sleep, sleep this time unbroken by dreams of a child dying in his arms—

Stop that. What happened is done, and no changing it.

But of course King Aedh had been too eager to return to Fremainn to tarry, understandably uneasy about being too long away from his court.

And from Eithne, too, Ardagh thought with a smile. *Sorcha.*

Ae yes, Sorcha. She waited as well. "What's that structure?" Ardagh asked to take his mind from sudden uneasy thoughts. "That plain stone tower?"

Aedh straightened in the saddle to peer through the forest. "Part of a ruined hill fort. One of those dating from the bad old days of Pagandom—your pardon, Prince Ardagh. That one would be . . . och, I can't place a name to it. I imagine Donnchadh of Clonarch could; we're nearly on his land. Not quite ruined at that," he added in a more speculative tone. "The wall looks pretty much still defensible. Lax of Donnchadh to let it stand."

"In case some petty lordling might try making himself at home in there?"

"Exactly. Well, if Donnchadh won't do the work . . ." Aedh shrugged. "A pity to tear the thing down after it's stood so long, but that's what I'll have to set someone to do. We can't have—"

"Gervinus!" Ardagh exclaimed, too startled by the sudden *feel* of peril to get the words out right. "A trap—beware—treason!"

The attack came crashing down on them, grim warriors charging in on all sides. "Odran mac Daire!" Aedh shouted in sudden recognition. "And Muirgheas mac Art, as well—how many more of you traitors are there? How many have come to be killed?"

Brave words. But the king's battle-weary, decimated force was in no shape for another fight, not so soon. "To the fort!" Aedh commanded, and began cutting his way through, his men hastily flanking him. Seized by the same desperate ferocity as Aedh—and by the sheer panic of a Sidhe surrounded by yet more iron—Ardagh slashed and slashed and slashed, one small, sane part of his mind noting, *Well now, here's the battle frenzy you wanted. A bit late, but still useful.*

Suddenly he was through the enemy, suddenly they were all through and riding like madmen for the safety of the hill fort. They thundered up through the narrow path formed by a double ring of earthen ramparts overgrown by grass and weeds to the thick stone wall that stood above, curving along the rim of the hill.

"Gate's still intact," Cadwal noted breathlessly. "Good old oak, lasts forever."

"Let's hope the bolt's lasted as well!" Aedh shot back. "Och, and the hinges! Ha, yes, they have," he added as a team of frantic warriors managed to pry the gate open. "Now if only the bolt's still inside . . ."

They raced through into a small forest of weeds, out of

which the tower rose like a rock from a tangled green sea. Ardagh noticed piles of broken stone lying everywhere, and wondered wildly if that meant the whole wall was about to crumble. There was a desperate scurrying of men leaping from their horses to slam the gate shut again. "The bolt—" "There—" "Get the damned thing back in its socket—yes, yes, it's holding, slam it shut—there!"

"Good enough," Aedh said breathlessly. "For the moment. Isn't going to hold anyone off for long, but at least they can only come after us a few at a time thanks to the ramparts. You, you, and you," his finger stabbed at warriors, "go look along the walls. Make sure there aren't any other weak points. You and you, go see what condition that tower's in; see if we can use it as a final refuge if need be. Spy out how many men are out there, too. The rest of you—ha, here they come. Let's see what we can do about holding them off."

Ardagh heard the enemy pounding at the gate and, suddenly inspired, said, "As you say, they can only come up through the ramparts a few at a time."

Cadwal grinned, clearly catching his idea. "True enough. They want in? Let's give them their wish."

The enemy must have believed their pounding had finally caused the gate to fly open of its own accord. They came rushing in—and met the swords of the waiting defenders. The first to enter died quickly, the next to follow tried too late to pull back and failed, trapped between the fallen dead before them and the living warriors coming up behind. After a mad time of skirmishing, the would-be attackers frantically managed to withdraw back down the narrow way between the ramparts, and Aedh's men shoved the dead back outside, then slammed the gate shut and bolted it once more.

"That little dance will keep them back for now," Aedh began, "but—Prince Ardagh? Are you hurt?"

Ardagh had staggered back, letting himself sag to the ground, back against the tower. Head down, he managed a shaky, "No." If he said anything more, the prince knew he was going to be ignominiously sick; he certainly couldn't explain that too much iron had sickened him.

To Ardagh's relief, the king turned away. "Ah, here are my searchers. The wall?"

"Wall's secure enough," one of the men answered, gesturing, "shaped like a horseshoe. Curves around on both sides of us without a break, then ends where the land drops sharply away. No one's coming up that way," he added, "not without wings."

Aedh nodded. "Whoever built this fort must have seen Dun Aengus. Same configuration. And the tower?"

"Sound enough. Probably could hold off an army, sure enough."

"And is that what we're going to have to do?"

The warriors shifted uneasily, glancing at each other. "Can't say for sure," one began, "because of the way the ramparts curve, and all the forest behind them. Don't really know how many men are out there. But there's another problem, a big one. There are a few pools of rainwater within the walls that look clean enough, good for maybe a day or so if we ration it. But there's no steady source of water anywhere in the fort. Well's gone dry."

"Now we know why the place was abandoned." The king smiled without humor. "One way or another, I think this is going to be a short siege." He glanced about at his grim, worn, battle-weary men. "Make the wounded as comfortable as you can. The rest of you, rest while we've got the respite."

Ardagh, body finally back under control, struggled to his feet. Aedh frowned. "And where are you going?"

"To the tower top. I wish to see for myself how many foes are out there."

Cadwal muttered something about "Now he can see through forest and earth as well as night," but he followed Ardagh up the narrow, crumbling stone stairway to the top. Catching his breath, the prince looked up. There must have originally been a roof to this tower, but it had long ago fallen apart. Leaning warily on a windowsill, Cadwal complained, "Not much room up here. Not very secure, either."

"Watch where you step," Ardagh said absently. "The floor's almost as rotten as the roof." He hadn't really wanted to be followed; the senses he was using had little to do with physical sight.

"I count forty," Cadwal said after a moment. "But I have a feeling I'm not seeing all of them."

"You're not." Fifty . . . sixty-five . . . seventy-five men . . . ae, no. "There are at least a full eighty warriors lurking out there."

"You're sure? Yes?" The mercenary shook his head. "Don't know how you do it, but . . . damn. That's twice the number of Aedh's force, and not weakened by battle, either."

"Or trapped in a fort without food or water. *Not* a good situation," Ardagh added dryly. *And what, oh what am I doing caught in the middle of it?*

He straightened, staring. That was Odran down there, Ardagh realized with a sudden jolt of angry strength, Odran the child-stealer, sitting his horse just outside the curve of the wall, fancying himself quite safe. Aching with the memory of another child who hadn't been rescued, a child who had died in his arms, the prince snatched up a rock, hefting it experimentally. He was already almost as weary as the humans and still sickened from the aftereffects of iron. It was foolish to waste any of his scanty store of Power. And yet . . . ae, what a tempting target!

Too tempting. He let fly, putting more than a bit of magical persuasion on the throw. The rock hit Odran neatly on the side of the head, tumbling him from his horse.

"Och, good shot!" Cadwal crowed. "Spectacular shot— here, now, what—"

Ardagh felt the mercenary's strong arms steady him as he staggered, breathless with the sudden loss of magical strength, then quickly let go, as if Cadwal had abruptly remembered this was a prince—or was all at once uneasy. Ardagh clutched at the windowsill, cursing himself for a fool, struggling to catch his breath and hide the struggle from Cadwal.

Who was staring at him. "That was quite an amazing throw," the mercenary said warily. "Almost too amazing."

Still winded, Ardagh only shrugged. "Worth it," he

managed at last, trying to sound like a mundane warrior who'd done some stupidly spectacular feat of strength. "Put some fear into them. They're withdrawing out of range."

It was just the right matter-of-fact tone. Cadwal might still be wondering, but he only grunted. "Of course they are. They don't have to do anything risky, just wait. With almost no food or water in here . . ." He shook his head. "Come on. Let's go tell King Aedh the bad news and get it over with."

Aedh, to give him credit, showed no apparent sign of despair. But he took Ardagh and Cadwal aside, as casually as though merely discussing the weather. "We're lucky the worst of the wounded are back at Kilfenora," he murmured. "None of the men we have here are badly hurt; they can still fight. What's bothering me the most about this," the king added, "aside from the obvious problems at hand, is that it takes time to set up such an ambush. It can hardly have been mounted on a sudden whim. And yet the traitors couldn't have known we were going to meet the Lochlannach where and when we did."

"Except," Ardagh said, "by sorcery."

"Och, that again!" Aedh glared at him. "I heard you shout Bishop Gervinus' name. But you don't see him out there, do you?"

"He would hardly put himself into danger needlessly. That doesn't mean he isn't—"

"You can't possibly believe he was behind all this." The king quickly held up a hand before Ardagh could reply. "And even if you do, never mind that now. We have more important matters to discuss. Cadwal, we've been through some rough times together over the years."

"We have that," the mercenary agreed warily.

"And in all those times you've always been a loyal follower to me. More loyal, as it turns out, than certain of my own people."

Cadwal frowned. "What are you saying?"

"That I release you from our contract, you and your men. The quarrel those traitors have with me doesn't include you.

If you ride down from here with a flag of truce, you can surely—"

"Do what?" the mercenary snapped. "Abandon you? Now?"

"Cadwal—"

"No! Look you, I am not going all softly self-sacrificing. Never have been that type of fool, and that's one reason I've survived. But in all the years I've been a mercenary, you've been the only man to treat me as though I and my men were still worthy of honor. No way I'm going to up and run now."

Ardagh, too weary to be more than bemused at human codes of honor, knew only that he didn't want to fight and face more iron. Mm, yes . . . "We may not need to fight," the prince said, considering. "Or die, for that matter."

Aedh's glance was wry. "We haven't got many choices. Three, to be precise. One: we risk all in a charge down the hill—"

"Suicide," Cadwal cut in, "pure suicide."

"Probably. The second choice: wait them out. Which, of course, is a joke, and not a very funny one. We have three, maybe four days of rations, if we parcel them out carefully. After that—och, well, we can always slaughter the horses if it comes to that, but with weary, wounded men and not much water we're not going to be holding out very long.

"The third and final choice isn't much better: send someone out to get help. Which is impossible. Anyone who thinks he could get safely past all those folks sitting out there just waiting to cut him down is welcoming his own death."

Cadwal snorted. "With open arms. Besides, I figure that even if we're lucky enough to get a good supply of rainwater to eke things out, we've still got only about six days, seven if we kill the horses. What help could he find in that short a time? Donnchadh of Clonach?"

Ardagh straightened. "Why not? His land is nearest, is it not? And he's one of the High King's vassals."

"So," the mercenary reminded him with a jerk of a hand, "are those."

"Did you see him out there?"

"No, but—"

"No," Aedh agreed. "That's not his way. Donnchadh's a hesitating sort when his flesh and blood aren't involved; we all know that. He'd wait to see who was winning before committing himself."

"The man tried to kill you!" Cadwal protested. "Or have you forgotten that bungled ambush? The one where we found our foreign friend here?"

"I haven't forgotten," the king said serenely. "And neither have I nor Donnchadh forgotten that his son, too, tried to kill me. And was spared. And was returned, nice and safe, to Papa after that pretty, honor-protecting duel. Donnchadh won't be comfortable with the thought of being in my debt. And he just might be persuaded to help—if he thought it was in his best interest. But getting *to* him's the trick."

"I could do it." Ardagh frowned at the humans' startled stares. "Don't look at me like that. I'm not being stupidly heroic, and I assure you I'm in no mood for suicide. But," he added with a sharp little smile, "you must surely have learned by now that I can pass where others cannot. My night vision, as you both keep noting, is sharp. And I don't wish to die trapped any more than do you."

"There is that," Aedh mused. "Your odd abilities, I mean. There isn't a one of us you haven't startled with those cat-like stalks and sudden appearances. You certainly can see like a cat, too. And if anyone can sway Donnchadh with smooth words . . . yes. If you're willing to accept the risk, so be it. As soon as it's fully night."

"Agreed," the prince said, and headed off to try to snatch some rest till then.

Ardagh stole silently down through the maze of earthen ramparts, pleased that the moon had chosen to hide itself behind a thick layer of clouds. Easy to slip past humans at night, when their day-oriented senses were muffled; much simpler, though, to do it without any troublesome moon-light to betray him.

The prince paused once or twice, avoiding the occasional wakeful guard, to catch his breath. He was still weary even after that sadly abbreviated rest, more weary than he would ever have admitted. *Once you reach the forest, you can take some strength from it. You simply have to reach it.*

Most of the humans were asleep. What, Ardagh wondered suddenly, if he tried his own magical attack on them? A surge of Power, perhaps, to frighten their horses or . . .

A surge of Power, when he was already weary. Clever, very clever. Besides, Ardagh snarled at himself, he had already squandered too much Power by felling Odran. And with so much interference from all the iron the humans bore, any spell he tried would probably hit him with a fatal backlash.

Ah well. Ardagh battled a sudden seductive inner voice whispering, *None of this is necessary, none of it. All you need to do is slip into the forest. Disappear. Leave these humans to fend for themselves.* It was tempting, Powers yes, very tempting. But if he abandoned them, that would surely mean the death of Aedh and everyone else in the fort, leave Eriu open to chaos—and turn Ardagh this time into a genuine oathbreaker.

No.

Donnchadh it was, then. The prince paused again, getting his bearings, knowing from what Aedh had told him that he wasn't very far from the boundaries of Clonach, then smiled, sensing faintly the aura of Donnchadh himself. Not far to go, indeed, especially if he could manage to "borrow" a horse along the way. From the enemy, perhaps?

Unfortunately, no. The traitor army's security seemed to be agreeably lax out here away out of range of those trapped in the fort—lax except where the horses were concerned. After prowling silently about the lines several times, Ardagh accepted that there wasn't a chance of stealing a horse without one of those very alert guards raising an alarm.

So be it. With a mental shrug, the prince dove into the forest as smoothly as a fish into a green-black sea and sighed in relief as its strength stole through him, calling to him, telling him *stay, recover, replenish Power.*

No. He had only a very short span of mortal time in which to reach Donnchadh and get the man to return with him.

This must wait. It took all his will to pull free from the forest's Powerful embrace, but the prince forced himself on through the night and the tangle of underbrush towards Clonach. Soon enough he would be—

Ardagh sprang back with a startled hiss, mind racing in wild, confused disbelief. Eirithan! It was impossible and yet he could not be mistaken, no, no, all at once he *felt* his brother's presence as strongly as though Eirithan was there before him!

And, with a sudden strong blaze of Power, Eirithan *was* there, standing proud and wary in the newly opened Portal. Ardagh staggered with the surge of hot anger, envy, jealousy flooding him. Ae, look at the man, look at him, so perfectly elegant, so perfectly Sidhe elegant, almost beyond bearing, not a hair of his golden head nor a line of his silken green robes out of place! The prince saw dismay flash in his brother's eyes and knew what Eirithan must be seeing in turn: a wild-haired, wild-eyed, rough-skinned barbarian in filthy hunting leathers. And that added new fuel to his anguished rage.

"What did you *expect* to see?" Ardagh snarled in their native tongue. "You knew full well into what you were sending me! And does the sight amuse you, brother? Am I entertaining enough for you like this? Ae, yes, and while we're on the subject, brother, what in the name of the Outer Dark are you doing here? Have you come to see for yourself if I'm still alive? How far into savagery I've fallen?"

He saw his brother flinch slightly, so small a movement a human would never have noticed it. "Not that," Eirithan murmured. "Never that. Whatever else you are, you are still my closest kin."

"By chance of Fate alone. Come, come, brother, no feigned softness, not here, not now. If it's not morbid curiosity that's drawn you here, what?" He heard his voice shaking, and fought in vain to control it. "Curse you, Eirithan, answer me! *Why are you here?*"

"For this one thing," his brother said quietly. "Ardagh, I have come to bring you home."

CHOICES

CHAPTER 30

"I have come to bring you home."

It was the last thing in all the Realms that Ardagh had expected to hear. Numb with the sudden sheer weight of shock, he could do nothing but stare and stare at Eirithan and finally gasp out, "Why?"

No emotion showed on the fine-boned face. "You are, as I've said, my closest kin."

"That didn't stop you from casting me into exile!"

"I did what seemed right and just at the time." Eirithan paused for the merest hairbreadth of time. "There is always the possibility I might have been wrong or acted in haste."

"Ae, yes, and there is always the possibility that swine, as the humans say, may turn to birds, but I don't see any roosting in the trees right now!"

Eirithan shuddered delicately at the indelicate human phrasing. "Ardagh, come. Time enough to discuss justice when you are back in our proper Realm."

He caught Ardagh by the hand before the startled prince could back away and pulled, just hard enough to force him to take a step forward towards Eirithan—and out of the human Realm. The prince angrily yanked his hand free, about to ask his brother what games he played. But before he could speak, the full magical glory that was his own native land washed over him, and Ardagh stood transfixed, head thrown back, so shaken with longing and wonder and joy in that instant that had Eirithan chosen to slay him, the prince knew he wouldn't have been able to raise a hand in his defense. *Powers, Powers, how I missed this, missed this so very terribly much, my own land, my own—*

Wait.

Suddenly sane again, Ardagh lowered his head, refusing to see the clear, bright wonder all around them, staring only at his brother. "You still haven't answered me, Eirithan. Why are you doing this?"

Eirithan's face was unreadable even to another Sidhe. "I wished it. That should be enough."

"That is *not* enough. Why do this?" Ardagh felt his own face harden into similarly cold lines. "Unless . . . you're having trouble, aren't you? Political trouble, perhaps, with those treacherous nobles. Something strong enough for you to seek help. Even from an exile."

"There is something of a disturbance in the Realm, yes," Eirithan admitted with cold, delicately vague honesty. "I wish you back, brother, to stand at my court as an honored aide."

" 'Honored aide,' " Ardagh echoed. "Not 'prince.' What of the sentence of exile, brother? Is that not to be lifted?"

"Of course it is. After you prove yourself fully worthy, the ban will be raised and—"

"In other words," the prince cut in bitterly, "no. It is not to be lifted. But then, you never meant for that to happen, did you?"

"Come now, brother, you are beginning to rant."

"Why should I not? You mean to use me as a tool, don't you? The only question is: how?"

"Not a tool." Eirithan said it with the tone of one patiently explaining things to a not-quite-bright child. "As I told you, you would be my honored aide. Ardagh, brother, enough of this foolishness. You've been among the human-kind too long; it's turned you wary as a wild thing. Come home with me, Ardagh. Your estate has been kept as it was. Your gardens are beautiful right now, so very bright with blossom, sweet with fragrance. See them, Ardagh, see their beauty. Stroll along their peaceful paths. Hear the sweet songs your

odd little Ninet plays. It can be yours again, Ardagh. Yours.
Only come with me."

Ae, Powers, he *had* been away too long; he'd forgotten
just how persuasive Sidhe charm-words could be. Teeth
clenched, Ardagh fought to ignore the longing the words
sent raging through him.

"You want your gardens' peace, Ardagh, I see it on your
face. You want it so very much. And it can be yours. If you
only come with me. One small thing to do, brother, one
small, small thing. All you need to do is come with me."

Ardagh's mind felt sluggish and slow as Eirithan continued his gentle croon, but the prince managed to wonder,
*Why does Eirithan need me? This "honored aide" pretense
is so shallow it's transparent. What does he want? And why
won't he tell me—*

He had it. All the glamour of Eirithan's words fell away
from him as Ardagh cut bluntly into the croon with, "All
that nonsense about 'my closest blood kin' means only one
thing. You're worried, aren't you? Ha, yes, you must be
worried nearly to death if you're willing to risk keeping me
at your side!"

"My poor brother. The humans really *have* warped your
thoughts, so very suspicious you've become."

"Have I, now? I don't think so. I don't think it's any mere
'disturbance' bothering you, either. No, you're terrified that
one of those treacherous nobles you once pampered is going
to manage a spell sly enough to get past your defenses."

"You exaggerate the peril. These are . . . somewhat uncertain times, surely, but tranquility will return. And there is
always danger, of course, even in the most peaceful of
Realms. Every ruler faces it. But you—"

"Me, indeed. As far as magic's concerned, we're very
closely related, half-kin or no. Ties of blood and all that.
With me forever at court, it would be simple enough for
you to confuse any magics aimed at you so that they would
strike me instead!"

"I repeat, you exaggerate. Granted, the post would not
be without its risks, but the rewards would be quite splendid. And, since you seem to have become so prickly on the

subject of honor, let me assure you that it would be a highly honorable post."

"A highly honorable grave!"

"Brother, please. If you've survived living among the humans so long, you are far too clever to fail now."

"And swine, as I say, can fly. All right, then. Pretend I'm that supernaturally clever. Pretend that I do your work and survive. And peace returns. What then? When is my exile to be lifted?"

"I told you, once you have proven yourself worthy—"

"*Like hell!*" Ardagh snapped in the human tongue. "What happens to your 'honored aide' when he's no longer needed? Enslavement? Or am I merely to be once more accused of treason and discarded?"

"I never said that. I never said any of that."

"No," Ardagh agreed, suddenly achingly weary of the whole conversation. "Of course you didn't. Only humans lie. Our kind merely circumvents the truth. All right, brother: a pact. I don't want to see our land torn by war, either. If you truly wish my aid, swear that you will first help me help the humans to whom I've given *my* word."

Eirithan frowned in distaste. "You gave your word to *those?* What vows you might have sworn to those animals hardly concerns me."

Ardagh sighed. "And so you prove yourself. And so you show how little you think of my honor. One more attempt: swear to me, brother. Swear that you will, indeed, lift the sentence of exile within a fixed, definite time, that you will, indeed, return me to my full estate."

"What nonsense is this? I have already offered you—"

"Swear it!"

"I have already said it! Once you have proved yourself—"

"No! Swear it now: a fixed, definite time!"

"I will not be pushed."

"And *I* will not be used! Curse you, Eirithan," Ardagh hissed, "for offering me false hope. Curse you for betraying me. Curse you to the endless Outer Dark for what harm you've done me and our land both—and may it be the traitors' hands that send you there!"

No point in attacking his brother or in trying to push past him into the Sidhe Realm; guards were almost certainly hovering just out of sight. Instead, turning sharply away before Eirithan could see his tears, Ardagh threw himself back into the human Realm and felt the Portal shut behind him. Staggering with the renewed pain of loss, the prince fell to his knees, then threw back his head with a howl that had in it all the rage and grief and loneliness within him.

The last echoes died away. The forest grew still, and then the normal little night noises, the chirps and whirrs and rustlings started up again. Ardagh shuddered, wrapping his arms about himself, then shuddered again and, with a sharp burst of frantic energy, scrambled back to his feet. Insane to scream like that, to let everyone within who knew how far a range hear him. If he was lucky, the prince thought with bitter humor, they would take it for the cry of a wild beast. Or a demon.

Ae, Powers. Ardagh determinedly wiped his face dry. He never should have let himself believe Eirithan, not even for the smallest of moments. But . . . he had wanted to believe so badly. With the glory of his own land wrapped about him, he had wanted to believe all could yet be well.

What had made him suddenly remember his vow to the humans?

Ironic that something like that should have saved him; if it hadn't been for the memory of that oath, he probably would have been so overwhelmed with longing for home despite all his doubts that Eirithan would have snared him.

What was, was. There would be, the prince told himself, trying to believe he hadn't sunk so low he could lie to himself, there would be another, truer chance to go home. Somehow. Somewhere.

But for now, Ardagh knew he could only do one thing: fulfill his vow and bring aid to the humans. With a savage oath, he set out for Donnchadh's realm.

Gervinus woke with a shout, staring blindly into the night, the grimoire a hard, reassuring presence clutched to his heart. There had been a cry, a wild, terrible cry, somewhere out there—out where? Where was he? What was he doing in the middle of—of forest, empty forest, all alone and—

The bishop gave a soft, shaken sigh. Now he remembered. Or thought he did; memory wasn't quite the dependable tool it should be these days. He was alone because he had insisted on it.

But why? That's what I can't remember. I said something about . . . about a spell . . . yes, a spell that could only be worked away from the others. For safety's sake.

But what spell? There's no need for sorcery now! They have Aedh penned. It's just a short wait before they have him dead.

Why would I want to be working sorcery now?

Gervinus looked down at the grimoire in dawning horror. He hadn't been in control at that point. The sorcery had. It had wanted to be used, no, it had insisted on being used, and he—he hadn't been able to resist.

With a cry of disgust, the bishop hurled the grimoire from him, hearing it crash into the bushes, then sat huddled in the darkness. This had been happening too often lately, these eerie lapses. But not again, never. He would be in control. He would be in control of himself, his mind, his body, his will. He would be in control.

And yet . . . and yet . . . it was foolish to throw away one's only weapon before the battle. One could never tell when such a weapon might be needed, particularly since things were likely to become chaotic after Aedh's death. He would need strength if he was to remain in charge. Strength beyond the merely human.

Strength he had just tossed aside. Gasping in sudden panic, Gervinus went in search of the grimoire, stabbing his hands on thorns, tearing his clothing, bruising his feet.

Where is it? Jesu-in-whom-I-don't-believe, where is it?

Just when he was sure it had melted into nothingness, one bloody hand closed upon a cold, hard something. With a sob of relief, Gervinus snatched up the grimoire and clutched it to him.

He would be calm. He would be in control. Sitting

huddled and alone in the night, the bishop vowed it. Come
what may, he would remain in control.

"Will you *please* stop that pacing?"

Donnchadh froze at that, glaring back at Derval where
she sat with her inevitable sewing. She stared right back
at him, cold-eyed as anything out of a tale of the Sidhe.
She should have been born *a Sidhe,* he thought, *heartless
and soulless as the stories say. No, or born in the olden days
when she could have been a warrior queen.* Ha, and then
he would probably have found himself battling her for the
crown. Maybe even losing—no, dammit! "What *would* you
have me do?"

"Act! Attack! Your men are armed and waiting for the
signal, yet here you wait. The others are out there doing
your work for you."

"That's exactly the point. Look you, wife, my men and I
are ready to march at a word, as you say. But what point is
there in risking all for naught?" Donnchadh found he had
started pacing nervously once more, and forced himself to
stand stock-still, staring out the window at nothing, anything but Derval. "No, no, far better to wait, see who is
stronger, who is weaker. If you make alliance with someone stronger than you, he controls you. If he's weaker, why
bother with the alliance at all?"

"You babble. Aedh is besieged. This is your best chance
to be rid of him forever."

"Yes, but what of the others? They all wish the crown as
well as I. If I join them now, I will only have to face them
later if I'm to seize the crown."

Derval gave a small, sharp cry of impatience. "You will
need to face them eventually, husband!"

"Yes, but better, far better, as I say, to wait. Wait till after
they're all weakened by battle—and I am not."

"Coward."

He whirled in sudden hot rage at that, ready to strike.
But the sight of Derval's chill face froze his anger as it always
did. And as he always did, he thought that she would most
likely welcome him striking her, yes, and then probably see

to it someone stabbed him in his sleep or poisoned his drink.
If she didn't do the deed herself.

Letting his hand fall limply to his side, Donnchadh turned
away, muttering, "Cautious, rather. There is no cowardice
in being prudent."

"There is nothing prudent in—" Derval broke off with
an impatient hiss. "Now what is that?"

Donnchadh glanced down to the courtyard. "A messenger. Riding alone. He could be bringing us news of how
the siege goes."

"Well then, don't just stand there!" Derval snapped. "Have
him brought to us so we can hear what news he brings."

"We," Donnchadh thought. *"Us."* But he issued the summons.

The man who entered was tall and slender, graceful as
a wild thing and, despite the stains of battle and travel on
him, beautiful, so strikingly handsome with those fine, high
cheekbones and sleek black hair that Donnchadh heard
Derval draw her breath in sharply in appreciation, and felt
a keen little flame of jealousy at the sound. The jealous fire
brightened when he saw the stranger's slanted green gaze
go straight to Derval. But the look wasn't so much in admiration, Donnchadh realized with a touch of surprise, as in
appraisal.

And to his utter astonishment, he heard the man murmur, "Poor lady. Born in the wrong time and place. No outlet
for your strength here but in plots and bitterness."

Derval stiffened as though he'd slapped her. "What nonsense is this? Who are you?"

Donnchadh held up a hand. "I know you, don't I?" he
asked sharply, and the stranger smiled, so charmingly that
the astonished king felt it quite melt the stirrings of anger
he'd been feeling.

"You may have seen me a time or two. Not you, lady,
alas," the stranger added with a smooth, courteous little bow.
"I was part of the entourage of High King Aedh when he
set free your son. I am Prince Ardagh Lithanial, whom some
have called Prince of Cathay, and I have come in the High
King's name."

"Why?" Derval snapped.

The prince's green gaze turned again to her, and Donnchadh was amazed to see her shrink back in her chair. "Because, as you both know well, your liege lord is being held under siege by traitors. Surely I am not to number you among those traitors."

Donnchadh stiffened. "What do you mean?"

That earned him a second charming smile, but one with a hint of ice beneath the warmth. "Why, my lord king, I have seen your men all armed and waiting to ride. Please, let us not play silly games with words. Which is it to be, King Donnchadh? Which side shall you choose?"

"It is not for you," Donnchadh blustered, "prince though you claim to be, to lecture me."

"No lecture, King Donnchadh. Just a thought: who was it held your son captive? Who was it had every legal right to slay him as a would-be regicide? Particularly since that son's father had almost certainly once set a would-be fatal ambush?"

"I never—"

"Ah, but we are not here to debate past Might Have Beens. Hear but this and consider: who was it held your son and your son's life in his hands, yet spared him? You are no raw, untrained boy, King Donnchadh. You know as well as I and he that your duel with King Aedh was deliberately devised to end with no honor lost to either side. Will you lose honor now?"

The suddenness of that final statement caught Donnchadh off balance.

Not so Derval. "You have no right to say such things!" she exploded.

"Have I not?" the prince asked mildly. "Which one of the two of you was it had secret dealings with the High King's foes? Ae, yes, I know of that. Which one of you was it made quiet, treacherous pacts?"

Donnchadh turned in shock to his wife. "You did this? You plotted behind my back and never said a word to me?"

"Don't be a fool, husband. It was for you I did it."

"But you went behind my back! Why?" The long-suppressed words came pouring out before he could stop them. Nor, Donnchadh realized, did he really want to stop them. "Look you, I've always given you your own way because I hate a battlefield in the home. If you wanted to insult me when we were alone, I kept my peace. Maybe that was stupid of me, maybe that's why you hold me in such contempt—no! Don't interrupt! You *do* hold me in contempt, you make that clear with every look, every word. You see me as weak—well, devil take you, I should have long ago beaten that thought out of your head, mother of my sons though you are! Why did you do it? Did you think me so feebleminded I couldn't be included in your plots?"

She must have been shocked by his words, she had to be shocked by them, but to Donnchadh's growing rage not a trace of concern marred her lovely face. "Hush, now, husband," she crooned. "I never thought you weak. And I meant no harm. As king you have so much weighing you down. I merely wished to take some of the burden from you and—"

"Take some of the burden from me! Don't you see what you've done? It's one thing to call me a fool when we're alone together. But by plotting without my consent—without even my knowledge, damn your lying soul—you've made me look like a fool in the eyes of others, a—a spineless fool who can't even act on his own but has to hide behind his wife's skirts! And I cannot allow that to happen!"

For the first time he saw some genuine alarm flicker in her eyes. And it was glorious. "That's right, Derval," he roared. "Fear me. At a word from me you're cast aside, thrust into some isolated nunnery, and I'm free to find me a gentler, sweeter mate!"

"You would never dare—"

"Wouldn't I? Try me, Derval, try me! How long were you planning to keep me ignorant? Ha, yes, and what other plots might you be weaving even now?"

"N-no others," she began desperately, but Donnchadh turned his back on her. The Prince of Cathay, or whatever he styled himself, was waiting in apparent tranquility, as if totally undisturbed by what he heard. The sight of that elegantly calm figure only increased Donnchadh's rage.

"Away from here!" he snapped at the prince. "I have chosen. I will ride with you. Now. And," Donnchadh added over his shoulder, "may the devil tear anyone who tries to stop me!"

THE FINAL STORM

CHAPTER 31

As they rode out from King Donnchadh's fortress, followed by a fiery, noisy troop of mounted warriors, Ardagh glanced back once over his shoulder to see Derval standing silently against a column, her eyes those of a woman whose plans have all fallen to ruin. It had been a wild guess he'd made about her working plots behind her husband's back, but once he'd said it, Ardagh had hardly been surprised to learn he'd guessed right.

She should *have been born in a different time and place, a place that would have let her use her intellect freely, not coop it within some restrictive role that could only lead to the terrible coldness, the ugly self-hatred I saw.*

Would Sorcha grow like that? The sudden, unexpected thought made him shudder and think, *Powers prevent!* And yet, Sidhe honesty made him continue, what else was there for Sorcha in this world, this society, but the same caging-in of her talents, the same turning at last to bitterness?

No, not that, not for her.

What, then?

This is ridiculous! Ardagh snapped at himself. Ridiculous to worry about such things—ridiculous to have any soft thoughts at all when riding back into battle.

Ae, yes. Another battle. An utterly weary side of him shrank at the thought. Too much had been happening lately, from combat-by-sword to combat-of-wits with Eirithan, too

much even for a Sidhe to endure. He wanted nothing so
much as to curl up someplace soft and safe and do absolutely
nothing. But ahead lay the ancient fort, and ahead were the
besiegers. And ahead was the inevitable confrontation.

So be it, Ardagh thought with determined bravado. *I've
escaped iron-damage twice so far within the last few days;
let's see if I can manage it one more time.*

He shot a sly sideways glance at Donnchadh. The man
had been almost absurdly easy to control and influence, all
fear and bluster. He would fight, though, Ardagh had no
doubt of that. Donnchadh's warriors had the hard-edged,
almost too eager look of men who had been waiting to do
something to the point of frustration. They would fight, too,
and fight well, if for no other reason than to let off all that
pent-up energy.

Good. At least someone *will be energetic.*

The distance seemed far shorter when one was riding
all the way, and riding the open road rather than weaving
one's way through the underbrush. "There it is," Ardagh
said, pointing out the tower's top rising above the trees.

"I know," Donnchadh said shortly, and without any pre-
amble gave the signal for a full-out charge. It was a charge
on foot, of course—Ardagh had already learned it was
impossible to mount a successful cavalry charge when stir-
rupless saddles were the norm—but no less swift and fierce
for that. Ardagh, swept along in the sudden surge of warriors, all shouting and clashing weapons, had no choice but
to whip out his sword as the wave came crashing down on
the startled besiegers.

Ha, yes, they were caught totally by surprise! Look at
them scurrying about like so many insects, shouting in alarm,
snatching up weapons, struggling to fight back—and there
came Aedh and his men down from the fortress, yelling with
fierce joy as they trapped the traitors just as he'd planned.

The traitors, yes! Ardagh felt his blade cut flesh again
and yet again and heard himself laugh in sudden battle rage.
Even if these weren't those who had betrayed *him,* it was
still wonderful, fiercely wonderful, to cut them down, to
slay them, to utterly, utterly destroy them—

Powers.

The prince fought his way back, literally and figuratively, out of the main crush of battle, gasping and stunned at his own ferocity and so sickened from the accumulated effect of too much iron in too short a time that he could barely stay on his feet. He staggered aside into welcome under-brush, where he could sink to his knees, huddling in mis-ery and trying not to out-and-out faint, without anyone spying him. This was not his battle, these were not his people, he'd done enough for them as it was, and they—he—they—

Gradually the worst of the sickness passed. Head no longer aching so foully, senses no longer swimming with nausea, Ardagh dared straighten slowly, still on his knees, and take in steadying lungfuls of air.

He froze. "No, ae, no . . ."

With a great effort, the prince scrambled back to his feet, listening with senses far beyond the physical, and groaned. Not Gervinus, not now.

Yes. Now. There must be a new battle. And this time, he knew with Sidhe fatalism, it most certainly was going to be his.

Gervinus, staring intently into a tiny forest pool, cried out in angry protest at what he saw. No, no, and no! The siege could not be so easily broken, help could not be arriving so easily!

But there it was: the suddenly attacking army was catching the besiegers totally off-guard, tearing into their ranks, smashing them down before they could even try to defend themselves. And here came that accursed Aedh down from his sanctuary to finish the job, trapping the besiegers between two forces, crushing them into the earth.

Gervinus gasped. In among the attackers was Prince Ardagh! Yes, yes, although the image was wavery and unsure, there was no mistaking that mane of black hair. Prince Ardagh, indeed, always Prince Ardagh, always there to block every plan—

"Damn him. *Damn him!*" All this work, all these careful

alliances and persuasions, all this soothing and pretending—all this for *nothing!*

No, the grimoire whispered to him, *not for nothing, not while there is still another force to be met.*

Sorcery. Gervinus stared at the grimoire, wondering. If he used sorcery now, would it not be an obvious thing to all? He didn't want to be the cause of a new union—a united force out to slay the sorcerer!

Do you want to be left with nothing? If you strike now, strike swiftly, powerfully, none will suspect. Destroy the enemy now and you can still win.

Arridu.

Yes, yes, that was it: make it look like a natural disaster, or even a demonic one, yes, even better, make it look as though the demon had been attracted to the battle and only he, Gervinus, Bishop Gervinus, holy Bishop Gervinus, had repulsed it, had saved humanity—yes, oh yes, it would work!

Water. He needed clear, still water. Gervinus scrambled to his feet, looking wildly about for a moment before he realized that the very pool he'd been using for scrying would serve. Why hadn't he realized something so very obvious? Where was his vaunted self-control? *What was happening to him?*

No matter. No matter. He was still the master of the grimoire, not it, he. He was still the master of Arridu. He would summon the demon and all would be well. Time enough for the luxury of worry when he had the throne. Thrusting his ringed hand into the water, Gervinus began the Words of summoning. Even though his head was beginning to pound so fiercely he could barely hear his own words, he continued the chant, summoning, "Arridu, Arridu, *Arridu.*"

The air had turned chill around him, chill and damp. A dank wind stirred his robes. *"I am here,"* a voice said softly. *"What would you?"*

He must be careful. The demon would detect even the slightest weakness, the smallest inconsistency. But Gervinus couldn't seem to find any words but, "Blood for you, Arridu, lives for you."

"Your *life, little human? Is it to be* your *life I take?*"

"No!" Sweet Jesu, he must be more wary! "My life is not yours for the taking, Arridu, by your name and the ring I bear, my life is not yours."

It might have been the stirring of the slowly rising storm winds, it might have been a demon's humorless laugh. "*As you will it, human. Who, then, shall be my prey? Hurry; I am bored with this Realm.*"

The storm clouds loomed up over him, the storm winds swirled savagely about him, nearly sweeping him from his feet—no, not merely wind but Power, raw Power swirling about him in all its terrible might till he couldn't think, he couldn't act, he couldn't do anything but gasp out, "All of them! All but me! And Ardagh, Prince Ardagh—be sure he dies as well!"

"*This one command I am most glad to fulfill,*" the demon purred, but whatever else Arridu might have added was lost in the sudden crash of thunder. Staggered by wind, blinded by lightning, Gervinus stood lost in terrible, terrified joy as all about him endless, boundless demonic Power raged.

As he hurried through the forest, Ardagh *felt* the first stirrings of a chill, alien Power—demonic Power. With a little thrill of alarm, he recognized it as emanating from the being that had attacked him once before and nearly slain him with a scratch: the demon that had a token of his blood.

But not enough to work me any harm, he assured himself, *or I'd already be dead. But what is the thing doing here and why—*

A sudden wild gust of wind buffeted him, hitting so sharply it nearly knocked him from his feet, whipping his hair painfully across his face. The prince clawed his vision free of the stinging black strands, glancing up in new alarm. The sky was boiling up with heavy black storm clouds, too swiftly, too fiercely, far darker than any earthly clouds could ever be. The bright day vanished under the weight of them, leaving behind only the faintest ugly grey-green glow.

Lightning split the darkness so suddenly that Ardagh jumped. It slashed down again and yet again, like so many blue-white, sorcerous Swords of Fire, and savage *cracks* told him of trees being struck down all around. The winds came screaming down on him in full fury, so fierce they nearly tore the air from his lungs. Thunder roared and boomed as if the very Realm was being torn apart.

This is no mere summoning! Ardagh realized in horror. *No, no, there's too much Power here, wild Power—Gervinus has lost control of the demon!*

Did the man know? Did the man care? Half-dazed by noise and blinding light, stumbling under the nearly solid curtains of rain, Ardagh staggered forward, head down against the press of wind. He must reach Gervinus. Whether or not the bishop knew what he did, or was even still sane, he was the only one who could hope to check this storm— quite literally—of hell.

The prince slipped on rain-slick rocks suddenly and went to his knees with jarring force. Looking breathlessly up, nearly blinded by rain plastering his hair to his face, Ardagh saw Gervinus standing alone, out of the forest, on the crest of a hill. Lightning blazed all about him, but he showed not the slightest sign he was aware of peril, and a chill stole through the prince at the sight.

Mad. He is quite mad. Sorcery has broken his mind.

Not quite. Gervinus turned as though somehow, over the roar of wind and earth-splitting crash of thunder, he had heard Ardagh approach. As he pointed at the prince, a sudden flash of lightning glinted off his eyes and his ring.

That ring! Ardagh knew with Sidhe certainty, *That ring is the source of his power over the demon!*

But Gervinus was shrieking, "He is here! Destroy him!"

Ardagh could have sworn he heard the hiss of a chill, hating voice beneath the storm's roar: *"Most gladly."* The prince scrambled hastily to his feet, but before he could begin so much as a word of a Shielding Spell, the storm's rage struck. He was hurled off his feet as easily as if he was a child's toy, thrown to the ground with bruising force. Breathless, he struggled to rise. The demonic storm almost let him make it to his feet, then casually threw him aside, slamming him back to the ground. Ardagh heard himself cry out with pain, and that hurt all the more, because even trying to draw a breath made his chest seem to burn.

Demon intends to play . . . till it kills me . . .

Not, he vowed, without a fight. Biting back a groan as muscles protested the movement, Ardagh rolled over onto his side, hoping his body was hiding from the demon the fact that he was fumbling for the hilt of his sword with maddeningly unresponsive hands.

He had it. With an effort that forced a new cry from him, Ardagh dragged the blade free and lunged blindly up. This time it was the demon who screamed. He *felt* its panic blaze along his nerves, but his wild slash met with nothing but air. A blast of wind sent him staggering helplessly backwards, ending up against something reassuringly hard and firm— an upthrust rock. Ardagh went into as convincing a fighting stance as he could manage, trying not to gasp with effort, trying to hold his sword steady, feeling his hair slap at his face as the wind whirled about him. Frantically guessing where the demon would be in the next second, Ardagh lunged again, and felt the blade brush something that felt almost like flesh.

But this time there was no scream, no panic. This time the demon . . . laughed.

"No, little thing. I have tasted your blood—"

Somewhere within him Ardagh found the strength to shout back, "Not enough to give you power over me!"

"Enough to keep you from harming me again with Shachshakax metal!"

Savage wind slammed into Ardagh's arm, tearing the blade from his hand.

Powers, no!

"You see, little thing? You are defenseless. Now enjoy the slowness of your death."

The wind's pressure increased and increased again, pressing him ever more fiercely against the rock. He was being slowly crushed! Pinned helplessly, nearly sobbing with the effort, Ardagh took the only course open and threw himself sideways and down, falling full-length, clenching his teeth against the impact. Twisting about, glancing up, hair half-blinding him, he caught a glimpse of Gervinus standing on the hilltop, the only movement visible to him the dark cloak whipping in the wind. Lost in trance? No, no, right now Gervinus was one with the demon, Gervinus *was* the demon, and it was that cursed ring that joined them.

What good was it to know that? Ardagh had no strength left, none. His body was ablaze, he could barely draw a breath without pain, and there was nothing to do but wait to be slain.

To be slain, yes, and to know as he died that the demon's rage would continue to blaze out across Eriu, killing all he knew, Sorcha and Eithne, Fothad, little Fainche, all who lived. . . .

No, he would not, could not let so much harm come from this! A weapon . . . he must have a weapon . . . With the smallest stab of defiance, Ardagh remembered that he still had his dagger.

Yes, but what good was it? The demon had already shown it could no longer be harmed by Faerie metal—

Cadwal. Why should he be thinking of Cadwal now, and how the mercenary had taught him knifeplay, that "down and dirty" knifeplay. . . . Hardly realizing what he was doing, Ardagh crawled painfully forward, knowing the demon would be delighted by what must look like a futile attempt to escape, hoping the thing would be amused enough not to stop him, crawled painfully forward. . . .

"Gervinus." It came out as a rasping croak, barely audible.

But Gervinus heard. The bishop turned sharply—

And Ardagh lunged up with the knife with all that was left of his strength, in that moment seeing only Cadwal, hearing Cadwal's words: *"Up under the ribs, up to the heart, that's the way to do it. Hit as many times as you have to after that, but if you get that first thrust right, he won't be getting away."* Ironic, that it should all come down to this, no high and proud Sidhe magics in the end, only something so very rough, so very human. But Cadwal would be proud of him because the angle was right, the knife was right, and even if Ardagh would be sickened at the thought of what he was doing if he was thinking clearly at all, the priest's lifeblood was spilling out hot over his hand.

Gervinus stared, only that, wide-eyed not so much with fear or pain as with sheer astonishment. "No," he said as indignantly as if Ardagh were some peasant who'd affronted him. "No."

Blood came with the words. As suddenly as if a rope holding him upright had been cut, Gervinus curled over the knife and fell lifeless. Ardagh fell beside the body, tearing the dagger free, stabbing blindly at the ring on the bishop's hand, again and again—

The ring shattered. And with it, the link from the human to the hellish Realm shattered as well. Quite undramatically, the demon was no longer there. Quite undramatically, the storm no longer existed. Clouds sped by overhead, parting to let sunlight glint down. Somewhere, a bird began to chirp tentatively, then sing, the sound thin and sweet and somehow hopeful.

"How very trite," Ardagh heard himself say.

And then he fell forward into night.

AFTERMATH

CHAPTER 32

Ardagh hadn't expected to wake at all, let alone wake in a bed, his own bed in his own guest house, aching in every bit of him and so worn he could not have raised his head from the pillow, but undeniably alive.

And being watched. He raised eyelids that seemed to have picked up their own unexpected weight, and found himself looking up at King Aedh, seated at his bedside. The king's face wore an odd mix of worry and bemusement and his eyes were completely unreadable. Ardagh tried and failed to speak, and Aedh waved to an obsequious servant, who brought water for the grateful prince, then retreated from the bedside and then the entire guest house at an imperative gesture from Aedh. Ardagh waited warily, but all the king said to him was a flat: "Cathay."

A sudden sharp stab of panic shot through the prince. If Aedh chose to attack him, even to have him slain, there wasn't anything Ardagh was going to be able to do to stop him. "I never claimed to come from there."

Aedh paused, considering, then shook his head. "No. I don't think you ever did, at that. You merely let us go on thinking it. Why?"

"It seemed wisest."

"Did it? Where are you from, then? And, while we're on the subject, exactly who and what are you?"

Heart pounding, Ardagh fought to keep his face in its

proper calm Sidhe mask, suspecting he wasn't succeeding
too well in his current weakness. "You saw, then."

"Some. The end of it. The . . . whatever that evil thing
was. And how it vanished when you slew Gervinus. Gervinus
was the one who caused that storm, wasn't he?"

Ardagh nodded slightly.

"Dammit, man," Aedh added reluctantly, "you were right
about him all along. He really had turned from God to evil."

The prince tried to shrug, then decided against that when
tightly wrapped but still sore ribs protested. Seeing his in-
voluntary wince, the king assured him lightly, "Nothing's
broken. A few bones are cracked a bit, as you might have
gathered from those wrappings, a few muscles the worse
for wear, and there's some most spectacular bruising. Nothing, Eithne and my physicians assure me, that won't heal."

Easy to make light of injuries you aren't feeling!

But for all his casual tone of voice, Aedh's eyes held no
warmth. "I repeat: Who are you? And what?"

Powers help him, how was he going to get out of this
trap? Ardagh fought with his tired mind in vain; he was
simply too sore and weary to think subtly enough. "I really
am Ardagh Lithanial," the prince said in surrender. "I really
am a prince. Of," Ardagh added, watching Aedh warily, "the
Sidhe."

That didn't get the explosion he'd expected. The only sign
of Aedh's shock was his sharply indrawn breath; there was,
Ardagh thought, a great deal to be said for royal training.
"Well," the king said after a moment, and "well," again.

"You suspected it, didn't you?"

"Yes. No. Och, man, I don't know what I suspected! It
is asking much of me to accept! But," he added with just
the barest hint of humor before the prince could think of
anything to say, "it would also explain a good deal, wouldn't
it? That fantastic night vision of yours, for one thing." Aedh
began ticking items off on his fingers. "Your gift for moving so impossibly silently and getting into wherever you wish
to be. Your refusal to let a child come to harm. Those eerie,
too-green eyes of yours and that almost inhuman—no, no,
definitely inhuman—beauty. Your everlasting, unshakable

truthfulness. A whole catalogue of what humans claim are Sidhe traits. You . . . really *can't* lie, can you?" Aedh asked suddenly. "Not even if you wished it?"

Ardagh sighed. "Believe me, King Aedh, my life here would have been much simpler if I could."

"I'm sure. A prince of the Sidhe . . ." Aedh shook his head. "I've heard all the old stories, of course; who hasn't? But I never thought they—you—those people existed!"

"You do believe me."

"I don't seem to have much of an alternative, do I? The world's a great deal stranger than I ever expected, it seems." Aedh paused. "So now, prince of the Sidhe, you can't lie. I'll accept that; there's been too much evidence of your truthfulness." He leaned forward slightly, face all at once grim. "Then you'll be telling me the truth when I ask you what I asked when we first met."

"I don't—"

"Back then, I didn't really worry about the possibility of your brother or his agents coming after you, not all the way from Cathay. But now things are very different. If the tales are true, any of the Sidhe can step from Realm to Realm as easily as a man passes through a doorway."

"Not quite that easily. And," Ardagh added bitterly, "not every Sidhe."

"I'm not interested in the techniques of it. Is my land in any danger from your brother?"

Ardagh flinched—catching his breath at the painful twinges that cost him—at the thought of that last, agonizing meeting with Eirithan. "No," he said, meeting Aedh's gaze steadily. "He will not cross into this Realm or have any dealings here. Eirithan's loathing for it is far too great."

"You're sure."

"I give you my word." *I am, after all, of far more use to him as a living tool—* No. He wasn't about to tell Aedh that. Instead, Ardagh continued, "There was far more danger to Eriu from the storm than from out of the Sidhe Realm."

"Och, yes, the storm," Aedh murmured. "I dread to learn just how much damage the cursed, hellish thing did across the land. How many it may have slain. Prince Ardagh, your people are said to be innate magicians. Just how much magic do you wield?"

Ardagh just barely kept from flinching again. How could he possibly answer . . . yes. He saw what Aedh meant. "Not as much as I'd like, not in this Realm," the prince admitted. "Not so much that I could ever be used as a weapon by or against you."

Was that sigh of relief or regret? "And how many here know the truth about you?"

"Your warriors, surely—"

"No. The way the storm was raging, I think I was the only one who got any clear glimpses of your battle. But who else in Fremainn knows about you?"

Ardagh hesitated again, considering how he might shield Queen Eithne. "Aside from you," he said slowly, "there is the Lady Sorcha. Cadwal . . . I'm sure that he suspects, particularly now that he has some free time in which to ponder, but I doubt he'll admit anything lest his men think he's gone soft in the head, as he'd put it. What about you? Will you—"

"Tell everyone something this fantastic?" Aedh snorted. "Do you want all of Fremainn to think I've gone soft in the head?"

Ardagh lay in silence for a moment, once more all too well aware of his helplessness and how easy it would be just now for the king to be rid of him. "What happens now?" he asked at last.

"To you, you mean? That is the question, isn't it? I won't deny I'd be more easy in my mind if you were—ah—someone other than what you are."

"If I were human, you mean? I'm afraid I can't oblige you there."

Aedh laughed shortly. "Och, no, I would think not. You are as you are. And as you are," he added more seriously, "you've never once offered any threat to me or mine. I owe you my life, Prince Ardagh, and the life of my son, and very possibly the lives of all here." The king got suddenly to his feet. "Your secret is my secret—mostly because I don't want hysteria about you spreading throughout Fremainn. I don't doubt the truth will slip out, bit by bit, no matter what we do, but that's not in our hands."

"Then you are saying—"

"Yes. You are still my guest. Now get some sleep before I have Eithne down on my head for endangering your health."

Ardagh smiled at that. *Easy enough to obey,* he thought, and slid back into a drowse.

He woke. Once more someone was at his bedside, and Ardagh forced open his eyelids to see: "Sorcha!"

"Hush." She reached out a hand to gently brush black strands back from his face. Her fingers stroked his hair for a moment. "I thought it would feel that silky," she said in a satisfied tone, drawing back her hand.

"You shouldn't be here. Not alone with me."

"Probably not. Even though," Sorcha added critically, "you don't look as though you could so much as lift your head off the pillow, let alone damage my honor. Don't worry," she continued blandly, "I have no intention of compromising your honor, either."

He started to chuckle, stopped with a gasp. "Don't make me laugh. I'm too sore for that."

"Och, I'm sorry. Ardagh, you're a hero, you know."

"Not intentionally. Things simply happened as they would."

"You're a hero," she repeated. "And don't be so self-deprecating. We aren't your people; you owed us nothing. You *could* merely have run off and left everyone to their fate."

"I considered it."

"Stop that! You didn't, and that's the thing." Sorcha paused, biting her lip. "When they carried you home, all torn and battered, I thought my heart would stop. Ardagh, I love you. Ha," she added triumphantly, "you don't have the strength to turn away, do you? You have to listen."

"Sorcha . . ."

"I know, I know, we've been over all the problems already. Yes, we're of two different races. Maybe you won't find a way home, maybe you will. Maybe you'll go alone. Maybe," she added, voice quavering a bit, "I'll go with you."

He drew his breath in sharply at that, stunned with delight, but before he could speak, Sorcha waved a hasty hand. "What will be will be, and neither one of us are, thank the dear, sweet, loving Lord, prophets. But right now we don't have to make any final decisions. And until the time comes when we do, there will be, the Lord willing, a stretch of nice, happy, ordinary days. I don't know about you, Ardagh Lithanial, but I have no intention of wasting any of them."

She bent to brush her lips against his. It hurt, it hurt so much it brought the tears to his eyes, but Ardagh managed to bring his aching arms up to draw her down to him and hold her fast against his chest. "I love you," he murmured into the mass of her red hair, rejoicing in his sudden joy. "I have never loved before, but I do love you, Sorcha ni Fothad, I do love you."

He was never going to lose the longing to end his exile. Ardagh knew that. But whatever happened in this strange, foreign human Realm, whatever was yet to come, for now he had a place, a home, a love.

For now, he was truly content.

AFTERWORD

This book is, of course, not to be taken for true history. However, a fair amount of it is, indeed, based on fact, or at least extrapolated from what little was written down in the 8th century A.D. There really was a High King Aedh, son of the saintly Niall, who came to the throne somewhere between 795 and 797 (when he was formally ordained by the Irish Church); the exact date of his crowning is uncertain. Like many an Irish ruler before and after him, he seems to have spent much of his twenty-five-year reign in battle, keeping this king and that at least partially in line. Many of the exploits mentioned in this book actually occurred, including his splitting of Meath between the princely claimants, though his attack on the Viking raiders is pure fiction.

The name of Aedh's wife is unknown to us, but the *Annals of the Kingdom of Ireland* do state that he had a son, Niall, who came to the throne after his death. They also mention the name of Fothad mac Ailin, who was first Aedh's tutor and then his chief poet and minister. Whether or not Fothad had any children is open to conjecture; I have chosen to give him a daughter.

Eriu is an ancient name for Ireland, which in the time of King Aedh was still densely forested; lengthy human occupation and the need of timber for houses and ships led to significant deforestation up to the present time both in Ireland and Great Britain.

Lochlannach is, of course, the Gaelic name for the Vikings. Viking raids were just beginning during Aedh's reign, though they amounted to little more than isolated attacks for the first twenty years or so; it wasn't until the 830s that they became an organized menace.

One of the main natural events recorded during Aedh's reign was a savage thunderstorm in about 799 A.D. It was so severe and deadly a storm that it was considered supernatural. In this book, of course, it is!

The land of Ireland has always been associated with various fairy legends, including those of the Sidhe, who are often described as living in the Hollow Hills, or using those hills, or sometimes wells, as portals from the human world into Faerie. There are numerous legends about the Folk in general and King Finvarra in specific; many of them deal with his more or less friendly relations with humans.

While a complete list of all the references consulted would be tediously long, some of the main sources are listed below:

Best, Michael R. and Frank H. Brightman. *The Book of Secrets of Albertus Magnus*. Oxford: Oxford University Press, 1973.

Byrne, Francis John. *Irish Kings and High-Kings*. London: B. T. Batsford Ltd., 1973.

Dames, Michael. *Mythic Ireland*. London: Thames and Hudson, 1992.

De Paor, Laim. *The Peoples of Ireland From Prehistory to Modern Times*. Indiana: Notre Dame Press, 1986.

Donovan, John O., trans. *Annals of the Kingdom of Ireland*, 7 volumes. New York: AMS Press, 1966.

Drew, Katherine Fischer. *The Laws of the Salian Franks*. Philadelphia: University of Pennsylvania Press, 1991.

Gerald of Wales, translated by John J. O'Meara. *The History and Topography of Ireland*. New York and London: Penguin Books, 1982. First published in 1195.

Kelly, Fergus. *A Guide to Early Irish Law*. Dublin: Dublin Institute for Advanced Studies, 1988.

Newark, Tim. *Celtic Warriors: 400 BC–AD 1600*. Poole: Blandford Press, 1986.

O'Carroll, Niall. *The Forests of Ireland: History, Distribution and Silviculture*. Dublin: Turoe Press, 1984.

O'Farrell, Padraic. *Before the Devil Knows You're Dead: Irish Blessings, Toasts & Curses*. Dublin: The Mercier Press, 1993.

O hOgain, Dr. Daithi. *Myth, Legend & Romance: An Encyclopedia of the Irish Folk Tradition*. New York: Prentice Hall Press, 1991.

Ross, Anne. *The Pagan Celts*. Totowa: Barnes & Noble Books, 1986. Previously published as *Everyday Life of the Pagan Celts*.

Scott, Michael, ed. *An Irish Herbal*. Dublin: Anna Livia Press, 1991.

Streit, Jakob. *Sun and Cross: From Megalithic Culture to Early Christianity in Ireland*. Edinburgh: Floris Books, 1977.

Weir, Hugh W. L., ed. *Ireland—A Thousand Kings*. Whitegate: Ballinakella Press, n.d.

White, Carolyn. *A History of Irish Fairies*. Dublin: The Mercier Press, 1976.

Wilde, Lady. *Irish Cures, Mystic Charms & Superstitions*. New York: Sterling Publishing Co., Inc., 1891.

A PREVIEW
FROM
CETAGANDA

A NEW VORKOSIGAN ADVENTURE

BY

LOIS McMASTER BUJOLD

COMING SOON
TO A BOOKSTORE
NEAR YOU

FROM BAEN BOOKS

CETAGANDA

The players (in order of appearance):

Vorob'yev, *Barrayaran ambassador to Cetaganda*

A Barrayaran sergeant, *chauffeur to the Barrayar delegation*

Miles Naismith Vorkosigan, 22-year old scion of the Barrayaran Regent, temporarily on assignment to the embassy at Cetaganda

Ivan Vorpatril, *his cousin, a promising young officer*

haut Rian Degtiar, *Servant of the Celestial Lady, and Handmaiden of the Star Crèche of Cetaganda*

Ba Lura, *the Celestial Lady's most senior servitor*

Mia Maz, *member of the Vervani delegation to Cetaganda*

Assorted Cetagandan nobles, ladies, functionaries; guests from various planets.

The scene: *Cetaganda, on the way to and at an event associated with a state funeral.*

"The proper name for the Cetagandan imperial residence is the Celestial Garden," said Vorob'yev, "but all the galactics just call it Xanadu. You'll see why in a moment. Duvi, take the scenic approach."

"Yes, my lord," returned the young sergeant who was driving. He altered the control program. The Barrayaran embassy aircar banked, and shot through a shining stalagmite array of city towers.

"*Gently*, if you please, Duvi. My stomach, at this hour of the morning . . ."

"Yes, my lord." Regretfully, the driver slowed them to a saner pace. They dipped, wove around a building that Miles estimated must have been a kilometer high, and rose again. The horizon dropped away.

"Woah," said Ivan. "That's the biggest force dome I've ever seen. I didn't know they could expand them to that size."

"It absorbs the output of an entire generating plant," said Vorob'yev, "for the dome alone. Another for the interior."

A flattened opalescent bubble six kilometers across reflected the late morning sun of Eta Ceta. It lay in the midst of the city like a vast egg in a bowl, a pearl beyond price. It was ringed first by a kilometer-wide park with trees, then by a street reflecting silver, then by another park, then by an ordinary street, thick with traffic. From this, eight wide boulevards fanned out like the spokes of a wheel, centering the city. Centering the universe, Miles gained the impression. The effect was doubtless intended.

"The ceremony today is in some measure a dress rehearsal for the final one in a week and a half," Vorob'yev went on, "since absolutely everyone will be there, ghem-lords, haut-lords, galactics and all. There will likely be organizational delays. As long as they're not on our part. I spent a week of hard negotiating to get you your official rankings and place in this."

"Which is?" said Miles.

"You two will be placed equivalently to second-order

ghem-lords." Vorob'yev shrugged. "It was the best I could do."

In the mob, though toward the front of it. The better to watch without being much noticed himself, Miles supposed. Today, that seemed like a good idea. All three of them, Vorob'yev, Ivan, and himself, were wearing their respective House mourning uniforms, logos and decorations of rank stitched in black silk on black cloth. Maximum formal, since they were to be in the Imperial presence itself. Miles ordinarily liked his Vorkosigan House uniform, whether the original brown and silver or this somber and elegant version, because the tall boots not only allowed but required him to dispense with the leg braces. But getting the boots on over his swollen burns this morning had been ... painful. He was going to be limping more noticeably than usual, even tanked as he was on pain-killers. *I'll remember this, Yenaro.*

They spiraled down to a landing by the most southerly dome entrance, fronted by a landing lot already crowded with other vehicles. Vorob'yev dismissed the driver and aircar.

"We keep no escort, my lord?" Miles said doubtfully, watching it go, and awkwardly shifting the long polished maplewood box he carried.

Vorob'yev shook his head. "Not for security purposes. No one but the Cetagandan emperor himself could arrange an assassination inside the Celestial Garden, and if he wished to have you eliminated here, a regiment of bodyguards would do you no good."

Some very tall men in the dress uniforms of the Cetagandan Imperial Guard vetted them through the dome locks. The guardsmen shunted them toward a collection of float-pallets set up as open cars, with white silky upholstered seats, the color of Cetagandan Imperial mourning. Each ambassadorial party was bowed on board by what looked to be senior servants in white and gray. The robotically-routed float-cars set off at a sedate pace a handspan above the white-jade-paved walkways winding through a vast arboretum and botanical garden. Here and there Miles saw the rooftops of scattered and hidden pavilions peeking through the trees. All the buildings were low and private, except for some elaborate towers poking up in the center of the magic circle, almost three kilometers away. Though the sun shone outside in an Eta Ceta spring day, the weather inside the dome was set to a gray, cloudy, and appropriately mournful dampness, promising, but doubtless not delivering, rain.

At length they wafted to a sprawling pavilion just to the west of the central towers, where another servant bowed them out of the car and directed them inside, along with a dozen other delegations. Miles stared around, trying to identify them all.

The Marilacans, yes, there was the silver-haired Bernaux, some green-clad people who might be Jacksonians, a delegation from Aslund which included their chief of state—even they had only two guards, disarmed—the Betan ambassadoress in a black-on-purple brocade jacket and matching sarong, all streaming in to honor this one dead woman who would never have met them face to face when alive. *Surreal* seemed an understatement. Miles felt like he'd crossed the border into Faerie, and when they emerged this afternoon, a hundred years would have passed outside. The galactics had to pause at the doorway to make way for the party of a haut-lord satrap governor. *He* had an escort of a dozen ghem-guards, Miles noted, in full formal face paint, orange, green, and white swirls.

The decor inside was surprisingly simple—tasteful, Miles supposed—tending heavily to the organic, arrangements of live flowers and plants and little fountains, as if bringing the garden indoors. The connecting halls were hushed, not echoing, yet one's voice carried clearly. They'd done something extraordinary with acoustics. More palace servants circulated offering food and drinks to the guests.

A pair of pearl-colored spheres drifted at a walking

pace across the far end of one hall, and Miles blinked at his first glimpse of haut-ladies. Sort of.

Outside of their very private quarters haut-women all hid themselves behind personal force-shields, usually generated, Miles had been told, from a float-chair. The shields could be made any color, according to the mood or whim of the wearer, but today would all be white for the occasion. The haut-lady could see out with perfect clarity, but no one could see in. Or reach in, or penetrate the barrier with stunner, plasma, or nerve disruptor fire, or small projectile weapons or minor explosions. True, the force screen also eliminated the opportunity to fire out, but that seemed not to be a haut-lady concern. The shield could be cut in half with a gravitic imploder lance, Miles supposed, but the imploders' bulky power packs, massing several hundred kilos, made them strictly field ordnance, not hand weapons.

Inside their bubbles, the haut-women could be wearing anything. Did they ever cheat? Slop around in old clothes and comfy slippers when they were supposed to be dressed up? Go nude to garden parties? Who could tell?

A tall elderly man in the pure white robes reserved for the haut- and ghem-lords approached the Barrayaran party. His features were austere, his skin finely wrinkled and almost transparent. He was the Cetagandan equivalent of an Imperial major-domo, apparently, though with a much more flowery title, for after collecting their credentials from Vorob'yev he provided them with exact instructions as to their place and timing in the upcoming procession. His attitude conveyed that outlanders might be hopelessly gauche, but if one repeated the directions in a firm tone and made them simple enough, there was a chance of getting through this ceremony without disgrace.

He looked down his hawk-beak nose at the polished box. "And this is your gift, Lord Vorkosigan?"

Miles managed to unlatch the box and open it for display without dropping it. Within, nestled on a black velvet bed, lay an old, nicked sword. "This is the gift selected from his collection by my Emperor, Gregor Vorbarra, in honor of your late Empress. It is the sword his Imperial ancestor Dorca Vorbarra the Just carried in the First Cetagandan War." One of several, but no need to go into that. "A priceless and irreplaceable historical artifact. Here is its documentation of provenance."

"Oh," the major-domo's feathery white brows lifted almost despite themselves. He took the packet, sealed with Gregor's personal mark, with more respect. "Please convey my Imperial master's thanks to yours." He half-bowed, and withdrew.

"*That* worked well," said Vorob'yev with satisfaction.

"I should bloody think so," growled Miles. "Breaks my heart." He handed off the box to Ivan to juggle for a while.

Nothing seemed to be happening just yet—organizational delays, Miles supposed. He drifted away from Ivan and Vorob'yev in search of a hot drink. He was on the point of capturing something steaming and, he hoped, non-sedating, from a passing tray when a quiet voice at his elbow intoned, "Lord Vorkosigan?"

He turned, and stifled an indrawn breath. A short and rather androgynous elderly . . . woman?—stood by his side, dressed in the gray and white of Xanadu's service staff. Her head was bald as an egg, her face devoid of hair. Not even eyebrows. "Yes . . . ma'am?"

"Ba," she said in the tone of one offering a polite correction. "A lady wishes to speak with you. Would you accompany me, please?"

"Uh . . . sure." She turned and paced soundlessly away, and he followed in alert anticipation. A lady? With luck, it might be Mia Maz of the Vervani delegation, who ought to be around somewhere in this mob of a thousand people. He was developing some urgent questions for her. *No eyebrows? I was expecting a contact sometime, but . . . here?*

They exited the hall. Passing out of sight of Vorob'yev and Ivan stretched Miles's nerves still further. He followed the gliding servant down a couple of corridors, and across a little open garden thick with moss and tiny flowers misted with dew. The noises from the reception hall still carried faintly through the damp air. They entered a small building, open to the garden on two sides and floored with dark wood that made his black boots echo unevenly in time with his limping stride. In a dim recess of the pavilion, a woman-sized pearlescent sphere floated a few centimeters above the polished floor, which reflected an inverted halo from its light.

"Leave us," a voice from the sphere directed the servant, who bowed and withdrew, eyes downcast. The transmission through the force screen gave the voice a low, flat timbre.

The silence lengthened. Maybe she'd never seen a physically imperfect man before. Miles bowed, and waited, trying to look cool and suave, and not stunned and wildly curious.

"So, Lord Vorkosigan," came the voice again at last. "Here I am."

"Er . . . quite." Miles hesitated. "And just who are you, milady, besides a very pretty soap-bubble?"

There was a longer pause, then, "I am the haut Rian Degtiar. Servant of the Celestial Lady, and Handmaiden of the Star Crèche."

Another flowery haut-title that gave no clue to its function. He could name every ghem-lord on the Cetagandan General Staff, all the satrap governors and their ghem-officers, but this female haut-babble was new to him. But the Celestial Lady was the polite name for the late Empress haut Lisbet Degtiar, and that name at least he knew—

"You are a relative of the late Dowager Empress, milady?"

"I am of her genomic constellation, yes. Three generations removed. I have served her half my life."

A lady-in-waiting, all right. One of the old Empress's personal retinue, then, the most inward of insiders. *Very* high rank, probably very aged as well. "Uh . . . you're not related to a ghem-lord named Yenaro, by chance, are you?"

"Who?" Even through the force screen the voice conveyed utter bafflement.

"Never mind. Clearly not important." His legs were beginning to throb. Getting the damn boots back off when he returned to the embassy was going to be an even better trick than getting them on had been. "I could not help noticing your serving woman. Are there many folk around here with no hair?"

"It is not a woman. It is Ba."

"Ba?"

"The neuter ones, the Emperor's high-slaves. In his Celestial Father's time it was the fashion to make them smooth like that."

Ah. Genetically-engineered, genderless servants. He'd heard rumors about them, mostly connected, illogically enough, with sexual scenarios that had more to do with the teller's hopeful fantasies than any likely reality. But they were reputed to be a race utterly loyal to the lord who had, after all, literally created them. "So . . . not all Ba are hairless, but all the hairless ones are Ba?" he worked it out.

"Yes . . ." More silence, then, "Why have you come to the Celestial Garden, Lord Vorkosigan?"

His brow wrinkled. "To hold up Barrayar's honor in this circu—um, solemn procession, and to present your late Empress's bier-gift. I'm an envoy. By appointment of Emperor Gregor Vorbarra, whom *I* serve. In my own small way."

Another, longer pause. "You mock me in my misery."

"*What?*"

"What do you *want*, Lord Vorkosigan?"

"What do *I* want? You called me here, Lady, isn't it the other way around?" He rubbed his neck, tried again. "Er . . . can I help you, by chance?"

"*You?!*"

Her astonished tone stung him. "Yeah, me! I'm not as . . ." *incompetent as I look*, "I've been known to accomplish a thing or two, in my time. But if you won't give me a clue as to what this is all about, I can't. I will if I do know but I can't if I don't. Don't you see." Now he had confused himself, tongue-tangled. "Look, can we start this conversation over?" He bowed low. "Good day, I am Lord Miles Vorkosigan of Barrayar. How may I assist you, milady?"

"Thief—!"

The light dawned at last. "*Oh*. Oh, no. I am a Vorkosigan, and no thief, milady. Though as possibly a recipient of stolen property, I may be a fence," he allowed judiciously.

More baffled silence; perhaps she was not familiar with criminal jargon. Miles went on a little desperately, "Have you, uh, by chance lost an object? Rod-shaped electronic device with a bird-crest seal on the cap?"

"You have it!" Her voice was a wail of dismay.

"Well, not *on* me."

Her voice went low, throaty, desperate. "You still have it. You must return it to me."

"Gladly, if you can prove it belongs to you. I certainly don't pretend it belongs to me," he added pointedly.

"You would do this . . . for nothing?"

"For the honor of my name, and, er . . . I *am* ImpSec. I'd do almost anything for information. Satisfy my curiosity, and the deed is done."

Her voice came back in a shocked whisper, "You mean you don't even know what it *is*?"

The silence stretched for so long after that, he was beginning to be afraid the old lady had fainted dead away in there. Processional music wafted faintly through the air from the great pavilion.

"Oh, shi—er, oh. That damn parade is starting, and I'm supposed to be near the front. Milady, how can I reach you?"

"You can't." Her voice was suddenly breathless. "I

have to go too. I'll send for you." The white bubble rose,
and began to float away.

"Where? When—?" The music was building toward
the start-cue.

"Say nothing of this!"

He managed a sketchy bow at her retreating maybe-
back, and began hobbling hastily across the garden. He
had a horrible feeling he was about to be very publicly late.

When he wended his way back into the reception area,
he found the scene was every bit as bad as he'd feared.
A line of people was advancing to the main exit, toward
the tower buildings, and Vorob'yev in the Barrayaran delegation's place was dragging his feet, creating an obvious
gap, and staring around urgently. He spotted Miles and
mouthed silently, *Hurry up, dammit!* Miles hobbled
faster, feeling as if every eye in the room was on him.

Ivan, with an exasperated look on his face, handed
over the box to him as he arrived. "Where the hell were
you all this time, in the lav? I looked there—"

"Shh. Tell you later. I've just had the most bizarre
. . ." Miles struggled with the heavy maplewood box, and
straightened it around into an appropriate presentational
position. He marched forward across a courtyard paved
with more carved jade, catching up at last with the delegation in front of them just as they reached the door to
one of the high-towered buildings. They all filed into an
echoing rotunda. Miles spied a few white bubbles in the
line ahead, but there was no telling if one was his old
haut-lady. The game-plan called for everyone to slowly
circle the bier, genuflect, and lay their gifts in a spiral
pattern in order of seniority/status/clout, and file out the
opposite doors to the northern pavilion (for the haut-
lords and ghem-lords), or the eastern pavilion (for the
galactic ambassadors) where a funeral luncheon would
be served.

But the steady procession stopped, and began to pile
up in the wide arched doorways. From the rotunda ahead,
instead of quiet music and hushed, shuffling footsteps, a

startled babble poured. Voices were raised in sharp
astonishment, then other voices in even sharper command.

"What's gone wrong?" Ivan wondered, craning his
neck. "Did somebody faint or something?"

Since Miles's eye-level view was of the shoulders of
the man ahead of him, he could scarcely answer this.
With a lurch, the line began to proceed again. It reached
the rotunda, but then was shunted out a door immedi-
ately to the left. A ghem-commander stood at the inter-
section, directing traffic with low-voiced instructions,
repeated over and over, "Please retain your gifts and
proceed directly around the outside walkway to the Eastern Pavilion, please retain your gifts and proceed directly
to the Eastern Pavilion, all will be re-ordered presently,
please retain—"

At the center of the rotunda, above everyone's heads
on a great catafalque, lay the Dowager Empress in state.
Even in death outlander eyes were not invited to look
upon her. Her bier was surrounded by a force-bubble,
made translucent; only a shadow of her form was visible
through it, as if through gauze, a white-clad, slight, sleeping ghost. A line of mixed ghem-guards apparently just
drafted from the passing satrap governors stood in a row
from catafalque to wall on either side of the bier,
shielding something else from the passing eyes.

Miles couldn't stand it. *After all, they can't massacre
me here in front of everybody, can they?* He jammed
the maplewood box at Ivan, and ducked under the elbow
of the ghem-officer trying to shoo everyone out the other
door. Smiling pleasantly, his hands held open and empty,
he slipped between two startled ghem-guards, who were
clearly not expecting such a rude and impudent move.

On the other side of the catafalque, in the position
reserved for the first gift of the haut-lord of highest status, lay a dead body. Its throat was cut, and quantities
of fresh red blood pooled on the shimmering green malachite floor all around, soaking into its gray and white
palace servitor's uniform. A thin jeweled knife was

clutched rigorously in its out-flung right hand. *It* was exactly the term for the corpse, too. A bald, eyebrowless, man-shaped creature, elderly but not frail ... Miles recognized their intruder from the personnel pod even without the false hair. His own heart seemed to stop in astonishment.

Somebody's just raised the stakes in this little game.

The highest-ranking ghem-officer in the room swooped down upon him. Even through the swirl of face paint his smile was fixed, the look of a man constrained to be polite to someone he would more naturally have preferred to bludgeon to the pavement. "Lord Vorkosigan, would you re-join your delegation, please?"

"Of course. Who was that poor fellow?"

The ghem-commander made little herding motions at him—the Cetagandan was not fool enough to actually touch him, of course—and Miles allowed himself to be moved off. Grateful, irate, and flustered, the man was actually surprised into an unguarded reply. "It is Ba Lura, the Celestial Lady's most senior servitor. The Ba has served her for sixty years and more—it seems to have wished to follow on and serve her in death as well. A most tasteless gesture, to do it *here* ..." The ghem-commander buffeted Miles near enough to the again-stopped line of delegates for Ivan's long arm to reach out, grab him, and pull him in, and march him doorward with a firm fist in the middle of his back.

"What the hell is going *on*?" Ivan bent his head to hiss in Miles's ear from behind.

And where were you when the murder took place, Lord Vorkosigan? Except that it didn't look like a murder, it really did look like a suicide. Done in a most archaic manner. Less than thirty minutes ago. While he had been off talking with the mysterious white bubble, who might or might not have been haut Rian Degtiar, how the hell was he to tell? The corridor seemed to be spinning, but Miles supposed it was only his brain.

"You should not have gotten out of line, my lord," said Vorob'yev severely. "Ah ... what was it you saw?"

Miles's lip curled, but he tamped it back down. "One of the late Dowager Empress's oldest Ba servants has just cut its throat at the foot of her bier. I didn't know the Cetagandans made a fashion of human sacrifice. Not officially, anyway."

Vorob'yev's lips pursed in a soundless whistle, then flashed a brief, instantly stifled grin. "How *awkward* for them," he purred. "They are going to have an interesting scramble, trying to retrieve *this* ceremony."

Yes. So if the creature was so loyal, why did it arrange what it must have known would be a major embarrassment for its masters? Posthumous revenge? Admittedly, with Cetagandans that's the safest kind. . . .

By the time they completed an interminable hike around the outside of the central towers to the pavilion on the eastern side, Miles's legs were killing him. In a huge hall, the several hundred galactic delegates were being seated at tables by an army of servitors, all moving just a little faster than strict dignity would have preferred. Since some of the bier-gifts the other delegates carried were even bulkier than the Barrayarans' maplewood box, the seating was going slowly and more awkwardly than planned, with a lot of people jumping up and down and rearranging themselves, to the servitors' evident dismay. Somewhere deep in the bowels of the building Miles pictured a squadron of harried Cetagandan cooks swearing many colorful and obscene Cetagandan oaths.

Miles spotted the Vervani delegation being seated about a third of the way across the room. He took advantage of the confusion to slip out of his assigned chair, weave around several tables, and try to seize a word with Mia Maz.

He stood by her elbow, and smiled tensely. "Good afternoon, m'lady Maz. I have to talk—"

"Lord Vorkosigan! I tried to talk with you—" They cut across each other's greetings.

"You first," he ducked his head at her.

"I tried to call you at your embassy earlier, but you'd

already left. What in the world happened in the rotunda, do you have any idea? For the Cetagandans to alter a ceremony of this magnitude in the middle—it's unheard of."

"They didn't exactly have a choice. Well, I suppose they could have ignored the body and just carried on around it—*I* think that would have been much more impressive, personally—but evidently they decided to clean it up first." Again Miles repeated what he was beginning to think of as "the official version" of Ba Lura's suicide. He had the total attention of everyone within earshot. To hell with it, the rumors would be flying soon enough no matter what he said or didn't say.

"Did you have any luck with that little research question I posed to you last night?" Miles continued. "I, uh . . . don't think this is the time or place to discuss it, but . . ."

"Yes, and yes," Maz said.

And not over any holovid transmission channel on this planet, either, Miles thought, *supposedly secured or not.* "Can you stop by the Barrayaran Embassy, directly after this? We'll . . . take tea, or something."

"I think that would be very appropriate," Maz said. She watched him with newly intensified curiosity in her dark eyes.

"I need a lesson in etiquette," Miles added, for the benefit of their interested nearby listeners.

Maz's eyes twinkled in something that might have been suppressed amusement. "So I have heard it said, my lord," she murmured.

"By—" *whom?* he choked off. *Vorob'yev, I fear.* " 'Bye," he finished instead, rapped the table cheerily, and retreated back to his proper place. Vorob'yev watched Miles seat himself with a slightly dangerous look in his eyes that suggested he was thinking of putting a leash on the peripatetic young envoy soon, but he made no comment aloud.

By the time they had eaten their way through about twenty courses of tiny delicacies, which more than made up in numbers what they lacked in volume, the Cetagandans had reorganized themselves. The haut-lord major-domo was apparently one of those commanders who was never more masterly than when in retreat, for he managed to get everyone marshaled in the correct order of seniority again even though the line was now being cycled through the rotunda in reverse. One sensed the major-domo would be cutting *his* throat later, in the proper place and with the proper ceremony, and not in this dreadful harum-scarum fashion.

Miles laid down the maplewood box on the malachite floor in the second turning of the growing spiral of gifts, about a meter from where Ba Lura had poured out its life. The unmarked, perfectly polished floor wasn't even damp. And had the Cetagandan security people had time to do a forensics scan before the clean-up? Or had someone been counting on the hasty destruction of the subtler evidence? *Damn, I wish I could have been in charge of this, just now.*

The white float cars were waiting on the other side of the eastern pavilion, to carry the emissaries back to the gates of the Celestial Garden. The entire ceremony had run only about an hour late, but Miles's sense of time was inverted from his first whimsical vision of Xanadu as Faerie. He felt as if a hundred years had gone by inside the dome, while only a morning had passed in the outside world. He winced painfully in the bright afternoon light, as Vorob'yev's sergeant-driver brought the embassy aircar to their pick-up point. Miles fell gratefully into his seat.

I think they're going to have to cut these bloody boots off, when we get back home.

CETAGANDA
by Lois McMaster Bujold

**Available in hardcover
January 1996 from Baen Books**